DISCONNECTED
by J. Cafesin
-

I0565046

-

Entropy Publishing
August 2016
-
-

DISCONNECTED is a work of non-fiction. Recognized names, characters, places, and events portrayed in this novel are true, according to the author's recollection. Certain names have been changed to protect individual identities.

-

Entropy Publications, San Francisco, CA

query@entropypublishing.com

-

Entropy Press® is a registered trademark of Entropy Publications, LLC.

-

Library of Congress Cataloging-in-Publication Data is available.

-

ISBN-13: 978-0692248959 (Entropy Press)

ISBN-10: 0692248951

Subjects LCSH: Women—United States—Los Angeles Roits—Hollywood Feminism—History—21 Century—Romance—Dating—Memoir

-

Printed in the U.S.A

First Edition: July, 2014

Second Edition: August, 2016

-

Cover design by TargetMediaDesign

-
-

1

Chapter 1

10/30/91

Intuition is a flash of insight. Neither telepathy, nor stroke of divinity, its enlightenment comes from empirical evidence, consciously or unconsciously attained. Intuition may not tell you what you want to hear, but if ignored, you're basically fucking yourself.

It's hard to tell what's happening at first. The video is blurry, shot at night, and in black and white. I can make out a police car with its headlights on, lighting up a group of cops loosely encircling a guy trying to get up off the ground. The video sharpens to clarity as a cop, wielding a baton, slams it full force into the guy's head, like he's batting a T-ball. The guy goes down again. The image jitters, as if whoever is filming felt the blow. It's always shown with no sound, leaving the newscaster to narrate the scene.

"Shocking! Deeply disturbing footage," Stan Chambers, the sage of the KTLA Morning News, manages to mix the right amount of righteous indignation with urgency in his delivery. "This is an obvious case of racial profiling, and blatant police brutality," Stan insists. So much for unbiased reporting.

Video pulls back to reveal two officers relentlessly clubbing the guy on the ground. He curls onto his side to avoid the blows, then rolls to his other side in a fetal position as the pummeling continues. An officer among the many standing around watching the beating yells and gestures at guy to lay face down. He does, rolls onto his belly and stills. The beating stops, and for a moment there's peace, like no one knows what to do next.

"Mr King was savagely beaten by LAPD officers..." and Rodney King's mug shots come on-screen. Only then is it obvious he's Black. His right eye is swollen shut, his cheeks and forehead bloody. White butterfly bandages above his thick brows stand out against his dark skin.

"So, what are you doing right now?" Lee asked me. I'd forgotten he was on the line. His question felt invasive, verging on lewd, like he was peeping into my bedroom.

I'd clicked on the TV after prompting him to "Tell me about being Lee," and he began reciting the same script as the twenty guys before him. Thirty-something, athletic, successful entrepreneur,' at a great space in his life.' All he wanted (not 'needed'—'wanted' makes one better adjusted) was someone to share his wonderful life with. My intuition bridled. How fulfilling could his life possibly be, if, like me, he was looking for love in personal ads in the L.A. Daily News?

"Is that the TV I hear, or are you with someone?" He asked casually, but there was an edge of 'why did you call me if you're with somebody.'

"Just me. Well, and my roommate, who's probably still sleeping. Oh, and my dog, of course." I muted the TV, looked over at Face curled in her beanbag bed, whimpering and twitching, lost in a doggy dream. Made me feel safer somehow, declaring I had allies on hand.

The video demands my attention when one of the loitering cops near Rodney savagely stomps on his head. King's bulbous body writhes on the ground with the blow. Police resume beating him, alternating between baton blows and violent kicks to his head and back. Miraculously, he manages to sit up, tries to shield himself from the relentless pummeling. Clearly dazed, he sits on the ground holding his head, then a half dozen cops pounce on him at once, throw him on his stomach, pull his arms behind him, and cuff him.

"I don't have a roommate. Or a dog either. But I like dogs. What kind of dog do you have?"

"A Shepard pound hound," I announced with a hint of bravado. "Seven years old and at the top of her form. She's a bit of a brat. Somewhat possessive, though she generally likes most everyone I do."

Lee chuckled, like he got my implication. "So, tell me more about being Rachel."

I flashed a tempered grin he'd turned my question to him back on me."What would you like to know?"

Rodney King can be seen hogtied and writhing on the ground through the group of cops standing around him. Camera pulls back to reveal several police cars exiting the parking lot and driving away. A brief passing tension as I envisioned one of them driving over King's head and crushing it in. I wondered if Rodney thought of it right then.

"Hmm..." Lee mused. "Let's start with something simple. You into the whole workout craze? Biking, hiking, any sports?"

I smiled again, knowing his angle. The main concern of women when blind dating is that the guy's a psycho-killer. Guys want to know if the woman is fat.

"I play racquetball."

"Really? I do too. Well, used to. Started playing in high school. Kind of gave it up after college, but I'd love to get back into it. Great game. Quick. Focused. Rather brash, though. Haven't met a lot of women that are into it. It ain't exactly tennis."

"I suck at tennis. My mind drifts with the pacing." It was true racquetball was not a popular sport among women. But it bugged me he pointed it out, as if suggesting women were weak. "I'm pretty sure I can give most guys a fairly good workout on a racquetball court though."

Strike one, was his 'at a great space in his life,' monologue. Strike two, the first thing he wants to know about me is what every other heterosexual guy wants to know before meeting, and it ain't my I.Q.

Verging on strike three with his sexist slam, I considered how to end the call politely.

"Are you one of those women who's only satisfied with the victory when you compete with men?"

"I play for the calorie burn, so I don't like to stop rallies for servers. I generally don't play for points." Racquetball was my only healthy fix over bouts with bulimia and speed. Heroin thin was in, according to the media, and my mother— the authority on proper façades. "Are you like most guys whose manhood hinges on winning?"

"Touché." Lee laughed. "I'll play you. Anytime. And we don't have to keep score. I can probably give you a workout too, and I sure could use one." He paused, and I heard the unmistakable sound of a lighter flicking, and then him taking a hit off a joint.

Definite strike three. *Say thanks for the chat and hang up!* But I didn't. "What are you doing right now?"

He hesitated, exhaled a whistling sigh. "Hmm...I asked you first. What are *you* doing right now?"

I considered lying. I just didn't have the energy to fabricate something glib right then. "Let's see...before I called you, I was scribbling some thoughts before starting my day." I dare not confess Lonely became so choking I called my Daily News mailbox one last time. Lee's was the only message, and came last week, close to a month after every other response.

"So, you're a writer," Lee said, with an oo-la-la edge. "Poetry? Fiction? You a novelist?"

"Nope. Just journaling."

"Ah, as in keeping a diary? Or are you penning a memoir?" His continued focus on me felt unnerving. I was usually the one interviewing. With just the simplest of prompts, most men blatted on about themselves, turning few to none of my questions around. Twenty-three phone chats, and the five men from my ad that I met 'for coffee,' which I don't drink, were equally self-absorbed, as men tend to be, ensconced atop the social order for eons.

"I stopped keeping a diary when I was ten. And a *memoir* is an oxymoron, at best, as memory is faulty— a construct of the writer's perception of their past." I tried to channel Dorothy Parker, but surely sounded more pretentious than clever. "Honestly, I was just screwing around with prose."

"Sounds like a good read. Must be fun, screwing around in your head." He paused, and I swear, I felt him smiling. "I envy creative people, I mean."

I smiled. "I must admit, making it with my muse tops out my list of favorite things to do. Reliable entertainment without complications." *Like masturbation*, but I didn't say it.

"Imagination as an endless source of self-contained amusement. I like it." He paused."Well, you seem normal enough. Intriguing, even. Why is it you're still single if you don't want to be?"

I heard him hit the joint again and felt the draw of desire, that part of my brain that craved escape from fear and want, and the weight of my ordinary life. "My mother tells me I'm too...much. My sister would say I want too much." I matched his directness with purpose but suddenly felt exposed with my confession."What about you? Why are you still single?"

"I'm not."

Strike FOUR— Walk. HANG UP!

"But we filed for divorce back in February."

A married (soon to be divorced or not) stoner (he was sure to be blatantly getting buzzed at 9:00 in the morning), was not the knight I'd been holding out for. My intuition screamed at me to dismiss this man. *Say goodbye and hang up.* But I didn't.

"We've been separated almost a year now. I haven't seen or spoken to her for over nine months. Just waiting on the final papers."

"I don't date married men." It made my skin crawl when illicit lovers were blithely complicit in the corruption of a marriage. And I had no intention of becoming a casualty of a divorcee's inability to keep his commitments.

"I don't date married women. My marriage is over. If you're worried about that, don't be." He spoke softly but with conviction.

"OK." But it wasn't. "Look, you sound like a really nice guy—"

"And you sound like a very bright lady, and I'd love to get together for coffee or something, get acquainted in person."

I sighed. "I told you, I don't 'get acquainted' with married guys." *Or stoners*, but I didn't say it.

"I get it," he said with humor. "How about we just play racquetball then? There's a club on Ventura near Vineland with regulation courts. Racquet World, I think it's called. I'm off by 3:00 most every afternoon. Play you tomorrow if you're available."

Say bye bye and HANG UP, my intuition said clearly.

But I didn't.

I unmuted the TV and watched the handful of police left in the parking lot meander around Rodney, still hogtied face down on the ground.

"...captured by accident while testing a new video camera, and given exclusively to KTLA, we first aired this footage back in early March, and it has sparked a national debate..." Stan has a hint of glee in his rich tenor, but keeps it out of his expression as camera is back on him at the news desk. The anchor is secretly salivating, picturing where to display his Peabody.

That was where the video clip always ended, and the viewer was left wondering what the evil cops would do to poor Rodney next. A perfect cliffhanger, edited to insight outrage. And it did. I understood that racial equality was still fiction, like equal rights for women, but I could not sanction the media canonizing a violent felon just because he was Black. Still, the countless times the horrific scene aired, daily, the clip always commanded my attention. It was like watching *A Clockwork Orange*, or a train wreck about to happen.

-

Chapter 2

It was clear Lee was better than me within the first five minutes. By a lot. He commanded center court and kept me running. His strokes landed the small blue ball with loud, hollow bangs against the white walls that echoed in the expansive enclosure. He was impressive to watch, had great timing, and was so focused on the ball, at times it seemed as if he were sucking energy from the room, then using it to power each hit.

"You play well," he said humbly after an extended rally. He bounced the ball on the glossy hardwood floor in instead of putting it in play. Maybe 5'9", baby-face, he was pudgy—what's called 'stocky' on a guy, though likely labeled 'fat' on a woman.

"And you're an amazing player," I conceded breathless. "Though you were a bit vague about your skill level on the phone. I'm trying not to feel set up here."

His full lips took on this arresting, ear-to-ear grin. "Thought you said it's all about the workout." He ran his hand through his full head of thick, chestnut hair—unusual for mid-30's men, with so many balding by then.

"And you're definitely giving me one," I practically panted. "Thanks for agreeing not to play for points."

"No problem. Not stopping for serves keeps it fast and fluid. I like it. Very zen." He bounced the ball a few more times then held it, looked at me and stuck out his tongue in feigned exhaustion. "You're giving me a hell of a workout." He held the ball up. "You ready?"

I nodded, though I wasn't sure I was. His green eyes stayed focused on me until an instant before he put the ball in motion.

He backed off a bit, played less aggressively, syncing us into a smooth, even rhythm. Each rally seem to last longer, and the longer they lasted the more charged they became, a visceral energy gathering between us with each hit that extended the play.

"Great rallies today. I really enjoyed that," he said while we cooled down with Diet Cokes in the club lobby.

"Me too. It was fun. Thanks for the game."

"Thank you." And he raised his Diet Coke can and we toasted. "To fun," Lee said with a grin, then sipped his soda. "I'd like to start having more of it, actually."

I tensed, waiting for the come-on my intuition told me he'd deliver when he asked me to play ball.

"I'd like to get back into playing more often. Just joined the club, in fact." He flashed an arch of his brow. "Would you be into playing on a regular basis, a couple times a week maybe? You can play as my guest. Free. It's one of the membership perks."

I was down to a few games a month since Jon moved in with Mary. I was back to starving myself chasing thin. I'd been putting ads in The Recycler and notices on the peg boards at local clubs, but I'd yet to find anyone to partner with. Lee's offer was very generous. He was right in front of me, leaning on the opposite wall in the short, narrow hallway to the outdoor tennis courts. His gray t-shirt, tucked haphazardly in his loose black athletic shorts looked blue from the light of the soda machine next to him, as did his face, right out of Dutch masterpiece, or a Nike ad. If he turned out to reliable, he was better than I'd hoped for. And I needed a consistent racquetball partner if I hoped to maintain a body worth noticing among the beautiful people in L.A.

"You clearly play way better than me. You sure I won't bore you?" Why he wanted to play with me was still vague. But his expression of awe when we first met in the lobby told me he'd likely be open for more than just racquetball partners.

"I have serious doubts you could ever bore me, Rachel." Lee expression took on his Cheshire grin. "You kept me on my toes today. And that's what I'm looking for. I'm hoping to get back in shape, especially now that I'm back to being single."

Was that the come-on? Or was he just stating a fact about the build required to compete with Hollywood's standard of chic.

"Why did you run that ad?" he asked flatly.

I stared back at him, feigned ignorance to thwart embarrassment. "Sorry?"

"Well," he began cautiously. "It seems to me you could date any guy you want."

If it was a come-on, it was the best I'd heard. He sounded like he was stating a fact. Not one of the guys I'd met through my personal ad had ever asked why I placed it. I smiled, then reminded myself I was there to play ball, and nothing more. Lee watched me. Despite his Pillsbury Dough boy build, he really was quite cute. "How old are you, again?"

"Almost thirty nine." His brow furrowed with mock irritation. "Now would you please answer my question? Why did you place that ad?"

"To find what it said, which, as it's turning out, seems to be way harder to come by than a racquetball partner." I gave him a wily grin.

"'Attractive, passionate, creative pro, 5'7", 135, 33, SWF, seeks, imaginative, passionate, pragmatic, independent thinker, with a wild and crazy heart.'" Lee quoted my ad word for word with a haughty smile. "That's me."

"'Who's ready for the real thing.'" I quoted the rest, and returned his cheeky grin. I had no intention of discussing my ad with him since I wasn't there to date Lee. I had no interest in spending a lifetime with a partner who lost the internal battle against his cravings more than I did. I was looking for long and lean, single, and [for the most part] clean.

He took another drink of his soda then looked at the clock on the wall behind the lobby counter. "Look, we just played almost two hours, practically non-stop. It's almost 6:00 and I'm starving. Come get some dinner with me. I'd love your company. And I really hate eating alone."

I hesitated, took a sip of my soda. Racquetball partner was one thing, but beyond that felt like adultery. "Sorry. I told you, I don't go out with married guys."

"And I told you, I'm getting divorced, and just waiting on the final papers." He studied me. "Besides, I'm not asking you on a date. We're just two friends having dinner and then we'll call it a night. I have to be up at 4:00 in the morning to deal with back east clients, so I generally go to bed pretty early. How about it? We've earned a good meal tonight."

I eyed him, but couldn't resist smiling. His last remark was characteristically female, like he knew what it felt like to count every calorie.

"Jerry's Deli is right around the corner and they have great sandwiches, soups, salads. My treat, to celebrate my new membership here, and our new partnership." He drank the last of his soda and tossed the can in the trash next to the soda machine. "Come on. Join me, if you've got nothing else going on. I'm lusting after a pastrami on rye."

My stomach rumbled. No need to rush back to my empty house. My roommate had been staying at her boyfriend's for the last month. Having dinner with my new racquetball partner seemed harmless. And eating an actual meal was far more preferable than one more dry baked potato topped with carrot sticks— the dog, and TV my only companions for the evening. And to Lee's point, we earned dinner after that workout. "Friends only, right?" I watched him careful for any change in demeanor.

"Just friends." He held up his index and middle finger in the Boy Scout salute. And the smile that spread across his face was infectious.

I followed Lee's silver Mercedes west on Ventura, towards Jerry's, and the setting sun. Even with the heater blasting I was freezing with the passenger window half open. Face was in doggy bliss though, her long snout stuck out as far as possible, craning her neck to snuffle in the cool, crisp air, her jowls puffed with wind. I smiled, glad to have her with me, continually enamored by her unfettered joy in just being.

The orange sunset lit up the smoke intermittently billowing from the sunroof of his Mercedes. The sweet smell of colitas floated into my

14

car and sparked my relentless craving for a buzz— that sublime lightness of being— for just an evening shutting out fear and Lonely, and engaging exclusively with my muse.

Lee accelerated through the light at Laurel Canyon just before it turned orange. I was right behind him, then a BMW cut me off and I slammed on my brakes to avoid hitting him. The idiot turned left in front of me, leaving me at the intersection just as orange turned to red. Waiting for the green light, reason went to battle with desire inside me. Racquetball, even the occasional dinner after a game could spark a friendship, as I had with Jon, but intuition insisted that was as far as I should ever take it with Lee.

Halloween, 1991, Los Angeles was typically clear and crisp out. As a native of the land of perpetual sunshine, I'd never missed trick-or-treating from bad weather. A fanatic fan of all things sweet, I used to be so excited for this day to come every year, though I probably shouldn't have been. My weight issues were surely caused by my inability to control what I ate. Paradoxically, through most of my youth, eating, preferably in front of the TV, felt more like the solution to feeling sad.

A beater car slowed to pace me as I took my place in the line of cars turning into the deli. Primered and dented, I couldn't make out the car model, or see the driver through the tinted windows. I called Face in and rolled up the windows, practically held my breath till they passed. Though Studio City was considered one of the better suburbs of L.A., even with the recent drive-by there, violence was spreading everywhere.

Heavy, audible sigh of relief when I finally pulled into Jerry's parking lot, then waited another five minutes for the valet—wearing only a Tarzan loin cloth (with the build to pull it off) to give me a parking pass for the business center lot. I pulled into the nearest available spot in the office complex, retrieved the pen stuck inside the metal coil of the spiral notebook on the passenger seat and flipped open the black cardboard cover to a blank page. As with all entries, I titled the prose simply by date.

10/31/91

Ah, to be a dog...to be so idyllically simple to thoroughly enjoy living instead of suffocating under the weight of fabricated complexities.

Closed the notebook, gave Face a quick scratch on the white diamond marking on her muzzle, locked my car and went to meet Lee. Several cars down the row of parked cars I was passing, a guy was hunched over the front of a Datsun Z. He was dressed in a fringed leather jacket, his jeans gathered around his calves, his bare white ass pumped back and forth as he humped the woman under him. She lay splayed on the long hood, panting and moaning, her sparkly blue party dress gathered up past her hips, her legs wrapped around his waist.

Neither seemed to noticed me. I took off running, passed the next row of parked cars, and the next, finally slowing to walk when I got to the deli's crowded entryway.

Lee stood by the wrought iron bench near the deli's entrance, a dozen or more people loosely gathered near him. All were White,

16

mid-20s to late 50s, in-shape, and in vogue—dressed tight and revealing, some even in costume, likely on their way to a party after their appearance at the frequented studio industry hangout. I still wore my skin-tight black leggings, topped with a loose black T, my standard racquetball wear. If I'd meant to impress, I never would have agreed to play ball our first meeting.

"That took a while," Lee said dryly. "Started to think you changed your mind and went home." There was a hint of anger in his tone. "I put our name down for a table already."

"Thanks." And I should have left it at that, but I felt a need to defend my honor. "I told you I'd meet you here, and I do what I say. Took me 15 minutes to get a spot in the business lot. Where'd you park?"

"Across the street." He stared at me with glassy eyes. "I have an in with the parking gods." He flashed a quick grin, which lightened his initial contention. "Anyway, glad you made it." His dark hair blended into the folds of the hooded sweatshirt he'd put on and framed his baby face. He looked like one of the Sibyls surrounding God in the painting on the Sistine Chapel.

A hostess came outside dressed as a maid from The Rocky Horror Picture Show, with the tiny flared skirt and 4" spiked heels, and called Lee's name. Our table was ready. It was packed inside, and loud. The deli was one large, bright dining room, complete with the classic chrome lined linoleum bar and rotating stools. The hostess led us through the crowds and seated us at a small maroon vinyl booth along the back wall. And for the moment we both got caught up in the bizarre.

A naked man, except for his feathered cap, groin and ass, was being escorted out of the restaurant by a large Black bouncer. He stopped before exiting, took off his cap and bowed to a woman about to pass him in the narrow entryway lined with glass cabinets full of treats. Both Lee and I laughed. He had a deep, resonant laugh. I liked it.

"It's definitely manic in here," he said, surveying the scene. "Thanks for coming, joining me for dinner tonight. Sorry about the timing."

"Don't be. The floor show is way more entertaining than another night of TV." I'd never have confessed this if I was looking to garner his interest, but I didn't have to pretend to be busy. I wasn't looking to impress Lee.

He chuckled knowingly. "I totally get it. I'm there. I've been hiding in my condo for a year now, since being back on my own. My friends are all on my case to get out and about. Which is why I was looking in the personals." He kept his focus on me as a slender young waitress/model/actress dressed as a Playboy bunny, floppy ears, bushy tail and all came to our table.

She was gorgeous—long, slender legs, her flat belly accentuated her perky breasts. Her cleavage demanded notice as she bent to hear us, but Lee looked at me as he ordered a pastrami on rye, and stayed fixed on me while I ordered a Cobb salad. He kept his eyes on me as the waitress straightened, stuck her notepad into her waistband and turned away.

"I hope you don't mind my asking," Lee said. "I'm wondering what kind of response you got to your ad?"

"Why?" I smiled. "Thinking of putting one up?

"Well, as my racquetball partner, would you recommend it? I mean, were the guys, like...normal?"

"What's your metric? Are you normal?" I teased. "I don't think any were psycho-killers, if that's what you mean. But most were on par with all the other self-appointed omnipotent males I've met." I heard myself say it aloud, and Lee laugh. I babbled on to cover the slam. "I only met a few of the guys for coffee. And I went out with just one, and only once."

"And who was this lucky guy? And why didn't you keep dating him?" Lee kept the conversation on me, as he had on the phone our first exchange. It was unique being on the other side of the interview. Felt...nice.

So I described a date from the previous weekend with a lawyer, who after meeting for coffee called back and asked me out. It got more complicated than intended to explain why even though he took me to Dar Maghreb on the Strip for dinner, I had no desire for a second date with a guy who insisted the homeless were out there because they're lazy, and in America we all have the same opportunities.

"The silver spoon up his ass clearly affected his brain." I joked, sort of. "From our chemistry to our environment, we are mostly the hand we're dealt."

"Spoken like a true cynic."

"I prefer realist."

"That's what all cynics say."

I smiled. So did Lee.

"Some would argue we have free will," Lee said. "We choose what to believe, how to be, who to love."

"Well, that's poetic and all, but most people adopt their parent's religion without ever considering what they believe. And how we behave is usually more reaction than conscious choice." I knew I was coming off strong, an egregious sin in women, according to my father, the purveyor of human behavior. Lee stared at me with rapt attention, unlike most men who seemed to mentally check out when I expressed an opinion. "And maybe we choose who to love, but we can't choose for that person to love us back." I was referring to Michael choosing Allison over me, but Lee's expression hardened.

"So, you believe our lives are predestined then?"

"No. Not at all. The laws of physics withstanding, we have quite a range of choice. People rise from poverty, overcome adversity all the time."

"Yes. But most people don't."

"Ah... You make my point. Thank you." I gave him a cheeky grin. I felt no need to be sparkly but not too bright with Lee, as the media, and social convention insisted women should be.

"Your date was unworthy of you, my dear. You're better off without him. You deserve someone who shares your vision, and passion, so you can't help but love him back." His green eyes were speckled with brown. They were large, the lids weighted but not sleepy, what my mother called 'bedroom eyes.' His long lashes nearly touched the base of his brow. "So, the lawyer's out?"

"Yup."

A scream of delight and everyone clapped as rock legends Jim Morrison and Kurt Cobain entered the deli. The actor who played Jim looked familiar but I couldn't place him. Kurt Cobain looked identical to the real one—strung out and rail thin. He fell into the lap of a stylish middle-aged woman sitting at a small table along the front windows of the restaurant, and kissed her, on the lips, until her husband, or date pulled him off. He left her smiling, though, and even more so when the crowd cheered as the musical duo were shadowed to their booth by the big Black bouncer.

A tall, trim young waiter, every bit as gorgeous as the waitress, dressed in swim trunks and a Hawaiian shirt delivered our meals. "Enjoy," he said with a quick glance to each of us then gave a little bow and left. One of the few remaining perks of L.A. was all the beautiful people on display. Just going to the store was like a fashion show, with eighty percent of the population that had come to Hollywood seeking fame perpetually auditioning.

"Struggling actor, or lead in a pop band." Lee grinned, then picked up half of his five inch thick sandwich and took a big bite. He ate ravenously, and with sheer delight. "Mmm. Excellent." He took another bite and I started on my salad.

We were quiet for a moment while we ate and watched the floor show. I assumed his exaggerated appreciation for his sandwich was for my benefit and would wane, but it didn't. Lee savored each bite like the very first, bite after bite without restraint. He ate like my father did, like I would have liked to eat, and probably would have, if I were a man.

Conversation came easily, without hesitation or awkward silences. We kept it light, talked about favorite shows, movies, books, our interests. We had an even exchange, his focused attention and continual barrage of questions fully engaging. An hour or more went by in what felt like only minutes since we'd been seated. There were moments when the room and mayhem disappeared, like we were the only two people in there, absorbed in each other, chatting away while we ate.

Lee finished everything on his plate from the coleslaw to the bagel chips and pickles. I left a few forkfuls of my salad, as is Weight Watchers' recommendation for at least the perception of controlled eating.

"So," he said, dropping his paper napkin on his empty plate. He sipped his water, then held the glass on the table between us with both hands, watching me intently. "I assume you're back to looking for 'the real thing. The white picket fence, the whole nine yards?"

I knew I was breaking a supreme law of dating edict engaging in dialog of marriage and kids on a first meeting, even in the abstract. But I could say anything to Lee— be as flagrantly honest as I wanted to be. We weren't on a date. "I've never been into fences. I prefer a lot of land around me, a safe haven for a family, flush with trees and spectacular views of the Pacific. I fantasize about the Zuma cliffs, or the rolling hills north of San Francisco."

"It's gorgeous up there, to be sure. But pricey." His Cheshire grin emerged. "Lucky I'm good at making money." He paused, possibly to drive the point home. "Turns out shipping freight is very lucrative."

Blanked on a witty retort as our waitress came by, collected our plates and left the bill. Lee picked it up immediately, glanced at the check, took a $50 bill from his wallet and dropped it on the table as he stood.

The bill couldn't have been more than $20. He was peacocking, or he was an advocate for waiters and had money to burn. Regardless, our server got lucky Lee paid the check tonight. I sagged with the weight of perpetually impending poverty. Freelancing paid my bills, but it would never get me that house in Marin, or the kind of cash it takes to raise kids. I followed him out of the packed deli. We emerged from the noise and mayhem, and I sucked in the crisp night air, suddenly free of the tension from the crowd.

Thanks again for dinner. It was fun." It surprised me how much I meant it.

"For me, too," he said. "Thanks for joining me tonight. Nicest evening I've had in quite some time."

"Me, too," slipped out and my face got hot. "Guess I'll see ya on the court next Tuesday at 4:00," I said more than asked, hoping he still wanted to partner.

"I'll be there. Look forward to it. Be ready to get it on next week." The Cheshire cat was back.

I smiled at his double speak. Wit was smart, and intelligence tantalized.

-

Chapter 3

Lee was already on the court, rallying by himself when I arrived at 4:00p.m. on Tuesday. We played for an hour and a half until thudded pounding on the thick door disrupted us, and we were forced to abdicate our court to the next reservation.

Sweat soaked and still breathless, we chatted over Diet Cokes in the lobby. He spoke about his weekend alone at home, boredom and guilt motivating him to spend multiple hours each day playing the $5,000 electronic keyboard he'd recently purchased. Then he asked me about my weekend.

I told him I worked on a novel from a script I started in film school. And I read, I said, but lied. I didn't tell him I'd wasted much of the weekend watching TV and getting off to sate the relentless ache of loneliness.

"Great rallies today. You really had me running, which is precisely what I need. I'm looking forward to getting back in shape." He took a drink from the frosted can and leaned against the wall behind him. "Gained like fifty pounds during the two years I was married. I've lost about thirty since we separated. Have around twenty more to go, though this last bit's been a bitch to drop."

I was awestruck by his frankness, his willingness to confess a typically female struggle. In the 1990s thin was mandatory in women, but men not so much, especially if they made a lot of money, which Lee had indicated he did.

"Truth is, I'm kind of a connoisseur." He flashed an arch of his brow. "Not exactly in the traditional sense. I just love food."

I laughed. "Me too. My dad turned me on to the joys of eating early on, so I was kind of pudgy growing up. Took a lot of crap for it too, from kids at school, even from my mom. Lost a bunch of weight in high school, with the help of Black Beauties," I confessed, probably because he had.

"They were pharms, back in the 70s, right? But women were starving themselves to death, if I'm remembering right."

"Yup. FDA pulled them from the market. Too bad, but better fat than dead, I guess." I half smiled. Shrugged. "I use racquetball in lieu of speed now. Fat is worse than leprosy, at least for a woman, especially in L.A."

"It's true that men aren't under the same body scrutiny as women. But if a guy is fat, he's not going to attract women like you, even with a lot of money." Lee eyed me. "You can have most any guy you want, Rachel, with that nouveau-punk wild-child look you've got going. You're really quite beautiful," He said boldly, and as statements of fact, without sexual innuendo.

I laughed to cover my embarrassment. "Right." Lee was teasing, or being patronizing, or he was crazy. I could pass as L.A. trendy, but I was not beautiful.

"You are beautiful," he said again, as if reading my mind. "You just have to believe it."

25

"Belief doesn't make god real."

"Ah. The cynic."

"No. *Realist*." I smiled. His eyes virtually twinkled as his Cheshire grin slowly appeared, a visceral awareness we were connected through a private joke we'd already established. I looked away, at the stud behind the front counter watching us.

"Don't you see the way men look at you?" Lee looked at the attendant, who went back to folding towels.

"Oh, he's just a big flirt. I'm sure he stares at all the women that come in here. He's probably an actor, or rocker or something— always looking for fans."

Lee sighed, and shook his head. "Whatever." He watched me, then took a long draw off his soda. "I wanta show you something." He put his Diet Coke on the floor and pulled out some stapled papers from his gym bag, then flipped through them to the last page and handed them to me. "I just got them from my lawyer today, pulled them from my mailbox on my way here."

They were his divorce papers, signed by both him and his wife on the last page, along with the impending date of 11/14/91 in the box with the L.A. County court stamp. I handed them back to him. "Wow. I'm sorry."

"I'm not. We should never have been together and I'm glad it's over. Now we can both move on." He put the papers back in his bag, picked up his soda and took a long draw. "On November 14th my marriage is officially over." He took another drink then looked at me.

"Join me for dinner tonight and help me celebrate, unless you've got something else going." He looked at me, waiting for an excuse or confirmation.

"Technically, you've got a week until you're *officially* divorced. And I'm not too sure it's appropriate to celebrate the dissolution of a lifetime commitment."

He eyed me with a hint of disdain. "It's more like a relief to have eradicated a malignancy." His expression softened. "Come get some pasta at Maria's with me, Ray. We earned it after that workout. And you know I hate eating alone. You like Italian?"

Moving at 80 on the 101, I lost Lee in traffic somewhere in front of me as it compacted. I slowed when I saw the river of red tail lights coming on a half mile ahead.

I heard the screeching of brakes, the boom! Then the bending of metal, the shattering of glass before realizing the compact in front of me hadn't slowed with the traffic and slammed into the sedan in front of them so hard they ended up on top of it.

I slammed on my brakes barely missing hitting the sedan under the compact, then watched my rear view and braced for the car in back of me to connect, but they managed to move around me. Most everyone on the freeway slowed to a crawl. The door to the sedan opened, but no one got out. That's when I noticed the flames lapping the undercarriage of the compact. And no one was coming out of there either.

"Fuck." About the last thing I wanted to do was get out of my car and get hit by a passing truck. I looked around frantically. Cars moved around the accident slowly as they ogled the scene, but no one stopped to help. "Fuck!"

It took me a moment before I was able to get out of my car without getting hit. I heard the high-pitch screaming of a child as soon as I opened my car door, and saw a kid in the back seat of the compact trying to open the crumpled door. I moved in front of my car, and to the right side of the accident as the female driver, who I assumed was the mom, moved to the passenger door and began kicking at it until it popped open with a sickening crunch.

"Hand him to me!" I shouted to her, lifting my arms. I felt the heat of the fire as a child scrambled out of the compact, practically falling onto me. Maybe 5, or a bit older, he was heavy and it took all my strength and will to hold onto him. He gripped my hair and wrapped his legs around my waist. The mom scrambled forward with a baby in her arms. I couldn't hold both, so I opened the passenger door of the sedan. The driver sat in his car. He looked at me dazed. Blood trickled into his eye from his forehead. "Can you move?" I yelled to make sure he could hear me.

He stared at me, then finally nodded.

"The car on top yours is on fire," I screamed at him. "There's people inside. Help me get 'em out!"

He just sat there staring at me.

"MOVE NOW! I need you help!" I screamed.

The boy clung to me as the driver of the sedan came to my side and helped the mom with an infant in her arms down and onto the freeway. The flames were licking the base of the compact's doors as I carried him across the two lanes of the freeway, the bloody sedan driver stopping traffic until we were all safely on the side of the road.

I set the boy down on the wide freeway railing and checked to make sure he was OK. Then I focused on the mom and child. The woman was Indian, from India, as were her kids, and spoke broken English, but I managed to get that even though her upper arm had a wide bleeding gash, she was well enough to care for her baby, which seemed fine. I asked the sedan driver if he was OK, and he mumbled a response I didn't get but I assumed since he was able to respond he was at least sentient. Then I stopped traffic again and ran back to my car to get my t-shirt.

The police showed up along with a firetruck and an ambulance as I was wrapping the woman's arm. I explained what I'd witnessed to the cops, then left the scene without goodbyes. No point in lingering now that everyone was being taken care of. I'd been driving virtually daily since I was 15 and had seen plenty of accidents. I'd stopped to help in only a few since most were minor and I'd have merely been an additional distraction. This was no minor accident, but no one died, or seemed permanently injured I told myself as I pulled into traffic on the 101, trying to convince myself to stop trembling.

I aggressively wove through traffic to get to Maria's to meet Lee. Twenty minutes had passed since we'd left the club. I hoped he hadn't assumed I stood him up and left. The only parking space was several blocks from the restaurant, and I ran to Maria's arriving breathless and sweaty, and right into Lee as he was leaving.

"I'm so sorry," I managed, approaching him just outside Maria's. He still wore the loose navy shorts he played in, and had put on his black, hooded pullover.

"Where have you been? You were right behind me—" he began, then cut himself off. "Whoa. What happened? You OK?"

"There was a car accident," I started, but had to swallow back bile. "I really need some water."

"Absolutely." Lee slid his hand in mine and led me back into the restaurant. "Table for two, please," he told the anorexic hostess. She led us back to a small square wooden table next to an ivy covered column in the outdoor patio. He held my hand till we sat on opposite side of the table.

I told him what happened in detail, continually sipping my water so I wouldn't throw up.

"Jesus," Lee said. "You could have been blown to bits. Whatever compelled you to risk your life like that?"

"Tad over-dramatic, don't ya think? Cars only explode in the movies. Besides, one of those kids could grow up to cure cancer, or initiate world peace or something. Never know." I flashed a wan smile.

"A cynic and an idealist. Must be a continual battle inside your head between the realist and the dreamer."

I eyed him. "You bet." His insight was shockingly astute, but bordered creepy, especially for a guy. I sipped my water, then took a deep breath to slow my racing heart. "I'm just glad everyone was OK. We all got damn lucky no one got killed out there today." I pictured the terrified kid, and the mom's torn up arm, and the sedan driver's head bleeding. And suddenly bile rose fast and I was sure I was going to barf. "Can we just drop it? I don't want to think about it anymore. I really hate gore."

Lee's glassy eyes were still fixed on me, but I couldn't tell if he was high. Jealously consumed me again, with the notion he was buzzed, and I sat there fighting myself over asking him if he knew where I could connect.

"You want a drink?" he asked. "Seems to me you could use one right now. I don't generally drink, but I'll share a bottle of wine if you'd like."

"I don't drink, actually." I wondered, if like everyone else, he assumed I was in AA. "Can't stand the taste of alcohol." I stuck my tongue out to emphasize my point. "Liquor has this revolting edge that everyone said I'd grow into but I never have."

"Wow. Me neither. And beyond the taste, I never liked the buzz. Too mind numbing. Hard to fathom why most everyone I know, or have ever met, frankly, drinks, and way beyond the social lubricant they all claim it to be."

"It's astounding where the mind will go to rationalize bad behavior." I smiled, finally calming.

He laughed, this deep, wickedly-knowing chortle. "Touché."

His eyes fixed on mine and I felt the tangible connection between us, almost electric, like plugging in, a profound understanding, a spark of shared knowledge. "I think you're like the only adult I've ever met who doesn't like alcohol. I'm always the odd one out with friends, when we go to dinner or especially to a club. Even with my family. My father insists toasting with water invalidates the sentiments."

"Well, no offense to your old man, but the sentiment is the toast, no matter what's in the glass." Lee assured me, then picked up his water glass and raised it. I followed his lead and we clinked our glasses, the words validating me, connecting us again.

He really was quite cute, even with his short stature, and the pudgy thing he had going on. And he wasn't married anymore..."So weed is your only indulgence?" I asked, intuition knowing the answer.

"I have many." He flashed a reticent grin. "If you're talking outside chemistry, weed's the only thing I've stuck with over the years. Tried a lot of the stuff going around high school, like everyone else. But like alcohol, they took me too far out there."

"How often do you get high?" I asked, even though I knew the answer to this too.

"Occasionally. Maybe a few times a month. On the weekends mostly, I guess. A frivolous indulgence at best." He answered without hesitation. "I generally wait for something good to come around, buy an ounce and smoke it till it's gone. Hard to find good smoke these days with so much Mexican crap flooding the market."

I stared at him, tried to see into him, if he believed himself, if I believed him. I wanted to. The voice in my head labeling him a stoner *could* be wrong.

A young waitress wearing tight black slacks, a white blouse and a red bow-tie appeared at our table. She flicked her long, tawny hair back over her shoulder and gave Lee a flirtatious smile. "Hi. Welcome to Maria's. What can I get you to drink?"

Lee smiled, then nodded for me to order first, and mirrored my canonical choice—black tea with milk, the English way. The waitress left and Lee opened his menu. "The best thing they make here is their Angel Hair Pomodoro. It's light, but very tasty."

I read along in my menu. Pomodoro sounded like L.A. chic for spaghetti. Expensive 'pasta' was all the rage lately. "Sounds good." Spaghetti was among my top favorites, but a rare high-calorie treat, though allowable after our workout this afternoon.

The patio was surrounded by high stone walls covered in ivy. Soft light glittered from the small white bulbs woven through the trellis overhead, and the candles in the red jars in the center of each table. The rich aroma of roasting garlic, and the subtle, sweet scent of Italian herbs and spices permeated the air and teased my taste buds.

"God, it smells great in here." Lee's face tilted upwards and he took a long, deep breath. He'd read my mind again.

Our waitress came back with our teas and Lee ordered for both of us, including a chopped salad to share, looking at me to confirm.

When she left, he focused his attention back on me. "So, you don't drink. Are you one of the rare few of our "Me" generation who's resisted sharing a joint, or even popping their mother's little helpers?"

Ah, a moment of truth. I could cop to all the way, or hide behind the façade of 'normal,' as I did with most people. "I smoke weed occasionally, though it's been a while. My connection abandoned his lucrative dealing career for a record deal about a month ago." I paused, hoping he may offer his contact, but he didn't. "I did a bit of speed in high school and college. Probably like you, I tried a lot chemistry, but the downs weren't worth the highs," I began, still debating how far to take it.

"For me, either. I never got into speed, or hallucinogens. Too taxing on the body."

"Marijuana's a hallucinogen."

"Well, it's an opiate derivative, and a mild one at that. It's not like heroin, or even opium. And it's not addictive like those drugs are."

That was a debate I wasn't about to engage in right then. "Well, I've never done heroin. Too afraid of needles, and that I'd like it too much and get hooked. And Mother's Little Helpers never interested me. Depressants aren't my thing. I can get down all by myself. According to my folks, I live there."

Lee narrowed his brows quizzically. "Wow. You don't seem like a depressive to me. Interesting your parents see you that way. Are you close with them?"

"Yes and no. I live only a couple miles from my parents' house, the one I grew up in. Studio City is great for freelancing. Thirty minutes to downtown or the beach during off-hours," I added, to assuage the impression I needed the security of living near my folks. "I spend a lot of time with my family, but I've always been the odd one out. For the longest time I thought I was secretly adopted."

Lee gave a quick, short laugh. "I used to wish I was." He took a sip of his tea. "And I must confess, sometimes I still hold out hope my real parents were a physicist and a college professor that died in some horrible car wreck when I was an infant."

"Jesus, and I thought I was dark," I joked, sort of. "I'm guessing you don't exactly get along with your folks?

"I get along with my dad okay. He lives in Arizona so we rarely see each other. My mom lives in Chicago. We hardly ever speak. I don't think she likes me very much. I think I remind her of my dad."

Red flag, my intuition waved. Any guy who thinks his mother doesn't like him is bound to harbor misogyny. "You have siblings?"

"An older sister. She lives in Oregon, with her female partner. My sister's a dyke." He stared at me, looking for my reaction, I guess.

"Does that bug you?" Didn't bug me, but his using the word 'dyke' instead of 'gay' seemed telling.

"Nope. Sexual orientation isn't a morality play for me. I've been an atheist since I was old enough to get that religion truly is the opiate of the masses, and a naive buzz at that. Doesn't take much to convince you to believe when you're looking for someone to save

35

you."

I stared at him, rather awestruck. To date, there wasn't a man I'd gone out with who attested to being a non-believer— one of the primary reasons I was still single. And while Lee's uniqueness impressed, I bridled at his arrogance. "I don't want to lead, or be shown the way. I want to share the journey."

He sipped his tea but didn't take his eyes off me. "Me too." He flashed a soft smile. "And I'm hoping with someone like you."

I stayed fixed on him, smiled softly, on the precipice of knowledge— knowing who Lee was, and desire—the man I suddenly found myself wanting him to be.

Our waitress delivered the salad, set it between us and gave Lee a perfect smile. "Enjoy," she said with a quick glance at me and left.

Lee started eating. He savored the bite almost lovingly, closed his eyes before swallowing then opened them and focused on me with a big happy grin. "Mmm. Lovely." He took another forkful, bigger, and before consuming the bite indicated with his fork for me to join him.

I did, savoring the lovely mix of veggies and greens covered in tangy, sweet Italian dressing. I generally felt shame eating in front of men, but salad was virtually guilt-free calorically.

"Thank you for joining me tonight. Other than the occasional meal with a few old friends, I've been kinda gun shy around new people since Sharon and I split."

"I've heard it feels like a death, when a marriage ends," though Lee didn't seem to be grieving at the moment. "I don't ever want to know what divorce feels like. When I give my word, especially on such a profound commitment for the rest of my life, I better be damn sure I'm prepared to keep it." Lee's expression harden, and felt the urge to recant, but instead took another bite to fill my mouth so nothing else derogatory would pop out.

"I did not, and still do not take marriage lightly," Lee said softly, but firmly. "I know Sharon and I never should have married. I knew it then. What I didn't know was how to walk away." He studied me a moment before he continued speaking. "I met her in Vegas when she was just 21, and a voluptuous, raving beauty. She was a dancer in one of those chorus line shows, a speed freak and cokehead. I didn't know how to help her." He shook his head as if with regret, and then delivered a compact discourse on why they were a bad match from the start. He made his ex sound crazy, subtly relieving himself of all culpability.

Watch out, intuition hissed. No matter how Lee rationalized his breakup, the fact was he made a profound promise he did not keep. In all probability, his word could not be trusted—a dangerous character flaw unlikely to change without some profound awakening, and his words did not indicate he'd had one. I kept hoping he'd admit to falling for the transient lure of beauty, then examine the cost and acknowledge the avalanche he'd helped perpetuate. But he didn't.

"Bad as it was, I was still prepared to see it through. It was Sharon that initiated the divorce." Lee glared at me with righteous

37

indignation, as if he knew the accusations in my head. "My ex-wife was having an affair with a business associate of mine and wanted out of our marriage." His glare softened. He shrugged, shook his head and looked away.

"Wow... How fucked up is that." The words kind of fell out of my mouth.

Lee scoffed. "Pretty fucked up."

"I'm sorry." I felt the sting of humility. If what he said was true, Lee didn't break his vows after all. His ex did, which absolved him of divorcing. "I'm really sorry that happened to you."

"Me too." A moment passed and his expression brightened. "I have learned, though. I can be taught! I now know I need to be with someone who's ready to commit to working at communicating— staying *connected*. Before I marry again, I have to trust my partner and I are on the same team, and we're looking to help each other be the best we can be. Till death do us part kind of thing." He half shrugged and gave me his single-dimpled smile. "Know what I mean?"

I did. He'd just recited my definition of Love. Lee was *too cute*. And I had the urge to lean across the small table, gather his face in my hands and kiss him right then.

The waitress appeared and served us our meals. Lee consumed the pasta with the same flourish as the salad. I took small bites, wrapping thin strands of capellini around my fork carefully before eating to savor each morsel.

"You like?" Lee asked with a quick raise of his brow.

"Yes. It's very nice."

We ate silently, almost reverently, sharing the same delectable experience. And I felt content, safely ensconced with Lee, a million miles from Lonely.

The silence didn't feel awkward, nor did it last long. Again, conversation flowed from favorite restaurants, foods, news gossip, in a smooth, even exchange. We lingered over our meals, enjoying our food, the evening, immersed in each other. It took conscious effort to leave some pasta on the plate instead of consuming every last bite and licking off the sauce. Lee finished every bite. Our waitress came back, took our dishes and left the bill, which Lee insisted on paying, leaving $50 in the black billfold.

He walked me to my car. It was dim, and cold, the air thick with evening haze that glowed around the stark streetlamps. I stopped when we got to my car. We both stood there, caught in that awkward moment not knowing what to do next.

"Thank you for another enjoyable evening." He stared at me, searching, then his eyes wandered to my lips. I anticipated the kiss and felt my walls go up. He'd agreed to just friends, and that's exactly where my intuition insisted we keep it.

As if reading me, he shoved his hands deep in the pocket on his pullover. "See ya on the courts on Thursday at 4:00," he said. "Drive safe."

"I will. And thanks again for dinner." I stepped off the curb, then moved around my Civic, unlocked my car door and opened it. "See ya Thursday. Goodnight." I got in and pulled away, leaving him standing on the curb.

My mind raced right along with my palpating heart on the drive home. If Lee really only used 'occasionally,' it could be he wasn't the addict I feared. And he didn't renege on his marriage if his ex-wife had broken the promise between them. Perhaps he wasn't the train wreck my intuition had conjured. He seemed everything I'd advertised for: Passionate, to be sure. And with his lack of religious orientation, obviously an independent thinker. Maybe my resistance to moving beyond friendship with Lee was merely fear *masquerading* as intuition.

Could Lee be my knight? I flashed on his baby face, smiling at me across the table tonight, and couldn't help smiling. I'd never fallen head over heels for a man, experienced that intense rush people talk about with new relationships. But from the moment I met Lee on the courts, and each encounter since, it was like being with someone I'd known a very long time. I'd heard friends talk about chemistry with this and that new guy they were dating. Whatever *that* meant. I assumed it was merely physical attraction, infatuation. Surely, they were confusing lust with love. But then, I wasn't factoring in chemistry. Powerful stuff. Dangerous stuff.

-

Chapter 4

Lee told me he had plans to go see *Other People's Money* with a friend on Thursday in the hall after playing ball. "I'd ask you to come, but you'll just come up with an excuse not to." He watched me intently, almost smugly.

He was right, of course. I had no intention of meeting his friends right then. "I'd like to, but I have to work. I'm on deadline with a direct mail campaign for my credit union client. I'm supposed to sell their low-income members that the $300 cash 'award' for refinancing their car is worth the thousands more it'll cost them to pay off their car loan."

"Excellent. Very plausible for on the fly." Lee drained his Diet Coke and tossed the can in the bin. "Ready to go?"

"I'm not bullshitting you, Lee. I really do have to work." We went outside and started down the front steps. I got that he was disappointed by his poker expression. "But even if I didn't, you're right. I wouldn't go out with you and your friend tonight. I hate being the third wheel, or making anyone feel like one. And, honestly, I'm not very social by nature."

"Rather be home, making it with your muse?" Lee virtually quoted me from our first conversation, validating me— he'd listened, heard me, and remembered what I'd said. He pointed a rectangular black remote at his Mercedes parked in the first space closest to the stairs. His car alarm disengaged with a chirp.

"Hang on a minute." Lee opened the driver's door and deposited his gym bag and racket, then retrieved his hooded sweatshirt from the back seat and put it on over his t-shirt. "On Tuesday you mentioned you'd lost your connection." He reached up to his visor, and I was surprised when he pull out a pack of Marlboro Reds. I'd assumed he didn't smoke cigarettes, then realize what was likely in the box as he flipped open the top and extracted a joint. "If I can't make your evening fun with a movie and some great company, at least I can help make it a little more surreal."

A visceral rush of lust, the hormone release scenting my skin in rich musk. I smiled, nodded, though the strength of my desire scared me, as did his offer. *See*, my intuition insisted. Reality cast a passing shadow on the moment, and mocked me my earlier fantasies about Lee. *He really is the addict you suspect.*

Lee put the joint in his mouth and lit it with a flat silver lighter. He sucked deftly, his movements smooth, practiced, pursing his full red lips softly in what looked like a sensual kiss. The rich scent wafted on the cold evening air as he handed me the J. I looked around the lot, packed with cars but vacant of people, then slipped the joint from his fingers and sucked deftly as well. The smoke filled my mouth and singed my throat with viscous sweetness. I suppressed a cough, my lungs tender after not smoking for almost a month, but couldn't help choking as I exhaled.

Lee gave me a quick, knowing grin as he slipped the cigarette pack back above the visor, then closed his door and engaged the car alarm. "Let's walk," he said, and we did. I took another hit and let the rush wash over me, suspending time, even space for a moment, disconnecting me from the cold, though I shivered compulsively before handing him the joint. As he slipped it from me, the warmth of his fingers momentarily radiated into my hand.

We stopped by my car so I could drop off my racket and get my jacket. Face woke up as I opened the hatchback, got up and shook out, then came to me with her sleepy face on, tail vaguely swishing, until she saw Lee. She brightened considerably at the prospect of a new friend. Her tail ramped to wide arcs, her smile undeniable.

"Well, who's this?" Lee asked affectionately, handed me the joint then stroked the dog between her ears and down her back. Face preened.

"Killer Dog Face. Meet Lee." I took another hit then handed him the joint as I retrieved my leather jacket on the passenger seat. "She goes by 'Face' though."

"Nice to meet you Face. You don't seem like a killer to me." He continued stroking her and she stood frozen with his touch. "You're just a big sweetie, aren't you."

"She is at that," I said, coming around to the back of the car again. "Stay in the car, baby. Watch out," I said to the dog then reached up to the open hatchback. Lee backed up and I shut Face inside. I caught her forlorn look as we walked away. A passing pang of guilt as I took the joint from Lee, but it wasn't safe for her to be running around on crowded Ventura Blvd at night.

I took a long draw, the smoke's chemistry tingling my scalp with tickling prickles. I smiled with the sensation, revealed in the warmth of my body heat reflecting back onto me, felt my shoulders loosen, my stride become casual, more gliding than walking. The buzz narrowed my focus and waylaid fear. Being single, alone and childless at 33 dissolved to the moment at hand with Lee.

"So, where'd you come up with Killer Dog Face?

"Killer as in cool. Dog because she is one. And Face after a term of endearment my mother calls me. I figured she deserved three names, like most people have."

"I see." Lee smiled. "Must be nice having a companion who's always glad to see you."

"It is. Face is probably the easiest relationship I've ever had. Dogs are simple. No hidden agendas. Easy to please. Just good company."

He took another deep hit, and again I had the impression he was kissing a lover. "Wow. I'd say that's a fairly accurate description of me, too," he said as he exhaled, and a playful grin emerged.

I smiled back. "Hmm, well, you don't seem all that simple to me."

His grin turned into a genuine smile. With the slightest bow of his head I got that he got that I, too, was paying attention— present when we were together.

We strolled along the boulevard, exchanging the joint. The shops were closed for the night. Cars whizzed by but the sidewalk was empty. No one walks in L.A. Few couples I knew really talked either, but Lee and I chatted non-stop, an even, fluid exchange again. We turned around at Bank of America, the digital clock in their window alarming Lee it was 6:30, and he'd agreed to meet his buddy at 7:00.

A midnight blue BMW slowed to pace us a block from the club. Tinted windows unrolled slowly. Young Black men peered from the passenger and back seat with blank expressions. I was scared out

44

of my mind, especially with the Rodney King beating being shown all the time, followed by angry on-the-street interviews, and drive-bys all over the news.

Lee slid his hand in mine and held it, took one last hit off the last bit of the joint, then flicked the roach into the gutter and glanced at them casually as we continued walking. "How ya doing, man? Nice night for a walk." He blew out a thin stream of smoke and spoke in an offhanded manner, showing no fear.

No response from anyone in the car but they stayed pacing us. My heart was coming through my chest. I anticipated the gun, and my mind played the scene of getting splattered with Lee's blood just before my body is riddled with bullets.

"Yo cracka," the passenger said, and I drew a sharp breath. Lee squeezed my hand, virtually pulling me to kept our casual pace. "Ya achin to score some real shit insteada that borda crap yo blowin, stinkin up this fine night?"

Lee looked at him. "Yo muthafucka," he said jokingly, probably smiling, though I couldn't see his expression. I think my jaw must have literally dropped and I braced for the bullet in my head. The guys expression stayed blank, then broke into a huge smile, his white teeth practically glowing against his dark skin and the night. "My lady here's been looking to cop," Lee continued casually. "Whatda ya got?" I almost stopped, but the way he glanced at me, practically glared, told me to keep walking and to play along.

"And a mighty fine bitch she is," the guy in the back seat said as the car pulled to the curb abruptly and the passenger got out. I stopped, paralyzed. Lee stopped too, let go of my hand and moved in front of me as the guy, a kid really, closer to teen than adult came up to us. He looked at Lee, then at me.

"I got like sixty on me," Lee said with authority, extracting his wallet from the back pocket of his gym shorts. He opened it widely so the guy could see Lee pull out the only cash, three $20 bills. "I'm willing to part with it all for the right bud. Don't wanta be disappointin my woman, if ya know what I mean."

The guy flashed his bright white smile again and looked at me. I scowled at him, trying to appear tougher than I felt. His smile softened, and his expression became so disarmingly charming I had to smile back. "We don't want no wrath of a piece like this, now do we. I's gots just what yo need, baby." He reached into the front pocket of his hooded sweatshirt and pulls out a small baggie of buds. "California gold. Home grown, straight from the Emerald Triangle. $35 an eighth, but I'll give ya a break at $60 for the quarter." He glanced around nervously. So did I, playing the scene of getting busted in a dope deal with the boys from the hood.

Cars whizzed by us as Lee examined the bud, then smelled it. I looked for cops. The dealer's driver was watching his rear view, until he saw me looking at him. Then he waggled his tongue at me.

Lee flicked the $60 he'd palmed in between his fingers and extended it to the dealer who plucked the bills from his hand. The dealer returned to his car. He got in and barely shut the door when the driver gunned the engine and they took off down Ventura, idiot laying half his tires on the road.

"I believe this is for you," Lee said, handing me the baggie of buds. "Can't guarantee the quality, but it sure smells good."

"Are you kidding me?" I managed while trying to slow my breathing and racing heart. "Why didn't you just ignore them?"

"They were dealers— what *you* said you were looking for the other night at dinner."

"I didn't mean bangers off the street. Jesus, Lee..." A group of cars drove by fairly slowly and I noticed a cop among them. The cop must have noticed us on the sidewalk because he slowed to a crawl just after passing.

Lee put the weed into the pocket of his sweatshirt, then slid his hand back in mine and we started walking again. "Where do you think your lilly-white dealers are getting their stash from. We just got it from the source, honey, at a third the price."

The cop trolled in front of us a few hundred feet. I wasn't sure if I was glad or scared of having a cop as our escort, afraid of the bangers coming back.

"Do you *usually* buy weed from roving street dealers?" I asked softly, but incredulously.

"First time, actually," Lee said, glancing at me. "I figured it was better to deal than get jacked, or worse. In case you haven't noticed, there's a lot of pissed off Black's right now. At least doing the deal we got something out of it instead of being the latest drive-by headline." We turned into the brightly lit parking lot of the racket club. "Customers are far more profitable than victims."

The cop took off down Ventura. What Lee said ricocheted in my head. Buying dope from that banger may in fact have been the best strategy to keeping everyone safe, and satisfied. He could well have been my hero tonight, saving us, me, from—"

"Well, that was fun," Lee said as we approached my car.

I didn't know if he meant the walk with me or the gang bangers, but didn't ask. I wanted outta there. I tried to will my heart to slow as I thanked him for the game, for the walk and the smoke, then unlocked my car to stop Face from whining.

"My pleasure. Truly," Lee said. "We on for next Tuesday?"

I opened my car door. "You bet." Lee was simply the best I'd played with yet. Face stuck her head out and continued to whine for attention until I stroked her. Lee did too and the dog preened, though he was looking at me while patting her.

His glassy eyes drifted from mine, looked beyond me, to the street. I turned to see a beater car cruise by the parking lot slowly. "Neighborhood's not what it used to be." Lee moved to hold my door, as if to usher me into my car. "I gotta take off. And you probably should too, before I leave the lot." He paused, waiting for me to get in. So I did. "I look forward to playing again. See ya Tuesday then. Have a good weekend." He shut my door, then turned away and waved without looking back as he walked to his car.

I felt a vague stab of rejection then wondered why as I started my car and left the club. I was the one who'd insisted on just friendship.

I wasn't sexually attracted to him. I preferred long and lean, and Lee was— not. His randomly scoring on the street from punk dealers was too casual to be new, unless he was that good a salesman, which made him even more dangerous to consider getting intimate with. And his practiced, passionate kiss off the joint earlier confirmed his using 'occasionally' really meant 'consistently.' Way beyond a *connoisseur*—with weed, his passion for food, and likely more, Lee was a user, an obsessive, compulsive addict. *No doubt about it,* intuition asserted. *Takes one to know one.* And my inner voice mocked me on the drive home for entertaining fantasies about him being Mr Right, when I knew Lee wasn't my knight our first conversation.

In my construct of the American Dream, addiction was not part of any scene. I needed a partner to be my strength, fill the void, give me ground. He'd be fit, disciplined, and motivate me to be, not join me in the mire of my obsessions. I wasn't blaming Lee for turning me on, responding to what I'd virtually asked for over dinner at Maria's. I felt grateful he'd provided me this moment of clarity. Lee was my mirror, not my knight, and he couldn't save me. The sting of Lonely suddenly lurked, but the buzz shut down feeling despondent, desperate— letting me focus solely on accomplishing the task at hand instead of pining over the family I didn't have or the fine arts career I'd yet to manifest.

Regardless that producing advertising campaigns was on the shallow end of socially redeeming, or that I was making my clients millions while I could barely pay my bills, freelancing afforded a living with no commute, and without the bullshit of office politics or sexist bosses. Equality was a joke in the 1990s. Even with a college

49

degree, most women went into teaching, psychology, nursing, or shilled makeup or real estate, or got stuck in an admin or some junior level position in departments run by men. And made half or less than our male counterparts. I was glad to be able to work from home, when I wanted to, in my own space. And right then doing freelance marketing seemed a practical, respectable career path as I sat at my drafting table and began spinning words that skated lies to make my rent.

-

Chapter 5

Lee called at 8:30 the next morning and asked me to join him and some friends for dinner at Spago's to help him ring in his 39th birthday. I wished him a happy birthday, then declined his invitation, of course. He laughed, said he knew I would.

"Then play racquetball with me tomorrow. I'm gonna need a workout after tonight's dinner. Come on. We should be playing at least three times a week anyway, ramp up the calorie burn here." Lee was clearly a salesman. He knew I played ball to get and stay lean. I could virtually feel him smiling through the wire.

"What time?" I inquired, smiling too.

Late Saturday afternoon Lee was on the last court available for the day. We played hard until the club kicked us off the court at 7:00, closing early on the weekends. He talked me into joining him for dinner at Hamburger Hamlet over Diet Cokes in the lobby while the staff cleaned up around us. It was his birthday *weekend* after all, and he didn't want to spend Saturday night home alone and bored.

"Come with me down to Laguna Beach tomorrow. I want to buy a piece of art for my condo. They have some great galleries down there. You can enlighten me with your knowledge of art history, put that useless degree, as you've mentioned, to use," Lee teased over his quarter pound double cheese and bacon burger.

He surprised me, first remembering what I'd said about my college education in a casual conversation weeks ago. Second, beyond just soliciting my knowledge, he was interested in art history, one of my passions. I looked down at my Chicken Caesar and suddenly resented the hell out of it, and me— my body— for storing everything I ate to fat, requiring I eat mostly salad to maintain trim, even with playing hard ball at least three days a week.

"Lee," I began, but hesitated, not wanting to hurt his feelings. "I really love playing racquetball with you. And I, too, would love to play more— three, four times a week if you're up for it."

"Love to." His eyes sort of twinkled, I think, and his full lips took on a tentative smile.

"Thing is, I don't want to lead you on." The twinkle in his eyes dimmed, so I tried to soften my delivery. "You're great company, and easy to be with, Lee. And I'd love to continue hanging out after we play, like we have been, like we are, as long as we keep it just friends." Truth was, he was glorious lightness in my persistent gloom, and more fun than I'd had with anyone in years, but I didn't say it, hoping to keep my message as unambiguous as possible.

51

His eyes glimmered again. "I enjoy hanging with you too, Ray. I love our connection, how much we have in common— that you *think*, and you don't drink, and you're not a blind believer." Lee flashed a quick grin. "You are wildly provocative, and wickedly evocative, my dear," he said, totally serious.

The compliment empowered me for a second, till trepidation countered. I got that he really wasn't hearing me. "Lee—"

"Look Ray, I'm happy to just hang out together when we can. No pressure, no worries, and with no expectations of anything beyond the friendship we're building." He kept his eyes fixed on mine, our connection only broken by the waiter clearing our plates. And even though my intuition knew his interest exceeded his words, I decided to believe him right then, and pretend we could just be friends.

On the 101 heading down to Laguna Beach at 10:00 a.m., Lee reached up to his visor and pulled out the Marlboro Red's box, extracted a joint, then flashed a grin. "Care to join me?"

Intuition mocked me. There was no doubt Lee was an addict. Friends we were becoming, and must surely remain. And since friendship was all we'd ever share, there was no need to wear a façade with Lee. I took the joint he extended and inhaled deeply, hoping to shut down my bewildering disappointment, and simply enjoy his company and the moment at hand. I relaxed into the soft leather seat, stared out at another sunny day in L.A., took a quick hit and handed Lee the J.

Driving under the influence of THC didn't phase me. In all the years I'd been driving high, or been with other drivers who are, if anything, weed seems to heighten caution behind the wheel. It knocked back flash anger at idiot drivers— a universe away from drunk, which seems to evoke blankness, or induce virulent testosterone reactions. Wasn't really all that concerned about a DUI either. I'd never known anyone detained or even ticketed for weed with the few cases I'd heard of someone getting pulled over while smoking. Apparently L.A. cops corroborated my observations of weed vs liquor while driving. And they should know, spending all day "scraping people off the road," a CHP officer once said to me about his job.

Lee got off the 405 at Newport Beach and took Hwy 1 down the coast, along the rim of the Pacific. I unrolled my window and sucked in the salty sweet air of my beautiful ocean. Down by the sea was my absolute favorite place to be. He turned me on to Brian Ferry, among the many tunes he'd complied onto the cassette we were listening to. I sang along softly to Phil Collins and Sting.

"Oh my god. Your voice is *fantastic*," he said after I finished singing *Long, Long Way to Go.*

"Thanks." My voice was one of the best bits about me. I had perfect pitch and entertained myself often.

"You should make a tape. Send it to producers. See if you can get any traction."

"Yeah. Along with a fine arts career. Music would leave me equally homeless."

Lee scoffed, shook his head. "I love this tune," he said, turning up the live version of *Hotel California*. "This song isn't really about California. The words are a commentary on the ephemeral women of L.A. Thank you, for not being one of them."

Don Henley's melodic tenor rang through the Bose stereo. "She got a lot of pretty, pretty boys she calls friends." I thought about Jon, and Tim, and Marc, and Michael, and now Lee. Most people swept into my life like waves, crashing in and slowly drifting out, and I wondered if Lee would be one of them. In my experience, eventually everyone moves on, even if they never leave Los Angeles.

Expensive homes began dotting the rolling hills as we came into Laguna. Hwy 1 became dotted with galleries and chic eateries. We indulged in pastries as walked the small seaside hamlet, and spent the afternoon examining some of the finest original art from around the world. Lee purchased an original Patrick Nagel for $5,500, a three by four foot ink and gauche drawing of a woman with short black hair, in a purple halter top walking a Doberman. He said it reminded him of me and Face.

We stopped at Crystal Cove on the way back and spent an hour or so combing the tide pools, then went to Balboa Island for frozen bananas. After a stroll on Newport beach, we took the car ferry across the harbor to get dinner. We indulged in teriyaki chicken with mudpie for dessert at The Chart House. I insisted on paying the bill, a gesture of friendship for his birthday, I'd told him, though it was more to even the field since he'd been continually treating me. I avoided choking over the $160 tab, left my credit card in the billfold and went to the bathroom, where I put a finger down my throat to get rid of the expensive calories I'd just consumed— a rare practice these days, when I've been particularly indulgent, like I was all day.

Lee pulled into my driveway close to 10:00p.m., blocking my roommates dented, dark green Chevy Vega. He put his car in park and looked at me, searching. "I had a great time today. Thank you for joining me, for turning me on to fine art, and for sharing my birthday weekend." His eyes drifted from mine to beyond me, and I followed his line of sight to Suzanne coming out the front door in a tizzy.

"Hi! Hellooo," she waved wildly. "I need to get out. Can you please move your car?" Wearing her usual black slacks and loose black long sleeve shirt which exaggerated her beanpole form, she carried a bunch of loose papers, dropping quite a few as she closed the front door behind her to keep Face inside. She bent to pick them up and dropped some more in the process. I couldn't help smiling with a shake of my head.

I looked back at Lee. He, too, was smiling at my roommates antics. "She's a bit scattered, but she's reliable with the rent, and a damn good musician." I suddenly felt pressured to get out of his car with Suzanne waiting for him to move it. "I really should get going. Happy birthday, again. And thanks for today." I opened the door to let her know I was coming, and Lee was going.

"Thank you. And for dinner too. See you tomorrow on the courts at 4:00? We're on for Mondays, Wednesdays and Fridays now, right?"

"You bet. Look forward to working off some of the gluttony we've been engaging in." I gave him a weak smile. "Well, goodnight." I got out of his car.

"Goodnight," he said softly.

I thought I sensed disappointment with his last look before I shut the door, though I may have been projecting the reaction I got from most guys. I had no intention of inviting Lee in and going to bed with him, as so many of my contemporaries did these days after a date or two. I'd had sex with five men so far, and only rarely for entertainment. I'd turned masturbation into a fine art, and did not need a man to satisfy me sexually. I've never confused sex and love, like so many women who give into lust harboring an unconscious hope for commitment. Our desire for sex is an evolutionary imperative. Fucking won't form a meaningful bond if none existed before the shared orgasm and momentary tenderness that follows.

After the last time with Jon, I decided the next guy I had sex with would be the last guy I'd ever sleep with. It wasn't exactly about waiting until marriage, but I was counting on my next sexual relationship to be with the man I intended to spend my life, and who was ready to make that kind of commitment to me. And my intuition assured me that would never be with Lee.

11/09/91

Obsession times two serves neither.

-

Chapter 6

For the next several weeks, Lee and I spent almost every day together. He called me most mornings before 9:00 to confirm racquetball on days we had a game, or to convince me to join him for dinner if we weren't playing ball. I didn't take much convincing. I thoroughly enjoyed being with him— felt alive, *awake* when we were together, wide awake, like I used to when I was a kid on adventures with Michael. After ball we'd turn the other on to a new restaurant, or meet up after work at an old favorite. I coped the check at the dives I consistently chose. He insisted on paying for the trendy places he picked, since he made five times my income, so he claimed. I humbly accepted his generosity, even though I knew it a bad practice with our *just friends* status.

On the weekends we ventured further—up to Hearst's Castle in San Simeon the Sunday after Laguna, then down to Sea World in San Diego the next. He always had weed, and always offered it. On the way to dinner after a game, or stuck in traffic on a Saturday, sharing a joint was in almost every scene. Our lives started to mesh together, and Lonely receded further each day. We didn't cross the line of friendship, sticking to a hug or a quick L.A. kiss when greeting or parting.

The Mercedes' headlights flashed through the bay window as his car pulled into my driveway at exactly 7:30 p.m. I'd been hesitant to accept his offer to help me cook tonight, afraid that inviting him to my place might give him the wrong message, especially with my roommate at her boyfriend's again. But being with Lee provided the desired distraction to the notion of being alone with my pervasive

57

dread all evening, anticipating Thanksgiving with my family. He emerged from his car and swung his black leather jacket over his shoulder, then walked the narrow pathway to my front door with casual confidence. He'd dropped quite a bit of weight in the few weeks we'd been playing ball. His stomach was flat under his soft white shirt that rippled with his stride, tucked into worn blue jeans that hugged his hips just right.

"Hi," I said as I opened the front door.

"Hi." He gave me a quick kiss before acknowledging Face wagging her tail wildly. Lee gave the dog an obligatory pat, their typical exchange when he greeted her at my car or front door. He tossed his jacket on the end of the couch and I lead him through the small dining room and back to the kitchen. "What are we making?"

"Apple pie. I have to wait till tomorrow to make the green bean casserole or it'll get mushy."

"Ahh. A knowledgeable chef I see. I really enjoy cooking, especially baking. I love the way it makes a house smell— that homey feeling it evokes."

"Me, too. I hate the cleanup, though."

"I don't really mind that, especially if it's a team effort— sharing the cooking and cleaning. I think it's only fair for partners to split everyday tasks. Halving the pain leaves more time to double the pleasure." He flashed me a quick grin. "I'm ready to start when you are." He stood by my grandmother's linoleum table where I had gathered most of the ingredients and utensils. "Just tell me what you need."

"Recipe is in that *Joy of Cooking* book. Page 55, I think." I filled the kettle for tea and waited for the water to boil. Lee found the correct page and got to work.

I pictured my father sitting at the head of the table in my parents' kitchen while my mother, after a full day teaching, cooked dinner and served it. After each meal my mom, sister and I cleaned up as dad read the paper or went to watch TV. At the very least, a life with Lee would not be a repeat of my parents' marriage.

The kettle whistle blew, like a warning to stop harboring such fantasies, and I smiled with the thought. I prepared our teas and brought the steaming mugs to the table before going to the fridge and retrieving the bowl of peeled and cut-up apples I'd prepared earlier. "I grew up with the promise women could become whatever we wanted to be. Except no one bothered to tell me that we can have it all, only as long as we do it all. Women *get* to have a career, but working or not, we still do the housework, cook the meals and raise the kids."

"Thing is, it's not only unfair to women, it screws the guy, too." Lee added flour then vigorously mashed the ingredients together, and didn't look at me as he continued with conviction. "It's fucking 1991, and women *still* makes less than half of what men do in the same damn job, so the guy is stuck with being the breadwinner, which sucks. I want to *be* with my kids, there for them, as intricately involved in their lives as my wife."

I was glad he was absorbed in his task and didn't notice my

enamored grin. I stood at the end of the linoleum table, perpendicular to him, mixing sugar, maple syrup, vanilla into the cut apples.

"Hope you don't mind if I use my hands." Lee set the fork down, went to the sink, washed and dried his hands then came back to the table and gathered the flaky chunks together, almost lovingly coaxing them into a sphere. He retrieve the rolling pin and cutting board at the end of the table, rubbed flour up and down the wood cylinder of the pin coating it in white, then rolled out the dough into a virtually perfect twelve inch circle.

"You've obviously done this before," I marveled.

"Many times. Sharon loved to cook. It was one of the few good things we did together, which is why I gained 50 pounds the two years we were married."

He may have believed his words, but I knew them a lie. Blaming his wife, ignoring his culpability in the care of his own body reminded me again why we must remain just friends.

"The trick to a perfect crust is in the handling." Lee retrieved the glass Pyrex and set it in front of him. "You have to get your fingers under the thin skin very gently," which he did as he spoke. "And in one fluid motion put it where it belongs. Then let it go." He separated his hands quickly over the Pyrex and the circle of dough covered the pie plate and fell softly into place. "Voila." He looked at me and smiled, then expertly fluted the edges between his nimble fingers around the rim of the dish.

I poured my apple mixture into his perfect crust, sprinkled brown sugar mixed with flour and pecans on top. He opened the preheated oven for me to put the pie in.

"Looks fabulous. Very professional. Save me a piece if you can," Lee said as we cleared the table and piled the sink with dirty dishes.

"It's unlikely. My family are big dessert people." I knew he'd be home and alone for Thanksgiving, and an acute stab of guilt motivated me to ask Lee to join our family dinner tomorrow.

"Then we'll have to make another pie soon, just for us. Shall we relax in the living room— put a buzz on?" Lee flashed his Cheshire grin.

The impulse to invite him to Thanksgiving vanished with his suggestion. Inviting a male *friend* to meet my family would surely come back to bite me. Lee was adorable, smart, witty, successful. He'd win my parent's affections and they'd spend the evening pondering what the hell was wrong with their daughter that I wasn't engaged to him yet.

I led the way into the living room. Lee sat on the couch and sparked a joint. I knelt at the fireplace, struck a match on the brick cladding and lit the pyramid of twigs and logs I'd set up earlier.

"Is that a backgammon board?" He pointed to the wood board I'd picked up in Athens ten years back. It sat on its side on the bookshelf against the opposite wall from the couch, folded into a thin, rectangular box. Only someone familiar with a Tavli board would know what it was.

61

"You play?" I asked, even though I knew the answer. He sucked on the joint deeply, deftly.

"Yeah, just so happens I do." He blew out a straight thin stream of smoke. It seemed to dance around his hand as he extended the joint to me when I joined him on the couch. "Care for a game?" Lee got up and got the board, brought it to the couch and placed it between us as he sat back down.

We passed the joint back and forth as we set up the board. Within moments everything slowed. The room glowed orange from the firelight, and warmed me. I felt safe with Lee there instead of hyper-aware of every car that passed or every creak of the house. Sweet scents of baking cinnamon and sugar wafted from the kitchen. The familiar pleasure of Lee's company sated me, and I relaxed and focused on the game. Within a few moves we established a fluid rhythm. And Lee was good, quick and intuitive, one of the smoothest I'd run across. But I was better.

"Where did you learn to play backgammon like this?" He wanted to know after I'd beaten him nine out of eleven games.

"In Greece. They call it Tavli, means 'table,' and it's a national past time there. I did a summer quarter at a college in Athens and played like seven hours a day."

"You play very well." He picked up the remains of the joint we'd left in the ashtray and lit it, took a hit and handed it to me. "I thought I was good at this game, but you're killing me."

"You've won two games. And you can clearly keep up with me. Most

Americans can't. You're really quite good." I meant it, but then realized it could be construed as patronizing. "I've just had a lot more practice." I took a hit to stop anything else condescending escaping my lips, then handed Lee the joint and excused myself to get the apple pie from the oven.

It looked like a cover shot for Good Housekeeping. Lee's fluted crust was flaky golden brown. Thick, steaming fruit juice bubbled and oozed through clusters of melted brown sugar and tips of baked apples. I think I may have actually salivated as I transferred the pie from the oven to the stove top, fighting the urge to serve Lee and I up a couple of slices. We deserved it, as it was our collective efforts that produced this perfect creation. And I could always buy a pie tomorrow if I didn't have time after working to make one...

I came back into the living room showering accolades for our team effort, proud I'd resisted the siren of sugar, the buzz providing me a moment's pause of resistance to ravenously digging in. Lee humbly credited my management skills as I resumed my position on the couch. I sat cross-legged in front of the backgammon board and we resumed playing.

Again, we established a fast, even rhythm, but this time it seemed charged. Lee's focus was intense, like with racquetball. I could feel him collecting and directing his attention to the game, competing with the fire for the oxygen in the room. No words passed between us as we played. Most games lasted only minutes, and our rate of play accelerated with each.

I finally yielded from exhaustion. "As much as I'm enjoying this, I'm done for the night." Other than Chris, my roommate in Athen's, I hadn't played anyone of Lee's caliber since the locals at the cafes in Kolonaki Square.

"What a rush playing fast like that!" Lee straightened his legs and sank back into the couch cushion almost breathless. "That was great, a total kick, even though you just won the last fifteen games in a row." He picked up the roach in the ashtray, lit it and sucked. "A cynic, an idealist, and now a ringer. You're like a modern-day Sally Bowles, ever the mystery, Ray." His eyes twinkled with mischief as he extended the joint to me. I declined, to avoid burning my fingers on the last bit of the J, uncertain if I should be flattered or insulted by his reference to the neurotic American played by Liza Minnelli in *Cabaret*. "Do you have any idea how much you could make in Vegas with this game?" He stared at me. His dark, wavy hair hung in his eyes. He looked like the lead in a punk band.

"The old Greek barfly who taught me how to play like this told me never gamble on Tavli." I felt a need to temper his exuberance. "So, of course I did, took a local for a lot of drachmas. Never got a penny of it, and lost a good opponent. I didn't see him at the cafe after that. The old man was right. Playing Tavli is about passing the time of day, relaxing with a friend, or should be."

"Bet that old barfly was broke, which is why he spent his days in a cafe instead of at his villa on some island." Lee said. "It'd practically be a sure win putting money on you in a Tavli tournament." He flashed a cocky grin that chilled me. "Seriously, I'll back ya with some cash if you wanta give it a go."

I stared at him. He wore a poker face, and I got he wasn't joking. "I think gambling is devoid of creativity and fundamentally corrosive." I wasn't trying to be contentious, but didn't really care that I was, irked he'd ignored the moral of my barfly parable. "Win or lose, you still lose. When you win, you're winning from some poor schmuck who can't afford to lose. When you lose, you *are* the poor schmuck. Across the board, it's lose lose."

"I agree. That's why I don't gamble anymore," he said, then looked away, as if he'd been caught in a lie. He took a quick hit before dropping the roach in the ashtray. "I quit years ago, but I took it pretty far out there before giving it up." He focused on stacking the game pieces in their narrow holders on the side of the board and didn't look up while he spoke. "Started my junior year of high school. My friends and I would go to Vegas on the weekends. I quit college my first semester and worked for my dad's shipping company, which is where I learned the trade, to support my gambling habit. By your age, I was in major debt, quite a bit of which I owed to my father for covering what I took from his company." Lee glanced at me.

"You mean stole?"

His brow tightened, and I felt a visceral change, like a wall was suddenly between us. "Yeah. I told you I took it pretty far out there. My dad was very cool about it though, got his partner not to prosecute so long as the money was repaid, which I did, in full. Still owe the government close to half a mill in back taxes though. And I blew the shit out of my credit, which is why I always pay with cash. My dad had to co-sign for just about everything I own, from the Mercedes to my condo." Lee shrugged. "It was all a long time ago."

Not to me. His confession was new, and deeply disturbing information. I flashed on my mother delivering her parable of warning when I was very young, telling me and my sister of her first husband, addicted to gambling and alcohol, abandoning her at 21, leaving her broke and virtually homeless with an infant son. I thought I heard my inner voice scream *run!* I heard Lee's words but they didn't really register, like he must be telling a story of someone else. "You owe *half a million dollars* in back taxes?"

"Well, a bit over $400 g's now. I've been paying it off for the last four years, and it'll be a non-issue in five more. Then I close the book on my gambling days." He huffed. "Not exactly where I wanted to be at this late date, but once the taxman is off my back I'll be set to start socking it away." Lee shook his head as if disgusted. "Never again," he vowed, more to himself than me, I think.

All our intimate talks and he'd never mentioned his gambling problem. He'd led me to believe he'd completed college and was flush with money— financially secure. I glared at him, but was mad at me. Lee's admission confirmed what he'd clearly demonstrated— with weed, with food, with racquetball, and with Tavli tonight— all *empirical evidence* of his obsessive nature. His gambling days may be in the past, but every part of me knew it an indicator of his future. Some people turned practically anything into an addiction, and I could not dismiss my intuition's insistence that, like me, Lee was among them. He too was looking to fill a void inside. I sighed. "It's late, and I've got to work in the morning."

Lee picked up the dice and held them up between his thumb and forefinger. "Any time you're ready for another game..." He gave me a gentle, teasing smile.

I believe we're already engaged in one, but I didn't say it. I put my hand under one side of the board and waited for Lee to release the dice. He hesitated a moment then tossed them in. I closed the box, picked it up as I stood and went to the bookcase to put the game away and some distance between us. "Thank you for your help tonight."

"My pleasure." Lee ran his hand through his thick hair.

"Mine too. It was fun." I tried to think of something to say to get him to leave without chasing him away. "I'll see ya Friday on the courts?"

"Look forward to it." He stood, inhaled deeply. "God, it smells great in here."

It did too, smoky; sweet; citrus and cinnamon wafting from the kitchen for the fire to consume. He lifted his jacket from the end of the couch and watched me as he put it on. His glassy eyes flickered, reflected the firelight.

I moved to the door then rested my hand on the brass knob. "Thanks again for coming, and helping, and everything." I opened the door and cold crept in.

He stood close, less than a foot between us, facing me. "Call me tomorrow after dinner if you want to hang out, put a buzz on, play Tavli or something." He gave Face the pat she'd been standing next to us waiting for, then looked back at me. "Tell me, where's the good in goodnight?" He stared at me as if awaiting my reply to his rhetorical question.

I shrugged, smiled. "Goodnight, Lee. Drive safe. See ya Friday."

He kept his eyes fixed on mine a moment, then said "Goodnight, Ray," gave a slight bow and turned away. He waved without looking back as he walked the narrow path, and with only a quick glance at me in the doorway, got in his car and left.

I shut the door and dead-bolted it. The house shuddered, the floor creaked. I was chilled straight through. Suzanne was back to practically living at Tony's, until, of course, she'd catch him making it with some groupie again. It was wild what so many women put up with to have someone to be with. Face shadowed me to the bathroom, lay by the doorjamb and waited, then followed me back down the dark hallway. The dog curled in her beanbag as I shut my bedroom door, closing us in before climbing into bed.

It was creepy quiet, except for the constant hum of traffic on the 101. And I felt scared and alone. Again. Still. A part of me regretted sending Lee away, but my intuition knew he was the freight train coming at me— I'd found my like kind, and mind in Lee. It was why I felt so connected to him. Like me, the siren of obsession was intertwined in his nature, with him every time he smoked a joint, hit a racquetball, rolled the dice. Ate. I could feel it. See it. My intuition screamed it, which is why we'd be poison for each other. Wasn't it Carl Jung that said, "You always fall in love with yourself?" Except I wanted a partner who was *better* than me.

-

Chapter 7

Lee woke me from a dreamless sleep at 8:30 Thursday morning. "Happy Thanksgiving!" His casual demeanor lightened the descending darkness over being with my family later.

I smiled. "Happy Thanksgiving." I lay in bed staring out the window at the fog shrouded morning and stroked Face, who stood almost frozen, pressed up against the side of the bed. The dog was totally satisfied, at peace. I envied her.

"Want to go see *Love Letters* Saturday night. It's at the Canon Theater in Beverly Hills, and it's closing the end of month, so it's this weekend or we miss it. Charlton Heston plays the lead, and even though he's a right-wing NRA nutcase, the reviews say he's pretty good. My pick, my treat."

It did sound like a treat. Local theater was usually excellent in L.A., with famous actors often playing the major roles, but way too expensive on my meager budget. "I haven't been to a play in ages," I mused aloud.

"Is that a yes, then?"

Almost every part of my wanted to say yes, but I didn't. Among his other indiscretions, Lee was clearly a lavish spendthrift, even though he was in massive debt with a half a mill tax bill, which made him at least frivolous, but more likely *dangerous* with money. And I felt weird about him taking me to something so extravagant. We weren't dating. The smarter part of me knew I should avoid adding to my mounting debt since I had no way of repaying Lee's generosity at the moment. *Think*, my intuition warned— *With everything given, something is owed.*

Lee sighed. "Look Ray, I get you want to keep it just friends right now, and I'm fine with that. Come see the play with me Saturday night. We can enjoy some theater, share a good meal, some stimulating dialog and pretend to be witty." His voice was lilted with humor. I could practically see his adorable grin through the phone.

I laughed. "Okay." I needed something to look forward to, a light at the end of another Thanksgiving of my mother's pinched expression of concern reserved for me alone, or my sister's sublime superiority she'd married into financial security and had graced my mom with three gorgeous grand kids. "I'd love to go see *Love Letters* with you Saturday night."

"Great! I'll reserve two tickets then." He paused. "One request."

"Go on."

"Would you wear a dress?"

So much for *just friends.* Clearly his interest was more than friendship. Reality mocked me that, of course, it had been his agenda since we'd met.

"Any dress. It doesn't have to be fancy or anything, just proper attire for the evening. And besides, you'd look stunning in a dress." He said it matter-of-factly, but I was sure I felt sexual innuendo traveling the line with his words.

"To date, only my mother has ever instructed me on what to wear," I said as evenly as possible. "Which invariably led to discord between us, and likely the beginning of our rather contentious relationship."

"Don't get riled. It's just a suggestion. The Canon Theater is pretty posh and people don't come in jeans. It's Beverly Hill on a Saturday night and everyone will be dressed to the nines."

Face rested her head on the bed and stared up at me with her big, brown eyes in hopes of getting more strokes, but I was done. "Thanks for the fashion tip on appropriate theater attire," I teased as I picked up my phone and took it with me as I got up, went to my work area and sat cross legged on the drafting chair.

"OK, OK I get it," Lee said with humor. "You have my solemn oath never to suggest attire again."

"Smart man." I set the cradle in my lap and the receiver between my ear and shoulder. "And he can be taught," I added jokingly, as I began inputting the copy I'd handwritten into *PageMaker* on the Mac that sat on the small table I'd built to match the height of my drafting table. We confirmed racquetball for tomorrow and disconnected.

I held the phone in my lap and stared out the side window at my neighbor's front yard. Morning dew on the pines, bushes, and enormous green lawn glittered with pinpoints of white light as the sun broke through the fog. Did Lee really see me as potentially stunning? I swept my hair away from my face, letting the soft strands run through my fingers, and for a second I touched beautiful. I could dress to impress, and in my head I played the scene, walking up to Lee in slow motion in the mid-length, maroon lace my sister gave me, imagining his drop-jaw expression. I couldn't help smiling then. Even though part of me suspected it a lie, being seen as beautiful made me *feel* beautiful.

The sweet, cloying scent of illness was veiled by the sharpness of cleanser in the antiseptic lobby of the Home. Chrome handrails lined the light pink walls. A hunched elderly man clutched onto the railing as he shuffled along in slow motion. Each step looked pained. Pasty white skin, his eyelids drooped over his small black eyes which seemed vacant, as if not only his body but his mind had abandoned him.

I took in the scene and was chilled to my core. Old scared me, sometimes worse than not getting there.

Grandma sat perched on the edge of the maroon love seat, her ill-fitting floral print polyester dress hung to her calves and gathered tightly around her short, crossed legs. She clutched the strap of her white vinyl purse between her bony hands resting in her lap.

"Well, it's about time," She sniped, as if I were late. It was 4:00 p.m., exactly when I was told to be there.

"You look lovely, Grandma." I leaned down and kissed my grandmother's soft white cheek. The old woman gave me a vain smile. At 84, she had flawless skin, virtually wrinkle-free, and her steel gray eyes were still rather piercing.

"And you look like you got your clothes at the Salvation Army. Why don't you dress properly?" She spoke in a clipped English accent though she'd lived in the States for over seventy years.

I wore my hole-free black jeans, and over-sized beige cotton shirt, which I actually tucked in. I even put on a bra for the occasion. The woman was delusional expecting more than that. "You ready to go,

Gram?"

She stood and straightened her dress, then squared her petite shoulders and rose her chin up. "I've been ready to get out of here since the day your mother stuck me in this place."

We walked to my Civic parked in the lot behind the building. I was annoyed by her bitterness, my mother's effort to her care more than sufficient in my view. It had been the right decision to have her committed. Gram almost killed herself overdosing on medication she'd mistakenly taken twice within minutes on more than a few occasions. She was losing her memory, and her once sharp mind could no longer manage life on her own.

It was getting dark, but bits of electric blue sky peeked through the thickening clouds. The air was crystal clean, sharp with moisture. A storm was coming. It was easy to feel in L.A., maybe because they're so rare. I settled Gram in the passenger seat then took a deep breath, sucked in the sweet wetness and released it slowly to shake off my growing anxiety.

"Try that lane, it's moving. Don't just sit here. Go around them. You should get off the freeway, the side streets are faster..." Grandma had a lot of suggestions though she'd never driven a day in her life. Between driving tips she talked incessantly about the 'crazy' people she now lived with. She swore her roommate stole her ruby necklace, one she claimed she got on Safari in Africa, though she'd never owned one and had never been anywhere but England until her teens, then the States the rest of her life. She was sure her neighbor across the hall was coming into her room at night to watch her sleep, though had no explanation why. Then she was sure she'd forgotten something back at the Home but couldn't remember what, then couldn't remember where we were going. She remembered after prompting, but then didn't want to go to her evil daughter's who had stolen everything she owned and had her 'put away.'

I pulled into my parents' driveway, alongside the row of rosebushes my mom and I had planted years back, a long narrow island of long-stem yellow and red roses that separated the neighbor's driveway from theirs. I stopped behind my sister's minivan, turned off the car, and looked at grandma who stared straight ahead, seemingly unaware we had arrived.

"You ready to go inside?"

"I told you, I'm not going in there. Why are we here?"

"For Thanksgiving, Gram, remember?"

"Well, I have nothing to be thankful for. Take me home."

"I'm sorry you feel that way." It was cliché and a lie and I felt stupid for saying it, parroting my mother's Pollyanna tripe. I considered telling grandma I know what hopeless feels like, and I too lived with a pervasive sadness and fear of the future, afraid of what's to be, or not to be. But there was no point really. Gram didn't acknowledge feelings, and she never showed fear. "Are you coming into the house with me or not?"

Grandma refused to get out of the car and I wasn't about to make her. She'd always been contentious, but she'd had a quick wit and delivered it with sharp humor, both of which left her years ago, as did the radiant beauty she once possessed. She was on the fringe

74

of life now, on her way out and almost invisible. Surely she felt it too. Maybe so many old people lose their mind because the reality of their marginal existence is just too degrading. And terror consumed me right then, bearing witness to my future.

I got out of my car and took a deep breath of crisp, wet air, then released it slowly as I went to the back of my Civic and lifted the hatchback, gathered the pie, and the green bean casserole I'd made this morning, then slammed the hatch shut and walked to my parents' Valley-ranch, single-story home.

Roasting turkey and smoky firewood wafted from inside as I stepped up onto the landing and then came through the iron screen door into the house I was raised, yet never really felt at home in. I passed the bookshelves neatly packed with encyclopedias and novels into the spacious, modern living room. A large open space wrapped around the centralized fireplace to the open dining area.

Dad tended the fire, poked an iron rod at the burning logs. Sparks flared and sucked up into the chimney. My brother-in-law, Larry, looked short and narrow standing next to my 6'3", 220 pound father, though both men looked remarkably alike, even with twenty five years between them. Each had speckled gray hair and short cropped beards and wire rim glasses. Dad wore navy Dockers and a long sleeve flannel shirt. As always, Larry looked like he'd just walked off the set of *The Big Chill*—Levi's, maroon Izod sweater, and those over-complicated sneakers.

"Hey." I announced. "Happy Thanksgiving." I set the food I'd brought on the slate bench that wrapped two sides of the fireplace, then kissed and hugged my father. He gathered me up in his big arms and drew me in against his barrel chest.

"Hello Baby." It was his only term of endearment for me. "Happy Thanksgiving." He released me and I felt abandoned midst the pack again.

"Hey Lar. How ya doing?" I inquired when he didn't.

"Good." That was it. Larry didn't turn my question around.

"Grandma's in the car and won't come out. Can you please go talk to her, dad?"

My father gave a heavy sigh and shook his head before handing the iron poker to Larry and going outside. Larry rested the end of the poker on the slate bench, held it like a staff and stared at the fire, clearly uninterested in engaging with me. He was a devout Jew, a conservative, directed, precise, with no interest in abstractions like feelings. And Larry dismissed most anyone who wasn't of like mind or income.

I collected my food and went into the kitchen. "Happy Thanksgiving everyone!" And that moment I felt glad to be there, to have family to be with. They were all I had, all I'd ever really had, as my mother so often reminded me. Everyone else came and went in L.A.

"Happy Thanksgiving," everyone said in unison, except Scott. My eight year old nephew sat at the kitchen table and consumed a finger full of the custard from the pumpkin roll he'd taken a scoop out of when he thought no one was looking.

Carrie sat in front of baby Adam strapped in the portable car seat on the kitchen table. She was feeding him spoonfuls of mushed up yams that dribbled out the side of his mouth. The gross factor didn't seem to faze her. Her mass of flaming red hair was pulled back into a tight braid and hung down her back practically to her waist. She wore a Spanish style gauze dress with a colorful, rather loud floral pattern of red roses, and mid-calf tan cowboy boots with sharply pointed tips.

I set the food down on the stove top above the oven where my six year old niece, Jessie, stood basting the turkey. Mom stood behind her, hand over her granddaughter's and together they squeezed the soft plastic ball, sucking up gravy into the tube then squirting it back on the bird.

"Happy Thanksgiving, Auntie Ray." Jessie looked adorably cute in her black velvet dress, her long, strawberry blond hair pulled back in a high ponytail.

"Happy Thanksgiving, baby." I whispered as I bent to kiss my niece's head, and before fully straightening I received my mother's quick kiss on the cheek. Mom was barely five feet, and shrinking with age.

"Happy Thanksgiving, Dolly." My mother had three terms of endearment for me. Dolly, Face, and 'my baby,' as I was her last born. "Is Grandma giving you grief?"

"She still in the car. Dad went to get her."

"Well, she wouldn't come in if I went out there." Her aged, sun baked skin glowed with beads of sweat that ran along the side of her gaunt face onto the brown plastic frame of her large glasses. "She only listens to your father." She took the baster from Jessie, pushed the turkey back in the oven and shut the door, then wiped her forehead on her shirtsleeve. "Go wash your hands, Jessie Rose," she instructed her granddaughter. "Then see if you can help your mother with the coleslaw."

"I'm feeding Adam now, mom." Carrie was in a huff. "I'll get to it in a minute. I told you I should have brought Mariana to help."

Mom didn't respond. She busied herself and tuned out, a technique she'd honed to avoid conflict. She got a carton of whipping cream from the fridge, poured the cream into a plastic bowl then set up the electric mixer.

I retrieved the coleslaw my sister brought from the fridge and took it back to the kitchen table. A baby bottle filled with dressing was on top of the cabbage mixture and I poured it over the shredded leaves until the bottle was drained. Jessie sat down at the table next to her older brother and started coloring, but within moments they were fighting, Scott hording the markers regardless of his sister's shrill protests. Carrie ignored them. Like our mother, Carrie had the ability to shut out what disturbed her. But the kids bickering annoyed the hell out of me.

"Knock it off, you guys." I spoke loudly to be heard over the mixer. "Scott, give your sister half the pens. And Jess, don't grab. *Ask*." I got Jessie's attention, but Scott grabbed the only pen Jessie had out of her small hand. She tried to grab it back nearly knocking a stack of dishes off the table. "Stop! Now! Both of you." The last bit sounded like I was screaming because mom had switched off the mixer. I grabbed half of Scott's markers and set them in front of Jess. Carrie looked up from feeding Adam and narrowed her eyes at me, but at least the kids stopped fighting.

"This is ridiculous, Mother." Carrie stood, wiped her son clean with the cloth she kept on her shoulder. "There is nothing for the kids to do here anymore. You don't even have cable. They don't want to be here. And I don't blame them. They can entertain themselves all day at home. We should just have Thanksgiving at my house from now on."

"No way," I protested. I'd never felt welcome in Carrie's home, always the unwanted guest she felt she *had* to invite. I looked at mom standing at the counter near the sink, poised with the mixer over the bowl of whipped cream. I recognized my mother's pinched expression and felt her rush of distress. "We've had it at home since we were born. Thanksgiving should be here."

"You have no idea what a total hassle it is dragging three kids everywhere." Carrie picked her son up out of the car seat and held him to her. "You only have yourself to worry about, Rachel. It's harder for everyone having it here. If you won't think of me, then at least think of mom."

I stared at my mother. "I am." Mom looked down, busied herself with the cream. Thanksgiving was the only holiday our mother still hosted. She'd mentioned many times how much she enjoyed preparing for it, looked forward to "having the whole family safe in the nest," even if just for a night. Carrie had co-opted all birthdays, Hallmark occasions and every Jewish holiday from Hanukkah to Passover at her 5,600 square foot McMansion in Agoura Hills.

Maids and caterers graced these parties which made it easier for all in some ways. But what Carrie didn't get is that everyone needs to feel needed, and slowly but surely she was robbing our mother of purpose, and pleasure.

"So, I hear you're dating that new guy you've been playing racquetball with." The words seemed to fall out of mom's mouth as if to fill the exaggerated hush.

I glared at my sister. When she called this morning to check on what I was bringing to dinner, I'd mentioned Lee helping me make the apple pie, and his invitation to see *Love Letters*— a defensive counter to Carrie's condescending comment that since I wasn't involved with anyone [and had the time], I should have cooked more. "Well, we're not exactly dating…"

"What do you call it then?" Carrie held her son and stroked his back in slow circles. "You've been playing racquetball for almost a month like every other day with him. And he's taking you to *Love Letters* Saturday night, in Beverly Hills. If that's not meant to impress, I don't know what is." Adam laid his little chin on her shoulder, looked at me, and burped. "I'm going to go put him down, mom."

"Night, beautiful." I whispered softly as he passed, his saucer blue eyes half-mast. And I was sucked into the black hole of want as I stood at the table tossing the coleslaw.

"Well, are you seeing him or not?" Mom handed each of the kids a whipped cream coated circle of blades. She used to give them to Carrie and me. My mouth literally watered as I watched Scott and Jessie lick off the cream.

"We're just friends, mom. We go out to dinner after racquetball sometimes, and we've hung out the last couple of weekends, but I really don't think it'll go anywhere."

"Why not? And how do you know this after a month?" Mom's thin, painted red lips stayed in a tight, flat line. "What's he do?"

"He runs his own company shipping freight. He's a consultant, sort of like me, but a lot more successful."

"And what's his name?"

I had my mother's attention, and smiled. "Lee."

"Does he have a last name?"

I knew why she was asking, of course. "Messer. Lee Messer."

"Messer..." She contemplated aloud as she scooped the whipped cream into a crystal serving goblet. Then her countenance filled with lightness and she smiled. "Isn't that Jewish?"

I shook my head, annoyed. I refrained from denoting him an atheist, afraid of dimming her brightness I was momentarily basking in. "What difference does it make, mother? A last name doesn't brand him a believer, and if he was I couldn't be with him. I'm still an atheist, mom."

"Then you're an idiot." She said it deadpan, like the words just fell out of her mouth without filtering through her brain. She didn't intend to be mean. It was almost an expression of endearment. She meant 'idiot' sort of like 'my beautiful baby...' "You condemn yourself to the fringes and then complain you're lonely. And I know you are. What woman wouldn't be still single at 33?" My mother had a way of proceeding from instinct rather than intellect, and was clueless how cutting her words were. "Why can't you just accept who you are and embrace your community like your sister. I guarantee if you did, you'd find the life you're still looking for." She shook her head and turned away to put the filled goblet in the fridge then went to the stove and stirred the pot of matzo ball soup.

"Living among the faithful whose belief in money supersedes the moral gospel they espouse isn't the community I'm looking for, mother." I sighed and shrugged my shoulders to shed my mounting tension. "And over scheduling every minute of the day with extraneous activities so I don't have time to think, or create anything, isn't the life I want either. I don't want to be Carrie, mom."

"I don't want you to be your sister, Rachel. I want you to be happy, and taken care of." She stared at me like she was stating the obvious, then her expression softened to empathy and she frowned. "My beautiful Face, why do you always insist on the hardest path."

I'd blown it again, pushed my mom away. Non-conformity was disruptive to the woman's psyche. And Lonely crept in, abandoning me to the outside again from the chasm now between us. I set the coleslaw aside, near Jessie. My niece was coloring a house with stickish smiling people inside. Scott's picture showed planes dropping bombs and people on the ground getting blown up. He looked up at me.

"I don't believe in God, grandma." He stared at me as he spoke to her.

"Oh, of course you do." Mom glared at me over the stove top but spoke to her grandson. "You don't know what you believe at eight."

"I did. I knew from the beginning of Saturday school what the rabbis were preaching was a bunch of crap." I was being combative, to be sure, but my mother was so dismissive, I felt the need to validate my nephew's pejorative statement. "And if religion is so damn important to family togetherness, why did it break up ours?" She'd chased away her first child, my half-brother, when Keith converted to Born Again Christianity to marry.

"You shut up now, Rachel. Don't encourage him." It was hard to see my mom's brown eyes glaring at me behind the large glasses, but I felt her irritation.

Mom busied herself, and I felt bad I'd come back at her so aggressively. Her reaction to Keith's conversion had fundamentally scared me. Though she didn't disown him exactly, she made it impossible for him to attend family occasions by proselytizing Judaism whenever we got together. She'd speak tirelessly on tradition, history, the culture Keith was *born* into regardless of his newly adopted beliefs, deeply offending his wife, who married my half-brother on the condition he convert to Christianity. The first and last time Keith brought his family to Thanksgiving, mom cornered his 4 year old son— her first grandchild— in the kitchen and preached to him that he was really a Jew, instead of the Christian my half-nephew was being raised. I feared the battle to come when, *if,* I had kids, since I had no intention of raising them with *any* religion.

"You two at it again?" Dad scowled at me as he came into the kitchen. I felt the familiar twinge of fear, not just from his size, but

83

growing up I'd felt the wrath of his temper. "You still fighting windmills, baby? Don't confuse your mother with facts, Rachel."

Mom stuck my tongue out at him in a coquettish kind of way, just the tip, childlike. Dad laughed.

"Grandma and Larry are cowering in the living room so they don't have to listen to you two go at each other. And I don't blame them." Dad went to the liquor cabinet above the utility closet in the pantry and got the big bottle of gin, brought it back in the kitchen and made martinis.

"We almost ready to sit down?" Carrie came into the kitchen and dad handed her his first completed drink. "Thank you, dad."

"Dinner will be ready in ten minutes." Mom opened the oven and pulled out the turkey. My seemingly fragile little mother was impressive to watch, straddling the open oven door and hauling that heavy bird onto the stove top. Could have made the cover shot for the November issue of Good Housekeeping. The turkey was golden brown, dripping with juice, and it smelled fantastic.

"For you, my dear." Dad handed mom a martini.

Mom wiped her hands, then the sweat from her face on the dishtowel and then took the wide rimmed glass with a gracious, "Thank you, honey." She leaned back against the counter and contentedly sipped her martini. "Why don't you girls start serving the salad."

Carrie put her drink on the linoleum counter top and got the salad from the fridge. "Jessie Rose. Please go into the dining room and get everyone to sit down for dinner. Scott, go help your sister, please." Her tone was as stern as her expression and her son only hesitated a second then followed his sister from the kitchen.

Jessie took her drawing to show off, but she and her brother left their mess of markers and pad pages scattered on the kitchen table. I began collecting them to make room for serving the salad. Carrie set the salad bowl on the table and glared at me.

"My children are Jewish. I'm raising them to have an identity and a community, both of which you seem to sorely lack. So keep your fucking mouth shut about what you believe, whatever the hell it is, or isn't, around my kids." She didn't give me time to respond. She grabbed her half-empty martini and walked out of the room.

I watched my sister disappear into the dining area. The satiny fabric of the heavy white drapes that covered the back glass wall of the living room glowed warm and shimmered with firelight. I heard Larry ask his wife if she was OK, and Carrie say "dandy," but she was "just so tired of her" (my) "crap."

Then grandma piped in with, "You're all full of crap."

I looked at my mom. She glared at me, then emptied her martini and put the glass in the sink behind her. Her displeasure wrapped her like a shroud and she transferred it as she spoke. "Please serve the salad now, Rachel Lynn."

I did. I turned my back on my mother and put salad onto plate after plate until the kitchen table had no space for more, then carried them two at a time and served everyone before sitting to eat. Larry

was touting his lucrative new strip-mall development in Malibu.
Carrie beamed proudly at her husband. Dad nodded with respect. I
shook my head but held my tongue. It was foolish to question the
need of another 7-11 obstructing the views and scarring the fragile
ecosystem along the coast to people who viewed personal wealth
as social progress. I knew my opinion was unwelcome among them.
Like grandma, I too was almost invisible, or at least wanted to be.
And I no longer felt glad to be there. We hadn't even gotten through
the salad this time before I wanted out.

My craving to get high grew exponentially as I crawled along in
traffic on the 101 in the rain after dropping grandma off. Brighter
than twilight from the streetlights, with five lanes of unfettered
highway, and it was beyond irritating how inane L.A. drivers became
when it rained. My ire rose with every ten minute mile, and I felt a
desperate need to shed the evening.

I called Lee a hundred times in my head, imagined him bringing over
some smoke, hanging out and playing Tavli all night. Talking.
Laughing. Sharing... Safe with someone who actually *liked* me. But
as I pulled in my driveway doubt crept in. Inviting him over at
10:00p.m. might imply I was asking him to stay the night, and I had
no intention of sleeping with Lee. Intercourse with him would not
fulfill me, or enhance the connection we already shared. It would
only complicate the friendship I was hoping to maintain.

-

Chapter 8

Had to cancel racquetball on Friday to find someone to restore my

Macintosh when it crashed attempting to draw the illustration I was creating for the monthly credit union newsletter. I spent the evening at the repair place in Hollywood, and $150 per meg for the additional RAM the salesman told me I needed to run Adobe Illustrator effectively. Continually upgrading my Mac was costing me more than I was making.

I was in the shower when my phone rang Saturday morning. I turned off the water and toweled off, listening to my machine cue up and deliver a voice. It surprised me how much I was hoping it was Lee, and how excited I was to see *Love Letters* with him this evening.

"I can't do a bike ride today." It was Lavonne. "And I won't be able to meet you for brunch." She lowered her voice to just above a whisper. "Joe and I got back together last night. I'm calling from his boat in Del Rey. He asked me to stay the weekend." Her tone was lilted with enthusiasm, and devoid of apology. "I'd say let's get together next weekend but with any luck I'll be busy. I'll call you during the week."

"Don't bother," I said aloud as I came into my bedroom. It was typical, even socially acceptable for women to abandon friends for a date. But still, it made me feel valueless.

Face came over, looking for strokes. I needed some too right then. I resented being the back-up plan to a man, especially a loser like Joe—an overpaid postal worker and beer-bellied sports fanatic, and at 37 he still lived with his mother. A week, a month down the line Lavonne would be calling to whine about feeling neglected and bored. Compared to Joe, Lee was a prince, whatever his failings.

I finished the newsletter to make deadline, leaving me no time to indulge in writing the short story I'd had in my head for weeks of a genie who gives two L.A. punks a shot at being more than bangers. I shut down the computer at 5:30 to get ready for the evening ahead. Pure bliss as the water streamed over me in the shower. The scalding liquid seared my skin, turning it bright red, the heat penetrating deep into my muscles. Physical pleasures— hot showers, jacuzzis, masturbation, back rubs were a good percentage of what made my life worth living.

It was almost dark out by the time I emerged from the bathroom with my hair blown dry, my eyebrows and chin plucked and my teeth brushed. I scavenged for what to wear. Dress, per his request, or pants... I went with something in-between, an '80s style *Flashdance* look— my big, burgundy silk blouse that fell to just below my butt, over sheer black tights. I decided against heels, choose my flat, black, pointy-toe boots to avoid the *Amazonian* look next to Lee.

I sucked in my stomach, threw back my shoulders and then combed both hands through my hair. It fell around my face in shiny waves. I looked tight, L.A. chic. Not beautiful, but not bad. It would have to do. I may not want to be with Lee, but I still wanted him to want me.

We exchanged a joint and listened to Brian Ferry's *Don't Stop the Dance* as Lee glided through the last few curves of Benedict Canyon. He'd said I looked 'stunning' when he'd arrived, promptly at 7:00p.m. "Simply stunning," were his exact words as he openly sized me up. He looked pretty cute, too, a skinny white tie against a loose black shirt tucked into black jeans, topped with his black leather jacket. Black is forever chic.

Women in evening gowns and men in business suits lingered on the curved red carpet that followed the line of the enormous marquee above. *Love Letters* in white cursive was scrawled across a ruby banner. The actor's names were printed across the top, Heston's considerably larger than his wife/actress Lydia Clarke, the other lead in the show.

Lee took a last hit off the joint, dropped it in the ashtray and suddenly punched the accelerator. He swung a sharp u-turn that instantly made me nauseous. I swallowed back barfing as he pulled into the parking space across the street from the theater where a Lincoln Continental had just pulled from the curb.

The queasy feeling returned about a third of the way through the play. The two actors on stage revealed their love story through letters, beginning as childhood sweethearts. Michael and I were big into letters after his family moved back east, right up until his last one, explaining why he'd proposed to someone else.

At intermission Lee led me outside for some fresh air, which turned out to be damp, freezing cold air.

"You okay? You look a little...white."

"I'm fine. Just cold." I huddled into myself, bit my lip to stave off tears, tried to swallow back the lump in my throat that always rose when I thought of Michael.

Lee moved close, put his arms around me and gently pulled me in. He was warm and snuggly, like a favorite quilt, and I rested my head on his shoulder. "If the play is upsetting you, we don't have to stay." He practically whispered in my ear.

I was humbled, grateful he was paying attention. I pulled back to look at him, met his eyes, momentarily shutting out the world around us. His soft, wavy dark hair framed his sculpted face, now becoming rather chiseled, with a strong, square jawline and high cheekbones as he dropped weight. Almost every part of me wanted to kiss him right then—fall into his arms, abandon what I knew was right and *be* with Lee, let him shelter me.

I looked away. One kiss would launch our relationship, past the friendship my intuition insisted we maintain. Lee'd been only kind. And I was basically using him, knowing he was hoping for more from me than I ever planned to give him. And I was suddenly encased in shame.

"Hey," he said softly, as if he'd felt my sadness, his expression tentative, questioning. The lights blinked to indicate the play was about to resume. "Say the word and we'll take off." He continued to scrutinize me. The lights blinked again.

"It's okay. It was just stuffy in there. I'm fine now. I'd like to see the rest." I wasn't sure I meant it, but I didn't want to spoil the show for him. I'd talk to him later about *us*. I'd explain that friendship was all I could ever offer him, how getting together would be a disaster for both of us, since two addicts would spend a lifetime enabling each other, and modeling obsession to our kids. And I absolutely refused to damn my children to addiction.

Letter after letter the lovers/actors read on the sparse stage unfolded two very different lives from me and Michael, but ignited memories of him anyway. I'd be married with kids by now, living the life I still sought if only I'd gone back east with him. Or maybe not. And I'd never know because I hadn't played that hand. At some point, tears welled and I turned my head away so Lee wouldn't see. He put his hand atop mine on the armrest, wove his fingers between mine and squeezed slightly. His warmth radiated through my hand and up my arm and spread through my body, giving me ground.

He held my hand to guide me through the packed crowd exiting the theater after the play, and all the way to his car, even opened the passenger door for me. I felt sated, safe, glad to be with him as I watched him come back around his Mercedes, suddenly dreading the relationship talk I was planning for the ride home. It was quite likely after I told him the truth, he'd want to part ways, move on, forgo our friendship, even stop playing ball. And right then it felt as if I couldn't bear losing him.

Lee got behind the wheel, shut his door and started the car. Then he pushed in the lighter, reached for the Marlboro box atop his visor and extracted a joint.

It felt like he slapped me. Lee was so close, yet so far from the man I needed him to be. A great playmate, to be sure, but he was not the facade he wore, nor the safe harbor in the life partner I sought.

He slid the box back onto his visor, then lit the joint when the lighter popped out as he pulled away from the curb. "Thought we might get a bite. I've been craving a piece of apple pie," he glanced at me with a wink. "The Apple Pan in Culver City has the best around, other than ours, of course. And they're open late." He handed me the J.

I sighed, resigned reason to privation. "I know the place. Sound's good." I took a deep hit and held it in my lungs hoping to feel the high as quickly as possible, let the buzz disconnected me from the intensity of my conflicted feelings. I handed him back the joint, then released the smoke slowly considering how to ease into the discussion of our *friendship* without causing it irrevocable damage. "I'm picking up the tab since you paid for the play."

He smiled. "Fair enough," he said, then his thick lips puckered softly around the joint like a passionate kiss. "I got the impression you didn't care for *Love Letters.*" Smoke came out with his words and got sucked out the sunroof.

"It's not that." *I'm scared out of my mind I'll be alone forever.* "The play reminded me of a guy I used to know. He lived around the corner from my parents' house when we were growing up. We were best friends for 30 years, until I called it quits."

"Why would you walk away from a *30 year* friendship?" He took another quick hit and handed me the joint.

"I didn't, exactly. Michael did, when he married his roommate." I took a long draw, smoke filling my lungs. My head tingled. Feelings dulled, regret distanced. "Took me four years after he married to finally figure out sharing our lives like we'd done since childhood wasn't serving anyone. His wife had to be his best friend, his most intimate confidant once he married. Not me anymore. For my 30th birthday present, I asked him never to contact me again. I had to let him go for both of us to move on."

"Wow. Harsh. For both of you, I'm betting." Lee turned off Wilshire and on to Robertson. Steel and glass monoliths became two-story brick facades with restaurants and beauty salons, then turned to liquor stores and tattoo parlors as we moved south. "I get it now. I know why you're still single." He half-laughed and shook his head. "The unbearable cost of love is losing it. And you're scared out of your mind of it happening again." He said it like a fact and did not look at me for confirmation.

Whitewashed buildings glowed blue from the harsh streetlights and flashed by like a cartoon backdrop. "Maybe. Partially, I guess. But there's more to it than that. Intellectually, I know I'll never have another relationship like it, from childhood forward, sharing everything, with no gender stereotyping, or resentments from past relationships." I took another hit to reinforce the disconnect. "The thing is, now that I know what's possible, I can't help wanting that level of intimacy." I handed him the joint. "Anything less now just won't do."

We stopped at a red light and Lee finally looked at me. "My god, girl, you really are a dreamer." He said it serious, but his eyes kind of twinkled with gentle humor. The light turned green. He followed the compact in front of us. "Michael's a hard act to follow, but I'll see what I can do." Lee glanced at me, fixed his eyes on mine for an instant before turning his attention back to driving.

I smiled, more outside than in, sitting there trying to figure out how to explain the boundaries I knew we should maintain without hurting him. Even high, reality assured me Lee could never replace Michael, but every other part of me wanted him to be my new best friend, my second chance. His kindness, his *interest*, the connection we shared, in moments even more intimate than with Michael, gave me ground. Obsessive, addicted, whatever, Lee made me feel valued and safe, and I was glad to be with him right then. Time slowed, stretching my intuition into inaudible echos as I relaxed into our now casual familiarity.

"I was raised in a White, middle-class suburb of Chicago. After my parents' divorced my mom couldn't afford both me and my sister, so my dad brought me out here when I was 12. My junior high school was mostly Latino and Black." Lee extinguished the tiny end of the joint and turned onto a residential street lined with small, single-story pueblo-style houses. "Since we're in the neighborhood, thought I'd swing by my old house, show you where I used to live." He turned onto another small street. The streetlights dimly lit the long front yards and pastel painted houses in eerie blue. "It wasn't the greatest area when I lived here. Hasn't changed much." His entire countenance tightened, from his jaw to his grip on the wheel when we noticed a group of seven, maybe ten Black guys gathered around a shinny black car, like a Camaro, in the driveway of a small house toward the middle of the block.

"That used to be Mr. Jackson's house. He and his wife worked at the studios, in props, and they'd decorate their yard with the coolest sets for every holiday. They were good people," Lee lamented. "They practically raised their grandson, even though he was a real wack job."

Lee pointed out his old house, cruised by slowly, and did not speed up as he passed the party house next. A fat guy holding a brown beer bottle moved down the driveway towards the street and glared at us as we passed in what felt like slow motion. I looked away and thought I saw something running across their front lawn then dart out into the street. Lee slammed on his brakes.

"Shit!" he snapped, and I frantically looked to see what he'd hit, if anything, because I didn't hear any impact. Lee looked around too, then in his rear view mirror, then took his foot off the brake and let the Mercedes roll. That's when I saw it, laying in the street. So did he. His eyes got wide, his expression sallow, but he didn't stop the car.

"What is that?" I asked, panic mounting, heart pounding.

"I don't know," Lee said cautiously. "I think it may be a dog."

"Stop the car!" I yelled, but he let it roll. "You can't just leave it there."

"They'll take care of it." He kept looking in his rear view mirrors, all of them. "We need to get out of here, Ray." And he began slowly accelerating.

"STOP!" I yelled louder, then opened the door, which was less dramatic than it sounds since the car was only going 10mph.

Lee slammed on his brakes again and I released my seat-belt and got out of the car before it came to a complete stop.

"Get back in the fucking car, Rachel," I heard Lee yell as I ran to the dog laying in the road several car lengths back. The gang from the party house were all watching us, but oddly, they stayed loosely gathered around the Camaro in driveway and didn't seem phased that we'd just hit their dog. In fact, a few of them were *laughing,* and

I was instantly filled with disgust, outrage.

It's eyes were open when I stopped within a yard of the short-haired black lab, having enough experience with dogs not to spook them by getting too close when they're injured. "Hey, baby," I said to the dog soothingly as I bent down, almost to the ground to get on his level.

The dog's nose incessantly twitched. He blinked a big, black marble eye at me. I put my hand in front of its snout and he licked it. "Good boy," I said softly. Then his tale started wagging.

"No. No. No. You're not supposed to *wag your tail*," a Black cop, in full uniform, though the shirt was unbuttoned exposing his ripped torso, walked up to me kneeling by the dog. A few of the guys from the group came meandering over, beers in hand, smiles plastered on a few faces. I stood, trying to look at tall as I could. "And you're not supposed to *lick* her," the cop added, glaring at the dog, comically exacerbated. "Get up. Come on. Get up, and get on outta here you mangy mutt," he casually commanded, and miraculously the dog did. Well, he got up anyway, then licked my hand again and stood there waiting for me to stroke him. So I did, stunned and thrilled the dog seemed fine.

"You OK, baby? You seem OK," I addressed the dog, who preened like Face with my touch. "I am *so* sorry." I began to the cop who looked more like an actor. "We didn't see him—"

"Oh, George Micheal is fine. He does this all the time. He's a stunt dog, always thinks he's training. He'd goes after anything if I let him. Get over here, George." The dog loped over to his master, who flashed an adorable dimpled white smile. "I'm his handler. Oh, and

I'm also a stunt double. I'm not really a cop. We were just coming home from the lot and he saw your car cruising by. Sorry if he freaked you out." He stroked Mr. Micheal vigorously. The dog clearly liked it, its tail up, ears back, butt raised. His shirt fell open as he leaned forward to pat the dog and only then do I notice he had a gun clipped to his hip, or a fake one, in a small leather case attached to the waistband of his pants.

I looked around the group of ten or more loosely gathered by us now. Many wore knowing smiles, and I was so glad the dog was fine I couldn't help smiling back. Several of them didn't look so enamored though.

"Whats you doen here, girl?" one guy said.

"Yo in the wrong hood, bitch," a woman sniped.

Lee came and stood next to me, slid his hand in mine. "We're good here, then. Dog's fine. We're all good?" he asked the cop/stuntman.

"We're tight, dude," the stuntman said. "Have a good night."

Lee nodded, then gently pulled me to start walking. The crowd dispersed. I heard a few chuckles, and grumbles, but no one bothered us as we got into his Mercedes and left.

"You OK?" Lee asked.

I hadn't had time to process what just happened. I'd simply reacted when I thought we'd hit the dog. *I* reacted. Lee didn't. He was ready to leave the animal lying in the road. And I suddenly felt ill.

"I'm feeling kind of sick, actually." I swallowed back the burning bile rising in my throat as we stopped at a red light. "And not so hungry anymore. Do you mind if we just head home?"

He frowned. "What's up? Is this about what just happened back there? We could have been seriously screwed. You get that, Rachel, right?"

"But we weren't."

"We got damn lucky. I couldn't stop any one of those guys from raping you, robbing us. It was ridiculous for you to get out of the car." He justified hitting a dog and not stopping to help it with scenarios of eminent danger.

"Maybe." There was nothing I could say to counter his position. The fact is, he may have been right, and we did get lucky. "Can we just call it a night?"

"Yeah. No problem." But he was clearly disappointed as he got on the 405, north.

I released a weighted sigh of relief up on the freeway, which was actually moving, making us less of a target in a drive-by. The trick was to never let anyone get too close. The infestation of people now inhabiting L.A. had destroyed the casual sunny siesta town I grew up in. Uncontrolled development turned paradise into a parking lot. I still clung to those languid times with Michael, when it took us 20 minutes to get to the beach, or we could get taquitos at night on Olivera Street without getting mugged. Then I heard Dylan's *Don't Think Twice* in my head, as I often did thinking of Michael. "*You just sorta wasted my precious time.*" I'd likely have found Mr. Right by now if in my 20s I'd been dating like my friends were, trying on relationships to find a fit. I was ensconced with Michael back then, pretending he'd commit to a partnership with me, knowing all along he wanted a wifey.

Wishing wouldn't turn Lee into my knight. He'd never be more than a temporary fix, and a corrosive one at that. And I thought about addressing this with him as I'd planned, but I had a splitting headache, and if I spoke more than a few words I was going to barf.

"I was trying to protect you tonight, Ray. You got a problem with that, we should talk about it. I want to keep an open forum between us."

"I know." I swallowed hard, pictured the dog he would have left to die, then fell into the void of cognitive dissidence. "I'm glad it all turned out OK. It's just late now, and I'm feeling really tired." *And shamed I'm doing to you what Michael did to me— wasting your precious time. And I want to talk to you about this but I'm feeling like shit, and afraid if I tell you you'll never be the partner I need you won't want to be my friend anymore.* "Sorry about the Apple Pan." *And I'd be so very lonely again without you.* "We can come back down here Monday or Wednesday after ball, or next weekend. Your call. My treat."

Lee shot me furrowed brows, his expression filled with doubt, but he didn't probe further. He lit another joint, then pushed in his lighter and the Brian Ferry CD. We shared the J and listened to the music most all the way home with only minor exchanges. Coming into the shimmering San Fernando Valley below Mulholland Drive, he reminded me of his scheduled bike ride with his friend, Mitch, along the strand from Venice to Huntington beach tomorrow. Lee asked me again if I'd like to join them. I declined, with the excuse of having to work. I considered elaborating, but I heard him sigh, sure he knew I'd lied, so I didn't make up any details.

Face was thrilled to see me when I came in the front door, and I felt the same for her. She was safe, so was I, and I stoked her with both hands along her spine to communicate my affection. In the scheme of things nothing really bad happened tonight. It was all rather surreal in fact, and I chucked with the memory of the hot cop and his *stunt* dog, George Michael, named after the pop singer, then vaguely wondered if the cop was gay, recalling his mannerisms, the way he spoke. It was hip, slick and trending to be gay (or bi) in L.A. the last couple of decades, even with the spread of AIDS.

-

Chapter 9

"My sister Colleen is in town with her partner for the wedding I told you about," Lee said on the phone early Friday morning. "I completely spaced out meeting them at The Baked Potato tonight after ball. She just called and reminded me. *Come* with me. My sister's partner, Arlene, is a real kick. I'm sure you'll like her. We can go straight from our game, since the restaurant is on Ventura, like three blocks from the club. I'd love you to join us. For once, just say 'yes.'"

I lay in bed stroking Face and staring out the side window at sunlight shimmering through the pines. Lee's voice was soothing, warming, like the comforter I snuggled under. I knew I should decline. If meeting his friends sent him, and/or them the wrong message, the same reasoning, even more so, applied to meeting his family.

"You'd really be helping me out," he continued. "My sister's been on my case since I separated. She's afraid I'm isolating too much."

"Are you?"

"Not since I met you."

I smiled, silently sharing his sentiments. He'd been distracting me from paralyzing loneliness since we'd met. Then recall summoned reason. The past few weeks I'd brought up the state of our relationship several times, iterating my commitment to just friendship between us. Lee had promised me he had no interest in a "rebound fling" after just divorcing, least of all with me, though intuition knew it a lie. His lavish attention, his consistent generosity, how he looked at me, the softness of his lips with his quick parting kisses told me he wanted more. The right thing would have been to walk away— end it, thank him for some great shared moments and then *go*, but I didn't. It felt as if I couldn't. After a month and a half of adventures, laughter, good food, great talks, easy company, and consistent hard ball keeping me lean, the idea of being without Lee filled me with the frigid cold I imagined accompanies death.

"Come on, Ray. If I'm the odd one out they'll spend most of dinner lecturing me on how to treat a woman, punctuated by weighted sighs of sympathy I'm back to being single. Help me out tonight and be the buffer between me and my sister."

To displace the image of my mother's pinched expression reserved exclusively for her still single daughter, I got the clicker from the nightstand and turned on the morning news. The distraction did not dilute the guilt motivating me to repay his generosity. The least I could do is be a friend when he needed one, so I reluctantly accepted Lee's invitation. The Rodney King video was on KTLA. Stan Chambers was reporting on the pending police brutality case being moved to the all-White, very conservative community of Simi Valley, followed by another of his 'travesty of justice,' diatribes. I shook my head in disgust, but I didn't turn it off as I got out of bed to began my day.

Of course we got high on the five minute drive from the courts to the Baked Potato in Universal City, which isn't a city, has no zip code, but is a group of businesses looking for cache' close to the studios atop the hill. The jazz club's façade was barn-like, black two by fours crisscrossing gaudy red paneling. A big box sign illuminated a brown comic potato holding music notes, the Baked Potato was scrawled across the side of the building in yellow neon.

Lee had made a reservation, and without delay the Glamour cover-girl hostess led us past the waiting crowds gathered at the entrance to our table. It was dark inside, no windows, the walls plastered with posters and photos of musicians and celebrities posing with the club owners. It held only twenty or so tables, in rows of five for prime viewing, most already filled. We were seated at the only corner booth in the place, along the farthest wall from the cramped stage. No musicians yet, and I was glad it was too early for the entertainment. Conversing over music isn't easy.

Lee seemed tense as he scanned the crowd, his eyes darting from person to person then finally landing on someone at the entrance. "Hey, there they are." He stood and waved to his sister and her partner as they emerged from the crowd now spilling into the dining room.

I stood to greet them as they approached the table. Colleen looked remarkably like Lee. She was about his height, and stocky—aka fat for a woman. She had long brown hair worn loose that fell over her shoulders and brushed the tops of her ample breasts. Arlene was lean, verging on petite, and virtually flat, with short, wavy auburn hair worn wild. They were both dressed casually, jeans and the like. Colleen's maroon sweatshirt had Northwestern printed across it, and upon inquiry she told me she got an MS in microbiology there in '78. Seated inside the dim club, she referred to her school days as 'life simplified,' and the real world as a statistician for the Bureau of Land Management akin to being stuck in the Ninth Circle of Hell in Dante's *Inferno*. She was smart, articulate, funny, and I liked Lee's sister.

Arlene was equally engaging. A veteran BLM commissioner, she vehemently expressed her anger at big lumber, and used mostly expletives to convey her frustrations with them "legally annihilating our forests," while we ate our stuffed potatoes filled with everything from bacon to salmon.

Colleen and Arlene did most of the talking during the meal. Lee and I listened attentively and questioned for clarity.

"Hey, why don't you both come up for New Year's?" Colleen asked. "We have a great ranch house nestled in the redwoods just outside Medford, Oregon. It'd be a blast to hang out together, cook some huge elaborate meal and play board games all night. We can watch the Rose Parade in the morning like we did when we were kids, remember Lee?"

"We'll clear out the solarium, put the inflatable mattress in there, make it cozy for you two," Arlene suggested. "It's a great space, and totally private in there."

Lee fixed his eyes on mine, searching. Hopeful, maybe?

"Oh God, I'm sorry." Arlene seemed suddenly mortified. "You aren't together, are you?" She glared at Lee, then at Colleen. "We thought you two were a couple."

"Lee told us all about you, raved about how smart you are, how you challenge him to think, unlike that flighty bitch ex-wife of his." Colleen glanced at her brother. "In all the years this kid's been dating, he's never been with anyone like you."

"His match, she means," Arlene chimed in. "You guys just seem so easy with each other."

Colleen meant it as a compliment, but it was really a slam on Lee. She inferred her brother had been with losers, either because he preferred women lesser than, as most men seemed to, or he couldn't get better.

Lee shook his head and looked out at the increasingly crowded room.

"You're both still welcome to come up for New Year's." Colleen said. "You can take the solarium, and Lee can sleep on the living room couch—"

"Absolutely," Arlene said enthusiastically. "Whatever you guys want to do, we can make it work."

Lee looked at me but he was expressionless, wore a poker face now.

"Actually, I'm going to Colorado in a couple weeks to be with a friend and her family for the holidays." I looked at the women as I spoke, knowing my words would likely hurt Lee. "It's an annual tradition, been going out there every year for years now."

There was an awkward silence, and then Colleen reiterated her offer to her brother alone. Both women spoke at great length about the astounding beauty of the Great Northwest, and suggested adventures from skiing to mountain biking to rafting.

"I'll let ya know if I can make it. I have to look at my calendar. Not sure what else is going on right now," Lee said lightly, but he avoided eye contact with me.

The opening band, before the actual band, both of whom I didn't know since I don't particularly like jazz, began playing. Four men in their mid-30s to late-50's were crowded on the stage, and they weren't bad, though very disruptive to conversation. We listened through the first set then Lee called for the check. He insisted on paying for everyone, put two $100 bills in the small black leather folder and then got up, paused for all of us to follow his lead, then led us out of the packed club.

 At the valet booth, Colleen and then Arlene hugged Lee, then each hugged me heartily, as if I were part of the family, or like they wished I would be.

The moment the valet shut my door, Lee punched in the lighter, reached above his visor for the Marlboro pack and then took out a joint as he put the Mercedes in motion. The lighter popped out and he lit it with a long, deep draw. He did not look at me as he blew out the smoke, put back the lighter, and pulled rather abruptly out of the club's driveway onto Ventura Blvd.

"What's going on? What are you so pissed about?"

He glanced at me but still wore his poker expression. "My sister doesn't have a clue about my relationships, marriage or otherwise. We didn't talk for seven years, and even now I hardly ever get into details with her because she always has something critical to say."

"Why do you care what your sister thinks, unless you think she's right?" It wasn't meant to cut, but then, maybe it was.

"About what? That I've never had a relationship worth a damn?" He paused. "Maybe that's what I'm trying to change with you." He didn't look at me with his delivery, but kept his focus on driving as he pulled into the racket club's almost empty parking lot.

Shit. About the last thing I wanted to do was hurt him. I'd not meant for our attraction to run this deep. I knew he wanted more from me all along. And I selfishly listened to his words, instead of his feelings. I should have laid it on the line a month ago, made sure he heard me, understood I didn't want more with him, ever.

He pulled along side my car and turned off his, then finally looked at me. His focus was intense, like with racquetball or Tavli, except now, on me. It felt wildly connected, like he was inside my head. Then he brought his hand to my cheek gently, pulled me in to meet him halfway and kissed me. His full lips spread heat through mine, his thick hand on my cheek sent warmth down my neck and into my chest and right down to my crotch, igniting the pleasure centers of my brain, which instantly went to war with the smarter part of me.

Lee pulled back, clearly picking up on my trepidation, then fixed his eyes on mine, focusing all his attention on me again to glean what I was feeling, except even I wasn't sure. He dropped his hand from my cheek, leaving it cold and I convulsively shivered. He caught it, smiled, then took another hit, like a Pavlovian response to the joint in his hand, then offered it to me. I declined with a shake of my head to rid myself of my duplicity.

"You know, I don't know if you're messing with my feelings on purpose or not. You invite me in, but keep me away." Lee paused, put the roach in the ashtray.

Ah. A moment of truth. Tell him what he wanted to hear and maintain our friendship, or share my fears and risk losing him. I'd fallen in love with Lee's beauty, yet knew his beast and was so overwhelmed with opposing voices in my head I was speechless.

"I need more from you, Ray." He sighed audibly. "I can't keep pretending this is enough for me. It's not. I want to be with you, all the way, in every way—show you how great we can be together.

And I'm not looking for just sex with you. I want to make love to you, Rachel. I've had many fuck buddies over the years, my dear. I want more with you than that." His eyes were locked on mine. "And though I'm not looking to marry you tomorrow, I want to be the last man, the only man you ever sleep with again." He paused, waiting, but I was still speechless, trying to formulate a response he would hear this time.

"It would be grand to live happily ever after with you, Lee. You know how much I love being with you. We've been together practically every day for the past month, and they've been some of the best times in my life ." I stopped there because I was repeating the same speech I'd delivered to him multiple times already, in which he'd said he was fine with remaining just friends. "But we'd be a disaster as a couple. We're both undeniable obsessives, forever teetering on the edge of self-control. Your 'frivolous indulgence' with weed is clearly an all day, everyday affair. And I'm with you, sweetie. I'd stay perpetually buzz if living numb actually made anything better in the long run. You're a self-proclaimed gambler, owe closed to half a million in back taxes. You own nothing, not your car, or condo, not even a credit card. You're clearly still irresponsible with money, spending it like you do. And I hardly make enough to support myself, let alone kids." I stayed fixed on him. He maintained a poker face, and I wondered if my words were getting through. "I'm 33 years old, Lee. I'm looking to find a man who's ready to father children *now*, has the means to support a family, and stopped living like a kid after he graduated college." I finally did the right thing and told him the unvarnished truth.

There was a pregnant pause between us, and he looked away. I literally felt him tightened, walled up and disconnect from me. "I told you I quit gambling, and that I'm dealing with my tax issues. And I object to the 'undeniable obsessive' remark. I can quit using weed any time. I don't believe in doomed to the affliction of addiction, like AA and NA and all the other bullshit Anonymous groups out there are peddling. Bad habits are just that— cast and fueled by poor choices based on a faulty premise. I take shit out there because I prefer living the extreme." He flashed a quick, punk grin. "But I can walk away from most anything when I choose to. And I don't get what the hell difference it makes anyway. Half the globe is on Prozac, or alcohol, or religion, or energy drinks and power bars. Most everyone uses something to get through the day."

"Whatever." Tension crept up my neck into the base of my head. "You are a master at rationalization, Lee," I practically whispered to suppress screaming at him. "And that's why you scare the hell out of me."

He laughed, derisively, or maybe I was projecting.

"It's not just about weed, Lee. People like us are consistent prey to instant gratification. I have a hard enough time fighting my own cravings. I don't have the energy to be the arbiter of yours too. As much as I love being with you, I don't want to end up hating you in a month or a year down the line because you possess the very same frailties I hate in myself."

He didn't look at me. I felt his separation as silence lingered, like an expanding wall between us.

"I'm sorry you feel that way." He sighed, shook his head but still didn't look at me. "I want to be with you, Rachel, but only if you want to be with me, not some version of who you want me to be." It seemed like he was going to say more, but didn't.

The truth of his words cut. Humbled. I felt myself crave him all the more as he withdrew. But I knew Lee wanted more than my mind and body. He wanted my heart and soul, and those I could not give him. He couldn't be trusted with them— to put me, even our potential children before his obsessions. "I'm sorry, Lee. We'd be a train wreck together. And I just can't afford to waste any more time on boys masquerading as men."

He looked away again, let the silence linger, a chasm now between us. "You know, I'm thinking we should stop hanging out so much then, give us both some time to find what we need." He paused, as if carefully choosing his words. "I'm sorry, Ray. Unless we're moving towards something more intimate, I'm going to have to move on."

I stopped breathing. My body tightened. Ground slipped away and I was suddenly free-falling. Warm tears slid down my cheeks before I knew I was crying. "Are you telling me you don't want to be friends anymore?" I knew it was right to let him walk, but I couldn't conceive of my life without him in it. "We can just play ball." I suggested softly, my voice small. Without racquetball we'd never see each other, maybe ever again.

"I think we need some time apart," Lee said softly. "I want a partner, too, Ray, a best friend to share my life. And I won't be looking for one if I'm spending all my time with you." He volleyed my words to Michael back at me. He looked at me, scrutinized me, and in that moment we connected again. We stayed fixed on each other and I

110

somehow knew he was giving me the moment to retract or modify what I'd just said and give us some hope for the future. But I didn't. I couldn't. It had already taken me way too long to do the right thing.

Lee shook his head and sighed, defeated. And he suddenly seemed a million miles away. "'A man never knows how to say goodbye.'"

His distance intensified my longing. "'And a woman never knows when to say it.'" I finished the quote from Helen Rowland, the early 20th century writer.

"Touché." He sighed again. "Rachel, you are brilliant, and beautiful, and broken, my dear, if you can't get beyond your fear." He waited for me to respond and when I didn't, couldn't, he finally spoke. "I guess we're done then. I'm gonna take off."

NO! Don't go, I wanted to beg, but didn't. Desperation pummeled reason, siding with Lee that weed was a non-issue I was making into a problem because I was afraid of commitment. I'd conjured the other issues as well. He was done with gambling, and was paying off his taxes, as he'd said. His ex was to blame for his divorce. His focus with racquetball, Tavli, food was passion, not obsession. But even desperation could not silence my intuition which flat out insisted anything beyond friendship with Lee would be emotional suicide. The void between us became a black hole.

"I'll miss you," he said softly. "I hope you find what you're looking for, get the life you want." He glanced at me as if we were passing strangers. "Take care of yourself." He started the engine. "Bye, Rachel."

I was being dismissed and dignity insisted I leave. After a moments pause I opened the car door. "Bye, Lee." I whispered, then counted to three, hoping he'd say something to stop me, but he didn't. I got out, shut the door, and the separation felt as if scissors cut the cord between us. I stood there watching Lee pull away, his headlights momentarily sweeping the half full parking lot, leaving blackness in their wake as he exited onto Ventura and drove away.

Then my skin started to crawl with the frenzied anxiety that comes from withdrawal.

-

Chapter 10

The weekend took a month to pass. No Lee, no friends available, and no weed to temper harsh reality. I stayed in bed, hid in my room with Face and TV for company, frozen in utter terror of life alone. I considered calling Lee every other second, telling him everything he wanted to hear, but didn't. Leading him on just to have a playmate was selfish, a waste of time at best, and sure to end badly for both of us.

Time slowed to a crawl, and like the clocks on classroom walls, sometimes it seemed to move backwards. Holiday specials with station breaks to news clips of Rodney King showed the best and worst of us, but the loving climaxes in the Hallmark films were always gloriously attained after miraculously overcoming any and all obstacles. Gotta love fiction.

The phone ringing woke me at 7:30 Monday morning. I'd been

hoping, then wishing, then begging the All I don't believe in that Lee would call. I imagined him confessing his love, professing his readiness to father children, promising to quit using with me in the New Year. He'd commit to working at becoming all that I needed— model self-discipline, healthy living, maybe finish his degree as a back up plan to running his own business, knowing how risky consulting can be. He was ready to become the master of his destiny instead of a slave to his addictions, and teach me how to be. I scoffed, shook my head at the cheesy climax I was conjuring. Truth was, we'd said everything there was to say. And I suddenly felt afraid to pick up the phone if it *was* Lee.

Fourth ring and the machine picked up.

"Hey, Rachel. This is Brian over at CBS, Television City."

I drew in a sharp breath, only then realizing I hadn't been breathing. I sat up in bed and put my pillow over the machines speaker but I heard Brian anyway.

"I'm hoping you're available to come in for the next few weeks." His teddy bear image came to mind. "We're on deadline for February sweeps and we need an art director to champion some of the new mid-season shows. We have a great lineup this year."

"Bullshit. Shut up!" I yelled at my machine. A 'great lineup.' Right. Another season that still portrayed women as either mothers, or evil, money grubbing whores, as in *Dallas*; or ditz chicks who need a man to save them, like in *Who's The Boss*, and virtually every other show and movie out there. And even me, to be fair, still looking for my knight, a hero to thwart Lonely, and rescue me from a barren existence teetering on poverty.

"Anyway, we could really use your expertise around here. Ring me up and let me know if you can come in today, or what your availability is through the New Year."

"Go away, Brian."

The machine clicked off. There was a discernible delay as the TV went to commercial, and for a second the bedroom was dead silent, like the room had been swallowed by a black hole, time slowing, stretching the years of isolation beyond any semblance of sanity. I noticed Face curled in her beanbag staring at me wide-eyed, rocket-ears straight up. The dog looked as scared as I felt.

The red light on my answering machine blinked it had recorded Brian's message. I'd stopped working in-house, full-time for CBS over a year back, when at the end of a meeting, after everyone else left, the married creative director grabbed my tit and then told me to "get ready" for him. With my knee to his groin, I threatened him with a lawsuit if he touched me again, but I quit that day. When I told Brian what happened, and that something needed to be done since this guy was sexually harassing the few women who worked there, he instructed me to put the CD's "minor indiscretions in perspective, and not take it so seriously."

Brian still called me into freelance when he was desperate, like now, with half his staff up in Mammoth or Tahoe for the holidays. Asshole. Even though the CD got laid off, along with half their marketing staff when they brought in computers, I felt and probably looked like shit. I had nothing clean to wear. And right about then I sure as hell wasn't about to walk that red carpet of the Artist's entrance, with all those tourists ogling to see if I was anyone famous, then enduring their scoffs confirming I wasn't a celebrity. I really was no one, nothing.

Dirty shirts, sweaters and jeans cascaded over the brim of the laundry basket on to the floor by the closet door. I couldn't recall the last time I'd washed more than my racquetball garb. And even clean, skin-tight stretchies and ripped t-shirts were inappropriate for a work environment.

No more Lee...I inhaled a shaky breath. Face came over and rested her head on the blanket waiting for strokes.

"We're on our own again, baby." Tears began again. "I'm sorry, but it's back to just you and me." I wiped my cheeks on the back of my hand then stroked the dog. Face licked the salty wetness from my fingers, enraptured, complete. Ah, to be a dog...

I stared out the side window at my neighbor's manicured lawn to find some ground. Lingering fog streamed through the palms and pines and cast the bedroom in light blue. *Tangled up in Blue*... I heard Dylan in my head, and crumpled inside. Tears streamed down my face again and I sat there with my hand over my mouth to stifle crying. Face curled back in her beanbag. Typical. Dogs are solipsists at heart.

The phone rang again. "Please, please, please be Lee..." I begged aloud.

"Hi, Dolly." My mom's cheerful lilt resonated from the machine's speaker. "Just wanted to check in, see if you're going to Colorado this year, or maybe staying home to be with friends." I exhaled as if she'd punched me. I'd told her about *Love Letters* the morning after seeing it, gave it rave reviews and painted a rosy picture of the evening, which I got a long time ago was my mother's preferred exchange. Like so many women of her day, and even today, it's expected we maintain a sunny facade. "Anyway, if you are staying in town this year, please think about joining us for our annual New Year's Eve get-together. It would make my evening having you home and safe with us to ring in the New Year. And please feel free to invite Lee! He's welcome. Well, let me know. Talk to you later." She disconnected without goodbye.

Run!

I'd been vacillating about going to the Rockies to spend Christmas with Chris and her family this year. I was thinking of spending the holidays with Lee, until his sister's invitation, and Lee's look of expectation, insisting I put some distance between us to maintain just friendship. No reason to stay in L.A. now. I could be shooting photography, conjuring stories, making it with my creative muse instead of hiding in my room, watching TV and getting off to blot out Lonely. And leaving town instead of working, I could avoid exploiting another *CBS Sunday Night Movie* about abused women or teens on drugs in the network's last, gasping attempt to recapture audience share lost to cable, video rentals, and emerging computer games way beyond Pac-Man.

I used the laundromat in the 7-11 strip mall a block from my parents' house since I'd moved out because it was convenient and safe. I was not welcome to do my laundry at their home, my mother informed me the day I left. Nor was I invited to show up for meals unannounced, nor stop by and raid the fridge. If I insisted on living on my own, then I should do just that, my mom had decreed. She wasn't thrilled about her 'baby' leaving the nest the same day her other daughter married and moved out, but there was no way in hell I could survive my parents without Carrie as the buffer between us. I was still a sophomore in college, and working full-time, though barely making rent, but I preferred living on the edge of homeless than with my folks who were convinced I was physically, mentally, and fundamentally... flawed.

I sat on the linoleum bench in the large, brightly lit room watching my clothes bob in thick, sudsy water in the industrial washer in front of me. The laundromat was empty, and mirrored my life. The spin cycle on the washer began and ramped in velocity with a high pitch whine. My clothes clung to the sides of the metal canister as it spun, opening a dark hole in the center. I wanted to jump in, hurt no more, want no more, be no more. I felt invisible. Cars parked in the lot on the other side of the glass wall and people went in and out of the 7-11 next door, but nobody even glanced my way.

My scalp tingled. It was hard to catch my breath. Felt like there was a weight on my chest. When my skin started prickling I got up and paced. I was having a panic attack, my mind racing with the notion that I'd never find a normal, stable man to be with because I wasn't normal— always at war with myself. *Breathe!* I did, slowly, deeply. *Chill*...I tried, but paralyzing fear of being alone forever left me falling again. I needed to find ground, support, to be seen, acknowledged, so I went outside to the pay phone on the wall between the laundromat and the 7-11 and called Jon. He picked up on the second ring.

"This is Jon. Talk to me." His resonant tone was familiar and soothing.

"Hi." I sounded maudlin even to myself.

"Hi. Wow. What's wrong?"

"Lee and I aren't together anymore."

"Since when did you two become a couple? I thought this guy was your new racquetball partner, my replacement."

"Well, we weren't exactly a couple, but I really liked him, Jon." I couldn't stop the flood of tears. I hid my face, stared at the phone. "I'm scared out of my mind I'll always be alone. And I may not be all that in love with people, but I hate alone." I spoke in a harsh whisper. "What if Lee was as good as I'll ever get, and I just chased him away?"

"Wait a minute. You told me you wanted a 'grown up,' a guy you can 'respect and trust'—your excuses for derailing me, if you may recall. From what you've told me, he's been, well, reckless, to say the least. You were right to let him go if he's not what you want, Ray, instead of ending up older, angrier, and back to alone years down the line on my side of the divorce stats."

"I 'derailed' you because you lied to me about being married, Jon." I said it louder than I meant to and a mid-40's woman passing by turned back and smiled knowingly, shaking her head sympathetically. "Lee doesn't want to be friends anymore, and that's what's really killing me. This last six weeks with him were a total blast. We clicked from the start, connected, you know, really enjoyed each other. If he wasn't so 'reckless,' I could've fallen in love with him, probably even harder than I ever did for Michael."

Jon's heavy sigh could be heard over a motorcycle pulling out of the lot. "I'm not sure what you wanta hear from me. Is Lee what you've been holding out for, Ray? Does he possess a 'clear head and open heart, model restraint, work towards excellence, and challenges you to do the same?'" Jon quoted me exactly and it surprised me he remembered what I'd said that first night we'd met seven years ago. "If that's Lee, then you owe him an apology. Call him and beg his forgiveness for whatever wrong you've done. If, however, you're looking to change him, mold him to what you want, or think you need, then move on."

His words literally hurt, and echoed Lee's Friday night. The sun broke through the fog and domed the scene in glaring white. My eyes started to tear, as they often did in the harsh L.A. sunlight, though I wasn't entirely sure I wasn't crying again. "I'm scared out of my fucking mind, Jon." I took my sunglasses from the inside pocket of my leather jacket and slid them on.

"I know, Ray. What I don't get is how your fear serves you."

I smiled. "Ah, my beautiful, rational, Jon. How nice it must be to have reason trump emotion with such ease. I require a lot of weed to disconnect, and even high I can't get to where you live, sweetie."

"I'd take that as a compliment, if I didn't know otherwise. You revel in

119

emotions, Ray. They're just another buzz to entertain that big brain of yours."

I couldn't help smiling. "Be nice, Jon. I just lost a good friend, a great racquetball partner, and on top of that, my only connection of late. Not my best day." I swallowed back the lump in my throat and refused to cry.

"Can't fix the former, but I can help you out with the latter." Jon rustled around as he spoke. "Picked up half an ounce of some amazing smoke couple weeks back. You can have whatever's left if you want it. I can drop it by your place on my way to work. Can't really hang out, but I can turn you on, and give you hug."

"You're a god, Jon. I'd love that. I'm at the laundromat by my folks' house."

"OK. See ya there in a bit, maybe fifteen or so."

"I'll be here. Thanks, J."

"Glad to be of service to a damsel in distress. Chow." Jon hung up.

I went back into the laundromat and waited for my clothes to spin dry and Jon to come by. The old Asian woman who owned the dry cleaners next door had filled the industrial washers with clothing and was waiting with a basket of dirty laundry to fill the one left that I was still using. She stood only feet away, eyes downcast, and did not look up though I openly stared at her, pressured by the woman's proximity.

The washer clicked off. I pulled out my clean, damp garments, piled them into a wire-frame cart, then put them into a wall dryer among the row of many, started the machine and sat on the peeling wood-laminate bench.

The old lady did not acknowledge me as she wheeled her empty cart out of the laundromat, now having commandeered all the industrial washers. The place was back to vacant. And I was alone again, only not really with Jon on his way. I craved weed almost as much as Lee. It, too, saved my from Lonely.

The parking spaces in front of the 7-11 were empty for what seemed unusually long. I tried to embrace the silence but it didn't work. The pings and dings of coins and such rattling around in the dryer annoyed the hell out of me, but there was no point in stopping the machine and collecting the all the change making noise. I couldn't do anything about zippers and buttons.

Accept the things you cannot change. The problem is knowing what's unchangeable. I could, in fact, put only soft clothes like sweaters and t-shirts in the dryer and hang dry anything with hard components, but there was no way I was doing that. Too much work, like trying to change Lee, though I still sat there considering the possibility.

I shook my head with contempt. I really was a desperate fool, and I felt small, stupid, invisible again. *Come on, Jon.* I anticipated the buzz, everything slowing, becoming surreal, disconnecting me from my pervasive fears, allowing me to plug into the unencumbered flow of ideas my brain gifted me when I got high. I watched my clothes spinning, flashes of red and emerald midst a tangle of black. I imagined what it'd feel like in that swirl of clothes, spinning, spinning,

spinning, out of control.

You are, reason hissed, if you think you can change anyone else but yourself. And even that's ify.

I stared out the glass wall. The fog had cleared to a perfect bright blue sky. Not a cloud in it. Sunshine and palm trees— L.A.'s magnificent façade.

A white Toyota Corolla pulled into the lot and it took me a second to remember Jon had recently traded up to a Jeep Cherokee. Half of Hollywood was suddenly enamored with 4 x 4s. And to work in the Industry you'd better be hip, slick and trendy. It's part of the price of admission.

Jon was a film editor, and worked all the time. Seven years ago he'd called me in response to a note I'd posted at the Coldwater Racquetball Club looking for 'C-B-level partners.' Jon and I were a good match. He was fast, kept me running and didn't care about keeping score. And he was gorgeous, classic chic in that Rob Lowe sort of way. After playing that first time, we shared dinner at Ocha Thai, and then took a three hour walk along Ventura to Encino and back. By midnight when we said goodnight, I returned his passionate kiss in kind, sure I could fall for him if not for my intuition needling me something was wrong with the perfect picture Jon presented.

When he called the next morning to arrange another game, his wife mistakenly picked up the extension and awkwardly introduced herself. Jon had neglected to tell me he was married, or that his wife was eight and a half months pregnant with their first child. Shot the shit out of *Happily Ever After* with Jon. We did institute playing ball two to three days a week though, and sometime after his divorce a year later we established an active friendship, and over the years a tight bond. He was my closest friend right then, till Lee came along, but trust him I did not. I knew, and Jon knew I knew, he thought with his little head over his big one all too often, which is why I'd never considered anything beyond friendship with him.

The dryer buzzed loudly and came to a slow stop. I stood and looked out the glass wall hoping to see Jon pulling up but no such luck. I got a metal basket, wheeled it over and opened the dryer door then pulled out an armful of warm clothing. They were soft and fluffy and smelled fresh and clean. I dropped them in the basket and went back for more.

"Is this mine?"

Startled, I banged my head on the metal rim of the dryer which sent a piercing blow through my skull as I stumbled back with an armful of clothes. I dumped them into the basket then rubbed the back of my head.

Jon examined his fleece shirt. I'd borrowed it and never gave it back to him. He stood on the other side of the open dryer door examining the shirt he'd removed from the basket between us.

"This is mine, isn't it? I've been looking for this for months."

"It's yours. Take it." I smiled. "It's clean." I finished clearing the dryer and shut the door. "Good to see ya."

"Good to see you too." He leaned across the basket and kissed me on the lips, closed mouth, a typical L.A. 'hey,' and then straightened, his eyes scanning me as he spoke. "You look great! Very tight. Playing a lot of ball works for you."

I frowned. "Except my partner just abandoned me." I wheeled the cart past him and over to the folding table. Jon followed. "Will you play with me, Jon. Go back to Tuesdays and Thursdays like we used to?"

"I'd love to play with you, Ray." He said it teasingly, moved up behind me and grabbed me around the waist with one arm. "Ooo, I miss playing with you. I do." He pressed up against me pushing my crotch into the edge of the linoleum shelf and gently moved his pelvis and hardening cock against the crack of my ass.

I whipped around and he backed up. "Knock it off, J." Jon had been an exception to the 'relationship required for sex' rule, and easily the best lover I'd ever had because I didn't care how he perceived me. It had always been just for fun, if neither of us was seeing anyone, with never any thought of commitment for either of us. We were safe, always used a condom, and those were about the only two rules. Ostensibly, neither of us was seeing anyone right then, so Jon wasn't out of line in his demonstrative display. But for some reason it felt dirty, made me feel cheap.

"So, you and Mary are through? Totally done and on to the next one?" I asked as I turned back to folding my clothes.

"We're done." Jon frowned, but his hazel eyes flickered with humor. "She said she couldn't trust that only my eyes wandered." He flung his fleece shirt on the bench against the glass wall. His tall, thin frame was Giacometti-like, silhouetted against the glare outside. "Confessing the past to cleanse the soul is highly overrated. The truth can really fuck up a functioning relationship." His straight brown hair hung past his shoulders and framed his gaunt face, his black t-shirt was tucked into worn blue jeans that hung on his slender hips like a GQ model. He held a black leather organizer under his arm. Very vogue. "I never should have told Mary that Lavonne and I split because of Allison." Jon flashed a quick, regretful grin, then put his organizer on the folding table next to me. He unzipped it and took out a pack of Marlboro Lights, extracted a cigarette and lit it, then pulled out a baggie of buds. "Here." He handed me the weed. "I hope it provides the diversion you need."

"Thanks. Looks yummy." I pocketed the baggie in my leather jacket.

"It is, trust me."

I did too, about the weed, anyway. Jon was a connoisseur of just about everything. He liked the best, and bought it, whether he could afford it or not. He took his first bankruptcy at 23, and was railing headlong into another one by 30 had he not landed the editing job at Universal Studios a couple years back through a friend who worked there. Knowing someone in the Industry is the most common ticket to entry.

"Mary was right. I don't know what's wrong with me. She's beautiful and smart and accomplished. And she still wasn't enough." Jon took a drag off the cigarette then exhaled it and the bright room clouded with harsh tobacco smoke. He delivered the cliché with Hollywood cadence, and gave a little shrug before zipping his black case and sticking it under his arm. He leaned back against the end of the folding table and stared outside.

"Maybe you're just not ready to settle down." *Or grow up*, but I didn't say it because he already knew it, and there was no reason to be contentious. "You know, Mary is a big time producer and gorgeous and all that, but honestly, she had a stick up her ass that went right through her brain. I love her 'success breeds success' rap, like no one knows who her daddy is. She really was a bitch, Jon. You're probably better off without her."

"Like you are without Lee?" He stared at me and cocked his head to one side.

Ouch. My cheeks flushed.

"Come on, Ray. I get that he lavished you with attention, was demonstrably generous and had all the emotional shit I so sorely lack. But 'just scratch the surface,' to quote you, and the full picture you've painted of Lee seems fairly screwed up to me. If what you've told me about him is true, then move on. Stick to your gut and find what you want."

He was right, of course, if I took out emotions like choking loneliness and gasping desperation. Jon did not feel these things. Losing Mary was more like losing an anchor than an appendage, though they'd lived together the last six months. He had no need of commitment. He could find someone to be with at his whim. And all counted with him, but none too much. By his own admission, Jon had never known Lonely, which I reverently envied.

"I've gotta jam." He leaned over and gave me a quick peck on the lips, then pushed off from the edge of the table. "Have a ten hour schedule today and I'm late." Jon was always running late. "Booked on *Married with Children* straight through New Year's or I'd say let's hang out, go up to Starwood's for New Year's eve. You got plans, or did they go away with Lee?"

"CBS asked me to come in but I'm thinking about going to Colorado early, hanging in the Rockies with Chris and her clan, escape the menagerie for a while."

Jon studied me. "Can't run from yourself, babe. Trust me. I keep trying but it never works."

My throat clamped. Tears fell. I couldn't stop them.

"Ah, Ray..." Jon pulled me in and hugged me in his warm yet separate way. "You're going to be fine." He spoke softly in my ear. "You still have many years to meet the right guy, make beautiful babies, and live happily ever after." Jon released me and we stood a foot from each other.

"That's you, Jon. Adorable, successful, athletic white male, Hollywood career track, and you've got the next 30 years or more before considered undesirable. I'm at negative three, and counting." I held up three fingers to accentuate my point.

He stared at me, like he was trying to get inside my head, but couldn't. He was too into his own to make the connection. "You worry me, kid. Hardcore coating with a marshmallow center." He sighed and shook his head. "You gonna be OK?"

"Yes, Jon." Anticipating the buzz I'd be putting on in 10 minutes made it almost true. "And thank you, for everything."

"You bet. What's mine is yours, save my fidelity, of course." He flashed a grin then pulled me in for a quick peck on the lips and released me, picked up his fleece shirt and walked backwards toward the door. "Happy New Year, Ray. Enjoy the smoke. Take good care and be safe out there."

I wished him a happy New Year and thanked him again as he turned and exited the laundromat. I watched him walk to his Jeep parked right in front of the glass wall, but he didn't acknowledge me as he got in his car and left. Jon was on to the next thing and I became virtually irrelevant.

-

Chapter 11

Las Vegas is like a sinister Disneyland. I'd hated the place since our family trip there when I was 10. Instead of awestruck by the bright lights and menagerie in the casinos like my sister was, all I could see were the worn, blank faces of old and young slumped at the tables and in front of the slot machines. I felt their desperation, and they grew uglier, morphing from normal to maniac, like Munch's *The Scream*.

Up on I-15 cruising past the city, the afternoon sun lit up the garish façades of the Strip, but the tall glass structures of downtown seemed to absorb more light than they reflected. I pictured Lee in one of the casinos, on a stool in front of a poker table, so absorbed in playing he doesn't notice he's turning into a rhinoceros.

Highway 15 starts getting beautiful around the southwest tip of Utah. Known as the Painted Desert, millions of years of sediment band the low hills in horizontal stripes of purple, brick-red, and blonde for miles before blending into thin yellow lines that lace the mammoth chocolate rocks of Zion. I marveled at nature's wonders, let it fill me up, ground me, like the buzz did, and Lee used to.

I stayed in the tiny town of Selina, Utah, that night, just off of the I-70 corridor through the Rocky Mountains. I was back on the road with the sunrise. It was eighteen degrees out so I didn't open the passenger window for Face to stick her nose out. The dog whined once, touched her wet snout to the cold glass and pulled back, then circled twice before plopping onto her sleeping bag in the back of the Civic.

I lit a joint and sucked it in to temper my trepidation over today's journey. The high desert of Utah stretches one hundred miles along I-70 with no services. Sagebrush plains sprinkled with dwarf trees lined enormous terraced slabs of decaying rock. Fifty miles in and the trees vanish. Tumbleweeds dance with the constant wind that howls through the low, flattop hills occasionally extruding from the vast wasteland of dirt. Lonely lives here.

I saw only one other car on the road in front of me, and saw no one behind me. The car ahead disappeared around a hill and for a moment I was alone on the highway, a metaphor for the present, but maybe my future too, damned to travel life alone. The notion cut, physically hurt, a deep, suffocating weight in my chest even high could not suppress. I could take it away in an instant, just miss the curve ahead, put the car in a ravine and kill the unrelenting longing.

And if no one ever found me, and no one cared I was gone, did I ever really exist? Had I not been buzzed I would have crumbled right then, but instead flashed a sardonic grin. Face was a great traveling companion— she didn't get fidgety or bored driving for hours on end— but she wasn't enough. I couldn't exactly discuss Descartes with my dog.

12/16/91 (driving)

A thousand miles from there,

And I'm still nowhere.

It takes at least forty miles into Colorado before the landscape gets lush. It's a gradual climb approaching the Rocky Mountains from the west. The snow-capped peaks can be seen from as far as the Utah desert, but the immensity of the Rockies can't be felt until weaving through them. Shrub trees turned to pine which seemed to grow with the surrounding mountains as I passed the tiny hamlet of No Name, irony at its finest, since No Name *is* the town's name. Snow crept down the steep slopes the higher I got, and by the time I reached Vail it blanketed the stunning panorama of 10,000 ft high peaks surrounding the resort town below. The highway was dry, with the occasional speckled gray mounds melting onto the road. I stopped only for gas and to let Face pee, then moved on quickly to avoid black ice that came with the night.

I got into Breckenridge mid-afternoon and parked in the Beaver Run Resort's heated garage to insure the dog's comfort. I stroked Face, told her to stay as I closed her in, then locked my car and crossed the glass enclosed overpass to the hotel entrance. I'd called Chris before leaving L.A., and we'd scheduled to meet at Tiffany's bar in the lobby when she got off work.

With almost an hour to kill, I chose a square wood table in the back of the bar and watched the skiers drink and flirt after their long day on the slopes. The ski-bunny blond waitress told me there was a $5 minimum after 4:00p.m. when I ordered just tea. After she delivered it, along with the check, she never came by again. The bar was filling fast. Skiers clomped in wearing their dripping gear then stripped it off after picking their spot and ordering drinks.

I watched, unseen by most, wanting to be noticed but not bothered. I was buzzed, though mildly by then. I pulled my spiral notebook from my backpack but prose failed to come to mind in any focused fashion after my long journey, so I sketched the room and the people in it. I was untouchable. Autonomous, almost invisible, safely nestled in the warm bar, making it with my muse.

"Wow. That's beautiful." A female voice said over my shoulder.

I startled, immersed in sketching a stunning male skier sitting near the bar. Maybe 25, he was on his fourth gin and lime, and either knew I was drawing him or was sitting that still because he was totally blasted. I looked up at the short, stout woman with coiffed, dyed brown hair who'd spoken. She was standing next to Chris. A very thin, middle-aged man with a bushy blond mustache stood on Chris' left. All three stared at my drawing then looked up in unison at the skier. I felt my face flush as he smiled back at us, and then at me with a knowing grin. I closed my notebook and got up to hug

Chris. I pictured her coming alone like always, her physical weight matching the weight of her demeanor. But when we separated and Chris looked up at me from her mere five feet, she seemed... happy. Dressed like her companions in casual work attire, her kinky yellow hair was pulled back in a French braid revealing her fair, freckled face, and made her normally gray eyes seem blue/green. She introduced me to her new boyfriend Rick, and their workmate, Shirley, as we all sat down.

"Are you a professional artist?" Shirley wanted to know.

"No." I didn't feel like engaging with strangers right then.

Rick's chair was beside Chris's. Their legs were touching and he held her hand in his lap. Though she was still plump for her small frame, and Rick was rail thin, practically concave, they seemed suited for each other, as if one completed the other, a yin/yang kind of thing. Though she'd mentioned him on the phone, I had no idea it was serious until that moment.

"You're very good. Where did you study?" Shirley asked me.

"Nowhere that counts. I just like to draw." I wasn't trying to be rude, but had no interest in rehashing my education and pretending it mattered.

"Rachel was an art student at the university in Greece where we met." Chris chimed in. "She carried this wooden board around everywhere, with sketches she was working on. Mostly nudes, if I recall correctly." She smiled at me, then at Rick, and I was consumed with envy.

132

We exchanged the basics— jobs, places of origin and the like. Rick went through three whiskey sours and two beers in the hour we sat there. He showed no sign of getting drunk, or even tipsy as he told wild stories about Vietnam, claiming to be a retired hit man for the Army, like Martin Sheen in *Apocalypse Now*, but it was hard to believe with his gentle demeanor. I asked questions once in a while, but more out of courtesy than interest. The gorgeous skier glanced at me every few minutes, probably to see if I was still watching him. I wondered what it felt like to be so completely comfortable inside your own body, to know you are beautiful, powerful— *male*— that the world is your oyster.

Chris informed me she'd been living with Rick for the past few months over her third gin and tonic. When we'd spoken on the phone she'd failed to mention I'd have her house to myself. I'd been looking forward to late night talks over Tavli, like we did as roommates in Greece, and the years I'd been staying with her for the holidays.

Shirley finally took off. Rick leaned over and kissed Chris on the lips, then stood and suggested we get dinner, but I begged off, claimed exhaustion. Watching their exchange of affection literally hurt. I couldn't wait to get out of there, up to her house, and away from them right then. We hugged goodbye and felt a visceral exchange between us that surprised me. Chris had never been demonstrative, and true to her German heritage had always maintained a composed stature and an appropriate distance. I smiled at my friend when we released but the invisible wall was back. She handed me her house keys, then invited me to join them after work tomorrow back at Tiffany's for Happy Hour. I accepted, thanked her again and

133

left, and without leaving the indoors traveled through hallways and glass enclosed bridges back to my car and waiting dog.

Face wildly wagged her tail tantalized by the scents of the forest as I pulled onto the snow dusted gravel drive and parked along the side a single-story, aging wood paneled house nestled in the eastern foothills of Breckenridge. She whined to get out and bolted as soon as I opened the hatchback.

"Get back here you crazy bitch," I yelled. And there was a heart-stopping moment when Face didn't appear upon command, but then she came barreling up the porch steps, wired, panting steam and waiting for me to unlock the back door slider and let her in.

It was as cold inside as out. And dark. Smashed my hip into the end of a narrow table and cursed. I finally found a light switch and lit up the quaint living room. The fireplace façade commanded the room with tightly fitted granite rocks that took up a third of the wall, its hearth big enough to curl in. A tan leather couch faced the fireplace six feet back, and in front of the couch was a long, low, knotty pine table. A large projection TV sat in the corner of the room, near the sliding glass doors I'd come in.

The TV remote was on the pine table. I retrieved it and clicked Power but the screen stayed dark. I pressed it again and again, then pressed the green button on the set itself but the TV did not come on. No TV! It couldn't be. My impulse was to run from there, get back in my car and find a motel for Face and me. But then I thought of the icy hill to get up here, and my half-bald tires and cruddy breaks, and reminded myself that any lodging in town this time of year was sure to be beyond my meager means, assuming anything was even available.

Face curled on the throw rug near the glass doors. I shivered as I dropped the clicker back on the table. No TV, and I sighed heavily, my warm breath condensing to steam. I glanced around for a heater box but spied none, then noticed the metal basket by the hearth stacked full of kindling and firewood. After checking to make sure the flue was open, I constructed a pyramid inside the fireplace then lit it and blew on it softly. The flame spread quickly, sparkling gold encasing the wood in quavering sheets. Within minutes the heat began burning my flesh and I put the heavy metal screen across the opening then went and sat on the couch, put my feet up on the low table and stared at the fire.

The crackle of the wood was now the only sound but did not fill the eerie quiet known only in remote areas. Beyond the buzz of any major city, in L.A. you can hear a freeway from just about anywhere. And right then I wished I was back there, with the perception of family and friends at hand, even knowing they did not fill, and often exaggerated the emptiness within. I got a joint from my camera case and lit it, the sweet smoke and familiar burn in my throat and lungs providing a psychosomatic buzz before the actual weed high.

What the hell am I doing here again, I wondered, staring at the flames consuming the logs. Eight years later and I'm still running up here. My contemporaries had moved on, from roadtrips to carpools, they were married and making babies and hanging with others of like kind. I was still doing the same old thing, running in circles on the little metal wheel. I should have stayed home, put that ad in the paper. But the Quest was exhausting and the idea of it daunting, especially after my recent sabbatical from the dating game hanging out with Lee.

I missed him. Most everything about him, from his powerful presence, to his Cheshire smile, his laconic laugh to the attention he lavished on me. If I'd agreed to give it a go with him he could be here with me now. We'd sit by the fire, share a joint, play Tavli and pass the night, maybe bake a pie and share it. We'd talk about everything and anything, just like we used to. He'd protect me from drunk skiers or whacked out locals who saw me drive up or heard me yelling for Face. They'd never throw one of the metal deck chairs through the sliding glass door and attack me if Lee were here.

The weed soothed, the fire warmed, and tired crept in as I wove my twisted fantasy. I made sure the screen was over the hearth, then checked the dead-bolt on the sliding glass door and went to bed. It was cold in Chris' bedroom and I huddled under the enormous patchwork quilt that spilled over the bedsides, almost to the floor. Every creak of the house or rustle of wind outside startled me. Again I wished I wasn't alone, that Chris was here with me, or somebody, anybody, *Lee*.

Face growled, low and menacing. It felt as if my heart stopped until I saw my dog still curled on the blanket I'd laid on the floor, twitching and growling in sleep, caught up in a dream.

"Face! Knock it off." I released the breath I'd been holding as the dog looked up at me, bewildered, then curled back into herself and closed her eyes.

I considered smoking another joint to put me to sleep but thought better of it. I'd be out of weed before the New Year. I'd promised myself I'd quit using then, nix it from my story. When I got back from Colorado I'd put another ad in the paper. It was a numbers game, after all. And to improve my odds of finding someone to be with that I respected, I was going to have to become someone I could respect. Drug-free, excuse-free, come the New Year I'd find more work, get the money together to move out of L.A. and up to the Bay, regardless of my mother's berating protestations I'd be abandoning the family moving away. Maybe starting anew would put me on the path to finally finding my knight, though somewhere deep inside my intuition insisted my perspective wasn't yet quite right— still looking for someone to save me.

-

Chapter 12

In the light of day the glass doors offered a spectacular view of the 14,000 ft craggy rim of the snow-capped Rockies. The magnificent granite mountains sloped down to the tiny hamlet of Breckenridge in the small valley below.

While waiting for the water to boil and admiring the grandeur of the view I noticed the three pronged head of the television cord on the hardwood floor and plugged it in. The kettle whistled in the kitchen. I made myself a cup of tea, then took the warm mug back into the living room, sat on the couch, picked up the remote and clicked on the TV.

Angelic voices swelled and a large church choir dressed in white robes belted out a hymn. It was a commercial for Midnight Mass at the Crystal Cathedral. I clicked through the 35 channels of cable and came upon *It's A Wonderful Life*, one of my all-time favorites. George was walking Mary home, promising her the moon. It seemed the only desirable men left were in the movies. Maybe that's the only place they'd ever been. I sipped my tea and tried to shed that reality, let the movie sweep me in. And it did, for the most part, relating to George's anguish when he wanted to end it all, and felt his torment when he was nobody, when he didn't exist.

I looked around the empty house. I really was invisible.

My camera case was on the pine table in front of me. I pulled a joint and smoked it and continued to watch TV after the movie ended, until I was high enough to hear my creative muse yelling at me to get off the damn couch and do something. I got my Nikon, called Face, and we went for a hike in the patchwork snow.

It was thirty degrees outside, a hot spell for winter up there. I was comfortably warm in a hooded sweatshirt and jeans, hiking boots and my leather jacket. The air was crisp and thin at two miles up. Face bound after squirrels and into piles of snow. Every few minutes she'd come looking for me, rocket ears straight up, big almond eyes shining with delight, tongue hanging out over bright white canines. I took a few shots of her for fun, then came to a clearing and focused on the panorama of mountains across the valley.

It was close to noon, the angle of the sun making the peeks look painted against a sheet of saturated blue. I'd been doing serious photography since my college days, long enough to know I'd never capture the depth of field in the massive granite slabs, or the mammoth slope of the mountain with the sunlight stripping shadows and flattening the scene. I took a couple shots anyway, then changed from wide angle to a telephoto lens and focused on the flora's colorful arrays peeking through the white patches of snow.

A couple hours later I was back in the isolated cabin with Face, the darkness descending outside and in. A white Trimline phone sat on the counter that divided the small kitchen from the living room.

Pick up the phone and call Lee. Beg forgiveness, promise to consider more than just friendship and invite him up to be with me. I flashed on scene after scene in my head, imagined exploring Estes Park and Telluride together, places I'd never venture alone in the Rockies in the mid-winter. I pictured laughing around a table in a cozy bistro with Chris and Rick, or making some elaborate meal with them and inviting a few of their friends. Intimate, joyous, sharing, caring, like a *Hallmark Holiday Special.*

The sun was set but the sky was still lit in blues and purples. I dreaded the evening of being the odd one out— an obligation and distraction from the one and only romance Chris had ever had, that I was aware of anyway. I sighed heavily, then got a joint from my camera case and lit it as I sat on the couch and clicked on the TV. And after a while the urgent need to call Lee left me.

I met up with Chris and Rick at Tiffany's a couple hours later. Almost a repeat of the previous evening except with just the two of them. We stayed in the bar for an hour, then Rick suggested we migrate into the hotel restaurant for dinner. With no legitimate excuse to beg off, I agreed.

Chris encapsulated the history of our friendship to Rick throughout dinner as if she'd never spoken of me to him before. In the small booth, over our tomato bisque in the dim diner, she explained in detail the flat we shared in Athens and the summer college program we attended there. She described learning Tavli together from the old man, and jokingly chided Rick for refusing to learn to play. She told him of our travels through most of Europe together and turned to me often with, "Do you remember..."

For the most part I did, though I wasn't all that interested in reminiscing. The restaurant was casual, the soup delicious, their company pleasant enough, but every time they snuggled against each other or exchanged a private joke I had to look away. I never dreamt Chris would end up with someone before me. By her own admission, she was a wallflower, and even she assumed she'd always be single. Watching her across the table sitting next to Rick, she seemed like a different person than the one I'd known the last thirteen years. No longer angry, she seemed content, even pretty. Her wiry hair seemed softer with the fine strands escaping the braid. Her head was still rather small to her body but her eyes seemed larger, and brighter.

I was consumed with jealousy again. Like most every other friend and family member, Chris sat across from me with her new beau's arm wrapped around her shoulders, poised to live happily ever after. Only I was still alone. *Loser. Old maid. Nothing, to no one.* And a flash of panic I'd always be single made me flush with heat. Sweat dripped from my forehead down the sides of my face.

I excused myself and went to the bathroom, filled the sink with cold water then stuck my face in and held it there. The parade of men I'd met the past few years flashed by. Most wore a bullshit bravado though they were balding, with soft bellies and mediocre careers, and satisfied watching TV all night after being served dinner. The very few with any promise, the smart, successful, active, attractive guys who sparked my interest initially, turned out to be mainly narcissists, more interested in how I reflected them, than in me. And then I flashed on Lee, and wondered where he fit in the pantheon. It didn't really matter. He, too, was now a memory.

My lungs burned and I straightened, gasping in air, looked in the mirror and flipped myself off. After a moment's hesitation I got some paper towels, dried off my face and then looked back in the mirror. My hair was a mess. My eyes seemed dark, and sad. I looked serious, somber, verging on morose. It was no wonder I was never any good at winning friends and influencing people. My parents were right, of course. Coveted women were sparkly and light, but I wasn't, never had been. "I hate you!" I practically yelled at myself, then splashed water from the sink onto the mirror. It dripped over my reflection, streaking down the mirror like tears.

A beleaguered mother pushing a stroller with a wailing infant entered the bathroom and compelled me to leave. She put her baby on the plastic pull down changing table as I wiped my eyes and face on my shirtsleeve and went out to the short hallway. And as irritating as that screeching child was, I still envied that mom for possessing the life I still sought.

I saw Rick and Chris kissing as I approached the booth. Eyes closed, they were lost in each other and didn't see me. I turned around and walked back towards the bathrooms, then paced the narrow hallway. I wanted to be anywhere but there. Chris had invited me out of habit this year, like a mercy fuck. My fading buzz was all that kept me from cracking up. My breathing was shallow and fast. My heart raced, reverberated in my throat. It felt as if I was becoming transparent, like it did in the laundromat a few days earlier, like if I disappeared no one would notice, or if they did, they wouldn't really care. I stared at the payphone on the wall, my brain searching for someone, anyone who might miss me, then picked up the receiver, punched in my calling card number and called my answering machine praying for someone who did, even if only my mother. It picked up on the first ring indicating I had a message. I fumbled in my jacket pocket for the small tone box then pressed the button to the receiver to cue the message.

"Hi. It's me. Lee." He paused. I gasped. "I miss you. I miss playing racquetball with you. And backgammon, and sharing great talks over meals. I miss our weekend adventures, and exploring new restaurants together. I miss your insights, and perceptions. I miss our connection." He sighed. "I've been thinking about it, about what you said. And I've come to the conclusion you're right. I'm probably not ready for the relationship you want right now. Clearly, I have some things to work out first. I hope we can stay friends and maybe even help each other get some of our shit together." He paused again. "Or maybe you'd prefer just racquetball and helping each other stay in shape. Either way, I'd love to see ya. Call me if you want to play some ball, or if you just want to talk." He paused for so long I thought he hung up, and I waited for the beep at the end of the message but it didn't come. "Hope to hear from ya." Then beep.

I stood there with the phone to my ear wanting more. My heart pounded hard and echoed in my chest. Lee was back! He had gallantly returned, once again rescuing me from the abyss.

Watch out! echoed from somewhere deep inside.

Fuck off, my childish rejoinder to the voice of reason.

"If you'd like to make a call, please hang up," said a woman's recorded voice, reminding me to hang up, and breathe.

I tried to come up with an excuse to exit the scene for a private setting to call Lee back on my way to rejoin Chris and Rick. They smiled at me with my return, but I knew it didn't really matter to either of them that I was there. But instead of envious, I suddenly felt glad for her, glad she'd finally found somebody.

On the way back to the cabin, and even while dialing Lee's number I rehearsed what to say. I'd let him know how glad I was to hear from him, how much our friendship meant to me, how much I too enjoyed our time together. I'd confess how much I missed him, how badly I wanted to be with him, assure him I too felt our connection—

The fourth ring his recorder came on, and deflated me. "This is Lee. Leave a message." Beep.

"Hi. It's me, Rachel. Got your message." My mind went blank. "Glad to hear from you. I'm calling from Colorado, a tiny town way up in the Rockies in the middle of nowhere. I'm staying with my friend, Chris, well, not exactly with her." I glanced around the empty house. "It's cold up here. Lonely followed me up this year. I wish you were here." I felt stupid I'd said it and wished I could take it back. "Oh well. Hope you're having fun in the warm L.A. sun. Love to talk." I gave him the number at the cabin, suddenly stuck for what else to say then added, "Well, take care. Hope we talk soon." I hung up, and waited. When he still hadn't returned my call by 1:00a.m. I went to bed, but it took an hour on that to fall asleep with my mind cycling over his message and my response, trying to figure out what I said wrong to chase him away again.

I was in the kitchen making tea and watching the morning news when the phone rang.

"Hi, it's me." Lee.

"Hi." I smiled.

"I'm glad you called back." He paused. "I wasn't sure you would. I'm glad you did."

"Me too."

"I miss you."

"Me too."

He gave a short laugh. "How's Colorado?"

"Cold." I sipped my tea and stared out the glass doors at the clouds pouring over the rim of the Rockies, intermittently blocking the sun. "And lonely." It just slipped out, but then, I didn't have to wear a face with Lee.

"I'm sorry. For me too. It's damn lonely here without you. I didn't realize you were leaving so soon. I thought you were going up there for Christmas."

"I was. But after our last night together I didn't feel like staying in L.A."

"Sorry about that. I really do want to stay friends, Ray. I hope we can still play racquetball, even do dinners, hang out and play Tavli when you get back here. Are you staying up there through New Year's?"

"That was the plan. I'll be with Chris at her parents in Delta through Christmas. They throw a holiday party for the entire town from Christmas day to a few days before New Years. We're down there through the weekend, then coming back up here for a small New Years eve party." I flashed back to last New Year's eve at Frankie's party watching everyone around me embrace at midnight, and then imagined a replay this year with Chris and Rick kissing while I'm standing there. I really had to get out of here before New Year's. "What are you doing for the holidays?"

"I'm thinking of going up to my sister's after Christmas, ring in the New Year with her and Arlene." He paused, and I thought I heard him take a hit off a joint. I scoffed silently, but with humor at my friend's 'indulgence,' getting high first thing in the morning. "How about you change your plans and meet me in Oregon, hang out with us for New Year's?"

He'd read my mind again, his casual offer saving me from another New Year's essentially alone. I couldn't wipe the coquettish smile off my face to save my life.

"If you leave there by the 30th, you can make it to Oregon by the 31st and we can ring in the New Year together."

Yes, almost escaped my lips, but but the better part of me interceded. "Look Lee, I'd love to join you and your family in Oregon to ring in the New Year. But I meant what I said last Friday night. I'm quitting weed at the beginning of the new year for good. Forever. I'm gonna practice living healthy, model restraint— discipline not addiction, and finding a man who does the same. As much as I love being with you, spending time together, I don't want to hurt you down the line. I don't see a future for us beyond friendship."

He sighed audibly. "Look, Ray. I know what you said the other night is right. I don't like it, but I know it's right. I have some shit to work out before I get seriously involved with anyone. I just got divorced. And I'm not ready to make another life commitment."

"I am, though...just not with you." I wasn't trying to hurt him, but his response seemed a non sequitur to my assertion.

"I know." His protracted silence seemed to suck the air from the room through the wire. And it hurt me knowing I'd just hurt him.

"I'm sorry."

"I know. But I get it. And I'd rather be a part of your life than not. I don't want to lose you, Rachel. You show me a path to who I want to be. I don't want to blow off our friendship."

"Me neither." But trepidation lingered, still wondering if he was really hearing me.

"Meet me at my sister's for New Year's. You can stay sleep in the solarium like she suggested. I'll take the couch in the living room." I heard him exhaled, pictured him blowing out a controlled thin stream of smoke, his punk grin lingering. "Come! It'll be fun. I promise. Meet me up there. I'm calling Colleen and telling her you're coming. The girls will be thrilled."

I pulled a joint and sparked it as I sat on the couch with my tea. We discussed places to see in Oregon while I watched the TV. I didn't care if Lee heard me getting high, especially since he was. I wore no facade with good friends, since they accepted me with my frailties, as I did them. Other then emotional support, in all likelihood their indiscretions, addictions or otherwise, would never directly impact me, or the family I hoped to create.

The morning news was on most every station, from local to CNN, several showing clips of Rodney King getting beaten then stills of his battered mug shots, and exaggerated reports of the "significant increase in drive-by shootings." And I was glad to be far from L.A., away from the insanity there, nestled in the Rockies and chatting with Lee, a million miles from Lonely.

-

Chapter 13

I spent Friday writing the short story of the genie and the gang bangers. I gave the tale a happy ending, which was unusual for me, usually focused on the dark. But the moral of the story, as all fairy tales need one, was that the choices we make lead to the life we live, and that a happy ending really is in our control.

In the evening I met up with Chris and Rick and a few of their workmates at Tiffany's. I relaxed into the casual exchange while they downed gins and beers. After their cronies took off, I joined Chris and Rick at Rick's flat. Rick went directly to bed. A hotel maintenance worker, he was on-call at 4:00 the next morning. Chris and I played Tavli late into the night, since, as an accountant she had weekends off and the holiday week to come. I didn't mention leaving before New Year's, but, truth was she most likely didn't care if I took off. I didn't tell her about going to Oregon for New Year's because I wasn't sure if I was yet, since staying in Colorado may be a better choice then getting back involved with Lee.

As excited as I was to see him, be with him, I felt apprehensive. While Lee provide me the ground I'd been missing with his attention alone, he wasn't exactly the greatest influence. After vacation, back in L.A., I'd have to limit our time together to racquetball, cycling the strand, productive activities that were cheap, or free. It was time to stop accumulating debt I couldn't reciprocate right now, and never, really, in the way I knew he wanted. Come the New Year I was done with weed, gorging on extravagant meals, unwittingly leading Lee on by accepting his invitations. It was time for me to make it on my own, and become who I wanted to be with. And that wasn't Lee, knowing he'd continue using, compulsively consuming, and modeling the addict I knew I had to abandon to actualize the life I still hoped for.

"—you're not even up yet. It's 9:00 already. I told you to be ready. I wanted to be on the road to my parents by now." Chris woke me from a sound sleep and nearly gave me a heart attack when she came into the bedroom Christmas Eve morning.

I bolted upright. "Sorry. Give me one minute." I got out of bed, slid on my jeans and a warm wool sweater over Marc's flannel shirt, then picked up my backpack off the cedar chest. "Let's go," I shot Chris a quick grin, called Face to come, and snatched my camera case off the kitchen counter as I followed her out the glass doors.

We sandwiched the dog as we piled into her white Chevy pick-up and headed over the Rocky Mountains to the tiny town of Delta, Colorado, where Chris was born and raised and her parents still lived. We were expected tonight for their annual Christmas Eve dinner.

I grew up watching the Christmas specials with John Denver sledding through the snow covered Rockies on the way to a family feast. I always wanted to be with him in that sled. L.A. in December is usually seventy-five degrees and sunny. My family celebrated Hanukkah, but it never had the cachet of Christmas. The sparkle of colored lights, the tree with all the presents underneath, I liked the glitter and glamour of it all. So I came to Colorado year after year to be a part of that scene. And though I never saw John Denver up here, it was one of those rare occasions I wasn't on the outside looking in.

A light snow started to fall and flakes flurried around us as Chris speed along I-70. I was glad for the chance to be with her alone. Rick was on-call all week for the rush of incoming skiers.

"Hey, Ray," Chris said. "I wanted to tell ya I'm sorry about Canada last spring, the entire road trip after your friend's wedding actually. I never should have agreed to it when I was so depressed after closing my firm."

"I'm sorry, too. I think we fed into each others depression. You're okay now though, back on your feet with this Beaver Run gig, right?"

"The job certainly helps me feel better about myself. Well, that and Prozac."

I smiled, again heard Lee's rejoinder the last night we were together. "Well, you seem really happy. Rick seems really nice. I'm glad you found someone to be with. I should be so lucky."

"Well, what about that guy you met from your ad? Lee, isn't it?"

"We're just friends. I like him a lot. He's a blast to hang out with." I smiled, picturing Lee's adorable baby face. "He says he wants more, but he's dangerous, Chris, an obsessive, like me. We could never be more than a fix for each other." I paused, took a deep breath and sighed to shed the truth of my words. "He professes to be an ex-gambler, but is in debt for close to half a million. He just got divorced from a two year marriage, and on top of all that he's a addict in denial. My gut tells me he's a little too screwed up to get seriously involved with."

"Aren't we all." She pressed in the lighter. "But Rick and I are better together then either of us are alone." She retrieved a pack of Marlboro Lights that was sliding back and forth on top of the metal dashboard, pulled out a cigarette, lit it and took a drag. "He's an alcoholic, ya know." She threw the pack back on top of the dash and reached behind her then pulled open the small back window a crack, but smoke still lingered in the cab. "He's full blown. Functioning, but an alcoholic nonetheless. I don't have to become one because Rick is."

I'd seen her put away two gin and tonics and at least a beer or two at Happy Hour night after night, which wasn't usual for Chris. I'd never known her to be a big drinker. "Well, whatever you're doing seems to be working for you. I hope it lasts."

"I don't know about Rick and I being together for the long run, but I am 35 years old and this is the first real boyfriend I have ever had. I am not going to be too critical. Live and let live. Carpé Diem, and all that," she quoted Robin William's in Dead Poet's Society. Chris took a final drag off her cigarette, rolled down her window and threw out the butt. Even though she closed it in seconds, icy air filled the inside of the truck and I shivered. "Look Rachel, Lee is the first guy you've been excited about in years. So he's not perfect. As you have said to me many times, we are all fatally flawed in one way or another. But a different way to see us is that we're all works in progress."

I smiled. Chris had never been profound, but was bordering that edge, throwing my own words back at me, with a twist. But living for just today was a fool's play. She'd been smoking since I'd known her, and would end up with lung cancer someday. If she missed that bullet, her weight issues, and now drinking excessively, daily, would certainly lead to major health problem not too far down the line. Regardless that she ignored her choices today would impact her future, and likely the lives she touched, they most certainly would.

Whether with diet, career, sex and/or in love— continually making poor choices and you're basically fucking your future self.

It stopped snowing by the time we got to her parents' sprawling ranch set in the middle of a hundred and fifty acres of chaparral wilderness. The dogs greeted us as we got out of the truck. Three chocolate Dobermans in their prime surrounded Face, but only Duchess, the youngest, would engage in play. The other dogs turned their attention to Chris and I and mooched for affection as they followed us into the house.

Chris exchanged hugs and kisses with family, and then her slender, attractive mother and her roguishly handsome father hugged me as if I were theirs. Her bear of a big brother, Jim, gave me a quick, tender embrace. Her older sister, Caroline, stayed on the suede couch and said 'Hi,' then inquired about my drive from the 'tar pit.' Six months pregnant at just 21, with a two year old son already in tow, Caroline eloped at 18 with the high school quarterback who permanently injured his knee his first game for Denver State. They'd been living on the government dime ever since.

For the next ten minutes straight she slammed L.A. for wrecking their economy and stealing Colorado's water. "I'm for turning off the tap and watching them all fry down there." Caroline took another big bite of apple pie drowning in vanilla ice cream, and either didn't care or was unaware of the health issues of being what looked like a hundred pounds overweight during pregnancy. "If they had any brains they'd all go back to where they came from, leave the place to the Beaners, Jews and Fags."

"When the barbarians come to your gate, you're welcome here,

Rachel," Jim said with shy smile.

"Thanks, Jim." I returned his smile and turned back to Caroline. Though I'd tolerated her slams over the years, they were getting uglier, longer, and words began spilling from my mouth. "People leave towns like these because technology and globalization are wiping out manufacturing jobs and killing the need for U.S. labor. They come to L.A. for work, and they don't leave whether they find it or not because it's better to be warm and broke than freezing alone back in the old home town that everyone moved to L.A. to get away from." My reasoning fell on deaf ears as Caroline's eyes veiled. She looked down at her plate then took another big bite of pie. Everyone was looking at us, and I felt bad for creating the riff, sort of. "Believe me, I too wish everyone stayed in Michigan, or New York, or Colorado, and you had your water and we had our land of plenty back." I sighed, slamming myself for engaging with her at all as I got up to greet Chris' grandparents, then joined the women in the kitchen to help prepare and serve dinner. The men watched football.

Glass eyes on the embalmed heads of clueless animals mounted on the walls of the guestroom glowed in the dim light from the lamp on the end table, next to the bed covered in bear skins. A buzz would surely help me dispel my disgust among the stuffed heads of deer, elk and even a mountain lion slaughter by man with gun looking to feel powerful. I slid a joint from my camera bag pocket and cracked the double hung window. Icy air flooded in as I lit the J and inhaled sharply, the heat of the smoke warming me inside and out. I moved the chest near the open window and sat on it to exhale directly thought the window opening, but it really didn't matter if smoke lingered in the room. Most everyone in Chris' family smoked cigarettes, including Caroline, even while pregnant. Their house was so saturated with tobacco smoke, the scent of weed would be indistinguishable.

It was one continual party for five straight days. Town folk streamed in and out daily, sharing in the holiday cheer. It snowed only that first night but it was cold, ten degrees or less most days. Other than brief walks with the dogs, and quick trips to the video or liquor store, we stayed inside. Chris and I helped cook and serve the meals, and in between played Tavli, watched movies and cable TV, and ate and ate and ate.

Initially I embraced the festivities. But it got harder to maintain cheerful after being introduced by her grandma to party-goers as 'Christine's little Jewish friend' for the twentieth time. I considered correcting her, confess to being an atheist, but that would only arouse judgment, and suspicion. Judaism, though foreign, was at least religion. Admitting to being a non-believer I'd be damning myself to the outside, obliterating one of the primary reasons I came here year after year.

-

Chapter 14

12/22/91

While intuition grants me foresight to the radiating effects of my actions, it's never really stopped me from continually making bad choices.

Between knowledge and change is the Grand fucking Canyon.

Monday morning I showed up at Rick's flat, my car packed, Face walked and fed. I told Chris I was going to the Bay. I didn't know why I lied. I wasn't sure it was a lie. I still had time to change my mind about meeting Lee at his sister's. Winnamucka, Nevada was the fork in the road. From there I could take Hwy 140 to Oregon, or stay on I-80 and go home. He'd said on the phone he was prepared for just friendship, but I knew it a lie. He'd tipped his hand when he admitted to wanting more. Of course, I knew what it was like to take anything over nothing— it's why I stayed friends with Michael for four years after he married.

I remembered Michael's call a few days after I got his letter explaining why he'd proposed to his roommate. "Allison told me we couldn't stay friends if I married you," he'd said. "I love her, like I do you, so I proposed, offered her the title of 'wife,' since you'll be my best friend for life."

I shook my head, disgusted I'd felt honored that he'd wanted to stay best friends. Even then I'd refused to acknowledge my relationship with Michael had really always been all about him. Taking something over nothing proved misguided at best, and a direction I had no intention of leading Lee. I pulled one of my three remaining joints from my camera bag and lit it as I left Breckenridge. Reports on the Weather Channel had said a storm was coming in from the Northwest, exactly the way I was headed. It wasn't snowing right then, though the roads were white with a fresh coat from last night.

Twenty or so miles west on I-70 the snow started falling in big, white flakes and within five miles had turned into a full blown blizzard, with

155

buffeting winds and white-out conditions crossing the Rockies. At one point I had to roll down my window to see I wasn't driving off the highway, my windshield so thick with wet snow my wipers froze in a coat of ice. Teeth chattering cold, fingers practically frozen to the wheel, I was finally able to keep my window rolled up when the snow let up around Salt Lake City.

Tension from the harrowing drive morphed into a relaxed surrealism with the storm clearing. Sparkling snow drifted across the blacktop in thick ribbons, like hundreds of ghostly sidewinders crossing the highway. The salt flats of western Utah stretched out around me in endless reverberating white against the bright orange horizon as I blazed along I-80 toward the setting sun under a blood red cloud deck.

My camera case was on the passenger seat next to me. I pulled off the highway onto a utility road and captured the moment, which took half a roll of film and about ten minutes of adjusting the aperture to get the best exposure. Back in the car, I blasted the heater to thwart gangrene. The pain was worth the potential gain though. I'd collected hundreds of beautiful slides over fifteen years of shooting, but every so often I'd stop time, freeze an extraordinary moment to share with those who weren't there to witness it.

I stopped at the Motel 6 in Elko, Nevada for the night. Inside the shabby room Face curled on the worn gray carpet outside the bathroom while I showered. Lee'd asked me to call him from the road, let him know when I'd likely be coming in to Oregon, but I felt afraid to talk to him right then, that he'd crawl inside my head and discover my doubt, still unsure of the fork in the road ahead. I lay on the mushy bed, clicked on the TV and settled on local news for the weather report but never got to hear the prediction, nor call Lee, the world fading to black within moments.

Sparklingly clear and frigid cold out, Face and I were back on the road at dawn the next morning. Stopped at a streetlight, ten TVs in the window of a pawn shop showed a heavy girl sitting cross-legged on a shabby bed, potato chip bags and ice cream containers scattered about her. Camera pulls back to reveal she's alone in some cruddy flat watching the ball drop in Times Square on an old TV. The image gnawed, mocked me as I got back on the interstate.

I lit my second to last joint and took several quick hits hoping the buzz would drown out my inner voice that was sure if I exited onto Hwy 95, I'd be taking the wrong fork in the road.

12/30/91 (driving)

What is the defining line of crazy?

When do you cross that line?

On what do you base your sanity?

I believe I may be losing mine.

I slid the pen back in the wire ring of the binder, closed the notebook, and took another hit before exiting I-80 at Winnamuca. A few more hits toasted the joint and stifled my inner chorus enough to

157

allow me to take pleasure in the ride. No point in second guessing my decision. I knew I wouldn't change my mind, fear of my nothingness descending again driving me. Desire to be with Lee, him wanting to be with me, had defeated all reason.

Desolate high-desert, Hwy 140 was mostly flat except for craggy hills in the far distance. Exploring new routes always entertained regardless of the terrain—an empowering adventure— a lone explorer of roads less traveled. And this one sure was. Maybe five cars passed in four hours, and I never came up on anyone until I got close to Lakeview, Oregon. Foliage and trees reappeared on the scene, and the drive got more and more stunning as the pines grew, changing scent and hue while passing through the northern rim of the Sierra Nevada's.

It was close to 3:00, sunny with a few puffy white clouds when I pulled into the Shell station just outside Klamath Falls. A balmy 48 degrees, according to the digital display on the monolithic steel structure in front of the Bank of America across the street. I soaked in the sunshine, basked in its warmth while filling the Civic, glad to be back in the West, excited to get to Medford.. I called Lee from the payphone next to a huge field while Face peed.

"Hi. This is Lee."

"Hi." I was surprised he answered his sister's phone. "It's me."

"Hey, you. Nice to hear ya. How was the drive?"

"It was great. When did you get up there?"

"Early last night. Where are you?"

158

"Some tiny town. I'm still about eighty miles from Medford."

"I'll give you directions how to get here. It's kind of complicated. Got a pen?"

"No. And I still have another hour on the road, so I'll call you again when I get into town and you can give me directions then, OK?"

"Good idea. Colleen and Arlene are at the store. They'll be back by the time you call and can give you much better directions than me." Lee paused, to take a hit off a joint. "Drive safely, and I'll talk to you soon." He exhaled. "Can't wait to see ya," he added like an afterthought. "Bye."

"Bye." I called Face, watched the dog romping toward me through the tall, tan grass, disappearing then reappearing like a lioness in the savanna with the setting sun behind her.

Back on the highway I smoked my last joint and imagined the evening ahead. I pictured The Big Chill, all of us cooking, then cleaning up while dancing around his sister's huge, country kitchen to a rock-n-roll score. Cut to full rotation of the four of us toasting in the New Year with champagne, and I don't even like champagne. See what too much Hollywood can do?

I took another hit and savored it, let the smoke linger in my mouth before inhaling. I was going to miss the sweet, smoky flavor of weed. I switched tapes to Brian Ferry's Don't Stop the Dance, his creamy sax mirroring the smooth, winding roads. I'd miss the way music sounded high, like being plugged into the sound board, or being the board. I shuddered with pleasure at the vibration of music

159

running through me, then caught the intoxicating sweet scent of sex. Along with weed providing a conduit to my creativity, I'd profoundly miss getting off buzzed.

My plan to quit using wasn't exactly at 12:01a.m. To avoid straying too far from the accord with myself, I laid down some specifics as I finished my last joint. I'd get high with Lee and his family tonight, then again tomorrow to christen the New Year with them, then leave mid-day. I'd allow myself the rest of the road trip to use, then be done. And I laughed as I flashed on Jeff Goldbloom in The Big Chill: "I don't know anyone who can get through the day without two or three juicy rationalizations."

Twilight encroached, the sky a mix of reds and blues, silhouetting the huge old redwoods into sleeping giants. I felt small, like a bug scurrying silently at their rooted feet as I pulled off the highway a few miles from Medford to call Colleen's. I stood at the payphone outside the mini-mart and let it ring quite some time but got no answer.

I went inside and made a cup of Earl Gray, paid and then went back outside and called again. Still no answer. And this time I let it ring even longer. Okay... So they were outside, took a walk, went back to the store for something. I got back in my car and sipped my tea, stared at the payphone. Ten minutes later I called again and only hung up when I lost count after thirty rings.

Secured my cup between my legs and drove into town. The place was deserted. I stopped at the only diner open, ordered a slice of lemon meringue pie from the tall, thin waitress, wearing a red Santa hat pinned to her dyed platinum hair and sporting crimson lipstick. I waited for her to come back with the slice, took one bite and

160

savored it before going to the payphone on the wall between the bathrooms and calling Colleen's again. Still no answer. Where the hell were they? Lee knew I'd be in by 5:00 on the outside. I called Information but Colleen Messer, at the same number I'd written on the pink post-it, had no address listed.

I went back to my table. By this time it was 5:30, and dark out. I felt pissed, and scared, and looked around the room, tried to focus on the moment at hand to ground me. The diner was a large rectangular room. It wasn't crowded. Mostly older white couples probably there for the senior discount. Christmas tinsel hung off the chair-rail molding that wrapped the room six feet up the walls. Faux-antique decorative plates set in plastic mistletoe on the fireplace mantle in the back completed the Americana scene.

God, what am I doing here?

My waitress delivered my check with a peppy 'Happy New Year,' and a genuine smile. At 6:00p.m. they announced over the P.A. they were closing for the holiday, and I got why she was so cheery. Before leaving the diner I called Colleen's house again. No answer. I must have let it ring fifty times. I called my machine. No messages. Then I called Lee's machine and left one. "Where are you? I have been calling your sisters for two hours and no one answers. I hope everyone's okay, no one's in the hospital or anything." I said sincerely. "I'm in Medford, waiting on directions from you. Please call my machine as soon as you get this message and let me know what's going on."

Waiting for Face to pee in the open field in back of the diner, I felt more scared than anything else at that point. Any number of horrific things could have happened, from car accidents to heart attacks to random acts of violence. There was no reason to assume he was avoiding me, as I cycled over our recent phone conversations line for line. He'd invited me of his own volition. We'd spoken only hours earlier and he'd reiterated he was excited to see me. Something must have happened. And I felt afraid for him, then for me when I noticed most of the cars had left the parking lot. I whistled for Face, we got in my car and I went looking for another open diner, and smoked a roach among several in the ashtray to slow my racing heart.

I spied the brightly lit truck stop ahead. The parking lot was filled with Mack trucks, and I felt small in my Honda Civic as I navigated between them. I parked and extinguished the remains of the joint in the ashtray. I had only a few roaches left, enough to roll maybe one small J. And just beyond the buzz lurked the darkness. Until right then I'd never spent New Year's Eve by myself.

The diner was stark and grimy, the air thick with smoke and the smell of burnt grease. They had a miniature plastic pine tree, blinking with small red and green lights sitting on the counter by the cash register. That was the extent of their holiday decorations. The payphones were near the entrance. It was freezing by the door with people coming in and out as I stood there calling Colleen's. No answer. Tried my machine again. No messages. My buzz was fading and I was barely able to defer my tears.

I got a booth and ordered a cup of tea from the old haggard waitress, then forced myself to focus on what had to be done instead of crying over what was. I'd get a motel and stay the night, leave first thing in the morning for L.A. There was no point in me staying without being able to reach him or his sister. I'd find out what happened down the line if I just kept calling Colleen's. Images of Lee dying of a heart attack, the EMT zipping the body bag, Colleen and Arlene crying as he's wheeled from their house looped in my head. It was likely I'd never see Lee again. If he died, of course. But if he didn't, without a damn good reason he'd not called me back there was no point in rekindling our friendship. Instead of returning home to racquetball, and a great Tavli partner, an occasional dinner or movie companion, and a confidant I could talk to about almost anything, I was now going home to nobody. My eyes burned, my vision blurred and a few tears escaped. No matter how I spun the future, I was the fat girl in some cruddy flat alone on New Year's Eve.

It was 9:00p.m. when the little truck stop cafe closed for the holiday. My waitress let me use the payphone one more time before she locked up. After calling Colleen's again, I left another message on Lee's machine that I hoped everything was okay, and that I was going to find a motel in the area for the night and would be leaving in the morning and I'd appreciate a heads-up on what happened.

There was nothing open and the streets were empty through Medford. The place wasn't exactly a roaring metropolis. I locked Face in the car with food and water. She settled in her sleeping bag as I slammed the hatch then went to checked into the Knights Inn Motel. In the shabby room I called Colleen's again and listened to her phone ring while forcing myself to breathe, and I finally hung up, then called my machine one more time to check my messages.

"I am so sorry!" Lee's passionate delivery resonated on the recording. "Arlene's dog, Etheridge, pulled the phone cord out of the wall. We didn't know. I waited and waited for you to call. I got really worried, but Colleen kept saying that you were a big girl and used to traveling alone and not to freak out about it. Finally I tried calling my machine to see if you left any messages. That's when we realized the phone was out." He paused.

I hung up. Exhaustion suddenly engulfed me. I released the deep, shaky breath it felt as if I'd been holding all night, then got up and paced. To slow my heart, mind, and escalating ire, I rolled one last joint out of the roaches I'd collected, but held off sparking it, instead leaving it in the glass ashtray for after a bath. I replayed his message in my head again and again, wrestling with the disconnect between his simple explanation and why it took him six hours to check his machine if he was so worried about me. I felt a twisted smile emerge, acknowledging the smarter part of me that was glad we'd missed each other tonight. If I believed in fate I'd call tonight another chance to get it right and stay away from Lee. Maybe we'd meet up in L.A., still play ball to stay in shape, but that would be all. No dinners. No movies. I absolutely had to quit Lee, or embrace him, us. Anything else was a prick tease, (whether he knew it or not) and I've always abhorred women who are, for debasing all women by promoting the myth that our sexuality is our greatest value.

The water was just shy of scalding when I eased in. The bath calmed me. It wasn't so bad, just me and my dog. I sat in the tub and listened to people outside on the walkway laughing and partying. Surprisingly, there was no longing. I was safe inside and reveled in the autonomy. I didn't have to put on a smile and pretend

I was having fun ringing in the New Year at some party or dance club with people who cared I was there about as much I wanted to be. I may never have been by myself on New Year's Eve, but that didn't mean I wasn't alone on quite a few of them, especially in recent years. I'd been using major holidays as a barometer— mirroring the media scenes somehow defined me as socially acceptable, normal. And I shook my head with the awakening, that it had taken me so long to get to. The truth was, participating in these festivities didn't validate, they undermined me. And I wasn't the poor fat girl watching the ball drop alone if I didn't share the holidays the way TV and movies depicted a young, single woman should. I was more than normal, if I chose to be, worked at becoming. And I scoffed aloud at my idiocy for buying into the media hype all these years, especially when I created it for a living.

The phone in my room rang at around 10:00p.m. I just laid in the bath. He could wait now, as it was most assuredly Lee since no one else knew where I was. He must have called the few motels around Medford to find me after hearing my last message. He let it continue ringing. I didn't move. It stopped. I smiled. A minute later it rang again. Still I didn't move. But this time he just let it ring. And the ringing was loud, and annoying. Finally I got up, pulled a towel from the metal rack and wrapped it around me as I went to answer the phone.

"Hello?" I said calmly into the receiver as I sat on the heavy, dark floral print drape-like fabric that covered the lumpy double bed.

"Hi." He paused, I guess checking my mood. I didn't say anything so he rushed on. "I am so sorry, Ray!" He paused again. I still didn't say anything, my eyes settling on the joint and box of matches in the glass ashtray on the nightstand. "I know you're really pissed right now. And I don't blame you. New Year's got totally wrecked, for all of us, and I'm sorry. What can I do to make it up to you? How about I come over there right now."

"I don't think that's a good idea." I retrieved the ashtray and put it on the bed next to me.

"I want to come. I want to make it up to you. Colleen and Arlene do too. They want you to come to breakfast in the morning. They both feel really bad. My sister was just trying to protect me, thinking maybe you decided not to show." He paused. I couldn't think of anything to say. "If I jam I can probably get there before midnight. The roads are icy, and it'll take me a while, but even if I'm there a minute before, I want to ring in the New Year with you, Ray."

"Please don't come, Lee. It's late and dangerous and I don't want to go back to worrying you got in a wreck. Tonight was a mistake. I get that, and I'm not mad. I just don't feel like celebrating New Year's Eve anymore. I'm getting ready to crawl into bed and watch a movie. Then I'm going to sleep so I can get up early and head home." I sparked the joint and took a deep hit.

The Unbearable Lightness of Being was starting on HBO. I had no interest in listening to his rationalizations, even if his 'my dog did it' excuse was true. In all likelihood, he was probably getting buzzed with the ladies while gorging, which tends to distract one's attention from the passing of time.

"You can't just leave tomorrow. You have to come to my sister's in

166

the morning, if not for my sake, then for theirs. Please don't be pissed." He paused again.

"I'm not," I exhaled, thought of adding more but had nothing else to say, then took another hit off the J. The growing buzz narrowed my focus to the opening of the movie.

"Then come over here tomorrow morning to ring in the New Year with us." He paused again and I was sure I heard him hitting a joint. "The girls went shopping in town this afternoon and spent a small fortune on an amazing spread for us. And my sister copped some truly spectacular local bud. Please come. Give us a chance to set things right." He paused again, waiting for my response but I didn't offer any. He was pulling me out of 1968 Czechoslovakia and into 1991 at some dive motel in Oregon. "If you don't come Colleen and Arlene will think you're mad at them for what happened tonight. Why do you want to make them feel bad when you're really mad at me?"

"I don't. And I'm not mad at you." I was more disheartened in me, chasing after Lee when I shouldn't be with him at all. "I'll let you know in the morning."

"I'll call you then, probably around 8:00 if that's OK."

"Fine."

"Good. Well, happy New Year. And I guess I'll talk to you in the morning then." He wanted to keep the conversation going. I didn't. I was done for the evening.

Tomáš and Tereza are arguing about his liaison with Sabina in the movie. Everything to Tomáš is relative, meaningless, he tells her to

167

justify his affair. Existence is full of unbearable lightness because it is brief, and entropic. Tereza, a photojournalist during the Soviet occupation of Prague, sees and records the turbulence around her. The violence and anger penetrate her, suck her into darkness. She fears her heaviness pushes Tomáš to other lighter, less complex women, and blames herself for driving him away.

Even high, the parallel wasn't lost on me, and I felt small, and sad for being the dark cloud of reality the filmmakers portrayed Tereza to be. It was no wonder mentally stable men, like her physician husband, Tomáš, were attracted to the silly, sexy, carefree Sabina, and not women like Tereza and me.

-

Chapter 15

The ringing phone woke me at 7:30 the next morning. "Shit" was the first word out of my mouth. If I believed in omens I'd have acknowledged it as a sign of the year to come.

"Rachel? Hi. This is Colleen."

"Oh. Hi." I sat up and took stock of the drab little room, sunlight cutting a sharp line through the thin opening between the heavy curtains.

"Happy New Year." She sounded cautiously cheerful.

"Happy New Year."

"First, I want to apologize about last night. I know Lee told you what happened with Etheridge. And it's not my brother's fault he didn't call you. I kept telling him you were an independent woman, and that women don't like to be coddled anymore, and you'd have called if you were coming. I honestly thought you'd just changed your mind. I was trying to protect my baby brother. I'm sorry. This whole mess is my fault."

"It's no big deal, Colleen. Really." I clicked on the TV. Of course the Rose Parade coverage had started, though the parade had not. Yet. I could feel the anticipation of the crowd gathering, recalling Michael and I camping on Colorado Blvd overnight for front row seats of the magnificent floats the next morning, the scent of roses preceding the parade by half an hour.

"Lee felt really bad about what happened last night. So do Arlene and I. We'd like to make it up to you, at least kick off the New Year right. Come over! We have a huge breakfast planned, with champagne, local smoked salmon and even caviar. Come. You won't be sorry." She sounded so sure. "The bacon is crisp, the omelets are made to order and the biscuits are baked from scratch, an old recipe from Arlene's great grandma."

Other than a six pack of mini powered-sugar donuts that I split with Face, and a pack of Corn Nuts, I'd been living on black tea, diet Coke and weed since I'd left Colorado two days earlier. My mouth literally watered with her enticing invitation. And truth was, I really liked them both, which is rare for me with most women, most people actually. "Sounds great. But I need to talk to your brother. Is he around?"

She hesitated. I waited. "He's on his way there now," she finally said.

"Seriously." It wasn't a question really. More like a reality check.

"Yeah. I told him not to let you leave and to convince you come for breakfast if for some reason I couldn't. But I'm hoping I'm your wake-up call, to give you time to get ready before Lee gets there. It's almost impossible to find this place, so he had to come there to lead you back here anyway. He left here 20 minutes ago, so he should be there soon." She paused. "Hope that's okay."

I half-laughed, since her question was arbitrary with Lee on his way. "I guess," I lied, sighed, suddenly feeling trapped. Sort of. It felt nice I mattered to them, that Lee had come to collect me before I'd even agreed to come. Very Hollywood.

"...won't be sorry. I promise," Colleen was saying on the line. "Say you'll come."

The battle in my head raged. LEAVE, the smarter part of me screamed, before Lee gets here. But when I peeked through the opening in the heavy drapes at the parking lot below, I saw his Mercedes pulling in and park next to my car.

I told Colleen her brother had arrived and we disconnected. The second I put the receiver in the cradle the phone rang again.

"Hi. Happy New Year." Lee said casually.

"Happy New Year."

"I'm here. In the lobby, as it is," he said cautiously. "You talk to

Colleen?"

"Yeah."

"You wanta come with me or follow me to her house?" he asked casually, and I felt him smiling through the phone.

"Give me ten minutes," I heard myself say. There was no point in holding a grudge and losing a good friend, and the best racquetball partner I've ever had, which I now desperately needed to get back in shape and then stay tight since I was going back to the dating game. And the notion provoked an instant headache. I put on Marc's flannel shirt tucked into worn jeans, my hiking boots and leather jacket completing my lumber jack look. While traveling I generally dressed to blend into the environment.

It was sunny, but dripping wet with morning due, crisp and cold outside. Lee was waiting for me by his car. He leaned against the back fender of his Mercedes, his hands tucked deep in the pockets of his leather jacket which he held tightly around him. His jeans hung on his hips, his thick chestnut hair was scattered in his eyes, and stuck out around a gray tweed English cap I'd not seen him wear before. He gave me a tentative smile as I approached. Lee's full, deep red lips, and the touch of pink in his cheeks enhancing his errant newsboy countenance. He looked 17. I'd forgotten how adorable he was. I couldn't help smiling back.

"I think I've missed that mischievous grin the most. Good to see ya, Ray. Happy New Year."

"Happy New Year, Lee. Good to see ya, too." I went to the back of

my car and opened the hatchback to avoid touching without making
the moment awkward. As cute as he was, I didn't feel like hugging
Lee, residual anger he'd abandon me last night still lingering.

Face preened with my strokes, then with my permission bound out
of the car and up to Lee wagging her tail wildly. He gave her a quick
pat before she took off to the grassy area that separated the street
from the parking lot in front of the motel, squatted and peed. I
deposited my pack in the back then my camera bag on the
passenger seat.

"Why don't you follow me," Lee said casually as he went around his
car to get in. "The roads are icy around some pretty nasty curves, so
don't drive like you usually do." He narrowed his brows at me in
mock seriousness, then got behind the wheel and shut his door.

I called Face and we got in my car and I followed Lee to his sister's
house. Agreeing to come was the right thing, I assured myself on
the drive there. Blowing off last night's debacle, and welcoming in
1992 with Lee and his family this morning seemed a far better
choice then burning my bridges with him, snubbing his family by
declining their invite and leaving him standing in the motel's parking
lot.

The roads weren't icy or particularly curvy to me, but I'd been driving
daily since I was 15, sometimes all day, for days in a row on roadtrips. Even did the two plus miles of switchbacks on Mullholland in
2.9 minutes in Michael's Porsche once, when he was back east
visiting his folks. I followed Lee well past the suburbs of Medford,
until only the occasional home could be glimpsed tucked into groves
of pine and redwoods. He finally turned left onto a dirt road which

wove through a thick patch of forest and opened to a clearing with a small, somewhat dilapidated clapboard house. He pulled his Mercedes in front of a brick and glass 'solarium,' obviously added on to the original structure. It was literally leaning, pulling away from the side of the house, cement haphazardly poured into the gap. I parked my car next to his, told Face to stay and joined him. He gave me a quick smile and looked away, and not a word passed between us as we went into the house.

Colleen and Arlene greeted us in the 'entryway,' which was four large tiles set into the cramped living room. Both women embraced me heartily and I felt welcome. The delectably sweet smell of pastry baking mixed with moldy dampness. Lee and I followed the women past the Christmas tree that took up a third of the room and blocked part of the kitchen threshold. The four of us gathered round a two-foot square butcher block 'island' (on rollers) in the center of the kitchen, where Arlene filled four glasses with champagne and we all toasted in the New Year.

Cut to camera POV and the scene matched the one I'd imagined on the drive from Breckenridge, though less grand. It didn't matter. I was living a Hollywood Holiday scene, but a sip of the bitter bubbly reminded me this moment would be short-lived. Only in holiday movies did the mismatched friends toasting in the New Year foreshadow them living happily ever after.

It was almost as cold inside as it was out. The house had no central heating, only a portable coil heater in the living room, and even with the oven on it didn't heat the kitchen much.. After another round of apologies and explanations, no one mentioned the previous night again. We relaxed into a casual conversation that flowed easily and morphed naturally. Even sensitive subjects were discussed openly, in stark contrast to Colorado. And I was glad I came.

After the last of the bruschetta appetizers topped with crab, melted Gouda, and black caviar, Colleen pulled a joint from a small wooden box on the shelf behind her that created the nook space for the small pine picnic table where the four of us sat.

"I want to show you both something after breakfast," Colleen said, handing me the joint across the table from her. "There's a fire road off of Route 199, which only the forest service can use. You won't believe the views from up there. You can see all the way out to the Pacific."

"It's called Pearsoll Peak," Arleen said as she got up and got the eggs from an old, bulky white fridge. "It's extraordinary. You can see the curve of the earth from up there."

I took a deep hit. I'd planned to leave after breakfast. I didn't know how to announce this without wrecking the moment, so I didn't say anything, instead took another hit and handed the joint to Lee sitting next to me.

"Remember that lightening storm up there last year?" Arlene more said than asked, and she and Colleen had an unspoken exchange, both smiling playfully at each other with their memories. "You guys have gotta see this place."

"It really is spectacular." Colleen chimed in as she got up, then pulled a big iron frying pan from the cabinet and set it on the stove top. "You've never seen anything like this."

"Sounds like a plan," Lee said, and looked at me. "I'm in. How 'bout you, Ray?"

"Does sound beautiful," I replied non-committal. But their description enticed. I love seeing places I've never been, especially ones I can't access on my own.

We all pitched in making omelets, cutting the peppers and scallions, grating the cheese, American and Swiss. Lee expertly manned the bacon sizzling on the griddle. We cleared our plates, and then our pallets with another joint as we all cleaned up.

I felt so bloated I could hardly breathe as I went out into the late-morning sunshine to give Face a plate of eggs and a couple slices of bacon. She was huddled in her sleeping bag but got up when I opened the hatchback. I stroked her as I set the plate down for her then sat in the back of my car, my feet dangling just above the ground. She gobbled up everything in less than a minute, seemingly without chewing, then lay on me and I patted her a few moments enjoying our calm connection until her big ears went up like rockets. She stood, her fur raised in a strip along her back, then with a low growl she bowed her head between her shoulder blades staring at the thick pine forest beyond the gravel clearing.

"Whoa. What's your problem?"

"Hi." Suddenly Lee was beside me.

Face's ears matted in submission and she wagged her tail wildly while I tried to restart my heart and catch my breath. Then her

175

rocket ears went up again and her tail went straight out behind her and she bolted out of the car and bound with fluid grace across the gravel and disappeared into the forest.

"Aren't you going after her? Or call her or something?" Lee asked, bewildered by my inaction.

"No. She only goes so far before she turns around and comes back. At least she has since the first time she went after something and couldn't find her way back to me. And she got lucky that day. My friend Jon found her. Since then she's never gone too far."

"She doesn't want to lose you again." Lee said. "Neither do I. Join us at Pearsoll Peak this afternoon. I'd love to share it with you., instead of being the third wheel with my sister and Arleen."

Boy, did I know how that felt, and I flashed on New Year's Eve last year at Frankie's.

"And it'd be a great photo opp," he flashed his Cheshire grin.

Face came out of the forest and lopped across the gravel towards me, tongue hanging out, and seemingly smiling. Lee stroked her back and I scratched the diamond marking on her head and she stood frozen between us.

"The view does sound extraordinary," I mused. "I'd love to see it up there."

Etheridge, a sleek, high strung racetrack-rescue greyhound came bounding out of the house right then, followed by Arlene.

"You guys ready to go?" she asked as Face met Etheridge in the middle of the gravel drive and the two dogs engaged in chase.

I looked at Lee. His green eyes were on me, alight with gentle humor, and at that moment I could foresee no reason why I shouldn't go with them to experience this spectacular scene. I'd leave when we returned, later that afternoon, maybe stay in Frankie's guestroom in Oakland if it got too late to go all the way to L.A. tonight.

Colleen insisted that Face stay in the house instead of cooped up in my car for another two hours. She shut the hallway and the kitchen doors, separating the dogs so they wouldn't wreck the place while we were gone, leaving Face the living room.

We piled into Arlene's Land Rover. I got shotgun because I get car sick if I'm not driving. We shared a joint winding along the Redwood Highway, simply the most beautiful road on the earth. Rich, vibrant emerald greens saturate the narrow canyon, the hills blanketed with old growth redwoods, some over 2,000 years old and twenty feet or more in diameter. The ground is covered with fallen limbs and fields of clover. Shards of bright sunlight cut through the 300 foot tall treetops, and the sky could only be seen above the thin band of the highway bordered by these graceful giants.

Moisture was heavy in the air but it smelled fresh, clean, and was quenching. I stared out, mesmerized as always when driving through this canyon. I glanced back at Lee a few times, mostly to retrieve the joint or hand it to him, his eyes glimmering with playful excitement. And I felt that charge, that connection between us sharing the extraordinary scene.

Arlene turned right off 199 and onto a dirt road with switch-backs up to the side of an enormous mountain. I was sure I was going to barf up all that breakfast, but then we reached the crest and the view opened to a snaking maze of mountain ranges drenched in forest green. The view was so unique, and so magnificent it captured all my attention even though the Land Rover was now bouncing along the hairpin turns of the ridge line.

We finally stopped at a clearing on the top of the highest peak. It was well after noon, the sun already arcing west, and windy enough to buck the car a bit. We all got out of the Rover to survey the scene. It was cold, but not freezing like Colorado, maybe forty degrees outside. We were a thousand feet above the fog line, patches still clinging in the valleys below, the tops of enormous redwoods peeked through like little nails on a fluffy bed. Trees blanketed range after range coating the coastal mountains in every shade of green imaginable.

"See it?" Colleen asked over my shoulder pointing to the horizon where the Pacific met the sky. "See the curve?"

The horizon line of the small strip of ocean that could be seen just beyond the last mountain range was not straight, not even close. The arc of the planet was clear from up there, like the view from a plane at 30,000 ft. The four of us stood in the clearing on top of the world scanning the panorama in awe.

"Oh my god," Lee whispered as if not to disrupt the scene.

I knew exactly how he felt. I'd never seen anything like it.

"See those huge, ugly brown patches where the trees have been cut away?" Arlene stood next to me and pointed to a hillside beyond.

On the mountainside near us and several more in view there were large patches where there were no trees, instead littered with stumps, and from a distance they looked like headstones. Below these treeless areas, massive swathes of fallen Redwoods lay like corpses.

"When they clear cut like that, the soil runs down the hill and literally suffocates the trees for hundreds of feet down the hillside," Arlene said.

"I spent the last six months compiling an EIR, got geologists to file addendums that proved clear cutting more of this area would have devastating effects," Colleen added. "The Forest Service awarded Evergreen Lumber the contract for clear cutting on Friday, right before the Christmas break."

I was suddenly aware of how cold it was up there. "I thought our National Forests were protected," I said indignantly.

"Most people do. It's actually only National Parks that are protected. The Forest Service is a bunch of bureaucrats bought off by big lumber. They keep pushing the boundaries of the Park lands, turning it into National Forest so they can cut more. The Good Ol' Boys have legalized rape."

"God, I had no idea," Lee mused.

I looked around at the exquisite mountains imagining a time when they would be stripped bare and shuttered. Colleen put her arm around Arlene's shoulder and pulled her in. The women stood huddled together against the cold.

"It's beautiful, but fucking freezing out here," Lee practically whispered and moved closer to me for warmth. I moved against him, body to body, and felt his heat, only then realizing how cold I was. My fingers were practically numb. I cupped my hands and blew on them, then Lee took my hand in both of his. Instant warmth, like a mitten, so I did not pull away, even after he gently laced his fingers with mine and held my hand.

We stood on the mountaintop experiencing the view. I waged an internal battle between staying cozy with Lee and capturing the moment forever, finally excusing myself, pulling away and instantly freezing without him as I went back to the Jeep and got my camera bag.

A tripod was required for the long exposure needed to clearly capture the scene. I extended the aluminum legs and set it near where everyone was still gathered then mounted my camera.

"Nice camera. Nikon. The best of the best," Lee said.

I smiled, glad he'd noticed. I'd worked hard to acquire the thousands of dollars of camera equipment I now possessed. I attached a 22mm lens and a plunger to the shutter release, then looked through the viewfinder.

My world narrowed to the view through the camera as I focused the lens on the horizon. I took a few shots, then straightened, smiled at Lee watching me. "Wanta see?"

He looked through the viewfinder and studied the scene through the camera a minute then straightened. "Beautiful." His lips looked blue.

"You guys ready to head back?" Colleen stood with Arlene huddled hand in hand. "Winter isn't the best time to be up here too long. I'm freezing my tits off. Let's go."

My nipples were painfully hard too, but I felt a need to capture the full panorama in this once in a lifetime opportunity. "Give me a minute for a few more shots?" I wasn't really asking, already moving the tripod with the mounted camera to another spot along the edge of the clearing.

"Take your time, but I'm waiting in the car," Arlene said. "Care to join me, honey?"

"Love, too." Colleen agreed. "You coming little brother?"

"You bet. I'm freezing my ass off. I'm outta here, my dear. Meet you back in the car."

I captured a full 180 degree panorama in eight overlapping shots, the setting sun casting long shadows sure to show off the depth of field in the scene. I almost dropped the Nikon and then the lens as I unscrewed them with frozen hands, but managed to get my gear back in my camera bag without damage then headed to the Rover.

"The prodigal artist returns," Lee said with a grin as I got into the passenger seat. "Thought we lost you to your muse out there."

"Better watch out for that bitch, Rachel." Colleen commented. "I think she may be trying to kill you, keeping you out there for the last twenty minutes in forty degrees."

"Twenty minutes?" I was aghast. "I wasn't out there but five, wasn't I?" I looked at each of them in turn and then at the digital clock in the stereo cassette player mounted in the dash, but 3:30 meant nothing to me since I had no idea when we got up there. "I'm really sorry. Why didn't you honk or something? I didn't mean to keeping you all waiting."

"We're fine in here," Lee said. "It was you we were worried about."

"And we wouldn't want to get in the way of great art." Colleen said.

Arlene put the Rover in gear and we left the clearing. "I've never even thought to bring a camera up here. Guess I figure I can come up and can see it whenever I want to."

"But it won't be the same tomorrow. The landscape is dynamic, always changing with the weather, seasons, politics, as you've said." I flashed on the clear cut graveyard.

"You're not kidding." Colleen chimed in from the back.

"What I captured today is unique to this moment in time, which can now be shared with others not here to see it. And if I did it right, not just glimpse the image visually, but experience it viscerally— feel the cold, the wind, the wetness, smell the rich earth, the redwoods, and be awestruck and humbled by the majestic beauty." I shrugged. "And if I really did it right, it'll help motivate people to join the fight to preserve all this."

"I told you she was a die-hard idealist." Lee said with gentle humor.

I glanced back at him, his expression filled with tenderness, but he didn't look right. His face was very red, his eyes watery and rather swollen.

"All artists are idealists," Colleen assured her brother.

He smiled. So did I, but had to face forward to avoid getting sick along the switchbacks descending the mountain. We were mostly quiet the rest of the way back. Either Lee or Colleen lit a joint and we passed it among us in silent reverie, lost in the passing scenery and the memories of the day.

I looked back at Lee when we got on route 199. "Are you okay?"

"Yeah. No." He gave me a wan smile. " I feel like shit. I think I might be getting sick."

Colleen reached out and felt his forehead. "Wow. You are hot. OK. As soon as we get back to the house I'll make you some chicken soup, and tea with honey and lemon."

"I don't want anything to eat, Col. And I hate tea with lemon. Mom always used to give it to us when we were sick and I hated it then and even more now because of the reference. I just want to get a room like we talked about, and go to sleep."

"You don't need to get a motel room, Lee." Arlene said. "I really don't like the idea of you driving when you're so sick. Just stay at our place tonight and we'll take care of you. Rachel, you're staying the night, right?"

I'd assumed we'd be back earlier and I'd have taken off by now. The long drive ahead loomed, but staying the night there didn't work for me either. It was freezing inside their house, and there were spiders in webs in every corner of every room. I hate spiders.

"I appreciate the offer," Lee said. "I love you both, but you need the heater in your room, and I really just want a warm place to sleep tonight. I'll be fine, Colleen. Don't worry about it."

It was almost dark by the time we got back to their house. I went to my car to put away my camera bag as everyone headed inside. Moments later, walking to the house, Lee came out of it. His mirthless expression did not mask his tension.

"You have to promise me you won't be totally mad."

Statements like that and you know you're fucked.

"It's no big deal, so don't freak out about it," he added as we walked to the house. "This is totally dealable, and no one got hurt which is what really counts, so don't have a meltdown."

My heart beat in my throat as I followed him into the living room. The room was a wreck, like a thief broke in and tore the place apart. Face went running from me. She tried to hide under the Christmas tree, knocking it over in the process. Colored lights exploded on to the floor, then they all went dead. Colleen ran to the wall socket and pulled out the plug. She and Arlene righted the tree while Face slinked to a corner of the room.

"Oh my god," fell out of my mouth. The carpet around the front door tiles was clawed to the floorboards. The blinds on three of the four windows were shredded all over the floor. The paint around two of the windows was scratched to the wood. I looked at Face shaking in a corner behind the fallen tree. "Get the fuck over here," I spoke in a low, growling tone then held her nose in the ripped carpet and in the shreds of the blinds all over the floor and told her NO! Then I pulled my dog by the collar to the front door, which wasn't easy with fifty pounds of resistance, and threw her out of the house then slammed the door shut, only then noticing the paint along the side and bottom of the front door was also clawed to the wood.

Colleen and Arlene tried to minimize their disappointment, but it wasn't working. They assured me it was no big deal, easy to fix and that I was forgiven but their faces revealed their anger as they surveyed the damage.

I felt horrible, apologized again and again. I promised to replace everything back to the way it was, knowing it would cost hundreds which I didn't exactly have to blow away. As angry as I was with my dog, her well-being was my responsibility. I excused myself from straightening up right then, went outside and whistled. Face came slinking up, her ears back in submission, tail down, practically between her legs. I growled at her, cussed a bit too, then put her in the car for her safety.

Etheridge came bounding out the front door seconds before Lee emerged. Face jumped out of the Civic and ran over to greet her and they happily engaged in chase. I felt myself seethe inside, considered putting my dog back in the car and shutting the hatchback, but what was the point. Bitch lived in the moment, and she'd never get why I was still mad.

Lee stood next to me and watched the dogs. "You okay?"

I gave him a vague smile and shrugged. "I'm really sorry my dog wrecked your sister's house. They must hate me."

"They don't hate you. And this isn't your fault, Ray. Etheridge probably went outside and Face wanted to join her so she tried to get out. And it's no big deal." It was hard to see his expression in the dim, ambient glow from the Christmas lights strung around the roof line of the house. "I'll cover the damages. Whatever it costs, I'll pay it gladly."

"Thanks, but I'll take care of it." I sat in the back of my Civic and watched Face suddenly abandon Etheridge and track something along the treeline. "She's my stupid dog. So what if she just damned me to copy writing for the next five months."

Lee laughed. "Then let me take care of it. I can afford it."

Technically, so could I, probably more than him since I didn't owe anything, to anyone— ever. My father ingrained in me that maintaining good credit was part of my social responsibility, and moral obligation to live up to my contractual agreements. I'd spent my adult life struggling to live debt free, often denying myself frivolities, like meals during lean times. I had maybe three grand in the bank, more than enough to cover the damages, but it would cut a big chunk out of all I had to my name. I sighed audibly. "I'm just so sick of living on the edge of broke."

Lee stared at me. "Not to worry, my dear. I'm right here, and I'll take care of you."

True or not, right then his words comforted.

"I'm staying at a motel tonight. My sister's house isn't exactly as advertised. Kind of surprised me too." He flashed an arch of his brow. "Froze my ass off last night, which is probably why I'm sick. I woke up from a nap yesterday afternoon with a spider on my eye. Freaked me out." He shuddered. "I just called a place about five miles up the road and reserved a room. I'm gonna stay there. If you decide to stay, you can crash here or at the motel with me. No pressure. I'm not hitting on you. Whatever you want to do is fine with me."

I couldn't just leave now, take off with their place a wreck from my dog. "Let's just get an assessment of the damage right now, see what needs to be done." I whistled for Face to come. She came inside with us and ate Etheridge's kibble as we finished tidying up the best we could. By then, it was after 6:00.

"We can go into town tomorrow and find replacements for the carpet and blinds," Colleen said as she pulled the phone book from the shelf while Arleen got leftovers from this morning and loaded the table with them, then distributed plates and silverware.

"And we have some leftover paint for the windows and door," Arleen said, looking at me. "We can start on it after dinner, or in the morning."

I'd planned to leave after breakfast this morning. Now I was obliged to stay at least another full day, possibly a couple to resolve the mess my dog had created. I felt like crying. Lee napped intermittently on the couch while Arleen and I sanded and painted the clawed areas. Coleen cleaned up our dinner dishes then made a list of the stores we'd need to visit tomorrow. It was almost 10:00 by the time we finished.

"That Tylenol didn't bring down your fever as much as I'd like," Colleen said to her brother after feeling his forehead. "How do you feel?"

"Like shit," Lee said. "My muscles are killing me. I really need to go lay down, Col." Lee stood, then put his hands on his knees, and his head down like he was trying not to pass out.

"You shouldn't be driving like this, Lee," Arleen said. "Especially at night, with the winding roads around here."

"And you shouldn't be alone tonight, either," Colleen chimed in. "You need someone to look after you. Stay here! You're staying here tonight, right, Rachel?"

Lee straightened and looked at me, pleading, I think. His eyes were red rimmed and puffy. His cheeks were crimson, his full lips ruby red. He looked completely spent, like he had no energy left to argue with his sister and Arleen.

"I'll stay with Lee tonight." I offered, looking at Lee. "I can follow him to the motel and stay with him the night, make sure he's OK."

Lee's grin spread slowly with his realization of my offer. "That works for me."

"Me too." Colleen said.

"Me three." Arlene added and flashed Colleen a quick smile.

I wasn't quite sure it worked for me, afraid of the implications of sharing a motel room, but at that point all I could do was hope he understood my gesture was limited to administering aid.

After giving Lee a spoonful of NyQuil, Colleen handed me a half full bottle of Vicodin with instructions to give him two before bed, then released her brother to my care. I followed Lee's Mercedes on the dark, single lane road, lecturing Face on where we fell in the pantheon of human economics the entire ten minute drive to the motel.

It appeared out of nowhere, light pierced the night around a sharp curve. A string of multicolored Christmas lights capped a nondescript, single story stucco structure with ten or so rooms set in a clearing in the middle of the forest. I followed Lee onto the gravel lot and parked next to him in front of the wooden walkway along the red doors of motel rooms.

"I need to let Face run around before locking her in the car all night," I said to Lee as he went to check-in.

"Okay," he said as he disappeared into the registration area.

Face moved at a quick, frenetic pace along the edge of a dark grove of huge trees. An icy breeze crackled the branches and I jumped at every sound straining to see into the forest, half expecting someone to come out wielding a knife. A few minutes later Lee came out of the lobby dangling a key and moved along the walkway.

"I'll meet you inside in a bit," I said, still waiting on Face to pick her spot.

"She can come in." Lee stood at the red door to room number 9 and inserted the key.

"No, she can't."

He laughed. "Whatever." He opened the door. "I'd stay out here with you but I'd really like to get inside if you don't mind. I'm fucking freezing."

"Go! I'll be fine." I meant it—and didn't, scared to be out there at night, alone. The place was right out of the movie Psycho.

"I'll leave it unlocked. See ya in a few." Lee disappeared inside.

I called Face to come and a few tense moments passed before the dog came out of the grove and glided into the open hatchback. She turned back to nuzzle for strokes and I scratched behind her big ears and along her back to her tail before telling her to lay down. She curled in her sleeping bag and I considered yelling at her once more, but there really was no point. The dog got that I was pissed but had long since forgotten why, kind of like most guys I've dated who vaguely remember the fight but can't recall what it was about.

Lee was asleep on the king size bed when I got inside.

Redwood panels lined the walls from the floor to the cream colored ceiling. A large color TV sat atop a long, low six-drawer knotty pine dresser against the wall opposite the bed. The room was cozy, and well insulated. It was warm in there.

I nixed the idea of TV as not to disturb Lee, washed up instead, then put on sweats and a t-shirt, turned off the lights and crawled in bed beside him.

Lee mumbled something, bringing me back from dozing. Then he said my name in a panic, then said it again. "Rachel! Watch out!"

I sat up and stared down at him. He was dreaming, talking in his sleep. He tossed a bit, and I heard my name again amidst more mumbling. I shuddered, creeped out. I called to him, even touched him but he did not wake, though he did settle into silence. I lay back down next to him, stared at the textured ceiling wondering what Lee was dreaming as I drifted off.

-

Chapter 16

The phone rang loud and brassy, waking me. I hustled off the bed and ran to answer it on the end table on Lee's side. He woke, startled, but managed to pick up the phone before I got it.

"Yeah." He spoke hoarsely then coughed, sat up and cleared his throat while he listened. "Better. Thanks. And don't worry about it. I'm usually up before now." He coughed again, then leaned back against the wood headboard and ran his free hand through his hair pulling it out of his eyes as he listened.

Feeling silly standing there, I went back to my side of the bed and crawled in then clicked on the TV. Local morning news was on the weather report.

"Give us half an hour." Lee spoke into the phone. "I want to shower. I sweat my guts out last night but I think the fever may have broken." He listened again, and I felt him watching me as Colleen's voice squeaked through the receiver, though I couldn't hear what she was saying. "I don't know. We can talk about it when we get there. See you in a few." Lee hung up, got off the bed and gave me a quick smile as he passed in front of me on his way to the bathroom, still fully clothed in jeans and his white, long sleeve shirt. "I'll be fifteen minutes, and we're out of here." He shut the bathroom door and I heard the shower go on.

Apparently there were no worries of him hitting on me. I felt relieved, even honored by his casual, androgynous demeanor. I dressed in jeans and my big gray knit sweater over my t-shirt, brought my duffel bag out to my car and let Face out for her morning pee. It was after 9:00, but the air was still cold and damp with tooley fog clinging to the ground and weaving through the trees. I tucked my hands in my jeans pockets and bounced up and down to get warm as I followed my dog along the edge of the forest. Lee came out of the room ten minutes later. I followed him to his sister's so Face wouldn't mess up his car with her muddy paws, was the excuse I gave, but I planned to leave directly after purchasing the items that needed replacing.

Both women were in the small kitchen cooking when we came in. Lee and I helped set the table. We indulged in a leisurely breakfast of homemade waffles, topped with fresh strawberries and whipped cream. After cleaning up, the four of us piled into Arlene's Land Rover taking the same positions as yesterday, and drove to Grant's Pass. We left Face in the garage with Ethridge's bean bag bed. Colleen lit a joint and we passed it around. Fifteen minutes later Arlene pulled into the True Value Hardware store parking lot.

We found no match for their existing ten year old carpet. After perusing several other stores with no success, it was decided the only alternative was to replace it entirely. At the new mammoth Home Depot warehouse, the size of which I'd not seen before, Colleen and Arlene agreed on a gray shag, and scheduled installers for the following week. With the carpet, the blinds and the string of Christmas lights, I dropped over eight hundred bucks before noon. I was verging on tears when we left the mega store. I really had to get out of there and back to work.

Lee took us to lunch at Debby's Diner. According to her name tag, Debby was serving us. Pixie hair cut and painted eyes, maybe in her late 20s-early 30s, tall and heavy, dressed in a classic mid-calf skirt and a tight pink cashmere sweater revealing the bulge at her waistline. Upon my inquiry, she confessed she didn't own the place. She'd taken the uniform and name tag of the last waitress years back, and her name was really Barbara Anne.

"Most everyone calls me Betty though." She set our teas, coffees and waters on the table of our booth. "A nickname for Betty Crocker, since I love to cook. Don't do much of it here, though, which is fine by me since I have five teenage boys and a hungry man at home and I'm cooking there all the time." She giggled like a schoolgirl.

"Five teenage boys?" Colleen was aghast. "You have them when you were like 15?"

"Had my first at 17. Beat my older sister, Charlotte, by four days." Debbie, or Betty, took her order pad from her skirt pocket and a pencil from behind her ear. "Now, what can I get for ya?"

After taking our orders the waitress strode away, head high, bounce in her step. I watched her placed our order on the metal turnstile and give a friendly smile to the cook in the kitchen as Colleen audibly scoffed.

"So many locals around here get married in or right out of high school and never leave. The women are like chattel, to serve the men, and pump out babies and don't get to college and never have careers so they're totally dependent and don't know any other way exists." Colleen spoke softly across the table.

"Small town mentality." Arlene added, her voice hushed. "Pisses me off. I was born and raised here, with all the Christian doctrine and stereotypical bullshit. I didn't buy into it. And I'm flat out angry at women who do."

I was too— thought women who propagated antiquated traditions unwittingly oppressed all women. But again, a part of me was torn, knowing having kids would limit my career pursuits if I wanted to actually be there to raise them. Sitting next to Lee watching Debby/Barbara/Betty, I felt a distinct yet growing envy. Our waitress buzzed about, and even overweight moved with grace, as if comfortable in her body as she poured coffee in front of a patron at the counter then topped it with cream and smiled before turning to the kitchen counter and gathering several lunch platters to deliver to other customers. Her stride was confident, her smiles welcoming, and given often. The woman seemed...happy, satisfied, on solid ground. And I still longed for what our oppressed waitress seemingly already possessed.

The conversation flowed on while Lee and his sister indulged in their cheese burgers and Arlene and I ate our salads. Colleen mentioned an impending storm, and suggested we all go cross-country skiing for the afternoon. I'd planned to leave on New Year's Day, then today after shopping, but the restricted area that both women touted of crystalline babbling brooks and aqua-marine lakes hidden in redwood laden mountains accessible only to Forest Service employees sounded too spectacular to miss.

I'd never been any good at skiing. Lee stayed by my side, even when I lagged behind, helping me up and brushing the snow off of me more times than I care to count. It was his first time cross-country skiing too, but he took to it a lot quicker than I did. He was encouraging and supportive when I got frustrated from falling. "Come on, get up. You can do it. I know you can," was his mantra to me all afternoon.

It snowed the entire time we were up in the Coastal Range limiting the photo opps without sunlight exaggerating depth of field. Stunning area though, with several small lakes surrounded by giant Redwoods and lush pines. We lit a huge fire on the bank of one of the lakes, under a Redwood canopy that kept the snow at bay, and we huddled around it for half hour or so while indulging in the pastries Lee had bought at the bakery next to the ski rental place. We watched the snow fall gently on the lake and spoke just above whispers as not to disrupt the silence. It started to get windy and colder, so we put the fire out, put our skis back on, and made our way back down the mountain.

We stopped for dinner at a small, country inn in the middle of the woods. The restaurant was a converted log cabin, complete with a huge fireplace. The hard rain hitting the wood porch outside sounded like a symphony. When the check came, Lee insisted on paying for everyone. Colleen sparked a joint on the way back to their house but Lee declined. His cheeks were crimson again, though he didn't look as bad as last night.

Well past 9:00, it was a bad idea to be traveling on wet roads for the twelve hour drive home through the night. I agreed to stay at the motel with Lee and leave early in the morning to head back to L.A. I took the dog's sleeping bag out of my Civic and told Face to come as I joined Lee in the motel room. He was rifling through his backpack, pulling out clean clothes when I came in.

"I'm beat. Being sick really took it out of me. I think the fever's coming back a bit. I'm gonna take a quick shower and go to bed. Hope you don't mind."

"No problem." I laid the sleeping bag by the dresser and Face curled onto it. "I'm really tired, too. Skiing, well, getting up from falling all day was exhausting." I flashed him a quasi grin.

He smiled back as he went into the bathroom and shut the door. I sat on the bed and flipped on the local news. Fifteen minutes later Lee crossed in from of the TV in a dark flannel shirt and boxer shorts and got into bed beside me.

"How ya feeling?" I clicked off the TV.

"Better. Thanks. Shower felt great."

"I'm next." I got up and collected clean clothes from my backpack.

"It's been a nice couple of days." He watched me. "I'm really glad you met me up here, Ray. It's a lot of fun hanging together again."

"For me, too. Thanks for inviting me."

"My pleasure. Glad you came." He yawned. "Love to share some recent epiphanies, but I'm really tired. Let's talk in the morning. Okay?"

"Okay."

"Goodnight." He rolled onto his side, away from me.

"Goodnight, Lee." I went into the bathroom and showered. When I came back in the room Lee was asleep.

I crawled into bed next to him. Too keyed up to sleep, I rolled onto my side and stared at him. He was on his back, his head tilted slightly towards me. He looked beautiful in sleep, his full red lips slightly parted, his hair falling over his forehead, mingling with his long dark lashes and framing his baby face. I imagined him waking, seeing me watching him, then reaching up and kissing me, softly at first, then with passion.

My desired surprised me. The last couple of days with him had been spectacular adventures. We were connected again, like before our falling out. I really loved being with Lee, more than most anyone before him. And I had the sudden urge to slap him upside the head right then for not being the grown up I wanted, and knew I needed.

Early morning I was outside in a gentle rain letting Face pick her spot. I was putting our stuff in my car when Lee came out to join me.

"My sister just called, asked if we wanted to come by for breakfast, then go up to Crater Lake today. Who would have guessed there's so much see in Oregon?"

"I'm taking off this morning, Lee. I have to get back to reality, get back home and back to work to cover the bills I've accumulated this vacation."

He frowned. "I thought we could stay through the weekend. And I told you I'd cover the damage Face caused. Come on. Stay."

"I can't. I really have to take off. I've been on the road for three weeks now. Vacation's over. It's time to get back to L.A."

"I was hoping we'd get a chance to talk before you left. Sorry for passing out on you last night, but I didn't realize you'd be taking off so early." He paused, looked at Face scouring the line of trees. "Thing is, I've been thinking a lot about what you said that night in my car, and on the phone with you in Colorado." He looked at me intently. "I totally get why you're afraid to be with me. And I'm completely on the page that everything you've said is right. It's time for me to stop acting like a kid and grow up. So, I'm gonna start controlling my spending, open a savings account and put money away, and pay the government off sooner than later to get them off my back. I want to start eating better, healthier, and play a lot of ball. And I'm following your lead and giving up weed when I get back to L.A."

My skin prickled with his assertion. I stared at him, tried to see into him. "You serious?"

"You bet. I can't promise I'll abandon it forever, but I'm going to prove to you, and me, that I'm not now, nor have I ever been addicted to weed." He stayed fixed on me, his expression resolute.

Tenderness stifled intuition's rejoinder not to move beyond friendship. He'd admitted I was right, that he wanted to change. All he needed was to be shown the way. And I was sure I loved him right then. Lee was dynamic, willing to change, 'a work in progress,' as Chris had said. We both were, and maybe, just maybe could be better together...

Lee stared at me, studied me, first my eyes, then lips, then back to my eyes, seemingly searching. "Come to breakfast at my sisters before you take off. Give you all a chance to say goodbye."

"I can't, Lee. It's a long drive and I want to get on the road. But please thank them both for me, and tell em how much I appreciated their hospitality, and how sorry I am for what my stupid dog did."

He smiled, shook his head. "I'll tell em. No worries." Water dripped off the ends of his hair. Only then did I notice it was raining.

I called Face to come before she was thoroughly soaked, hoping to avoid wet dog smell for the first fifty miles on the road, opened my hatchback and she glided in happily. Shepard's aren't fond of getting wet. I turned back to face Lee.

"I'll miss you," he said. "But I'll see ya in a few days in L.A." Then put his thick hand on the back of my neck, pulled me in and kissed my forehead, pressed his warm, full lips just above my brow sending heat through my face, into my chest, right down to my crotch.

Several beats passed before he pulled back, let his hand drop casually and pocketed them both in his jeans but kept his eyes on mine. "Drive safely."

"I will." My forehead was still warm and my crotch still tingled from his kiss as I unlocked my car door and opened it, my brain literally buzzing with adrenaline and pheromones. One last look before leaving, our eyes locked and I felt our electric connection, like he was inside my head.

His eyes sparkled with affection and humor. His chestnut hair cascaded to his shoulders in soft waves. His full lips revealed a hint of his Cheshire grin.

I reached out to him then, grasped his face in both my hands and kissed him, full on his lips. I couldn't help it. He wrapped his arms around my waist and pulled me to him. I slid my hands around the back of his neck as heat spread from his lips to mine, then into my cheeks. His hot tongue moved into my mouth and set my entire body tingling.

Hard to say how long we stood there kissing, but I noticed the rain pouring down on us the moment Lee did. We finally separated, soaking wet and laughing, then bid each other farewell. I got in my car and closed the door cutting the cord, but not the connection between us.

-

Chapter 17

On I-5 just south of Medford, hard, slushy rain demanded my focus to keep the Honda on the road. I felt anxious and craved a joint, then realized I'd just quit and craved it all the more. I was going back to L.A., like countless times before returning from traveling, but didn't feel that suffocating heaviness looming, anticipating being back there with Lee. He'd be back in Eagle Rock late Sunday night. We'd see each other Monday, play racquetball, our last game seeming eons ago, perhaps go out to dinner at Maria's after we played. It could be different between us now with Lee ready to be a grown up, working together to help each other be the best we can be. I was suddenly breathless with excitement by the possibility. I could hardly contain my delight harboring the notion the grueling search for my knight may be over. I merely had to cultivate the Prince I seemingly possessed.

At the rate I was going I wouldn't get home until after midnight— never a good time to be on the road in L.A. these days. It finally stopped raining as the Shasta Range descended to the mouth of the San Joaquin Valley just after Redding. Vast grasslands radiated golden light between the deep emerald groves of ancient walnut and oaks. Big, puffy explosions of gray clouds with blazing white outlines of sunlight were breaking up against the azure sky.

The sun had set when it started raining again about a hundred miles from L.A. Jerk drivers abound as traffic slowed to stop and go, making the slick roads even more dangerous. Rain pinged and sheeted off the windshield, balls of ice inside the droplets of water. Probably snowing up on the Grapevine. I wove through traffic to get to the pass before they closed it. Making my move around some asshole crawling along, I spotted a silver sedan, like Lee's Mercedes changing lanes two cars back in my rear view mirror. The car slipped into the fast lane several cars back and I lost sight of it, and laughed at my silly schoolgirl crush, imagining Lee everywhere.

Some idiot flashed their brights behind me. I was going as fast as I could without going through the car in front of me. I focused on the driver in my rear view mirror. I could tell it was a guy by the breath of his silhouette, but with his headlights reflecting the rain on windshields it was impossible to see his face. I could barely make out the vehicle he was driving, a gray or possibly silver sedan. He flashed his brights again and I cussed out aloud but put on my blinker to move to the right and let him pass to avoid being the victim of a drive-by. I looked over my shoulder to see if I was clear and saw the jerk driver move into the slow lane blocking my entry.

"Fine, asshole. Go around me." I watched the car moved along side me. Without the glare from his headlights I could easily see the car was a silver Mercedes, exactly like Lee's, actually, and pictured him behind the wheel smiling and waving at me, then realized he was real— Lee was next to me, pacing me on I-5.

Red brake lights flashed on the car in front of me commanding my attention by their sheer proximity. I slammed on my brakes and had to swerve into the right lane to avoid hitting them, grateful Lee had backed off beside me, giving me room to move in front of him.

The odds of us being on the same road at the same time were about a billion to one unless he'd followed me. The idea creeped me out a minute, then I discounted the notion since I hadn't seen a silver Mercedes anywhere on the road until now. A green sign for Twisselman Road Exit 1 mi ahead came and went, and I put on my blinker to indicate for Lee to follow me. He gave me a quick flash of his brights.

My wipers squealed across my windshield, like fingernails on chalkboard as I got off the highway. The rain had stopped but the air was dense with wetness and looked like swarms of tiny bugs gone berserk in my headlight. A few hundred yards from the interstate I pulled onto the dirt along Twisselman road. Lee pulled up behind me and left his lights on as he got out of his car and came over to mine. I turned off my engine, told Face to stay and got out to greet him.

"This is unreal. I can't believe this," he said as he approached. "The odds of meeting out here have got to be astronomical! I saw your car miles back but didn't believe it until I got in back of you and saw Face." We met in the middle, his surprised expression likely matching mine. "Good to see ya." Wide smile as he gathered me in his arms and spun me around and we both laughed. He put me down and stared at me, his eyes twinkling with wonder, and humor, and I felt the spark of our electric connection.

"This is so bizarre!" I said. Arbitrarily running across each other still needled me. "What are you doing here? I thought you were staying in Oregon for the weekend."

"Decided not to."

"Why?"

"I missed you the moment you left." He kept his eyes fixed on mine. "Didn't feel like staying without you. Stopped at my sister's, said goodbye and hit the road."

Same road, leaving Medford close to the same time, it was possible, even likely with the traffic he'd have caught up with me.

"I would have bet a billion to one against us meeting out here. Must be Kismet—we're meant to be together." Then he gathered my face in his hands. "I'm ready to be the man you need." He pulled me in and kissed me. His thick lips blanketed mine in warmth, then his tongue traced my lips and then slipped in between them. He held my face in his big hands and transferred his passion, his desire. My crotch tingled with the pressure of his hardness against me. I sucked in his tongue gently, then rhythmically, welcoming him.

Thunder sounded way off, then cracked loudly nearby and I felt it resonate in my chest. I pulled back from him to catch my breath and saw lightning flash over a nearby vineyard.

"Wow." Lee and I said in unison, like kids in wonder, then laughed.

The smell of ozone filled the air and suddenly lightning spread through the clouds above us like hundreds of long, fine, burning hairs. Thunder instantly followed with a loud fizzle of electricity.

"Oh my god! You see that?" I shouted to Lee, turning away to look around, taking in the view of silver lined thunderheads lit up by the almost full moon peeking through.

Lee howled like a wolf at the sky, then yelled, "Let's get out of here. I'm sure to lose you in traffic but I'll call you when I get home, or you call me." He turned away and so did I but he grabbed my hand and pulled me in again for a quick kiss, smiled as he released me and ran back to his Mercedes. "Drive safe."

"You too." I went back to my car. Face was up and in motion, edgy from the storm.

Lee flashed his brights and I waved as I got in my car and stroked the dog to calm her. She'd clawed my last car to the floorboards when I took her on a photo shoot to Blue Jay Way to capture a storm over L.A. As I swung the Civic around in a tight u-turn I assured Face in a calm, soothing voice everything was fine. Good. Great, in fact, though my cooing turned to cussing when I hit my brakes to avoid slamming into the dead stop traffic on I-5.

Lee followed me onto the packed interstate and stayed with me a few miles until traffic picked up again. I lost him as I wove around slower drivers on my mad dash to the Tejon pass, but I felt Lee back there, behind me, our connection still intact even with miles now between us.

-

Chapter 18

I crawled along in the rain on the Ventura Fwy for half an hour, though it was only three miles to my exit. I could've walked faster. Who are all you people? Why are you here, fucking up the freeway at midnight? Get out of my city! Gripping my wheel in frustration I thought about the vacation, all that had happened, but it was far away already, like something I'd dreamt. Then I thought of Lee, and smiled. I had someone to be with if I choose to, someone to watch over me, shelter me from the harsh reality that my home had become.

It was close to 1:00a.m. when I finally pulled into my driveway. It surprised me to see my roommate's car parked in front of the garage as I pulled in back of her, blocking her in.

Suzanne sat at the dining room table when Face and I came in the back door and through the kitchen. She stared out the bay windows stone still, dressed in her typical black attire.

"Hi." I greeted her, sensing her darkness. "Happy New Year!"

"Hi." Her tone verged on morose. She didn't even glance at me.

It was obvious my roommate had been crying. I stopped, unsure what to do next. Getting too personal with roommates always ended badly, but I sat down across from Suzanne at my cheap, pine-rimmed glass table anyway. Four houses and twenty five roommates later and I ought to know better, but watching someone crumbling, well, I couldn't just walk away. "What's going on Suzanne? You okay?" Clearly she wasn't.

"We broke up. Tony decided he was madly in love with some supermodel that's been all over him since his band went gold." Suzanne finally looked at me. She looked like a puppy after just getting kicked. Her straight, lifeless brown hair hung to her shoulders and hid too much of her face. Her flat brown eyes behind black, plastic-rim glasses were surrounded in red, her ashen cheeks streaked with wetness.

"Tony's an asshole, Suzanne." I tried to sound sympathetic. I'd never actually met the guy so I didn't want to totally slam him, especially if they got back together. "You are talented, smart, and adorable and he's blind if he can't see that." I kept my eyes on hers but she looked away, back out the window.

Only thirty, Suzanne was a brilliant singer and songwriter. She was a piano teacher for the money. Her unique sound was beyond standard rock or even punk and way too avant garde for the mainstream. She would forever be one of the background people you'll never know, but her sound will undoubtedly have a profound impact on music of the future. Of course Tony knew this, probably why he dated her. His band took Suzanne's original sound and made it commercial.

"But Tony promised to launch me. And now I'm back to nowhere, with no one. I'm back to being invisible." She looked back at me, pleading, scared, desperate, and looked away again.

Ouch. And I was suddenly so very grateful to Lee for saving me from obscurity, and the suffocating void my roommate was now trapped in. I watched Suzanne stare out the window. It was close to 1:30 in the morning by then. Exhausted from the drive, I tried to think of something to say to soothe her so I could exit the scene. "You're not invisible, Suzanne. And you are not alone. Besides friends and family who love you, you have your music. Engage with your muse. Let it steel you from the void. You know this. You don't need to be with Tony, or any guy to make it. Use all the intensity of your feelings right now and create a great tune that'll blow the doors off MCA. Tony and his band aren't the only players in town. This is L.A., not Pennsylvania. Practically everyone here is in, or connected to someone in music."

"And even if they're not, they think they are. Everyone out here is a musician or producer or director or writer or in 'The Industry.' It gets

207

so tiresome. But Tony was the real deal. The Chili Peppers are hot right now. And with Warner Brothers repping them, it's likely they'll get a lot hotter with the publicity machine behind them." She glanced at me then seemed to disconnect, as if a thought suddenly occurred to her. "Do you think it makes me a whore that I care more about losing my chance at fame than I do about losing Tony?"

If Suzanne was a tramp then I was surely one too. I wouldn't consider dating Lee if he didn't make good money, enough to support a family. Even owing what he did in back taxes, he still made more than I ever would freelancing. And if, by some miracle I landed a man's position as a creative director in an agency, my salary alone— far less than any man would get— would never cover the cost of raising kids in the better school districts of L.A. But no matter how much Lee had or made, I wouldn't be with him at all if he was fucking every groupie in town. Several times over the past couple of years Suzanne had come home crying after allegedly catching him with another woman.

"So now you're the tramp when he's plastered all over the rags with a different woman on his arm every issue, and not one of them, in two years, has ever been you. Doesn't that tell you something, Suzanne? It should tell you a lot." I knew I sounded harsh but I felt mad at my roommate right then. "You're better off without Tony, even if all you wanted him for was his connections. And if that's really the case, there's a hundred more like him in this town so all is not lost." I stood up to indicate the conversation was over. The whole context of it irritated me. It shamed all women when we tolerated abhorrent behavior from men just to stay with them.

In my room I replayed my four new messages. Jon and my mom wished me a happy New Year. Lavonne had broken up with Joe again and wanted to know if I was available to talk soon. The last message was from Lee.

"Call me when you get home, just to let me know you're safe. The grapevine was a bitch, wasn't it?"

I crawled into bed and called him. "Hi."

"Hi. When did you get home?"

"About a half hour ago. When did you?"

"Few minutes ago. How'd you like the snow coming over the pass?"

"It was totally cool, like moving at light speed through a star field."

"I knew you'd love it. Was thinking about you going through it, that you'd think it was beautiful." I felt his smile, our connection through the line. "Well, I'm glad you're back safe. What are you doing tomorrow?"

"Laundry. What about you?"

"Same. Wanta play some ball, then do dinner?"

"Love to. What time do you wanta play?"

"Let's try for around 3:00, but it's usually crowded on Saturdays. I'll call for courts in the morning and let you know."

"Okay."

"Well, get some sleep. Have sweet dreams and I'll talk to you tomorrow. Bye."

"Sweet dreams. Bye." I held the phone after he disconnected and listening to the dial tone for what seemed like minutes, but it was probably more like three seconds before I hung up. I heard Suzanne go into her room, felt the weight of her sadness with her footsteps, and retrieved my journal.

1/3/92

Andy Warhol was wrong. Fifteen minutes of fame is only for the select few. Most of us live and die in obscurity.

-

Chapter 19

Racquet World was packed, per usual after the holidays when everyone's racked with guilt for over-consuming. I could relate.

I saw Lee rallying through the little window of the court door, smooth and powerful as always. He was panting and sweating when he stopped to greet me as I came into the room and shut the heavy door behind me.

"Hey," was all he could manage as he tried to catch his breath, but his happy grin was all-telling and infectious.

"Hey." I smiled back. "How long you been here?" I pulled on my glove, slipped the racket cord around my wrist and spun it until it was tight.

"About half an hour. Came early to make sure we'd get a court." He stared at me, his green eyes penetrating, connecting us in the white, cavernous space, as if we were the only two people on earth. "This is harder than it looks after not playing for so long. You ready to rock?" Lee threw me the blue ball and positioned himself in the center of the court.

Hard didn't touch how it felt on that court within minutes. We were both sweating and gasping, moving in seemingly slow motion to what we use to before the three week break.

"This sucks," Lee wheezed. "I stop getting high and suddenly I can't breathe anymore. What's the deal with that?"

"You quit using then?" I stared at him. He gave me a gentle smile.

"I told you I would." His eyes were laughing, as if he was delighting in my pleasure. "Gave what I had to my sister before I left." Lee stood before me, sweat matting his hair to his forehead and streaking down his face then onto his loose gray t-shirt, hiding the slight bulge of his belly. His black gym shorts extended to his knees exposing his powerful calves. And though he stood waiting to play against me, we were finally on the same team.

"Ready to take this to the next level?" Lee asked, bouncing the ball a few more times.

"You bet." I flashed my broadest smile to let him know I got his double entendre. "Hit it."

He did, hard and low, the ball hit the front wall with a loud crack! that echoed though the vacant space. I returned his hit virtually as hard and low, and our volley stayed vivacious, hot, a sensual dance, the ball beating a sharp, pulsating rhythm that tingled inside me for the entire time it was in play. I finally landed a perfect dead ball, laying the ball down making it impossible to return.

"Aowww!" Lee yelled like a fan at a ballpark, then bowed to me in mock-humility.

We played for over an hour until I laid the ball down a third time, several minutes after the next players had knocked on the door indicating our time was up.

"Great hit. Good way to end it," the young, thin actor who played Doogie Howser— the genius kid doctor sitcom, said to me as he barged onto the court, clearly perturbed about waiting so long.

"She's a force to be reckoned with, for sure." Lee said to him.

"He taught me everything I know about this game." I told Doogie as I got my keys from the box set into the wall and handed Lee his wallet. A fat, somewhat slovenly young man with a long ponytail followed Doogie in.

"Seems this teacher could learn a thing or two from my student. When, exactly, did you master the dead ball, my dear?" Lee inquired as we exited the court.

"Just doing what you taught me, honey." I stood in the dim hallway watching Lee put his racket in his gym bag and retrieve his keys.

He straightened and looked at me. "You hungry?"

I was still breathing hard, uncertain how to respond. My best friend for the past two months stood before me, sweat-soaked and breathless, and adorable. But taking it slow sexually was mandatory. I needed time to see if he would follow through with his commitments to quit using and get his shit together, though with his recent efforts in response to my needs, I felt obliged to respond to his. I reached out then and pulled him to me, kissed him hard, long, parting his lips with my tongue and sucking him in. I slid my arms around his neck, pressed my body to his, felt his warm wetness against my cheeks and neck, tasted the salt from his sweat. He pushed himself against me, pinning me back against the outside wall of the court, his growing hardness tingling my crotch like the racquetball vibrating my ass every time it hit the other side of the wall.

Lee pulled back as a couple entered the hall talking. I was grateful for the distraction, so horny I almost came right there, and may have if we went back to kissing, but Lee took my hand, laced his fingers in mine, then picked up his gym bag and lead me from the club.

We spent Sunday in Santa Barbara., walking, talking, combed the beach for shells. We ate dinner at a charming sea food place overlooking the ocean, and didn't get back to L.A. until after 10:00p.m. I didn't ask him to come inside like last night when he came back to my house after Maria's and we played Tavli till 1:00 in this morning. He had to be up very early for his back east clients, and I had to be at CBS, so we decided to call it a night and meet up after work to play ball, then go to dinner, get back to our routine now

213

that vacation was truly over.

The week ahead seemed less daunting building something real with Lee, that mattered, my career in advertising a practical joke to creating a bond with him that could lead to a home of our own. I drove to CBS on Monday morning with little of the usual dread. Even walking down the red carpet to the Artist's Entrance, and overhearing some guy asking his wife if I was Winona Ryder didn't bother me. I was there to make money, nothing more, to pay my rent until I didn't need to anymore. I imagined my life with Lee— two kids, large yard with fruit trees and a studio for me. I'd spend the days writing, Lee at home as well, working from his home office while the kids are in school. Sometimes we'd share lunch, or skip it to get intimate. Later in the afternoon when the kids were doing homework, I'd pick some lemons and oranges to marinade the chicken for dinner. I smiled with the fantasy, holed up in Pat's office. Pat was in court ordered rehab after getting busted blowing a joint on the roof of Television City, according to Brian, the lead CD, who warned everyone not to go smoke out up there anymore, "now that L.A.'s turned into a police state."

I leafed through the project specs and groaned audibly over having to promote yet another overacted Brian Dennehy movie. Burden of Proof was based on a book by Scott Turow, a sort of sequel to his first novel, Presumed Innocent. Two books, and two screen deals, and the author was surely flush with money that bought him time to create whatever he wanted. I wondered if Turow had inheritance or financial support when he wrote his first book, or lived poor until he was discovered. And I dreamed I could be too, conjuring a career as an artist— writing fiction, shooting pics, building whatever I conceived. The fantasy felt hollow though, just cultivating my own genius. I needed to nurture a family, love and be loved by those who really know me.

Images from a beam scale to the columned facade of the Justice Building in D.C. helped me focus on creating the print campaign that would go into TV Guides, popular magazines and newspapers across the country. Even if I was never discovered, Lee had kindly assured me he'd be privileged to support our family. And reality or not, his generous offer delighted me.

1/7/92

When I was little, my father used to call me Marco, after the Dr Seuss character in I Think I Saw It On Mulberry Street. Marco is a compulsive storyteller who prefers fantasy to reality.

I expected for the first month or so, and in fact it played out that being straight with Lee was virtually the same as high with him. For most chronic users, the first few weeks straight are...refreshing. More awake. More socially aware— plugged in. Since marijuana's chemistry stores in fat cells, it leaves the body slowly, over weeks, easing withdrawal symptoms, unlike the intense cravings experienced in days, even hours sometimes when quitting hard drugs or alcohol. The initial abstention is so mild it has been mistakenly assumed weed isn't addicting. But four, five weeks down the abstinence road from smoking and life starts to grate. Irritate. Too sharp. Too real. And then the cravings descend like wolves and continually gnaw on the psyche.

The weeks flew by with afternoons playing ball then sharing dinners together, and on the weekends back to exploring the mountains to the sea. We lingered over meals, lacing our fingers on the table, held hands on long walks, kissed over games of Tavli and at stop lights, fondled teasingly on the racquetball court or stuck in traffic. We shared a passionate embrace at the end of each evening. And while Lee had become more attractive than ever before, another good thing about waiting to make it was building intimacy slowly generally prevented confusing lust with love.

Cozy in his Mercedes, winding through Benedict Cyn, we listened to a mix of Brian Ferry, Chris Isaak and Miles Davis on our way to dinner at Stratton's. He held my hand on the burl divider between our seats most of the way into the city, connecting us. Westwood Village was like a ghost town of its former vibrant self. Streets once packed with movie goers and tourists, specialty clothing stores and moderately priced restaurants, Westwood used to be the place to come for a film debut, to see or be seen. Now most shops closed early, many storefronts were empty, the streets virtually deserted since the displaced gangs from Pasadena's renovation found their way here. Two drive-by shootings last summer took out something like eight people and completed the White Flight from Westwood. Though the grand theater marquees still glitzed up the night, few people came to see movies here anymore. The crowds had thinned to mostly UCLA students and staff. The campus had reclaimed the Village.

Stratton's Bar and Grill was practically empty even though it was just after 7:00 on a Saturday night. Only two other couples sat at opposite ends of the enormous oak bar that ran the length of the restaurant. The room was square and cavernous with wood paneled walls all the way up to the crown molding framing the high, Crawford ceiling. It smelled of sizzling steak and wood smoke inside. Square tables filled the center of the room, surrounded by booths against three of the four walls.

A young, tall, slender waiter with red hair and a face full of freckles led Lee and I to a booth, and without welcoming us to the restaurant, abruptly asked if we wanted anything to drink. His blue eyes were sad, brooding, and I got the distinct impression our waiter was upset about something as he took our order and turned away.

"Whoa. What is his problem?" Lee said. "Looked like the dude was about to cry." He reached for my hand across the table.

"Yeah. I got that." I took Lee's hand, kept my eyes on his, tuning out the room around us.

"Either he didn't get the part—" Lee began.

"Or he just failed a mid-term—"

"Or broke up with his girlfriend."

"Or lost his dog."

"Nah. He'd be crying then. Bet ya ten to one it's the girlfriend." We watched our waiter filling cups with hot water then Lee looked back at me. "Thanks for choosing to be with me, Ray." He gave me an intimate smile and squeezed my hand.

"Thanks for choosing to be with me, Lee." I flashed him a soft smile, even though it was all fairly disgusting in that puppy love sort of way.

The waiter brought our teas to the table on a round tray. He glanced down at our entwined fingers as he distributed our steaming cups and then put a silver container filled with cream between us.

"Geez, you two look like you're really in love." The waiter spoke with the kid-like cadence of Ronny Howard, and his resemblance to Richie Cunningham of the sitcom Happy Days was remarkable. "You're really lucky to have each other."

"She's pretty amazing." Lee spoke to our waiter but never took his eyes off me. "And I feel lucky indeed to be with her." His eyes twinkled with delight and I beamed, emboldened by his declaration.

Lee ordered crab cakes, with two French onion soups to start and crème brûlée to finish. The room was dim but glimmered with golden light, candles flickering on every table. It felt like a fairytale in there, like we were on a movie set.

"So, do you think we're in love?" Lee let go of my my hand to prepare his tea, then sipped it. There was a hint of humor in his eyes over the rim of his cup, probing mine as he waited for my answer.

I knew the game. He was asking me to confirm our level of commitment first. And a battle ensued inside between giving him the answer he wanted to hear, and the truth.

His expression lost all lightness the longer I remained silent. His eyes seemed to dim and I felt him pulling back, withdrawing from me.

218

"I'm not sure what love is, Lee," I began. "I know I totally, completely, unequivocally enjoy being with you, and when I'm not I miss you." I studied him and caught a whisper of a smile. "Love, for me, isn't a state of being, it's an action. And sublime though attraction may be, the kind of love I'm looking to share with you is proven over time, time and time again by consistently being responsive to each others needs." I stared at him. "You ready for that?"

He was fixed on me. "Definitely."

I smiled, but said a silent prayer that Lee was ready for the real thing, through thick and thin, in sickness and health, to love and cherish till death do us part... I put my hand on the table hoping he'd take hold, and he did. He laced his fingers in mine connecting us again. I felt safe, coveted.

The waiter came back with our food. "I've been watching you guys. And you seem so easy with each other." Richie was very chatty as he set our dripping cheese-crusted soups down in front of us. "I just want to know the secret to your apparent success. How long have you guys been together?"

A slow smile spread across Lee's face. "About two weeks now. We've known each other for almost three months, but she was afraid of me." He spoke to me, not our waiter.

"Well, you guys look good together, you know, right I mean, like you belong with each other. Two sides of the same coin, kind of thing." He set two glasses filled with ice water on our table and tucked the serving tray under his arm as he straightened. "But I can't guarantee the accuracy of my perceptions anymore. I thought my girlfriend and

I would be together forever and the slut just dumped me for some cock-sucking, mother-fucking jock." He shook his head and sighed heavily.

"Wow. I'm sorry," I said.

"Me too." The waiter looked at our food. "Enjoy." He sulked away, head down, shoulders slumped.

Lee and I looked at each other and grimaced as discretely as possible.

"He may have been wrong about his ex-girlfriend, but he's not about us." Lee picked up his water glass and raised it for a toast. "To you and me—two sides of the same coin, my dear. Thank you for completing me."

We clinked glasses and sipped our water to consummate the toast, but in a flash of insight I heard distant intuition mock me. Two sides of the same coin ricocheted in my head until the sweet, salty, tangy flavor of the shimmering onion soup captivated me, as did Lee's company.

-

Chapter 20

1/18/92

My father continually needles me—unlike most everyone that occasionally puts the proverbial gun to their heads, I consistently go one step further and pull the trigger.

"Get off here." I instructed Lee to exit the freeway at Kanan Road on our way to my sister's house. It was close to 6:00p.m. but night glimmered in suburban twilight.

Lee was stylishly 'put together,' as my mother would surely notice, in his black Dockers and maroon sweater, his thick hair combed neatly but soft wisps still scattered in his eyes and framed his baby face.

"This was a stupid idea." I didn't want to hurt his feelings but couldn't hold in my growing anxiety. He'd accepted my sister's invitation when Carrie had called to inquire what I planned to bring to our father's 65th birthday party and Lee answered my phone. I'd anticipated this evening all week long, imagining finally being awarded my mother's look of loving approval, the one given so freely to my sister. Lee was charismatic, engaging, attentive, passionate— traits Carrie often complained her husband, Larry, sorely lacked. My family would welcome Lee in, one less obstacle between us.

"No worries, Ray. I won't disappoint. You'll be the belle of the ball tonight. I promise." He shot me a soft, knowing smile as he brought his Mercedes to a stop at the end of the off ramp. "You're going to have to tell me the way." He stared at me, waiting.

I stared back at him and then it occurred to me he was asking for directions. "Right. Turn right. Then over the hill and left at the second light."

His smile broadened again for just a second, then he looked away, focused back on driving. His jaw had literally dropped when I greeted him at my front door earlier. I wore my lace, maroon dress, the only clothing my sister ever bought me, for my 26th birthday, a week after Michael married. Unlike our mother's tailored choices, this dress was hot, tight around the tits and torso, flaring loosely from the hips to an inch below my knees.

We passed the glowing strip malls to the endless maze of houses that lined the rolling hills. Lee placed his hand gently on my knee to stop me from bouncing my leg. I clamped my hands around the chocolate cream pie I got at Marie Callender's to replace the chocolate mousse I didn't cook for the party. I forced myself to be still as we wove our way through the McMansions of the Morrison Ranch housing development. Lee turned down Carrie's short street, swung the car around at the end of the cul-de-sac and pulled up against the curb in front of my sister's white, eight bedroom, six bath, two-story, pre-fab colonial.

He turned off the car and looked at me. "You ready to go party?" He raised his eyebrows and flashed a grin, then retrieved a bottle of white wine from the back seat.

I gulped, shook my head.

Lee laughed. "They can't be all that bad, Ray. They produced you." His eyes kind of twinkled and he put his hand on my cheek a moment, gave me a quick kiss then released me, opened his door and got out.

I followed, and we walked side by side up the slate landings to my sister's massive oak doors. I glanced at Lee and his gentle smile fortified me. Then I pushed down on the long brass doorknob and opened the door onto the grand marble entryway of Carrie's house. A sweeping staircase graced the left wall and wrapped up to the second floor open hallway that bordered seven of the eight bedrooms. In the living room to the left, an enormous fire blazed in the huge marble fireplace casting an orange glow to the cavernous room.

Family and friends gathered in the entry and spilled into the dining room. I greeted my sister's lifelong girlfriend, Nancy, a regular fixture at festivities with a quick kiss. She introduced her husband and seven year old son to Lee. Next were the ever-present neighbors and their pre-teen daughter and punk teen son, followed by Grandma already sitting at the walnut dining table elaborately set for sixteen. I saw my mother standing with my dad and brother-in-law, in the back of the entryway. Mom had her public face on. It was hard to tell she felt anything beyond her sparkly façade until she spied Lee. Her countenance lit up with her genuine smile, like sun breaking through the morning fog she radiated her joy. I couldn't help smiling too as I led Lee down the hallway to meet my parents.

Carrie came from the kitchen to greet us. She wore a loose, tan cottony dress, mid-calf and cinched at the waist with a thick red bow. Her flaming red hair was pulled back with another thick red bow, the ends of the silken ribbon brushed her shoulders. She extended her hand and Lee shook it and introduced himself, and then he did the same with my parents and brother-in-law. After the canonical pleasantries, Carrie took the pie from me and excused herself to "orchestrate the meal," then went back to the kitchen.

My petite mother stood before me in a fitted navy dress and reasonably-heeled blue pumps, martini in hand. My father was next to her, big and imposing in his coal sweater and dark gray khaki's. He also held a martini in his huge hand, his long, artisan fingers spread around the wide rim of the glass.

Larry offered Lee a martini, but Lee declined, confessing he didn't care for them. My father took on an actor's pose as he began his dissertation on what makes a good martini, and then tried to convince Lee to have one.

"Ed, you are clearly a man of discerning taste." Lee nodded humbly but with humor. "I, however, am but a mere commoner and would much prefer a diet soda if one's available."

"You don't drink, Lee?" my father inquired politely.

I tensed, afraid my dad would vocalize his warped perspective: Never trust a man who doesn't drink, or anyone who doesn't like dogs.

"I think it's very smart not to drink." My mother came to Lee's defense. "It's just a lot of empty calories anyway." She took another sip of her martini. "But ooh. This is sooo good!" A wide, childlike smile spread across her face, dark eyes twinkled with humor.

"Your rousing endorsement makes it hard to resist, Ruth, but I'm the Designated Driver tonight and I take my title seriously, especially having your daughter with me." Lee smiled at her confidently, tenderly. "Precious cargo." He slid his hand in mine and squeezed, plain as day for all to see.

I blushed, looked away, at Larry, though I noticed my mother beaming. "Is the diet Coke in the outside fridge under the bar, or in the garage fridge?" I structured my question to motivate my brother-in-law to go get the soda himself, knowing the idea of me rooting around his house would unnerve him.

"I'll get them. And I'm sure Carrie could use some help with dinner, Rachel," Larry sniped as he went to retrieve the soda.

I left my parents to chat with Lee, certain he'd wow them. I went into the den and kissed Scott and Jessie hello, though the kids hardly noticed, lost in watching Back To The Future II on their home theater system. Lee winked at me when I passed him on my way to help Carrie display dinner. I smiled outside and in as I entered my sister's enormous country kitchen.

"Lee seems very nice." Carrie was at the oven unloading a cinnamon and pecan kugel casserole onto the hotplate built into the elaborate range top.

"He is." I didn't extrapolate, assuming my sister would inquire further.

"Can you help Maria with the stuff in the fridge?" She said it more like a command than request.

We had no further exchange. I helped unload the huge brushed steel refrigerator of its contents. Carrie manned the ovens and toasters. We crammed the butcher block island with platters of pastrami, roast turkey and beef, smoked whitefish and lox, cheese blintzes, caviar and crackers. We crowded more food onto the kitchen table already filled with several salad choices, plates of mushrooms topped with crab to sweets from cranberry/jello mold to hamantaschen. Stacks of plates to begin the food orgy were placed between two large wicker baskets with fresh bagels on the counter top dividing the cooking from the dining area. Carrie was the archetypal housewife. She knew how to stage a meal.

When everything was off the stove top and out of the ovens, freezers and fridges, the three of us paused and looked at our efforts. The amount of food in that kitchen bordered on obscene for a guest list of sixteen, four of which were children. What Carrie blew on excess that night alone would feed Maria's family back in Mexico for a month, and me for several months.

Carrie nodded approvingly and addressed her maid. "Gracias, Maria. Pienso que eso es todo para ahora. Nos serviremos nosotros mismos esta noche."

Maria glanced at me as she walked by, out of the kitchen across the back of the entry hall to her small bedroom off the den. I looked at my sister to inquire again why she didn't think it appropriate for Maria to eat with us, but Carrie was already on her way to the dining room where she invited everyone to get a plate and serve themselves dinner.

I preferred self-serve at my sister's. A lot less work than playing waitress, but festival seating was the perk. After Lee and I filled our plates we sat together at the far end of the mammoth dining room table, however, within a minute Larry sat at the head of the table perpendicular to Lee. My father followed Larry, set his plate piled high with food on the table and sat facing Lee and I, but continued talking only to Larry. He was on some diatribe again.

"…And if the queen had balls, she'd be king. Sanctions don't work with these people. We need to go in there with brute force and bomb the hell out of 'em, find out where Hussein is hiding and bring him down. The world is watching if we'll follow through—live on TV! The U.S. must not appear weak." My father looked at Lee then back at Larry. "If we don't stop the bad guys then what the hell was the Gulf War for?"

"To free Kuwait, which coalition forces accomplished last year, Ed." Larry gave him a tolerant grin, as young often do to old. "Sanctions will send the message we want Hussein out of Iraq."

"Mark my words, Saddam Hussein, and the fanatic Muslims he represents will come back to haunt us if we don't take him down now." He looked at Larry then Lee but not at me. My father never engaged women in political discussions.

"Personally, I'm not a big fan of war for conflict resolution." Lee looked at me then glanced at Larry but spoke to my father. "But I tend to agree with you, Ed. What was the point of going over there if we're going to be right back up against the same fascist dictatorship down the line? Of course, sanctions may help put pressure where needed to defeat Hussein's regime. Conversely, maybe after thousands of years as bedouins, most of the Middle-East just isn't ready for a capitalist democracy."

I choked on my Crescent roll. They all looked at me. I forced myself to swallow, and keep the smile off my face. Lee was playing them, taking all sides without ever stating a point of view, a sales technique for winning friends and influencing people.

"You know what I don't get?" I spoke to cover Lee's little joke and derail my father probing him further. "Dad, you're willing to pay the inexplicable price of war—for oil, instead of investing in alternative, renewable energy, or driving a Honda instead of your twelve miles to the gallon guzzling LeBaron. Why is that?" I stared at my dad but he surveyed his plate as he prepared a forkful of turkey and kugel without acknowledging me. A flash of anger overrode my shame. "And Larry, you support sanctions when surely you're aware they only hurt the poor while the regime hordes everything. The rich always take care of themselves, don't they, Lar." I delivered the words like bullets, meant to penetrate, but all I ever did was agitate.

"Do you have a better plan than sanctions, or war, Rachel?" Larry glared at me. "Our government has top minds working on it around the god-damn clock, but if you think you have an answer to the Middle East problem I'm sure they'd love to hear it. We'd all love to hear it."

I flushed, burned red hot inside, but kept my mouth shut. My father didn't look at me. He savored another bite of his turkey as if he hadn't heard the exchange. I couldn't look at Lee so I looked down, but felt the rest of the guests at the table watching us.

"A better plan might include the will of the voters to decide how to spend our tax dollars." Lee spoke to Larry and my father, but his words backed me. "After all, it's my hard earned cash and I'd like some say in where it's going. Investing in science, medicine, technology seems more fiscally responsible to me than blowing away countless more lives and billions of dollars annually to perpetuate our addiction to oil."

"So, you're a liberal." Larry said it with disdain.

Lee gave him a tolerant smile. "I'm a humanist."

My knight was a humanist.

I stared at him. Lee looked at me and I felt my smile match his. I looked back at Larry, then at my father still seemingly lost in his food, then got up and went into the kitchen to get a Diet Coke, and breathe.

I pulled a cold can from the fridge and stood at the sink looking out the kitchen windows at the dimly lit back patio. The jacuzzi glowed red and looked like molten lava the way the tub was sunk into the patio. A circle of wide clay tiles bordered the rim and separated the hot tub from the swimming pool which glowed phosphorus blue/green and stretched the length of the yard. The quarter acre manicured lawn that spread out to the left of the pool area faded to the night just beyond the ambient light from the house.

"Lee's really cute, and very charming. I see why you like him." Carrie came into the kitchen with half-full plates of scattered food, set them in the sink, then got the sponge and wiped away the endless parade of ants streaming along the splash guard of her granite counter top. "How are you guys doing?"

"Great. Lee's great. He really is a sweetie."

"Sweetie? Doesn't exactly sound like you're very serious about a 'sweetie.'"

I signed. "I don't know yet, Carrie. We're working on resolving some open issues before I'm ready to commit my life to the guy."

"Here we go." Carrie shook her head with an exaggerated sigh. "Everyone has issues, Rachel, especially if they're still single at your age. There seems to be something is wrong with everyone you date. Do you judge yourself that harshly?"

"Yes."

Carrie stared at me. "I believe you do, which is part of your problem." She shook her head again, then turned away and rinsed the dead ants off the sponge. "Maybe you should focus on what's right with Lee instead of what's wrong with him so you don't end up childless and alone." She squeezed the water out of the sponge and left it on the back of the stainless steel sink then turned back to me. "Look, do what you want to do. You always do. All I know is you're out of time, Rachel." She stared at me. "The struggling bohemian is only chic when you're young, hon. You ought to start living in the real world and realign your expectation with what you have to offer."

I searched her eyes for compassion, or at least some awareness of how devaluing her words were, but saw neither in Carrie's banal expression. My older sister stared back at me like I was the clueless one. I wanted to scream, "You know nothing of the real world, in your colonial McMansion with your honey and his money," but I didn't. Carrie married at 22, right out of college, went from living at the home she was raised in to a McMansion with her husband. She'd never paid a bill in her life, had access to endless cash which she spent lavishly, and didn't have a clue what the 'real world' was like for all but the privileged few. She was the harsh judge for a world she knew nothing of.

Carrie crossed in front of me and went back into the dining room. Moments later, I did too. I sat next to Lee and ate while listening to the boys argue politics, and then merge into religion, in which Lee joked about being an Apatheist, though acquiesced to my mother he was at least in part Jewish because his dad was a non-practicing Jew. At one point Lee suggested that the government legalize drugs and tax them like alcohol to help resolve the federal deficit, and my father jumped on that bandwagon as a staunch Republican who fervently believed in limited government intervention. But I knew, and Lee knew I knew that he was teasing me when he broached the subject.

After eating, Lee went to play Duke NukEm on the computer with my nephew, but the rest of the men sat there, waiting for coffee and dessert to be served. The women got up and started cleaning. Get up and help! I wanted to yell, but managed to refrain from saying anything else that challenged. Even in the 1990s men were considered kings of their castles, and most suburban families still modeled the 50s sitcom, Father Knows Best. And mine was no exception. I followed the ladies lead, gathered dinner plates scattered with unwanted remains and brought the appalling waste of food into the kitchen. Maria was back, doing the dishes stacked in the sink. Carrie retrieved the four layer lemon chiffon cake from the pink box on the counter top and loaded it with candles, then lit them. I followed her back into the dining room along with the other women singing Happy Birthday.

The party began breaking up a half hour or so after dessert was served. I wished my dad a happy birthday with a heartfelt hug and kissed my family goodbye. Lee shook hands with my father as he extended birthday wishes of health and a good year to come, and then shook Larry's hand. He kissed my mother and sister on the cheek, which seemed a little too familiar, though both women responded in kind.

Outside was cold and crisp. I blew steamy breaths on the way to Lee's car wishing I was exhaling smoke. I craved a buzz, as I so often did after being with my family, though I smiled with the image of my mother radiating joy as she gushed over how gorgeous, and smart, and sweet Lee was when she'd trapped me in the kitchen earlier while I was wrapping left-overs.

"That wasn't so bad, right?" Lee said as he opened the passenger door for me. "I, for one, rather enjoyed it. Great food. Good company. It was fun tonight, meeting your family."

I watched him, perplexed, as he went around his Mercedes. "Fun isn't a word I've associated with my family since I was 10, and rarely even then." I got in the car as he got behind the wheel and looked at me.

"Hey, at least your parents are still together, and your family is normal." He started the car, and let it roll down the hill to the stop sign.

I laughed. "Normal? You mean classically pedestrian?"

Lee laughed. "OK. Let's go with that."

Outside the occasional lights nestled in the Malibu Hills flashed by, but it was mostly dark beyond the light from the freeway. The Mercedes was a warm sanctuary. I was glad he'd come tonight, content to be with him, pleased by my mother's felicity. "Thank you for coming tonight. It was amusing with you there, watching you wrap them around your finger." I hadn't actually meant to say the last bit. I gave him a cocky smile and tried to soften the remark. "You were very impressive. Honestly, you made it tolerable. It was nice having someone on my side."

"I am, ya know, on your side."

"I know." For now, echoed my inner voice, but it was barely audible and may have been fear, not intuition. "Thank you, and not just for tonight." I took his hand and held it, connecting us. He flashed me a soft smile as he turned left onto the 101 and accelerated rapidly down the on-ramp, pinning me to my seat. We both hadn't used for over four weeks, but I hadn't brought it up virtually at all, and neither had he. I'd hardly ever craved a buzz, safely ensconced with Lee, except on rare occasions like this evening with my family. I was afraid of confessing my craving right then, of bringing up weed at all with him. MA meetings everyone sat around and talked about all their stoned adventures which always left me salivating to get high. It's no wonder the AA program's best kept secret is their appallingly low abstinence rates.

"I want to be with you, Ray. In every way. I'm ready. Are you?" Lee said as the San Fernando Valley opened up before us, lights twinkling like diamonds from the recent rain.

1/24/92

Men are the freight train comin at ya.

Women are the poison in your food.

-

Chapter 21

There was no reason to hold back now. He'd embraced the changes he'd said he'd make for almost a month now. It was only fair I embrace his needs as well.

His thick hair framed his twinkling eyes and full lips as he gathered my face in his hands and kissed me with passion, and hunger, in my bedroom. It felt as if he was devouring me, mouths connected, tongues mingling. I returned his fervent kiss in kind, drew his tongue into my mouth and sucked him in. Arousal perfumed the air with the thick sweet scent of sex. Lee unzipped my dress and pulled back, then slid his fingers along my collar bones until the dress fell off me and onto the carpet. He flashed me a quick smile then leaned in and kissed my breast along the curve of my bra, then slowly up the side of my neck as he undid the three clasps in the back. I shimmied out of my panties and left them on the floor as I assisted him in removing his clothing.

I surrendered to his maleness as he gently pushed me back onto my bed and lay on top of me, kissing me all the while, slowly at first, then with wild abandon, locking his lips to mine then breaking away and kissing my neck, my breasts, sucking on my nipple to the edge of pain, then back up to my lips again, swallowing me in. He slid to my side, ran his warm, thick hand over my nipples ever so slightly, arousing every part of me, and then buried his fingers in my pubic hair. The aroma of sex spiked and I almost came right then but Lee rolled away, onto his side and turned off the lamp on the bedside table, and I suddenly felt small, shy, ugly. Perhaps he thought my...voluptuous shape was revolting naked.

He rolled back towards me, and then he was on top of me again, his hard mound pushing into my crotch. We slowly worked into a natural rhythm, kissing all the while, and I got lost in the dizzying, touching frenzy until I felt him push inside of me.

"Wait." I pulled back. "We need a condom. Do you have one?"

He didn't answer, just stayed on top of me and continued rotating his hips gently.

"We can't have intercourse without one." My hands were on his chest. I looked into his eyes. The room was so dim they looked like black holes. "I don't want you inside me without a condom. You have any?"

There was a protracted silence. Lee rolled onto his back and for a second I thought he was pissed. "I don't have AIDS, Rachel. I'm not gay, and I've never slept with those kind of people."

"And what kind of people would that be, Lee?"

"You know, high risk people. Gays, bisexuals, heroin users. I don't have AIDS, or any STDs. You're going to have to trust me sooner or later, Ray." Lee pulled the quilt over himself. "Stopped carrying condoms when I was married. Didn't need em. Sharon was on the pill. You don't use birth control?"

"I tried taking the pill but it made me sick, and I haven't used my diaphragm in so long I wouldn't trust it. Shit! I can't believe this. I can go to Ralph's and get some. Take me ten minutes."

He leaned up on one elbow watching me, openly scrutinizing my naked body, the blanket covering him to his waist. "Forget it. Come here," Lee virtually commanded. "No worries, my dear." His tone was softer but I couldn't see his expression with only the soft glow of ambient streetlight. He grabbed me playfully, pulling me to him, pressed up against me as he slipped his hand around the back of my neck and then kissed me while he moved his free hand over my breast, my nipple, then slid his fingers lightly down my stomach and buried them in my pubic hair again. I gasped with pleasure. My breathing quickened. My heart pounded. My body flushed with heat and the scent of sex spiked again.

It took me about five seconds to get off. After the release I giggled with delight, then thanked him. He kissed me again and I sucked him in, reached down and took hold of his hard penis, his length just fitting the width of my hand.

And right then I realized it was Lee trying to hide something with the dark.

I held him, began pumping but he grabbed my wrist and stopped me.

"I'm good. I'll take it from here."

"Give me a chance," I said gently, still rather surprised by how small he was. The few men I'd been with had all been long and lean. I pushed him flat on his back and then ran my lips and the tip of my tongue up and down his short staff, then drew him into my mouth for a moment (something I rarely did to avoid gagging but felt no such threat with his size), and then withdrew, my mouth tight over the tip of his penis as I pulled back, replacing my mouth with my hand again.

Lee groaned. "Oh god," he exclaimed, got hard as a rock though never grew more than four, five inches in length tops before he ejaculated. "Thank you," he said and kissed me lightly.

I scurried off the bed and retrieved a towel from the bathroom. He wiped himself off, then bundled the towel into a tight ball and handed it to me as he pulled the blanket back over him. I tossed it into the laundry basket by the closet door then got back in bed and under the blankets to lay beside him. We snuggled in the afterglow of orgasm. Lee spooned me, put his arm over my side and let his hand rest on my belly. Warmth and contentment enveloped me. I laced my fingers in his. He squeezed my hand and pulled me tight.

"Tell me what names you like for a girl?" he asked.

"A girl, huh?" I played along. "Actually, I wouldn't mind having all boys. I've heard boys are a lot...less complicated than girls. And women really do have it a lot harder then men."

"I'd love a daughter, though, raise her to be strong, and proud, driven like any man, and shatter all the stereotypes of silly, helpless women. How does two boys and one girl sound, like your sister has?"

"OK. Fine. So what names do you like for boys?"

"Well, lets see. I like Benjamin, after Mr Franklin, since he was a pretty cool dude."

"My first full time job outta college my boss almost raped me at the company Christmas party. He went after his secretary after I kneed him in the crotch. His name was Ben. Benjamin Miller."

Lee pulled me to him again with a quick squeeze. "How about Thomas then, after our dear friend Edison. Tom for short."

I smiled. "I like Tom, and Tommy's cute for a boy. What about Kyle for our second son?"

"Kyle," he repeated it slowly. "What will his friends call him for short?"

"Ky. Nothing for kids to make fun of with that."

"I like it. Reminds me of a surfer dude. He'll fit right in here."

"I don't want to raise kids in L.A."

"Where do you want to go then?"

"North of San Francisco. Mill Valley, Novato maybe, a smaller, safer community."

"I love it up there. And I can run my business from just about anywhere. That's the beauty of it." He paused to kiss the back of my neck. "You can write, develop photos, build. We'll both have home offices so I can be there for our kids."

His words enchanted. And I was falling in love with idea of us. I wasn't destined to a life of loneliness and financial hardship. The future didn't have to be like the past, or worse if I stayed alone and childless. I could finally move on to what mattered, as all my contemporaries had done, and work at establishing a real life with Lee.

-

Chapter 22

In a diner a long time ago my waitress was talking to one of her regulars in the booth next to mine. He asked her why she was so chipper lately since she was usually rather serious. "I met a guy a month ago and we're good together. I have someone to share my life with now, the good and bad, which makes most everything better."

I know just what she meant.

The Rodney King trial was in motion, the video of his beating shown fifty times a day on every station, and L.A. had a lot of stations, the most in the world actually, even without cable. Everyone was on a hair trigger, especially with reports of random drive-bys almost daily. The cops were afraid of the public they were supposed to be protecting. My casual siesta town had become Crown Heights, Brooklyn. And though L.A. never had a true sense of community like Manhattan or Chicago, until Rodney King we basically got along. But after that video, the city I'd always known as home was beyond scary. It was ugly. Except I had Lee to shelter me from the evil outside, and even the darkness gathering within.

Little more than a grand to my name after paying my bills in the beginning of the month, including the extra on my Visa for my dog's indiscretions in Oregon, motivated me to get on the phone and find some paying gigs. February sweeps were in full swing and the studios no longer needed freelancers. Within a few days I had two projects, and between the credit union campaign and the bank merger package for my new client, I was busy all day. Lee and I met only for racquetball and/or dinner throughout the week, then I returned home to work, often staying up into the early morning hours to meet deadlines.

Friday evening after ball Lee suggested we go to Old Town Pasadena and try out one of the new trendy restaurants. Since his place was on the way, he asked we stop there so he could change out of his racquetball attire, and also show me his condo since I'd yet to see it. Instead of leaving my car in the lot to get ripped off or broken into after the club closed, or going backwards to my house to drop it off, I followed Lee to his place, a top floor loft of a sprawling three-story complex nestled in the foothills of Eagle Rock.

I followed him into the elevator and his warm thick hand slid to the back of my neck and pulled me in for a sensual kiss during the short ride up. Pure bliss from head to toe, we continued kissing even after the elevator door opened, stopping only when we noticed the couple waiting to get on. His condo was modest but clean, a narrow kitchen to the left of the entry beyond which opened up to the living room with an overstuffed leather couch, a giant projection TV, and a synthesizer with a full size piano keyboard hooked up to a complex stereo system. The Nagel painting of the woman and dog hung over the synthesizer. Across the room a sliding glass door opened up to a small concrete patio overlooking a garden with a large pool and small Jacuzzi three floors down.

He kissed me again on the balcony, then took my hand and led me up the stairs along the far wall to his bedroom. A three foot high glass wall topped with round brass railing ran along the open area of the loft overlooking the living room. The double bed, covered with a thick, white quilt, took up most of the space; the two small mission end tables on either side of it almost touched the opposing walls. Lee resumed kissing me and we eventually stripped and ended up in his bed. We explored and played with each other until I couldn't hold back much longer and asked for him to come inside me if he had a condom.

He rolled away and pulled out a gold-foiled coin, like chocolate Hanukkah gelt—a Trojan Magnum Gold condom from his end table drawer. I suppressed a giggle thinking of his size, and vaguely wondered if the condom would stay on him once he was inside me. He held the coin out to me with a teasing grin. I took the condom and peeled back one side of the gold foil and took out the moist rubber.

I felt clumsy and awkward as I tried to fit the long condom on him. Within moments his hard-on contracted, as did my heart. To avoid a total crash and burn for our second sexual encounter, I tossed the condom on the end table and gathered his cock in my hand, then my mouth, eventually arousing him again.

Lee moaned then grabbed for the condom and put it on, then virtually shoved me back on the bed and rolled on top of me, and then slammed himself inside me. He came an instant later. Even in the dim light from the courtyard I caught his haughty smile as he sank back on the bed and thanked me in a breathless whisper. A moment later, holding the condom around the base of his cock he got up and went into the bathroom to dispose of the condom.

Lee came back in a moment later, his dick flaccid, practically lost between his balls as he bent to kiss me, then he crawled under the covers next to me and moved his mouth to my breast and sucked gently. I closed my eyes as he slid his free hand down along my belly then pressed his palm into my crotch while tickling my nipples with his tongue. I moaned then gasped as the sudden surged of pleasure rippled through me. Lee gave me a soft, rather tentative smile. I put my hand on his face, pulled him in and kissed him, but there was a visceral disconnect.

The air was viscous between us when we finally cuddled up together.

"I'm sorry," he said quietly. "I'm really not used to using a condom. I never liked em. Makes it hard to feel you. On top of which, I don't think I've had sex without being buzzed in ten years."

The bed seemed to sag and swallow me up. We'd been clean for only six weeks, per my request, and it felt as if he was blaming me for prematurely ejaculating. But I let it ride. I didn't want to make him feel worse than he already did. "Well, I hope you weren't too disappointed." I tried to inject some levity, confident at least I'd gotten him off.

"You know I'm not." He squeezed me around the ribs so tightly for a second it was hard to breath. Then he brushed my hair back away from my neck and kissed it softly.

We lay spooning, but the silence felt like a wall between us until his stomach rumble loudly. He laughed. So did I, connecting us again.

"I'm starving. Let's go into Old Town and get something to eat." Lee gave me a quick kiss and got out of bed, went to his dresser along the glass wall and pulled out clean clothes. I borrowed a dark gray, long sleeve Polo shirt and a pair of his jeans, cinched at the waist with one of his belts, so I wouldn't have to put back on my sweaty skins and t-shirt.

We ate at some overpriced Italian place and window shopped along Colorado Blvd, recently renovated with high end clothing boutiques, home design shops and art galleries. The Santa Ana winds were up, the night cool, the air clean, sharp.

"Ever been up to Mt Wilson?" I asked as we were walking, hand in hand, back to his car.

He glanced at me, smiled. "No."

"Well, it ain't Pearsoll Peak, but the view's pretty spectacular from up there. On a clear night like this, with the full moon and all, you can see the entire L.A. basin all the way out to the Pacific. Wanta check it out?"

"Love to."

I drove his car on the winding, narrow roads up to the peak so I wouldn't bark up dinner, and I knew where I was going, having come up many times to shoot pics. It was a shame I didn't have my camera with me. Lee and I took the dirt path to the mountain rim and a sparkling sea of glittering gold spread out before us. L.A.'s vastness can only be seen from above, and only on the rare clear days. I often ventured to high place around the city when a storm was clearing or when the Santa Ana's were up to get the full view of the ever expanding menagerie I lived in.

"Oh my god," Lee said softly, standing on the edge of the mountain surveying the scene. "This is surreal. I had no idea this was 20 minutes from my house."

"Yeah, well, don't get too excited. You get this view up here maybe three times a year. The rest of the time it's foggy or too smoggy to see anything."

"Well, it's beautiful now, but fucking freezing," he said as he moved behind me, put his arms around me and pulled me in.

His body warmed me, outside and in. We stood huddled together in the fierce wind staring at the sweeping view of millions of pulsating lights blanketing the earth to the horizon and out to the dark silver sea. The full moon reflected on the Pacific and revealed the broad curve of the Santa Monica Bay.

"Thank you," Lee whispered in my ear.

"For what?"

"For turning me on to things—places, even ideas, ways of thinking I'd never have gotten to on my own."

I turned to him then, gathered his face in my hands and pulled him in for a passionate, sensual, loving kiss, trying to communicate how very glad I was to be with him, how empowered he made me feel, valued, safe in his embrace.

Lee fixed his eyes on mine when we separated, focused all his attention on me, into me. "I love you," he said with certainty.

"I love you, too." The words left my mouth before they processed in my head. But when I heard them, I absolutely believed them to be true.

Weeks passed in a radiant blur, sure to be our glory days, never again this new between us. We explored new places from Catalina Island to Death Valley, or visited favorites, like the outdoor Santa Monica Mall, then a walk along the cliff-side promenade overlooking the Pacific. Sometimes we'd just hang out, watch videos or play Tavli.

He stayed at my house on Friday and Saturday nights, limiting sex to the weekends. It wasn't bad, exactly, but it still wasn't great either with him continually whining over my insistence he use a condom. We'd have intercourse without protection when he pledged his fidelity to me alone, in front of witnesses, along with signing a marriage contract that betrothed his loyalty forever.

Lee became a regular at my family's functions. And we had a lot of them. Birthday parties, Purim, we even joined my sister and her husband for a few Friday night Shabbat dinners. And for the first time in as long as I could remember, they were...if not fun, at least entertaining. I wasn't the odd one out anymore, the single, sad, aging spinster. I was with Lee, and though still on the outside looking in at my family, I too, had a partner to shelter me.

I thought of Lee constantly when he wasn't around— what he'd said the night before that was cute or made me laugh, his adorable baby face, his punk, Cheshire grin. When I'd go shopping with a friend, I'd look in men's wear, buy Lee a sweater I thought he'd like instead of getting clothing I needed. I looked forward to being with him the moment we parted, and felt safe, and on solid ground when we were together regardless of our city crumbling around us.

Mid-March. The days were getting longer, warmer, the Rodney King trial hot, fueled by the media's coverage. Racial tension spiking throughout the city serving only reporters hungry for stories, which ironically they seemed to be creating.

Graffiti covered the sides of most every overpass. KILL ALL WHITE in red spray paint four feet high and ten feet long was scrawled on a concrete wall bordering the 101 as we drove through Hollywood. I looked at Lee driving. He stared out the windshield, either not noticing or at least not acknowledging the threat. He was doing 80mph, weaving smoothly through all four lanes of traffic without braking while managing to keep distance from other cars. Lee was an excellent driver, one of very few I'd known. Still, I thought I might barf passing Tinsel Town on our way to see his buddy, Mitchell, after racquetball on Friday night.

The giant glass cylinders of the Bonaventure Hotel appeared from behind the Union Bank tower as Lee got off the freeway and swung back over it on the 3rd Street off-ramp into downtown. Steel and glass office buildings lined the streets like any other city, but they were dwarfed compared to Manhattan. Between the skyscrapers were old brick buildings, though several of the office towers had been added directly on top of the old structures. But the most bizarre part about downtown Los Angeles was there was no one, literally no one walking on the streets.

It was just past 6:30, and though the sun had set half hour ago the streetlights lit the ghost town in perpetual twilight. Wholesale, finance, light manufacturing and some state offices were mostly what happened during the day in downtown L.A. Depending on what sector you worked determined where you went home to, but no one stayed here. Most restaurants served the lunch crowd and closed at night. Street gangs, homeless, and artists renting lofts were the only consistent residents other than the endless influx of Latino immigrants.

Mitchell's condo was on the 23rd floor of a skyscraper recently built across the street from the Music Center. It had been constructed, along with several other residents like it, when Mayor Bradley got it into his head that he could turn downtown L.A. into Manhattan West. For a year, maybe two, the price for a condo here was sky high, marketed as the new trendy place to live. That's when Mitchell had bought his. Unfortunately, it never caught on. No one wanted to live in a crime ridden, dirty, rat infested city. That's why they moved here from places like New York. The building Mitchell lived in was three quarter's empty. And now he couldn't sell it at even half the price he'd bought it for.

Mitchell shared all this as I gazed out the floor to ceiling windows in his living room. It was dizzying up there. Downtown sparkled, the expansive city beyond twinkling endlessly outward to the blackness of the Pacific. "It's beautiful, Mitchell."

"Well, I wouldn't want to be up here during an earthquake." Lee chimed in from the black leather couch.

"It's built on rollers. I was here during the '89 quake and it just swayed a lot. It's really quite safe." Mitchell handed Lee a can of Diet Coke, then extended another to me. "I wanta move out of here because it's really lonely." Nice looking, mid-thirties with dark brown eyes and brown hair worn short, slightly receding on the sides, Eastern European heritage, maybe ethnic Jew. He wore black jeans and a tight black tee-shirt that showed off his flat, toned stomach and braided muscles of his arms. "There's no one around and nothing to do. It's stupid to go for a walk at night. It's like asking to be mugged. You have to stay in or escape the area. Nothing is open except for the Pantry which never closes and caters to truckers and aging traveling salesman with food like brisket on mashed potatoes." Mitchell stood within inches, gave me an amused smile and sipped his white wine. He was tall, close to six feet and stood straight, though casually, like an athlete.

Lee sat on the couch popping grapes into his mouth, plucking them from a crystal bowl filled to the brim that sat on the Lucite table in front of him. He inquired about Mitchell's new cable TV show focused on the L.A. music scene. Apparently, twenty years playing guitar and a BA in Music Theory didn't pay off, so Mitchell gave up on being a rocker. He went back to school, got a MBA at UCLA and was now using his education and connections to market other musicians.

"Sounds like a worthy endeavor," I assured him, then looked at Lee to confirm but he scowled at me.

"So what's the plan, Mitch?" Lee said. "When are you offing this place and out of here?"

"I should be out by summer at the latest. Looking in the Valley mostly. Studio City area. I want a house this time. Four bedroom minimum. I can cover the down payment with what I get from this place."

"You ready to lay out close to a million?" Lee narrowed his brows at Mitch. "You oughta consider something smaller to start, think about going in with someone, sharing a place maybe."

"Oh, I'm looking to share, with a wife preferably." Mitchell smiled at me then looked back at Lee. "I'm not planning on staying single forever. Four bedrooms is a good starter house. I'm trying to get my life in order, ya know, stabilized. I want to have something to offer a woman when I find her."

"Fancy degrees and family money aren't enough anymore?" Lee shot Mitchell a quick look and they exchanged some shared knowledge then Lee looked at me. He pat the empty place next to him on the couch, like he was calling his dog, his bitch to come. But I didn't.

"So, how will you know when you've found the right woman?" I asked Mitch almost mockingly, it laughable he believed there was such a thing as the one. Lee may be my knight, but only because his timing was right and not because he was the only one for me. Reason assured me our obsessive natures would likely come to the fore again somewhere down the line, but I was out of time to find a man without glaring frailties that wanted to be with me, or to try and establish the intimate connection I felt virtually from the beginning with Lee.

"I don't believe in 'the right woman,' Rachel. I am eternally grateful to my family for showing me what real love is—that it's not a given with a marriage contract, but must be earned. Daily," Mitchell said. "My parents will be celebrating their 40th wedding anniversary in April. My older brother is married ten years and has two amazing kids. My twin sister is married four years now and has two year old twins that I'm mad about. Ask any one of them and I believe they'll tell you they're happy." Mitchell paused to sip his wine. "I hope, well, plan to model my family's examples."

That was probably the highest compliment I'd ever heard anyone say of their family. And I flashed on marrying into a family like Mitchell's that would adopt me into their fold and supplement all that was missing from mine. Lee sat perched on the edge of the couch draining the crystal bowl of grapes. I considered asking him if there was anyone in his family he'd like to emulate, but with what I knew of his history I doubted there was. And though I could sympathize, the notion felt rather disturbing.

"So, we going to dinner or what?" Lee smiled at me with his cheeks full, and vaguely reminded me of a chipmunk.

We agreed on Langer's, one of the oldest delis in L.A., just west of downtown across from McArthur Park. Urban legend had it that every year when they dredge the tiny lake they'd find at least a couple of dead bodies down there, which says something about the neighborhood, but Langer's was the only place open for miles worth eating at.

Lee ordered a corned beef sandwich dripping with jack cheese and mayonnaise. I ordered the smoked fish platter. Mitchell got an omelet, with fruit instead of the hash browns, and he and I shared some of our college experiences, then exchanged stories of our travels around Europe and the Middle East. Lee didn't have much to contribute since he'd never gone anywhere except for Vegas. I tried to orient the conversation to a common thread and focused on TV. Mitchell and I recapped our favorite episodes of Thirty-Something, then critiqued a new cop show, Law and Order, where sometimes the bad guys actually got away with the crime. Lee claimed he only watched Nick at Night, and was rather monosyllabic with his responses throughout the meal. He insisted on paying the bill and Mitchell didn't argue.

The boys sat at the baby grand piano in the corner of Mitchell's living room and played show tunes together. They weren't brilliant, but could follow a song and Lee goaded me into singing tunes from West Side Story, Man of LaMancha, and finally Funny Girl. Mitchell gushed over my voice and picked songs to keep me singing, but when Lee ran through his repertoire and went and sat on the couch, I feigned tired and quit.

"In olden days a glimpse of stocking was looked upon as something shocking, but now God knows, anything goes." Mitchell sang the classic tune with exaggerated cadence as he stood at the piano and played. "Good authors too who once knew better words, now only use four letter words, writing prose anything goes." He laughed and gestured for us to join him.

I joined Mitchell in the chorus but Lee did not. "The world has gone mad today, and good's bad today, and black's white today, and day's night today." We were spot on key and blended beautifully. "When most guys today, that women prize today are just silly gigolos." I stopped singing with Lee's piercing glare.

"And though I'm not a great romancer." Mitchell continued, though toned it down, as if tiptoeing around the lyrics. "I'm bound to answer when you propose, anything goes."

"Will there be an encore or are you ready to go?" Lee kept his eyes on mine.

He gave Mitchell some excuse about being tired and we left. He was silent going down in the elevator and remained so in the car driving home.

"What's going on, Lee? What are you so upset about?"

"Like you don't know." He snapped.

"No. I don't." But I did. I wanted him to talk to me instead of me having to pull it out of him, but he remained silent. "Am I supposed to guess or are you going to talk to me?"

"I saw the way you were looking at Mitchell."

"What are you talking about? I wasn't coming on to him in any way.

We were all screwing around with singing until you stopped—"

"I saw desire," he said flatly.

I flashed on lying then thought better of it. Can't build a foundation on lies. "I'd be lying if I said I don't respect Mitchell's choices, like getting degrees, traveling the world, looking for a house and planning for the future." I saw Lee's eyes narrow but he didn't look at me. "But I don't even know him. He's your friend, Lee. And I'd never date him, unless you like... died or something."

"Oh. So now you want to date him."

"I didn't say that."

"Do you know Mitchell's parents paid for his education, his rent, food, his dates, everything, so he took five years to graduate with a BA and another three on that for his MBA. He bought that condo with daddy's help too. He has a different job every other month. I make more money than he does, by a lot. I've given Mitchell thousands of dollars to get this cable show he told you about off the ground, and a year later I still haven't seen anything. Mitchell is a sponge. He mooches off of everyone."

"Wow. Those are pretty harsh words to say about a friend."

"All I'm saying is if I had the kind of support at home that he does, I'd probably have gone to college, and traveled the world too. I was on my own by 17 and have supported myself since the day I moved out of my father's house."

I felt miffed Lee expected kudos for gambling himself into debt since

I'd been on my own since 19, paid for college and traveling without any support from my family. "Lee, I am not interested in Mitchell." I said with certainty, though part of me knew I'd lied. Sometimes lying helps sustain a foundation.

"Right." He practically whispered then pushed on the CD changer and we listened to The Cars, Heartbeat City as we drove the rest of the way to my house with the music between us.

By the time we pulled into my driveway it was after 1:00a.m. but the lateness of the hour did not dissuade him from wanting to get it on. He got on top of me when we got into my bed and slammed his groin into mine again and again. I felt him get hard, paused our passion to pulled a condom from the wooden box on my nightstand and fumbled to slip it on him but he grabbed it out of my hand and did it himself. He was back on me, and then pushing inside me. Small though he was, it was still quite stimulating with him bumping and grinding against me. I hoped he'd stay inside me, connected, but he lost his hard-on almost instantly, a common occurrence if he didn't get off inside me within moments of putting the condom on. Lee rolled off me.

"I can't feel anything. It's like wearing a fucking glove. I can't feel you. I really hate this." He was mad, shamed. "I don't think I can do this. I can't continue like this. I feel inadequate, and I'm starting to resent you for it. Can we please just do it without the condom?" He wasn't really asking. "I'm absolutely sure it'll be better for both of us, Ray."

'You're not just sleeping with the guy, you are sleeping with everyone he's ever slept with,' the AIDS mantra was in my head, especially since Lee had previously confessed he hadn't worn a condom since high school.

"Look Rachel, if we're building a relationship on trust, you're just going to have to trust that I don't have AIDS or any STDs." He read my mind again. "I trust you."

It was easier to trust me, knowing I'd slept with only five guys in my entire life, all of which had been with a condom. "I trust you, Lee, but I'm pretty sure neither one of us is ready for me to get pregnant?"

"You're right on top of your period. I can always tell."

It was true. And he'd know if I lied just by the timing. "OK, I guess, just for tonight."

Lee rolled on top of me, put his hands on my breasts, leaned on his elbows and stared down at me as he pushed his pelvis into mine. I felt him stiffen and grow. Hard to make out his expression in the dim room but I thought I saw him smile as he entered me. Crushing me under his weight he pumped harder and faster. He came in a surge with a loud grunt. I couldn't wait for him to get out of me, off me so I could breathe. I arched my back and groaned, faking an orgasm, then put my hands on his shoulders and gently pushed him back. He took the hint and rolled off of me. I inhaled and exhaled sharply.

"Thank you." He kissed my forehead and snuggled into me. "I love you. I love the way you make me feel. We're finally on the road to something real. I was starting to think we'd never make it together if we couldn't get it on without a rubber between us."

I practically stopped breathing, the bed beneath me suddenly disappearing and I was free falling. Lee had considered breaking up because he hadn't fucked me to fruition. His implication was skin on skin intercourse tonight insured we'd have a tomorrow. But sex was an immature and fragile thread to hang a lifetime commitment on.

03/27/92

Sex is 5% of the relationship when it's good and 95% of the relationship when it's not.

-

Chapter 23

Saturday morning we headed east on the 134, up the hill towards Pasadena. Sunlight sparkled off most every surface slick with dew. We were on our way to Tucson to see his father and step-mother. The weekend trip was my spontaneous idea, as Lee hadn't ever visited his dad's place in Arizona, even after multiple requests to do so. And Mitchell's laudatory commentary on his family had me wondering the family I'd be marrying into with Lee, the other reason I'd motivated this road trip. It was also an easy excuse to escape my manic city for a couple of days. The escalating violence was invading my psyche of late, igniting my outrage daily with every altercation, especially without weed to disconnect from the anger around me. Reality was becoming too sharp, making me edgy most of the time. And though Lee sheltered me, it was hard to feel safe anywhere in L.A. these days.

We listened to music and chatted in our typical fluid fashion. I avoided bringing up my gnawing desire to get high, scared of Lee acknowledging his, lacking the strength to help him battle his cravings, and my own simultaneously. I didn't bring up last night's sex either, but felt afraid of repeating it. Unwanted pregnancy always haunted me with intercourse, birth control or not. I didn't want a repeat of my mother's early life with an abusive ex-husband who left her penniless with a genetically manic-depressive son.

Crossing the California border into Arizona, Lee expanded on his family history, first recapping what I knew of him growing up in Chicago until his parent's divorce, then about living with his dad in Culver City, a rather rough L.A. suburb from 13 to 18 yrs old. He too was laudatory of his father's achievements— starting his own business from nothing and turning it into a successful freight company.

"But that was years ago." He paused, glanced at me with what seemed like trepidation, then focused back on driving. "My dad was, well, compelled into making a deal with the devil for partial ownership in the Indian Casino he runs now— payback to the mob for gambling debts he accumulated in Vegas."

I think my jaw dropped, but I'm not sure. What he'd just said sounded more surreal than real and I was having a hard time processing it right then. I knew his dad had a shipping company, and had moved to Arizona with his wife right after Lee graduated high school, but that was it. He'd neglected to tell me about his father's gambling addiction. Till now.

"His 'business partners' take most of the profits, but my dad's not hurting, for sure. They set him up in Tucson after he was fired from the company he started for almost bankrupting the business to fund his gamble habit."

Like father like son? but I didn't voice it, nor did he address the parallel. And for the first time in a long time I heard my inner voice sneering at me for getting involved with Lee. "So you're father is in bed with the mafia?" And I flashed on Diane Keaton in The Godfather when she married Al Pacino.

He laughed. "I guess you can say that." He glanced at me with a quirky, guilty grin. "It's ain't like The Godfather, Ray." He chuckled. "The men who funded my dad's casino are legally putting up casinos across the country on Indian land since gambling is legal on reservations if the Native Council says it is. And while it's true these 'businessmen' may straddle the line of the law, they don't shoot people, or leave horse heads in anyone's bed."

His words didn't soothe me. I stared out at the straight highway, the desert around us flying by at 90mph. I'd imagined my partner's father as a doctor or college professor, and a wise, benevolent man at that, but Lee's original portrayal of his dad as a successful businessman sufficed. Though my parents were what society, and even Lee had deemed normal— still married, had remained faithful and coveted the classic parental roles, I was hoping to marry into a replacement family, one that cherished me as I was, as I did them, my husband's parents' moral compasses, and trusted caretakers for our kids. I felt a growing irritation with his revelation that he'd neglected to fill me in on the details of his father's exploits before, though I didn't confront him on his lack of disclosure, afraid of putting more distance between us.

We got into Tucson around sunset. It was windy, dusty, and cold as we crossed the parking lot of the Double Tree hotel and took refuge inside the large room with two double beds Lee's dad had booked and paid for. He'd left a message as well, to meet him at his casino for dinner so Lee could finally see his 'show,' instead of meeting up at the hotel as originally planned. I couldn't help resent the man before I'd even met him for choosing to exploit weakness in others, and modeling addiction to his son.

Lee put on his brights as we blazed through the black desert, lighting up the highway and scrub brush a few yards beyond, occasionally swerving to avoid a large tumbleweed that escaped the bramble along the side of the road. We continued along the arrow straight highway for about twenty minutes then came upon a huge sign in the middle of nowhere, blinking in five primary colors, ten feet across and at least six feet high flashing Apache Palace * WIN! WIN! WIN! * Bingo * Slots * Poker *

The huge dirt parking lot was packed with cars. The building looked like a re-purposed supermarket. Rectangle box, flat roof, glass front. Christmas lights were still strung around the top of the building, or perhaps they were a permanent part of the façade. Inside was dense with cigarette smoke which mingled with the stench of stale fried foods. At least three hundred people sat at fifteen or more long folding tables with benches on both sides, arranged in rows that took up most of the enormous, brightly lit room. Everyone had bingo cards in front of them and several neon colored, fat-tip felt markers. Food was strewn about in the center of the tables and most everyone was munching something greasy, from burgers to nachos dripping with orange cheese. Hardly anyone noticed Lee and I enter, seemingly focused on their game.

Along the back wall in the center of the room was a small stage with Christmas lights strung along the base of the deck. A man, a mix of Jackie Gleason and Vito Corleone, maybe 5' 9", at least 300 pounds, wearing a loud-print Hawaiian shirt and navy slacks stood on the platform yelling letters and numbers into a mic in an excited tone. He waved when he notice Lee and I by the entrance. The MC was Al, Lee's dad.

A few people in the crowd yelled "BINGO!" and held up their colorfully marked cards. Al handed the mic to his slender wife, easily twenty years his junior with a bad blond dye job, then came off the stage and went to each of the winners. After examining their card carefully he scrawled his initials flamboyantly across each with a big red marker. His gestures were gregarious, overly congratulatory though they'd won all of $10 bucks. He absolutely waddled when he moved. His eyes were narrow and sunken, his mouth tiny on his round face. He was sweating and panting when he finally approached us with a wide, welcoming grin.

"Good to see you! Glad you made it. Well?" His father gestured with both hands at the scene, like we were supposed to be impressed by all of it or something. Lee squeezed my hand before unlacing our fingers to shake his father's extended hand. I made a mental note they didn't hug. I didn't want them to, the notion they were close was horrifying right about then. Lee introduced us. I stuck out my hand to shake Al's and avoid anything more intimate, and managed to refrain from wiping my palm on my jeans to rid my hand of Al's sweaty touch.

Lee's dad suggested we have dinner at the 'lovely buffet' there, since he had to work tonight with the regular MC out sick. He lead us behind a floor to ceiling smoked glass patrician that blocked off a twenty foot wide area along the right side of the room. Slot machines lined the walls, and several small poker tables were stuffed inside this separated area. The 'buffet' was towards the back, and consisted of five metal pans filled with food floating in oil under hot lamps.

I fixed myself a small salad from the wilted lettuce in the bowl next to the bins and joined Lee and his dad at one of the four sticky plastic booths along the sides of the enclosure. Lee had a heap of greasy brisket on his plate, piled on top of mashed potatoes. Al had a large pile of spaghetti topped with meat sauce surrounded by several pieces of garlic bread. Father and son discussed Lee's business a few minutes then his dad moved the dialog onto his casino.

"This place is a gold mine. The Indians own 51%, making gambling legal on reservations since the casino is majority owned by the natives. I own the rest with some Vegas investors."

"Most Native Americans on reservations live meagerly on government subsidies. Why would they want to promote gambling to their own people?" I wasn't exactly trying to be contentious but didn't care if I was.

"Casinos are big business. Very profitable for everyone." Al sat across from us and glanced around the room as he continued. "Every resident on this reservation gets a monthly check from the profits made here."

I could see the large room though the glass partition. Mostly round, reddish-brown faces with rather blank expressions framed by straight dark hair streaked with gray. Most were over-weight and over 40, with bad teeth, and in worn clothing. "These people don't look like they're rolling in dough to me."

Al smiled a thin lipped grin. "It really is a shame with these folks. Ninety five percent of them are here every other night blowing their profits hoping to win big. Everyone's looking to get rich for doing nothing." Al shook his balding head. "Only one a night wins the $150 tournament game. The average loss weekly is over $300 bucks." He looked around the room again slowly, nodding and smiling at the few who caught his eye.

"Knowing this about your clientele, why do you provide them all this?" I felt Lee tighten next to me. He took his arm from the back of the booth behind me and held his tea with both hands.

"I'm offering entertainment, like television or the movies." Again Al gave me his thin lipped smile. "In fact, this casino is the only entertainment for miles around, especially since they don't even get cable out here."

"These people are schmucks." Lee said flatly. "They bought into a casino on their vast wasteland of property blinded by grand presentations of projected profits without considering the only clientele within thirty miles were their own people. With nothing better to do they come here and gamble away their minimal net profits after the investors takes their loan payment and grossly inflated operating costs. How exactly does this casino serve the Native Americans on this reservation, dad?"

"I'm not judging these people, son," Al defended. "Gambling is a personal choice. I chose to give it up a long time ago. When I retired from shipping I was approached by some club owners in Vegas to go in on this bingo deal, and after reviewing the financials I jumped at the opportunity. I'd have been a fool not to. These places really are gold mines."

Beyond a liar, the man clearly had no moral conscience.

Lee sighed, shook his head, took another bite of his brisket with a blob of mashed potato on top. Al segued the conversation to the home he'd recently had built, and raved about the growing opportunities for great properties in the area. Lee's stepmother, Betty, came over and introduced herself, hugged Lee with a warm hello then shook my hand with a friendly smile. She wore a rather loud, floral-print dress with a thick white plastic 60s-style belt pulled tight around her narrow waist, the gathered fabric making her breasts seem larger and hips broader than they were. She was sparkly and light, more mobile home park than city or suburb. We talked about virtually nothing for the next ten minutes, then Al and Betty went back to work after arranging where to meet for breakfast in the morning before we headed back to L.A.

I stepped out into the cold, crisp desert air and it felt like the entire building had been lifted off my shoulders until Lee took my hand. It was sweaty, like his dad's had been, and sent a cloying chill through me. I was glad when he released me when we got to his car.

He pushed in a Brian Ferry tape as we drove back to the hotel. Most times listening to music was a shared experience, but tonight it felt like a sound wall between us. Lee stared out at the highway, the high beams spotlighting only the road directly ahead in the vast darkness. He seemed a million miles away, and I felt afraid to engage him, of what he might say. Defend his father and I'd resent him, and feel even more afraid of his lineage than I already did.

'You don't just marry an individual, you marry their family,' echoed in my head as we came into Tucson. It was just after 10:00 and I didn't want to go back to the hotel straight away with even the possibility of getting into sex right then. I suggested we go get some dessert before going back to our room, perhaps a better forum to engage in sensitive dialog rather than in bed together with our sexual history to date.

It seemed the only thing open in all of Tucson was our hotel coffee shop. The short, slender, 30-something, dirty blond, deeply tanned hostess/waitress took us to a booth in the back and we ordered tea and two slices of lemon meringue pie.

"God, my dad looks terrible. He's gained so much weight. He looks so...old, and he's only 63. I'm really worried about him." That was all Lee had to say about the scene we'd just experienced.

"Well, maybe suggest he put less greasy food and more fruits and salads in his buffet. That may be a place to start." I was trying to be helpful, but got I wasn't when he looked at me and narrowed his brows, exasperated.

"He's always been overweight, but not like this. Ever. Pudgy, soft, like me maybe." Lee flashed a wayward grin. "But never fat like he is now. God, shoot me if I ever go there."

"No worries. I'll keep you on your toes." I smiled.

"You already do, my dear." Lee smiled. "Thank you for being here." He squeezed my hand, as if hanging on for dear life.

The waitress came back with our teas and pie slices. Lee lifted his fork as she set the five inch high piece of lemon meringue in front of him, took a big fork full and stuffed it in his mouth. And I flashed on Lee at 63 looking like his old man since they possessed the same short, bulky stature, and the propensity to...overindulge. He took another big bite of pie, opened wide and swept it off the fork and into his mouth, then slowly chewed, savoring the flavors as only connoisseurs of sensation do.

I nibbled at my piece of pie, the meringue rubbery, the lemon filling old and thick enough to cut, and listened as Lee regaled me with his family history. Betty had been his dad's secretary in his freight business from it's inception in Chicago. The last seven years of his father's marriage to Lee's mother, Al and Betty had been having an affair.

"My mom must have known. My dad would take off for days, sometimes weeks. My mom started drinking, was sullen all the time, got really distant. My father finally left her for good to be with Betty. He never paid a dime of support, left my mom basically broke, which is why I had to move to L.A. with him since she couldn't afford to take care of me and my sister on her own."

"Did you want to move in with your dad?"

"Not at first. But I had no choice really. I was 13, and my mom seemed perfectly fine to get rid of me. Not a lot of love lost between us to this day. I've always loved my dad though. He gave me a home, and helped me out in some really tough times. He gave me my career. Betty has always been really supportive too. She's a good lady."

A good lady? Somehow I doubted it. She was a willing participant in an affair that eventually tore Lee's family apart. I didn't challenge his comment though. About the last thing I wanted to do was hurt Lee. It wasn't his fault his step-mom was an adulterer, or that his father was a pig. Genetics were the luck of the draw, the ultimate gamble for us all.

I suggested indulging in the hotel jacuzzi before going back to our room. Close to an hour later when we got out of the hot tub we were both completely drained. We cuddled in bed for a few minutes, then Lee fell asleep. Perfect. I told myself the image of his old man would fade with distance and time, but I knew I was lying. Incorporating Al into my extended family image was simply inconceivable.

Lee was gone in the morning when I woke up. I checked for a note, then the bathroom, then the hotel gym and when I couldn't find him I went back to our room. He was setting a tray with two cups of tea and two bear claw donuts on top of the dresser.

"Hey beautiful." He smiled, kissed me quickly and handed me a cup of tea. "So, you ready to get out of here?" He took a big bite of a bear claw then handed the other to me, but I declined, though it did look yummy and tantalized. "It's really good. You sure?"

I nodded, busied myself packing my backpack so I couldn't see him stuffing lard and sugar in his mouth so early in the morning and right before breakfast. Lee was still somewhat...soft, and could easily go back to the Pillsbury Dough Boy look if he kept eating fatty foods without restraint. In April, my father was having his second bypass surgery in just four years, and I flashed on my mom harping on him with virtually everything he put in his mouth. How terrible it must be to live in fear of your husband's premature demise from his inability to control his obsessions.

We met Al and Betty at a deli in the north of town for breakfast. His father had ordered platters of smoked fish, bagels, fruits and sweet rolls. Betty hugged me like I was one of the family. So did Lee's dad, which wasn't a good thing before eating. Al bragged about the new casino they were planning for another reservation near Sedona. Betty was demure when she spoke with humbled pride of her secretarial job at the casino and helping Al on the floor at night. Something about her irked me. Maybe it was her frigid demeanor, or the way she'd applied her makeup— a thick foundation and cherry red lipstick made her seem like a mannequin. I got the impression that if we were in Nazi Germany she would be your best friend right up until the time she was turning you in.

"Much of my success I owe to my beautiful wife here, though it took me a while to come around to that. Betty's my little good luck charm." Al put his arm around his wife's slender shoulders and Betty smiled modestly as he squeezed her to him. "She's stuck with me through thick and thin."

Why Betty stayed with Al was a mystery to me. He was bottom of the barrel and I was sure the woman could have done much better.

She wasn't stupid, and I suspected was never desperate to mate since she claimed she had no desire to have children.

Two hours later we left the restaurant after Lee and his dad stopped arguing about the check, which his father eventually paid. We all hugged goodbye which creeped me out but I tried to shake it off in the car, actually glad to be heading back to L.A.

"God, he is such an asshole!" Lee pulled from the parking lot mad as hell. "Did you see the way he said, 'Of course all casinos are fixed,' like he was proud of it. I wonder if he ever stops to think about anyone but himself. I am so glad that I'm nothing like him." He shook his head. "He paid for everything, ya know. The hotel, breakfast this morning. It makes him feel like a big man throwing money around. It is so petty."

Lee insisted on paying for just about everything we did together. Another parallel to his father. And the foundation we'd been establishing seemed to be crumbling beneath me. I stare out the windshield so Lee wouldn't see my doubt.

"I know what you think of him. I know you think he's disgusting. To be honest, most of the time I do too." He sighed heavily.

I wasn't sure what to say, afraid of hurting his feelings any more than I unwittingly already was. "Well, Betty seems nice. And your dad's clearly successful. He seems like an intelligent man." That was about all the positives I could come up with, that were the truth anyway.

"Oh, he's smart alright. He knows how to screw you in a thousand different ways. Reminds me of the gun dealer who says he's not responsible if the gun he sells is used to kill innocent people. Right. Like what did the salesman think the guy was going to use an AK47 for, hunting Bambi?"

As he ranted, the image of Al faded, and I saw only Lee, the man I knew him to be— smart, compassionate, moral as his actions, words and passion attested. His thick, chestnut hair tussled onto his shoulders. It framed the profile of his soft but sculpted features and hung in the long dark lashes of his green eyes.

"Maybe you're like me," I joked to lighten him. "And you too were secretly adopted." Then I took his hand and held it to connect us. "And even if we are genetically linked to our parents, it doesn't mean we have to be like them. We are who we choose to be." But the line sounded right out of a movie and I knew it was bullshit. Reality is, most of us grow up to emulate our parents. Except I wanted my kids to be better than me. (And their kids better than them and so on, each generation healthier, stronger, smarter, extending life longer, giving us more and more time to maximize our potential and not only survive, but thrive.)

-

Chapter 24

Lee's friend Mike was coming into town from the bay and staying with Mitchell for the weekend. Lee invited them both to come by his place on Saturday night. Like Mitchell, they'd attended high school together, but Mike was a "techno geek," had gotten into Stanford and never came back to L.A. I invited Suzanne to join us. She declined, until I told my roommate about Mitchell's cable show. Network. Network. Network, I reminded her. By the end of the week two more of my friends and two more of Lee's had been added to the guest list.

I'd never hosted a gathering before. Neither had Lee. It kind of felt like our coming out party as a couple. I was excited, but nervous. The crowd would be diverse and I hoped everyone would get along. Saturday we shopped for three hours and Lee spent over $300 on party foods and liquor.

We spent the afternoon arranging platters of snacks. Jon was bringing the trendy new game Pictionary. My girlfriend, Lavonne, had just broke up with Joe again and was on the prowl. She brought the game, Scruples— a quick way to get into someone's psyche, she'd said. Lee had loaded the ten disc CD changer with everything from rock to pop to punk. Pizza rolls were still in the oven when Mitchell and Mike arrived.

Mitchell greeted me with a kiss on the cheek in the fashionable L.A. way then went into the kitchen to get a beer. Lee introduced me to Mike, who shook my hand while his eyes walked all over me, then he focused back on Lee.

"Hey, dude, Mitchell and I are looking to chill tonight. You got anything green around?" Mike was only a bit taller than Lee but slender. His hair was flat brown and cut short but unkempt. Beyond his wire-rimmed glasses, his eyes were brown, set rather close, pug nose, his features unremarkable. "I spent the last week trying to wow VC for funding and I really need to put a buzz on."

"No, Mike. I told you I quit for a while. I wasn't bullshitting." Lee looked at me and rolled his eyes.

"Well, can you call your neighbor then?" Mitchell was back, beer in hand. "Ask him if he'll sell us an eighth or something?"

"Carl only sells quarters, Mitch. And it's damn expensive, $80 or more." Lee turned away to open the door and welcomed in Jon and Lavonne. He greeted Jon with a shake of hands and Lavonne a kiss on the cheek upon my introduction. I kissed and hugged them both and led them into the living room.

"Hey Mike, you wanta go in on a quarter then?" Mitchell said loudly.

Mike took out his wallet. "I only got $45 on me. Can you cover the rest?"

"Yeah, I think." Mitchell looked in his wallet. "Hey Lee, loan us twenty bucks, would ya?"

Lee gave a sardonic laugh and shrugged. "I don't think Carl's even home you guys."

"Just try, dude, that's all we're asking," Mike insisted.

Lee looked at me as if to say, 'What else can I do?' then took out his wallet. "Can't this wait until later?" Lee handed Mike a $20.

Mike took the money, added it to the money he had in his hand and pocketed it. "Just call him, will ya?"

The doorbell rang again and Lee welcomed in Suzanne with a quick hug then went into the kitchen to get the Pizza rolls from the oven. I led my roommate into the living room and introduced everyone, including Mitchell who still lingered with Mike near the kitchen, clearly more interested in scoring than talking.

"Can you make that call to Carl like now, dude?" Mitch suggested.

The doorbell rang again and I answered it. Lee greeted a young married couple with handshakes and hugs then introduced, Shelly and Steve, associates he knew through his business. Shelly was eight and a half months pregnant and looked about ready to pop. I lead them into the living room and introduced them to my friends. I took drink requests and Lee and I went into the kitchen to pull beers and pour wine. The guests exchanged small talk but not as much as I'd like. Everyone seemed to be listening to Mitchell and Mike pester Lee.

"Should I just go next door, knock on the door and tell him I'm a friend of yours?" Mike asked.

"No, Mike. Not cool." Lee handed me a couple of beers which I delivered to Jon and Lavonne sitting on the couch.

"Then can you just make a quick trip over there?" Mitchell pestered.

Lee looked at me exasperated as he handed me the white wine he'd poured for Suzanne. "Me casa a su casa, everyone," he announced. "Please help yourself to food and drink." Then his eyes locked on mine. "I'll be right back," he said softly. "Come on Mike." And he went out the front door with Mike in tow.

Mitchell stayed a few feet from the door. I sat on the bench for the synthesizer, drank my Diet Coke and listened to people chat as I tried to rationalize Lee going to score. Shelly was closest to me, sat on the chaise lounge that extended from the couch, holding her pregnant belly. I inquired about their coming baby, but it was hard to pay attention looking at the door every other second hoping to see Lee come back in.

Lavonne saved me by joining into, and then taking over the conversation. Bless her. I watched my friend tuck a loose strand of her curly dark hair behind her ear and focus her blue eyes on Shelly, the way she used to look at Jon when he mattered to her, and me sometimes when I do. Her friendly, freckled face smiled a lot and laughter came easily and reflected her lightness.

Suzanne talked to Mitchell still standing near the kitchen. Jon and Steve were equally engaged. I smiled, glad for the scene, except for my missing boyfriend. Ten minutes later Lee and Mike returned. Carl came along too and brought this hippie-type couple, easily in their 60's, he claimed were his parents. I introduced myself, unsure if he was joking. Carl had shoulder length blond hair, blue-eyes, was tan and built, and beyond just a weed dealer, a big-wave surfer, he claimed. And he knew the best waves from the Wedge to Montecito so he wasn't a poser.

Lee joined me on the bench after he got himself a Diet Coke, his small condo quite crowded by then. "Hi." He leaned over casually and kissed me.

"Hi." I felt mad at him, but wasn't sure why. The noise level escalated substantially with the new arrivals and it was hard to hear Brian Ferry singing Don't Stop the Dance.

"You got any rolling papers, Lee?" Mike came out from the kitchen with a Heineken in hand.

"You're not smoking that in here." Shelly said, rubbing her swollen belly.

Mike just stared at her, and Lee didn't say anything, so I said, "Of course he's not going to smoke it in here. Right, Mike?" I glared at him.

"Oh, yeah." Mike finally said. "Right. Of course. We'll use the balcony. No problem." He looked at Lee. "So, what about those papers. Can you give me a hint or should I rummage?"

Lee had his poker face on, looked at me and shrugged. "I might have some papers in the junk drawer, the big one at the end of the counter."

Mike went to rummage. I looked down, embarrassed by the scene. Minutes later Mike, Mitchell, and soon-to-be-dad, Steve, went out to the balcony to share a joint. Shelly scoffed, shook her head, mentioned since pregnancy her husband had agreed to quit using around her, and was livid with him when the boys came back in, wouldn't let Steve touch her when he sat next to her and tried taking her hand. I wouldn't want to be in their car on their way home tonight.

Lavonne suggested we all play Scruples, ostensibly to unite the crowd. Everyone joined in. We made up our own rules, had everyone draw one card and answer the questions. And Lee and I agreed on most every answer except for the last one.

"If you could be anyone besides yourself for twenty four hours, who would that be?" Lee read his card aloud.

From Carl's 'mother' to Shelley, every woman there said they'd want to be a man for a day. Some said a famous man, some said any man, but each of us sought the experience of what it felt like to be male. In contrast, there wasn't a man in the room that wanted to be a woman. Not even Lee. Every guy there said some famous rock or sports star, or some macho movie star, or just plain rich, Mitchell added.

"I never want to be a woman." Lee said definitively. "Men have all the advantages. We get to have kids without the hassle of periods or the pain of childbirth. We don't have to choose between work and family, and even without a degree we make more money, and have way more career and advancement opportunities. We don't have to get off the ladder of success and wreck our earning potential to be the primary caretaker, so we never have to be dependent on anyone else to get by. I don't know why any man would want to be a woman, even for a day."

I looked around the room. Every guy was nodding and smiling. My skin prickled. Lee was right, of course. Men still ruled in our society, and the sexual equality I thought reachable in my lifetime suddenly seemed light years away.

Everyone mingled after playing Scruples. I sat on the edge of the coffee table and talked to Jon and Lavonne until I noticed Lee out on the balcony with Mike and Mitchell. I excused myself and went to be with my boyfriend, praying he wasn't getting high. He saw me coming towards the glass door before I reached it and smiled at me as I joined them.

It was cold out, the air full of mist and the sweet scent of weed. I actually salivated, my desire for a hit keeping my eyes on the joint like a mooching dog as Mike passed it to Mitchell. Lee leaned against the wall of the balcony, seemingly not partaking. The tall pines behind him bent in the breeze and I shivered, then moved in to snuggle. He hugged me, then released me.

"Why don't you go back inside and get warm." Lee said softly, like it was a suggestion for my welfare instead of the dismissal it was.

I looked at Mike and Mitchell, then back at Lee standing next to me. "Join me?" I suggested casually.

"Give me a minute. I'll be in soon." He smacked me on the ass playfully as I turned to go back in.

I glared at him as I went back inside. I thought I may cry, so I went into the kitchen and started cleaning up to avoid interacting. There was no way to tell if Lee was getting high with his friends, but it was likely he was. I too, wanted a buzz to achieve that sublime lightness, focusing on enjoying the moment instead of the dissolving grand plan of my life. But I'd made a promise to myself to quit, as Lee had to me. And I had every intention of keeping my word, though the smarter part of me knew it absurd to expect that of Lee.

I heard the three of them come back in a bit later. Lee didn't join me in the kitchen. He stayed in the living room and socialized. Suzanne was the first to go, giving Mitchell her number before leaving. She started a trend and by 3:00a.m. everyone had finally left.

"God, I thought they'd never leave." I shut the door on drunken Carl and his spacey parents.

"Me too. I think everyone had a good time though." Lee stood at the kitchen threshold staring at the mess in the living room. "Let's leave it for now. We can clean up in the morning." He held out his hand to me.

I hesitated, considered asking him if he got high with Mitch and Mike but didn't. I was too afraid he'd broken the pact between us, or knowing he lied if he used and said he didn't. I moved to him, took his hand and he led me up the stairs to his bedroom. I noticed the paperback of Lonesco's Rhinoceros on his end table as he gathered my face in his hands and kissed me.

"I'm not ready for sleep just yet. Wired from the party, I guess." He pressed his groin into mine and I felt his hardness, his intention now obvious. "See what you do to me?"

"More than happy to be with you, sweetie, but if you want to be inside me we're going to have to use a condom." After last weekend's adventures with his family, and tonight imbroglio with his friends, the idea of reproducing with Lee suddenly seemed...icky.

We had sex with a condom, but it took him quite a while to get off, leaving me raw inside. I lay next to him, staring at the ceiling. He rolled onto his side and looked down at me. I rolled away, onto my side so he wouldn't see my face and snuggled back into him to conceal the distance between us. Lee spooned me and whispered sweet nothings in my ear. He rambled on about our kids to come; Sara's graduation with her MBA from Stanford; Kyle finishing his doctorate in biology at Berkeley, on track for working on a cure for cancer.

Icy shards prickled my scalp and the distant voice of intuition pierced my consciousness denying I'd ever have children like these with Lee.

"So, when Kyle is 13, do you think he'll be a typical rebellious teen?" Lee continuing to play our now familiar game. "Or will we be privy to his life, among his trusted confidants?"

"I plan to be," I said wistfully, longingly. My vagina burned and it was hard to get into the game right then but I played anyway. "I'll do my damnedest to stay connected to my kids, and to prove to them again and again I can be trusted to be there for them."

"My kids?" Lee teased, sort of. I was sure I caught an edge in his tone.

"You know what I mean." I hadn't, couldn't say our kids.

"Good night." He rolled onto his back. Within a minute he was asleep. I stared at the ceiling. He'd scored for his friends tonight, most likely used with them. And though getting high 'occasionally,' didn't bother me, I knew that simply wasn't possible for Lee, or me. It was just a matter of time before he'd score for himself again. And I would have hated him right then for being the addict he'd denied he was, but I hated myself instead for believing him when I knew I shouldn't have.

-

Chapter 25

"So what did you think of Lee?" I asked Jon a few days after the party.

"I thought he was really nice." His tepid response was telling.

"Come on, Jon. Let's hear it."

"What do you want me to say? I liked him."

"But...?"

"Well, if you really want the truth, I don't see you guys making it for the long run."

Ouch. "Why?"

"I don't know, Ray. He seemed smart, like you said, but not as smart as you, intellectually, I mean. But that's not really the thing. It's like, when we talked he was trying to figure out what I wanted to hear instead of giving me his opinion. Like he knew you'd be asking me what I thought of him and he wanted to make sure I liked him. You know what I mean?"

"I guess. I'm not sure. Extrapolate."

"He's a consultant, essentially a salesman, right?"

"Right."

"Well, he's a damn good one if you want my opinion. All I'm saying is watch out."

"Watch out for what?"

"That he ain't selling you a bunch of crap. That what he says and what he is aren't two completely different things. I don't know. I just got the feeling that what I was looking at wasn't the full picture with Lee. Be careful. Anyway, I thought you weren't attracted to short, heavy-set guys."

"I'm usually not. I don't know what it is about him J. He makes me feel really special."

"I bet."

"What's that supposed to mean?"

"That's what makes him such a great salesman. He tells people what they want to hear. Look Ray, I don't want to see you get hurt. You had a lot of good reasons for your reservations. Why don't you have them anymore?"

"I do. I just want to give him a chance. You're the one who is always telling me that I expect too much from the men I date."

"That's true. Well, you know him better than I do. He seems nice enough, I guess," Jon said. "I hope he turns out to be everything you need. I really do. I want to see you happy with a good guy. You deserve it."

"And you don't think Lee is that guy?"

"I don't know him well enough yet. Just take it slow is all I'm suggesting. Get to know him through what he does, not what he says. That's going to take some time so try not to jump into this with your heart. Use your head." He was giving me the same speech I usually gave him, except I would say his dick instead of his heart. "You know all of this," he continued. "Do yourself a favor and take your own advice."

"Are you telling me I should walk away from Lee?"

"No. You asked me what I thought and I gave you my initial observation. I'm sure it's tainted by what you've been telling me since you met him. Maybe I'm even a little jealous you're falling in love, and not with me." He was trying to be kind, not a familiar space for Jon and he sounded corny instead, but I smiled at his attempt anyway.

4/13/92

Potential, like Intentions, or Love, are meaningless unless put into action.

Two weeks after our party, I was in bed writing in my journal and watching the KTLA Morning News. CHP officer Theodore Briseno was testifying against fellow officer Laurence Powell for beating Rodney King in clips of the ongoing trial when Lee called. Shelly gave birth to a healthy girl the night before and he suggested we go see the baby on the weekend. I'd never been a enamored with infants, often fretting over the early stages of parenting, concerned how I'd manage slobbering, smelly, crying newborns that couldn't communicate beyond screaming. But I agreed to go. I wanted to see how Lee would be with a baby.

Saturday evening we were on our way down to Shelly and Steve's house in Long Beach listening to the Pretenders. I looked at Lee focused on driving. His face was fuller, like when we first met, making his features seem rather puggish, and I caught a glimpse of his father's profile, and felt nauseous.

He insisted on getting dinner before seeing the baby. The only place open in downtown Long Beach was a small steak and seafood place across from the harbor. During the work week the streets of the second largest port in the country were filled with foreign sailors, contractors and day laborers, but like downtown L.A., at night and on the weekends the place was deserted.

The restaurant was practically empty except for the bar which was filled with local boaters knocking back beers and shots. Lee and I sat across from each other in a dim booth, a candle in a red jar flickered on the table between us.

As a starter Lee ordered a bowl of clam chowder and a side of mushrooms in garlic and butter. After finishing those he moved on to a full rack of beef ribs. He was enraptured as he consumed each bite. Red sauce dripped down his fingers and coated the sides of his mouth. He ate like an animal devouring a fresh kill. I felt sick watching him eat. His gorging scared me. Like my mom with my dad, I'd likely spend a lifetime on Lee's case to control his eating. And I wanted to smoke a joint so bad I could taste it.

Pay attention! Intuition herald, though I didn't want to hear it. Lee wasn't overweight because of his ex-wife, but probably had been, and would be for life. I counted every morsel of food I put in my mouth since losing weight in high school. I'd had bouts with Bulimia to purge myself from my lack of discipline, and Anorexia to prove to myself I could control my own behavior. I played racquetball not for the love of sports, or even the game, but for the calorie burn. I absolutely refused to go back to being heavy like I was growing up, not only because thin was in, and forever will be, but letting myself get fat again was wearing addiction on my sleeve, and I absolutely needed to achieve more than the sum of my weaknesses.

"So, what do you want to do tonight after we see the baby?" Lee asked, licking his fingers. "Personally, I'd like to go back to your place or mine, smoke a joint, hang out and relax." He didn't look at me. He gobbled a huge bite of potato salad.

"Okay..." My skin prickled. "I was thinking about a movie or something like that." I kept it light, assumed he was just sounding off, inside my head again, joining me in my cravings. "We can stop at Blockbuster on the way home, pick up a video and watch it at my place."

"What I really want to do is go home, call Carl and score, get high with you over some backgammon, maybe take a jacuzzi later as a prelude to unencumbered sex." He said it matter-of-factly, his poker face on.

"You're serious." I practically whispered.

"Well, yeah. Look Ray, we've been straight for almost four months now. And that's long enough for me to decide I like stoned better. I mean, being straight is fine, not an issue while I'm working, but in the evenings sometimes I just want to relax and smoke a joint. And I don't see what is wrong with indulging occasionally."

"You promised me you'd quit using. You gave me your word, Lee. Or was that just rhetoric to get me in bed?" I shook my head. "I assumed you were good to your word and ready to grow up."

"You know what happens when you assume..." but he didn't finish the idiom aloud. "Exactly how long was I supposed to quit to prove to you I'm not addicted to weed? I told you back in January it wouldn't be forever and I'd go back to indulging occasionally."

"Three and a half months straight after a lifetime of using is nothing. I thought the point of quitting was to prove to me and yourself that you aren't addicted. You go back to using now and you're proving you are." I couldn't watch him stuff another forkful in his mouth so I stared down at my plate scattered with greens from my Caesar salad. And I don't even like salad. "You just don't get it, do you?" I felt like crying.

"What I get is that you're trying to be controlling. Look, let's just forget it for right now and go see the baby. I don't feel like getting into it, okay?"

It wasn't really a question. He picked up the bill. I took it away from him, laid some money on the table and we walked out. We didn't say anything on the ride to Shelly and Steve's. We cooed over their infant for a half hour or so, which was surprisingly cute with his tuft of blond hair and wide blue eyes, then sat around and talked about nothing for another half hour and left.

The atmosphere was thick between us in the car. He blazed along the 710 at 80 mph, pushed in The Cars Heartbeat City CD and didn't speak. I didn't either. It felt like if I said anything at all he'd come undone.

"I think I'm just going to drop you off at home." Lee finally spoke as we passed Griffith Park. "I'm feeling really tired and I want to get to sleep. We'll talk in the morning, okay?"

Again, I knew it wasn't a question. I tightened inside, fear and outrage vying for position. "Lee, is it all about the chase for you?"

"What?"

"I mean, did you just want to prove to yourself you can get anyone you set your mind to by telling me what I wanted to hear? Or were you for real about wanting to be with me?"

He sighed heavily. "No, my dear. It's not about the chase. I really want to be with you, Rachel. But sometimes I get the feeling you don't really want to be with me. The way you were looking at me over dinner. I know you thought I was being a pig. You don't like what I eat. You don't want me getting high. You insist on a condom between us." He sighed again. "Look, forget it. I'm just tired. It's late. We can talk about this tomorrow."

I felt myself shriveling inside. I sat statue still hardly breathing, scared to speak, afraid he'd leave me forever if I uttered another word. I'd expected him to stay, like any Saturday night, hold me, spoon me, assure me everything was okay. I wanted him to want to change, to work at becoming what he'd promised me.

Lee turned into my driveway, pulled his Mercedes only up to the front door walkway, put it in Park and sat sullen behind the wheel.

"Are you sure you don't want to come in. I'll be nicer." I gave him a cheeky grin but he didn't acknowledge it.

"I just need some space tonight, Ray. Let's not make this into more than it is." He slid his hand around the back of my neck and pulled me in for a kiss, heartfelt but quick. "I'll see you tomorrow. We'll talk then. Okay?"

"Okay." But I still felt afraid. I wanted him to be the man to save me, provide the life and family I sought, be my knight, or at least to still believe he could be.

"Goodnight."

"Goodnight." I hesitated, then opened the car door and got out but turned back and bent down to see him. "You know Lee, there are moments I really love you."

He focused on me then and for a second I felt our connection. "To be honest my dear, moments may not be enough." His face hardened into his poker expression. Then Lee disconnected again, leaned over and shut the passenger door then backed out of the driveway.

I watched him pull onto the street and drive away, then went into the house, shut myself and Face in my bedroom and cried my eyes out. Lee was right. I was a judgmental bitch. He'd merely expressed the incessant desire for weed I too had been battling, and I'd indicted him for it. And even if he was suggesting he 'indulge occasionally,' would that really be so bad as long as it wasn't around me, or our kids.

Accept Lee for who he was or lose him. Lonely loomed, black and choking. My sister was right. I found fault with everyone I dated, from the pragmatists for being too detached, and quite frankly boring, to the creatives for being neurotic egomaniacs. Chris was right. We're all screwed up and I expected too much. And my parents were rightly enamored with Lee. He was the best thing I'd found in seven years, with an even more powerful connection than my childhood affections for Michael. And I prayed to hope I'd not chased him away.

It was lightly sprinkling, and what should have been a fifteen minute drive took almost an hour in crawling traffic to get to Lee's place. A black BMW with tinted windows crept alongside me like a spider. We jockeyed for first position in our respective lanes for a mile or so but when the Beemer's lane opened up allowing it to move ahead, it stayed pacing me.

Fuck. All I needed was to get shot before telling Lee I was sorry for tonight, for everything I'd done and said. A bullet to my head now would be a B-movie at best, a footnote among many between the headlines of the violence erupting all over L.A.

The BMW's driver and back windows opened simultaneously. Faces of at least three white boys looked comic green in the twilight from the headlights and freeway lamps. The guy in the back seat held what looked like beer bottles in both hands, an offering to me apparently, and yelled "Party! Party!" The driver and passenger pointed at the road sign for the Forest Lawn exit and yelled what looked like "Follow us!"

Trapped by the SUV in front of me and their Beemer on my right, I ignored them. Then one of them appeared through the sunroof, his body emerging from the vehicle to his waist. He waved wildly and when I continued to ignore him he threw a beer bottle at my car. I swerved into the breakdown lane and slammed on my brakes to avoid the bottle hitting my windshield, the car behind me just barely missing slamming into me. The BMW screeched away, the guy in the sunroof flipping me off as they went.

I tried to let go of my outrage as I stood at Lee's door and knocked. I thought I smelled pot, but then figured it must be his neighbor, Carl.

Lee opened the door and the smell of weed came rushing out into the hallway. "Hi. What are you doing here?" he asked casually, his green eyes glassy. When I didn't say anything he moved aside to let me in. "Come in if you want to."

"You're getting high," I managed.

"Yeah. Want to join me? Come in!" He gestured toward his living room.

I still didn't, couldn't move. It felt as if my blood was boiling. I didn't say anything in fear I'd come undone if I opened my mouth.

"Look, are you going to come in or not because I am not going to stand here with the door open for very much longer." He didn't say it mad, he spoke very matter-of-factly.

"I am afraid to."

"Afraid of what? Of pot? Of me? Of yourself? What are you afraid of, Ray?" He asked, more annoyed than anything else.

"I am afraid of you. I am afraid of myself. I am afraid if I come in I'll walk out high tonight and I don't want to get high anymore."

"Then don't. I'm not going to force you. Just come in. We can talk inside."

I heard the elevator ding, his condo right across from it. When the elevator door started to open I went into his flat. Lee shut the door and went into his kitchen where a bunch of weed was scattered in a box top. He glanced at me with his poker expression, completely disconnected, then went back to rolling a joint. I just stood there like an idiot watching.

"So, why are you here?" he asked as he licked the rolling paper and refined the joint between his fingers. He raised it in a toast at me before he stuck it in his mouth and sparked it. He took a deep hit, his expression taking on his Cheshire grin as he slowly exhaled.

I flipped. I smacked the joint out of his hand. Hard. It went flying into the living room and landed on the carpet still burning. Lee ran to get it. I went into the kitchen and wiped the counter clean in one pass. The buds of weed in the box top flew everywhere. "You fucking liar! I came over here to apologize to you, thank you for abstaining the last three and a half months, congratulate the achievement and beg forgiveness for denigrating it earlier. I came to give you the out with weed, to use occasionally if that's what you need, but you've already taken it. For how long, Lee? When did you go back to using? Or did you ever quit? And thanks for cluing me in mother-fucker!"

Lee ignored me, went in his kitchen holding the joint he'd retrieved then got on his knees to collect the buds scattered on the floor.

"I was straight up with you from the very beginning. You knew I didn't want to be with an addict. You promised me you were everything I've been holding out for. What happened to that?" My words pouring from my mouth like water through a dam. "I told you I need to be with someone disciplined, that I'm an obsessive like you, but you swore to me you weren't. Well, eating whatever you like without restraint isn't making me fat." I couldn't stop even knowing I was hurting him. "You said you were ready to grow up. You promised me you'd get your money shit together. How is blowing who knows how much on weed, and hundreds weekly on art you don't need and books you don't read getting it together?" It was a rhetorical question. "And how do you afford whatever your whim when you're $360,000 in debt?" I knew the answer to that too, but I managed to shut up.

"My money issues are not your concern, or at least they shouldn't be. I've treated you nicely, and that's all that matters." He didn't say it angry. He collected the weed from the floor and dropped in the box top.

"You really don't get it, do you." I stared at him in bewilderment but he didn't even glance at me. "If we're together, working towards forever, then every part of your life concerns me, from your addiction to weed, to your obsession with food, to your money problems. All of it. I'd hope my issues are of equal concern to you. I'm looking for total disclosure, complete transparency, not as a concept, a nice idea, but for real. I told you all this back when we first met, and again when you wanted to move beyond friendship. I thought you got it."

He took another hit off the joint and silently collected buds of weed.

I wanted to kick him in the head to get his attention but continued ranting instead. "And I'm not half as mad at you as I am at me. I'm an idiot falling for your crap, for not listening to my intuition when it told me you were just a good salesman, even to yourself— living in delusion about who you imagine you are but will never be."

"I'm not delusional, Rachel." He glanced at me then, his expression filled with arrogance and anger. "I'm your goddamn mirror, sweetie."

"Well, at least you got that right. And I'm yours, honey, reflecting you on your knees to obsession, modeling who I don't want to be, or be with." I walked out. Stormed out actually, slamming the door behind me.

I stood outside his door for quite some time, shaking, debating whether to go back in or not, hoping he'd come out, beg me to stay, agree to quit using again, call it a 'slip.' Maybe I was making a big deal out of nothing. Even if he was addicted to weed, if he was fully-functional, able to handle finances, family, and me, what did it matter? And I wanted to believe it, but didn't. My obsession with Lee was born out of desperation, in search of someone to save me from myself. I scoffed and shook my head at my idiocy, then pressed the down button on the elevator and when it opened to collect me for the third time, I got in and went home.

The red light on my answering machine was blinking when I got back after midnight. "Hi," Lee's voice sounded sad, not angry. "God, I guess I really blew it tonight. I know I promised you, and more importantly myself that I wouldn't get high and I blew it. I guess I am just not ready to quit yet. I know that's not what you want to hear. I don't know what to say to make things right between us. I'm sorry I let you down." He stopped, and I thought he hung up because there were several seconds of silence. "Call me. We need to talk." He paused again, then added quickly, "I really do love you, Rachel. Call me. Bye."

I dialed his number straight away, but hung up before connecting. My mind raced. I wanted to tell him I loved him and we would work things out together, but couldn't fathom how. He could never achieve the stability I sought in a partnership. He chose home alone to get high instead of being with me tonight. He'd choose using again and again over me. He had no intention of quitting weed. He didn't care about staying in shape, eating right, living healthy or getting his finances together. It was just a matter of time before he went back to gambling, assuming he wasn't doing it already. Lee was an addict, and I'd known this about him from our first phone conversation. Choose to stay with him and I'd have to settle on always being second to his siren of obsession. And my intuition clearly trumpeted, *You don't need Lee.*

4/16/92

Instant gratification is a hallmark of childhood, and addiction.

-

Chapter 26

The usual Sunday morning religious crap was on at 5:00a.m. *Meet The Press* came on PBS at 6:00, with legal experts discussing the Rodney King jury now in deliberation. When they showed the video beating for the fifth time in ten minutes, I flipped through the nine stations again.

I sat in bed, desire waging war with reason in my head. Shadows from old oaks and pines moved across the lush green of my neighbors manicured front lawn as the morning passed. It got harder to breathe with each passing minute I didn't hear from Lee. I was into my fourth rerun of Star Trek, The Next Generation when the phone rang around noon.

"Hi." Lee practically yelled into the phone.

"Hi. Where are you?" I heard traffic in the background.

"I'm at a phone booth somewhere in Griffith Park. Rode my bike here early this morning. I was up most of the night trying to figure out how to fit into— live up to who you want me to be." He didn't say anything while a blaring siren passed. "But I can't. You were right from the beginning. We shouldn't be together if you can't accept me as I am."

My breath caught in my throat. "Just tell me if you think I was wrong last night."

"This isn't about right and wrong, my dear. I'm not who you want, Ray. You've made that abundantly clear. And I don't see the point in pursuing a relationship from here. Do you?"

Yes! No. Vertigo. I felt like I was suffocating, drowning, falling down,

down, down into blackness. Until that moment I'd assumed it was my choice if we stayed together but realized right then he was ready to walk.

"Look, the bottom line is I need to be with someone who respects me and I don't feel you do. I don't see where we can go from here without a foundation of mutual respect."

"I respect you, Lee, in a lot of areas, from your business savvy to your generosity. If you're looking for blind adoration, I can't give you that."

"And I can't give you the security you're looking for. I'm not that guy with the supportive family who traveled Europe while going to college and now has a budding white-collar career. I'll never have a king for a father and I'll never be a valiant prince."

"I'm not asking you to be. I just want you to work at becoming who you promised me. Relationships are about compromise, Lee."

"Right back at ya, sweetie. I love you, Rachel. I want to be with you, but as me, not trying to be who you want me to be. And addict or not, you're right— I will rarely be a model of restraint since living on the edge of contained is infinitely more entertaining than taking the conventional route." There was levity in his tone, I felt it through the line, and couldn't help smiling, again reminded of the basis for our deep connection. "I like who I am, Ray. I'm sorry you don't."

I sighed heavily. "I love you, too, Lee. But I will always want to be more than I am, and want to be with a partner who does too." Regardless of the media rhetoric of the woman's role in society, or what my friends did, or my family thought, continuing to distort reality/intuition with desire/desperation suddenly didn't seemed doable anymore. Sadness consumed me, but I knew accepting Lee unconditionally would leave me constantly wanting. It was the life I already had, and Lee, in fact nobody, could save me from it... but me. "So, that's it then? We're over?" I heard my words as if someone else had spoken them. Life without Lee, letting him go completely was simply inconceivable, beyond withdrawal, on par with death.

A horn blared in the background and Lee was quiet for what seemed a long time. "I don't want to lose you, Ray, not after how far we've come. We can still be friends, or at least play racquetball if you want to..."

"I want to." And I want you to fight for me, be everything you promised me, or at least try to be, but I was pretty sure I didn't say it.

"I don't want to come to Passover tomorrow, though. It'd feel to weird if we're not together anymore, and I don't want to pretend."

"Okay." I pictured my mother's pinched expression and felt the lump rising in my throat, choking me as I considered Passover at my sister's without Lee.

"So, I guess I'll see you on the courts on Wednesday at the usual time?"

His promise we'd see each other sated me a bit. "Okay," I murmured.

"I wish it could be different between us."

"Me too. Makes me very sad." I tried to control the quiver in my voice.

"Me, too. Take care and I'll see ya Wednesday then." He didn't say anything else but stayed on the line. "Please hang up first," he finally said.

"I can't. I'm too scared." I need you. Please covet me, love me, shelter me.

"It'll be okay. I swear. You don't need me, Ray, or any man really. I honestly believe you of all women can thrive on your own, you just don't believe it yet. Follow your passion. Stick to your vision and create the life you want. You can, ya know. I promise." He paused, perhaps to give me a chance to respond, but I had no idea what to say to his cheerleader rhetoric. "I'm hanging up now." But he didn't. Finally he said quickly, "I'll see you Wednesday. Bye." Lee disconnected.

I held the phone trying to fight the rising panic that I was now only two months outside of 34 years old, and once again on my own, with no one, alone.

"If you wish to make a call, please hang up and dial—" I finally hung up with the recorded woman's voice reminding me my connection with Lee was over.

-

Chapter 27

"I just wanted to let you know that Lee isn't coming tonight," I told my sister on the phone the next morning.

"Why?"

"I don't think we're gonna make it. I need more than he can offer right now…probably ever."

She sighed heavily. "Whatever. But what I don't get why you keep sabotaging relationships, especially at your age."

"Carrie, there's a lot you don't know about Lee. He's not what he portrays himself to be."

"Nobody is, Rachel." She scoffed, like I was an idiot. "Larry and I think Lee's great. What's so bad about him?"

Ah, the critical question. Tell the whole truth and it was over with Lee for ever. "Lee's a gambler, like Aaron, mom's first husband. He owes close to half a million in back taxes to the IRS. He went bankrupt five years ago and has no credit, and no savings, but continues to spend money lavishly instead of paying off his debt. He's an obsessive, just like me, except he doesn't control his behavior, virtually ever. So, does Lee still seem like someone I ought to be setting up house with, Carrie?"

"Aaron Flint was a manic-depressive abuser, which is why mom left him. His gambling was only a small part of his issues. I don't get that Lee is violent or depressive."

Like my parents, my sister was so convinced I should to be with someone, she didn't really care who or what he was. It was devaluing in the extreme and I got mad. "Lee's a stoner, Carrie, an addict. He's been getting high since he was 12 years old and for the most part uses every day of his life. Is that a good enough reason why I shouldn't be with him?"

"Oh," she said. "Why didn't you tell me this about him before?"

"I don't know," I lied. "I thought we'd be able to work it out together, that I could help him grow up." A rising lump in my throat prevented me from continuing.

"I can't talk to you about this now." Her kids were fighting in the background. I heard dishes clacking and then Larry yelling at the kids to shut up. "I have twenty five people coming here tonight and I'm totally busy right now."

"Twenty four."

"Oh yeah. The table is already set for Lee. I'll have to change it, or you can when you get here. Come around 3:00. You can help me finish cooking and we can talk then. Okay?"

"Okay. See ya around 3:00."

I got to Carrie's just after 4:00. On my way to her kitchen I said "Hi" to the kids who barely acknowledge me, mesmerized in front of the TV watching Rugrats. Maria was washing dishes. Carrie was putting a matzo kugel in the oven.

"Hi. Sorry I'm late, but I had to finish a job that had to go out today. What can I do to help?"

"It's done," she remarked, clearly pissed off I was an hour late. "I have to go upstairs and get changed so we can't talk now," she said as she left the kitchen. "Oh, would you go take Lee's place off the table. I didn't get to it."

"How do I know which one it is?" I yelled after her as she went up the stairs.

"Read the seating cards." She disappeared into her bedroom. I went into the living room. Carrie and Larry, Lee and I were seated at the smaller table, set up in a T against the long table. I took Lee's setting away and almost crumbled, repeatedly swallowing back the lump in my throat so my sister wouldn't see me cry. I was going to look pathetic sitting alone at the head of the table with my sister and her husband. My mother and father were at the end of the long table. They'd have a perfect view of their daughters. The winner and the loser. Just great.

Walking into the kitchen with the place setting in my hand the doorbell rang. I handed the dishes to Maria and went to get the door. Enter mom and dad.

After kisses and hugs my mother looked around and asked, "Where's Lee?"

"He's not coming." I left it at that. She didn't.

"Why not?"

"We broke up."

"Why?"

"I really don't want to get into it, mom, okay?"

My niece and nephew came in to greet their grandparents right then and saved me from the third degree. I went upstairs to avoid them all. Carrie was putting on her makeup in her 'dressing' room the size of my bedroom. "Mom and dad are here."

"I heard. What'd you tell mom?"

"That Lee and I broke up. And I would prefer you didn't tell them what we talked about this morning." Just in case Lee and I ever got back together...

"I won't," she said to my refection in her wall to wall mirror. "I've been thinking about what you said this morning. Is Lee using affecting your sobriety?"

My sister, like my parents assumed I got clean in MA and never resumed using. Since I was back to abstinence, I answered with certainty. "No."

"Well, then I guess it goes back to what we've talked about before. You're never going to find the perfect guy, Rachel. Most men are boys at best, cloaked in bravado, and ego that needs massaging virtually daily. You've told me Lee's a successful businessman, and he can afford to support a family. Well, you can't. He treats you nicely, and he seems to genuinely care for you. I can see why his getting high scares you. But not everyone's an addict just because they use drugs. I mean, most everyone drinks, or is taking something to help them cope, or sleep, or function."

"Carrie, why are you pushing this relationship so hard?"

"You're almost 34 years old, Rachel, and you haven't had a real relationship since Michael. Lee is the first man in a long time you seemed to like that likes you. You hardly have any time left to meet someone and have a family. Do you really want to risk spending the rest of your life alone and childless while you search for a perfect fit that doesn't exist." She focused on me in the mirror. "God, I'm sorry," she said turning around to my tear streaked face. "I just want you to find someone to share your life with, have kids and be happy."

"I know," I practically whispered, wiped my face, looked at myself in the mirror and wanted to cry again. My eyes were red-rimmed and surrounded in darkness, my entire countenance looked so very sad. We heard the doorbell ring and then people coming into the house greeting each other.

"I have to go downstairs now." She stared at me. "You gonna be okay?"

"Yeah. I'm fine." I wasn't though. I couldn't swallow back the lump in my throat threatening to suffocate me.

"Good. Wash your face and try to look happy. I worked really hard on this dinner and I want it to be special for everyone. Please don't be sad in front of my guests." She didn't mean it mean. Carrie was just that way. Totally and completely self-absorbed. If what she'd said of most men was true, she and Larry were merely two sides of the same coin, and yet another relationship I had no intention or desire to emulate. She was probably right that the partnership I envisioned didn't actually exist yet.

She left the bathroom and went downstairs to greet everyone. I heard more people coming in and the crowd downstairs grew noisy with gaiety. I ran some cold water in the sink and stuck my face in it, wondering if one could drown themselves in a bathroom sink. Dead— feeling no more felt eminently more attractive than my daunting future right then. I kept my face submerged until instinct took over and I stood up gasping in fresh air. I buried my face in one of her plush purple towels, then combed my hair and looked at myself in the mirror again. My eyes still looked puffy and sad, but I plastered a smile across my face and went down to join the happy crowd.

After a few brief exchanges, I hid in the kitchen and helped Maria put the finishing touches on dinner. It felt like if I opened my mouth I'd start crying, which I was desperately trying to avoid. I didn't want to spoil my sister's party. We all took our seats and Carrie started the two hour service. Twenty minutes into it I couldn't sit there another second as the only single adult at the table, and subjected to my mother's sympathy every time she looked at me. I went into the bathroom. Tears came immediately. I stayed in the bathroom for a good fifteen minutes, finally got the crying under control, rinsed my face off yet again, and then went into the kitchen to make myself a cup of tea. My mother came in a few minutes later, her pinched expression plastered on her face.

"What is going on with you?" Her words felt like projectiles. "Your sister worked very hard on this dinner. Do you really want to spoil it for her?"

"No, mom. I'm sorry." I preferred her 'don't ask, don't tell' policy better. I didn't say anything. I felt small enough as it was.

"Is this about Lee?" She stood two feet from me. I moved to the counter and sat on it to put distance between us. She followed me over though, stood directly in front of me so I was trapped up there on the counter top.

"I thought you weren't seeing him anymore."

I felt tears welling. Damn. "I'm not." I'm back to alone. "I'm not seeing anyone." I fought to not to cry, swallowed hard, wiped my eyes with my palm. "And I'm scared out of my mind I'll be alone forever, mom, and miss the chance to have kids, have a family of my own." I couldn't talk anymore. I sat there and cried.

"Ah. Rachel Lynn..." She sighed. Her expression softened as she watched me, though her eyes were hard to see with her glasses reflecting the kitchen lights. "Then I have only one question for you."

I suddenly felt trapped, though I don't know why. Whatever she asked I was going to lie anyway. "What?"

"Do you want to fix it with Lee? Because if you can, maybe you should. I was so pleased to see you with someone. You seemed to have such a nice connection."

"My issue with Lee was never our connection."

"Well then, maybe it's time you focus more on the positives between you. Your dad and I thought Lee was great. And he was clearly enamored with you. And at this stage in the game, dolly, maybe you should learn how to be more accepting." Her typical lemons into lemonade response. "My beautiful baby, you'll never find someone to be with by critically examining everything."

"That's not fair, mother. You don't understand who Lee is—"

"And I don't want to know." She folded her arms across her chest, leaned back against the butcher block behind her. "Let me tell you something about relationships, missy. They aren't supposed to make your life harder. They're supposed to be a calm harbor, someplace you feel comfortable, and secure in. We all want a safe place to come home to. If that can't be with Lee, then stop wasting energy on him and go out and find someone who will be a haven for you, and to whom you can provide the same."

"That's exactly what I'm trying to find, mom. And I've been looking for like a decade now." I shook my head and looked away, feeling the distance growing between us. According to my mother, I was still single was because I was being unreasonable wanting more than what I saw of most marriages. I sighed. "I really have to get out of L.A., to someplace less expensive, less pretentious, like up to the Bay."

"There's nothing in San Francisco that isn't here, except family and friends that loves you. How can you move from your home, from people who care about you, away from your sister and the kids? You can't be part of their lives hundreds of miles away. And wherever you go, you take you with you, dolly," she sniped, again implying her daughter needed fixing.

What I don't take is you, but I didn't say it, of course. "Carrie's kids don't need me, mother. They hardly know I exist." The kettle whistled, which stopped me from deconstructing her Pollyanna version of our family dynamics with facts.

She straightened, stared at me through her thick glasses. "Get yourself a cup of tea, go wash your face, put on a smile and then join us in the living room please." She moved aside so I could move off the counter. When I jumped down in front of her, she gave me a hug. It took all my will not to start crying again, and maybe she felt that because she quickly released me, held my face in her hands just a moment, and turned away and went back to the party.

I got my tea, washed my face and went back to the table. Carrie was leading the crowd in song. She didn't look at me when I sat down. She kept a smile on her face as she strummed her guitar. My mother stared at me with concerned contempt. I was spoiling Carrie's big night. Larry sat next to me. He poured me a full glass of wine when we got to the part in the service that honors 'the fruit of the vine.'

"Go ahead. It will make you feel better, swear to God," he whispered.

Anything to make Carrie and my mother happy. I practically gagged as downed the entire glass after the prayer. Larry filled my glass almost to the rim again, looked at me and grinned. He poured another full glass for himself too. I finished the second glass by the end of the second prayer. He filled my glass to the top again for the third prayer. After the toast I drank that one too. By the time dinner was served I was feeling fine. Actually, to be more precise, I wasn't feeling anything, which was fine with me. I chatted amicably with the guests, played Nintendo with the kids, sang with my sister after dinner. Everyone was entertained. My mother was pleased with my performance. My sister was glad I'd "snapped out of it."

I stayed until dessert was finished and the liquor buzz all but gone, and was the first to leave my sister's party. Like a mouse in a maze, I ran down the halls of my brain as I drove back to my empty house, my empty life, searching for something to save me from the descending darkness.

Later in bed, I wrote another personal ad for the Daily News:

Attractive, passionate, creative pro, 33, SWF, seeks SM who thinks with his brain instead of his dick; who wants a wife that's more than a doting mother who doubles as his whore; a man looking to be challenged to achieve more than he can conceive, and who's grown up enough to understand commitment and compromise are vital for a lasting relationship, and is ready to practice both.

The actual ad I placed in the paper the following morning simply read:

Attractive, passionate, creative pro, 33, SWF, 5'7", 135, active and in-shape seeks professional, kind, attractive, thinking SM, 30-40 who is ready for the real thing.

I hoped my vague and limited descriptors, along with nixing the anger would broaden my response rate. The rest of the day until late that night, then up again at dawn on Wednesday I focused on the direct mail campaign I was creating, meant to soothe the ruffled feathers of customers who would lose half their services, and be charged for the rest, when my credit union client merged with Bank of the West. Beyond feeling small and slimy, Lonely lurked, black threatening to consume me. The only thing that held it at bay and allowed me to function was meeting Lee for racquetball later in the day.

He was on the court, volleying with himself, but when I came through the heavy door he stopped. "Hi." He stood in the center of the white walled room, already sweating, his gray t-shirt saturated around the collar. "You okay?"

"Yeah." I was humbled his first words were concern for me. Seeing him on the court per usual, it was as if nothing had changed between us. "You?"

"I guess. What do you say we play for points today? I think you're ready. Don't you?" He bounced the ball on the floor with his racquet after delivering the challenge. He wore a poker face but I was absolutely sure there was humor in there.

I slipped on my glove, twirled the cord at the end of the racquet around my wrist as tight as it would go and gripped the handle. "Is it important?"

"Not important. But it could be educational, ya know, see how far you've come. One game for points. How about it?"

He slaughtered me, placed the ball everywhere I was not, commanded center court and had me running the entire game. I didn't get one point. I'd known he was better than me, but I had no idea Lee could play that well. Easily an A player, he'd been dumbing it down for me. And I got mad. I insisted we keep score the next game too, to prove to him and myself that I could challenge him, if not with control, at least with endurance. I didn't want to give him an excuse to stop playing ball with me. I didn't want to lose him. I played as focused and hard as I could. It took me until our third game to get any points, and game after game I never got beyond ten before he took me.

A knock on our door two hours later didn't stop us from playing but then two big guys barged through the heavy door and claimed the court as theirs. I retrieved my wallet from the wall cubby as Lee went out. I met him in the hall, watched him towel off sweat.

"Well, that was educational. I learned I'm still an oafish clown at this and you're some ace pro."

He laughed, threw the towel around the back of his neck and held the ends as he looked at me. "You are no clown at racquetball, my dear. If you were, I wouldn't waste my time playing you. I'd put you up against any solid B player, and I'm talking about guys. When you're focused you touch A sometimes, more and more actually."

"Not enough to beat you."

"You already have, honey." Lee stayed fixed on me a moment then bent to put his towel in his gym bag. "Truth is, you'll be able to take me in racquetball sooner than later if we keep playing."

"I'll be here, if you will. I love playing with you." I gave him a shy smile, hoping he got the double entendre.

He smiled but it faded as his eyes drifted to a couple at the other end of the hall going into a court. "I'd do a soda but I've gotta take off. See you here Friday?"

"Yeah." Disappointment mingled with exhaustion and I leaned into the wall behind me for support. I'd hoped to hang out after playing, possibly find a space to be friends again. "See ya Friday."

"Good. Look forward to it." Lee picked up his gym bag, put the strap over his shoulder then walked away, waved without looking back as he went down the hall and disappeared past the entryway.

I missed him the moment he was gone, and would have pined for him all night long had I not seen him lighting a joint as he drove by me on his way to exit the parking lot. It sparked a Pavlovian carving for a buzz, but also reminded me that weed was one of Lee's many obsessions that ignited mine, confirming why it unwise for us to hang out anymore.

-

Chapter 28

Got home from racquetball, flopped on my bed and flipped on the TV. A middle-age White male reporter spoke in this very excited tone "—that two of the three cops were acquitted of all charges, and one was acquitted of all but one charge in which the jury was hung." He stood on the steps of the L.A. courthouse yelling over an angry crowd. "We are expecting an official statement from Mayor Bradley on this obvious miscarriage of justice..."

I switched the channel. Another reporter standing outside the Simi Valley courthouse was repeating the verdict. He spoke in the same amped manner, like he couldn't get the words out fast enough.

"We're all shocked. This is unbelievable," the young, White reporter exclaimed. "I don't know about you folks out there, but after seeing that videotape there is no doubt the police used excessive force. The results were obviously prejudiced by the all White jury in this upper middle class neighborhood of Simi Valley."

So much for unbiased reporting.

It got worse station to station, minute by minute. The press retried the case, live, and found the jurors guilty of racism, the courts suspect of jury rigging for moving the venue, and convicted the cops for excessive force. Reporters stated opinions as if facts, made Rodney King into a hero, even though he was a violent, thieving drunk.

Click. On ABC a bunch of people were shoving each other in back of a reporter speaking excitedly into the camera, and a part of me hoped that reporter would get his head bashed in. My phone rang and I clicked off the TV.

"Are you watching this?" my mother asked.

"No, it was making me ill so I turned it off."

"Well all hell's breaking loose downtown. They just dragged some poor man out of his truck, and there's a bunch of Black men smashing his head in. Oh my god…" her voice trailed off. Someone on my mom's TV in the background was screaming, "Terrible, terrible pictures! The only thing this guy did was enter the area. Being White is his only crime!"

I couldn't resist. Click. POV from a helicopter, circling above a red

Mack truck stopped in the center of an intersection. A White man was on the ground, on his knees a few feet from the open door of the truck. Several Black men moved around him, then one ran up behind him and slugged him in the back. He stumbled but managed to get to his feet, then another Black guy came up and pitched something into the side of his head.

"Ah! The man is down again!" the reporter yelled over the thrumming chopper blades as the Black guy pranced away with his arms in the air like Score!, both hands flipping the bird. "What was that?...Some sort of rock, possibly a brick," the reporter mused as camera pulls in on the man laying in the street, blood now appearing near his head on the pavement.

"Can you believe what is happening here?" I'd forgotten my mom was on the phone. "I don't want you going out tonight. They're dragging every White person out of their car. Stay in your house. Do you hear me young lady?"

"Mother, no one is dragging everyone anywhere. The media is sensationalizing this to death." I sat on the edge of my bed feeling my blood boil witnessing this beaten, bloody man on the ground reaching out for help while passersby just watched him.

"The man is obviously seriously wounded. And no one is helping him," the reporter yelled as camera pulled in closer on the guy's bloody face. He grasped at the air as if he was blind. Some Black guy stood just beyond the man's reach, filming him.

"What is wrong with that cameraman?" I seethed, disgusted. "Why isn't anyone helping this guy? What the hell is wrong with these people!?"

"Listen missy. Black people are very upset right now. And they have a right to be. We all saw that tape, what those policemen did. They deserved to be punished and weren't."

"Rodney King is an asshole, mother, a violent felon, arrested multiple times for beating on women and robbery. This is a guy who clearly doesn't give a shit about anyone but himself. I don't know what really happened that night from what we saw of that video. Every one of those jurors saw that tape in it's entirety at least five hundred times. The public saw a five second clip from the media's point of view. I wasn't in that courtroom, mom. And neither were you."

"I know what I saw," she said definitively, which was good enough for her.

"No, you don't. That's my point. And even assuming a miscarriage of justice happened here, then we have the right to peacefully protest the ruling, even file a civil lawsuit, but it doesn't give anyone permission to arbitrarily attack people. And the press, and our dear mayor, don't have the right to yell fire in the theater because they don't like the outcome of this case. There must be a better path to justice than inciting a riot."

"I'm not going to discuss this with you now. You always make things so complicated. Don't go out tonight. You hear me? Stay home! I'll talk to you in the morning." She hung up. No, "bye," or "chow." Just click.

"...No police or emergency personnel on the scene. None have been seen anywhere in the area," said the reporter in his voice-over commentary with camera still on the bloody man as he slithered on his back towards his big rig. No one helped him. Two Black women casual glanced at him desperately groping for his truck door as they walked by.

And I wanted to hit those bitches in the head with a brick right then. These people weren't human, and didn't deserve to exist among our race. OUR race. The Human Race.

Click. I flipped through the channels, hoping the beating was an isolated incident. Another helicopter's POV of a bunch of Black guys kicking another White guy on the ground. He lay faced down several feet from a white truck stopped in an intersection, the truck door open wide. A Black guy in a white t-shirt and black cargo pants ran up to the guy on the ground, lifted something large over his head then threw it down on the defenseless man.

"Oh no! NO! He's bleeding, unconscious in the street," voice-over of reporter as the scene unfolded. "Hit the siren, Doug." What sounded like a police siren goes off. "Ah, this is tragic. The man is unconscious in the street. And people are still coming up and throwing things at this poor individual, whose only crime is being White."

I stared at the screen, my growing horror overshadowing even my outrage. This was beyond crazy. This was L.A. What happened to the paradise I grew up in, filled with casual, friendly, sun-drenched locals co-existing in racially mixed neighborhoods. My public schools were predominantly White, but there were Blacks, Asians,

Latinos. L.A. had never been divided by race— only income. Until now.

"Ah, no," the reporter said. "They're taking everything from his truck. The man is being looted..."

It was surreal watching a Black guy bend over the beaten man on the ground and lift his wallet from his pants pocket then run away. Several other Black guys were coming out of the back of the truck carrying stuff, running past the driver still motionless in the street.

"This isn't happening," I heard myself whisper. "This can't be happening."

Hal Fishman on KTLA news was in studio talking to reporters stationed around L.A. "What's that, Carlos?" Camera back on their trusty reporter in front of the L.A. courthouse. "Okay. We're getting some live reports down the street at the Criminal Courts building of rioting. What?... Stay with us folks. We're live and unedited here...Yes. Yes. It's been confirmed. A riot has broken out at Central and Vermont. We're sending a sky unit there now...And wait! A woman has been shot in a drive-by in East L.A. at Lincoln..."

Click.

I flipped through every station including PBS, hoping one station had the sense to be showing Rosanne re-runs, but none were. Finally I turned it off. The silence that followed sucked me in and I stared blankly into space. Blackness descended, not the usual suffocating shroud of Lonely, but the bottomless pit of hopelessness.

I tried to work, lay out articles of drivel on loan rates and housing

314

starts, and why in this depressed economy it was a good time to buy. Bankers were on par, maybe even more self-absorbed than thieving Rodney. They worked the system to legally steal. And I was helping them. I shook my head, disgusted. The notable artist and quotable writer I sought to become to contribute to our evolution was a delusion of grandeur. I was just a narcissist, and like most everyone else merely a cog in a twisted system beyond my influence.

The most powerful craving to cop a buzz that I'd experience since quitting consumed me. I needed to disconnect from the piercing, ugly reality. One call and Lee would bring over some bud. I'd have my best friend back to thwart the blackness. We'd get lost in playing Tavli the rest of the night— unplug from the world outside gone mad. I stared at my phone on the end table. Just pick up the phone...

Stay in that room another minute and I'd have called Lee. I abandoned work and took Face for a walk. It was almost 9:00 by then, a warm spring evening, but outside was eerie. There were hardly any cars on the road and almost no freeway noise, which was very strange, since no matter where you live in L.A., you can always hear the constant thrum of traffic.

Face went bouncing around from yard to yard, lost in the smells of squirrels, and mice, and pee from other dogs, happily searching for a playmate. Why couldn't people be more like my dog? What is wrong with us? Where was our compassion, since we all knew sadness, loneliness, fear? I felt tears flow down my cheeks. Stop it! I dried my eyes with the back of my sweater sleeve, but when I blinked more tears fell. Don't do this! It doesn't matter. It won't affect you if you don't let it, I told myself, many miles, and light years away from the madness downtown.

"FUCK!" I yelled at the top of my lungs. I turned around, walked back to my house and curled on my bed in shame. My outrage, my anger towards the ignorant that were rioting and looting— reflected them.

I woke to sirens at 7:00 the next morning and lay in bed listening to one after another blaring in a rush somewhere. The newsletter needed to go to the printer by 4:00p.m. Fed-Ex. I should have been out of bed already but felt afraid to get up. I lay there half awake, trying to pretend that it was just another sunny day in L.A., then my phone rang.

"Hi." Lee said. "You alright?"

"Yeah. How about you?" I managed, my heart suddenly beating fast and loud, reverberating in my throat.

"Yeah. Well, sort of. Are you watching the news?"

"Nope. What's up?" I got out of bed, went over to the drafting table, and started organizing what needed to get done.

"Turn it on. They're burning down L.A. You won't believe what is going on out there."

"I don't think I want to know."

"Just turn it on. You've gotta see this."

I retrieved the remote and flipped on the TV. KTLA usually had comedy news from 6:00 to 9:00a.m. Not this morning. All the usual faces were sullen. SkyCam was showing buildings on fire from the chopper's POV. Roving street reporters were filming hordes of Blacks and Latinos stealing everything from electronic equipment to bags of groceries. Some had backed their cars up to broken windows and were cleaning out the store fronts, then driving away. No police were around, which the reporters boldly announced from one location to another. The way the media was showing it, it looked like we were living in Beirut.

"Can you believe this?" Lee asked.

"Yeah...No...This is too weird." I stood glued to the set showing a helicopter's perspective of a huge warehouse engulfed in flames somewhere near LAX. "Oh my god, I know where that is...Shit! Lee, I've gotta call my printer. The warehouse they're showing is right near his shop. I'll talk to you later, okay?"

"Yeah. Call me back after you talk to him, assuming you talk to him."

"Okay. Bye." I hung up and dialed Lloyd.

"Southland Printing." Lloyd's son and business partner answered the phone.

"Steven! You're there."

"Rachel?"

"Yeah. You guys okay down there?"

"For this minute we are, but the police came by and told us to lock up and get out. We're shutting down the presses right now. Don't send the job today. It's gonna have to wait."

Great. For the first time in eight years in business on my own I was going to miss a deadline. "Yeah, okay. Do you know how long you'll be down?"

"I don't even know if we'll have a place to come back to. They're burning down buildings two blocks from us."

"I know. They're showing it on TV now. Are you guys insured?"

"Not for civil unrest. Look, I've gotta go. We were supposed to be outta here an hour ago. Call back tomorrow. Hopefully, we'll be back up by then."

"Okay. Hey, Steven, take care. Be safe out there."

"Right. Where is safe now exactly?" Steven gave a quick, sardonic laugh. "Take it easy, Ray."

Lloyd and his son Steven ran a small print shop in the middle of industrial Inglewood. They'd started out small, had recently expanded and even took on a few employees. Black and Latino employees to be exact. They worked long hours, were honest, good people and didn't deserve this shit. Why anyone would want to hurt them was beyond me, and cut deep, like someone stabbed me.

Don't do this. It doesn't matter. Don't care. And the powerful craving for a buzz teased my pleasure centers again, testing my resolve to stay sober to this sharp new reality. One call to Lee... Then it occurred to me I was going to be late delivering to my client, so I called them instead.

"We're sorry. Because of the riots we will be closed until further notice," the recording said. "Please leave a message. Beep." I left a message for my contact explaining the hold-up in completing the job and promised to call back with any updates.

On TV Skycam's POV was showing thin plumes of smoke rising into the orange sky throughout the city as the camera panned from downtown to the coast. The phone rang again startling me from the strikingly bleak image.

"Hi." Lee. "Is your printer alright?"

"Yeah. He had to close though. I can't get a hold of anyone at the credit union either, so I guess I'm off the hook for today."

"Me too. They've stopped all trucks and trains coming into the city so I had to tell my clients they won't get their freight on time. Not a good morning. The dickheads looting and rioting are totally screwing with my business. I don't give a shit what their problem is. I wish they'd all fucking kill each other and be done with it."

"Jesus, Lee. Not enough violence for you already?" But I knew how he felt which is why the reflection put me on the defensive.

"Don't give me shit, Ray. You're right back there, aren't you? Letting that black hole gobble you up again. You can't control this, my dear. This really isn't even your problem. Take a day off. Relax and enjoy

319

it. Just let it go."

"Right. Can you tell me how, exactly, it's not supposed to bug me that our city just turned into a war zone?" I shook my head, disgusted. Of course he could relax and enjoy, getting buzzed all day, narrowing his focus to whatever struck him. I wanted some so bad I could almost taste the sweet smoke, and had to hang up to stop myself from asking him to bring some weed over. "I've gotta go. I want to finish the job I'm working on, just in case they reopen and I can messenger it over later. Are we still playing ball tomorrow?"

"Yeah. But we've got to be outta there and off the road by 6:00 with the curfew on," Lee reminded me.

A curfew in L.A.? It was ludicrous. Part of me was with Lee, wishing the assholes tearing apart my city would all die. It took most of my will to go back to working. My better self would have turned off the TV, but I didn't. I couldn't. L.A. was coming undone just the other side of my windows but it was like watching the Gulf War unfold halfway across the globe. I had to stay tuned-in to find out who was going to get bombed next.

It was well after dark when an explosion rattled my window just shy of breaking them. Suzanne wasn't home and I was scared out of my mind when I told Face to stay and went outside to look for the source of the noise. The street was empty, presumably from the curfew. A bright orange glow down the block turned out to be the Ralph's supermarket on fire. White and yellow flames danced out of the huge glass storefront and lit up the night as a firetruck came blaring down the street, lights blazing.

Several neighbors had gathered in a tight circle on the sidewalk, their white skin practically glowing under the florescent street lamps. They talked quietly among themselves but as I approached they parted slightly and welcomed me in so I couldn't avoid them.

"Stupid lowlifes," my next-door neighbor practically spit. "Destroying their own neighborhood is bad enough. Now they have to come here and destroy ours too."

"And the stealing! It just goes to show they can't be trusted," the old lady from across the street exclaimed.

"I'm not saying that the jury was right," said my neighbor's husband. "But that sure doesn't give them the right to go out and hurt innocent people."

"I don't know what they're trying to prove," my neighbor said, shaking her head. "All it's proving to me is these people are aggressive and violent and deserve whatever they get. Poor and ignorant is no excuse for barbaric. They should go back to the hole they crawled out of—"

"Ship em back to Africa and Mexico," someone said.

I listened silently as I watched Ralph's burn. A part of me was pleased the store befell disaster. The management sucked, the usual wait in line fifteen minutes or more. The produce was overpriced, and usually overripe. Served em right. I left the neighbors to snipe among themselves.

Back home every station was showing minorities looting business, throwing molotov cocktails at storefronts, or beating up White people. And as much as I'd have liked to hate my neighbors for feeling as they did, I could not discount that monster of blind, feckless rage now festering in me. I paced between the bed and the TV trying to rid myself my gnawing anxiety I wanted to peel my skin off, rid me of me. Face watched me, rocket ears straight up, her eye wide with wonder. My scalp prickled, my heart pounded. I broke into a sweat and felt as if I might pass out, or puke.

I went into the bathroom and splashed my face with cold water, then looked in the mirror. "Don't do this, Rachel. Don't believe what you see on TV. It is not reality." I stared at myself but felt no relation to the person staring back at me. All I could see in my head were interviews with angry Blacks, their faces twisted with hate as they yelled into camera exclaiming adoration for their new hero Rodney King. "Those stupid sons-a-bitches," I heard myself say to the person in the mirror, then covered my mouth in horror. I was my neighbors right then. "You're the stupid sonofabitch," I yelled, again filled with self-loathing forcing me to turn away from my reflection.

I went back into my room and turned off the TV. It was silent inside and outside.

Except for the sound of running water.

What the hell was that? It wasn't raining. The sprinklers weren't on yet. I checked the kitchen, and the back yard, then went outside, around the side of house and stepped in a muddy puddle. After clearing some bushes below the bathroom window, I notice a small geyser coming up from the crawl space underneath the house. A pipe had obviously broken. Shit. Tonight of all nights.

I went back inside and called the Department of Water and Power. My water bill was already over $100 a month, and I wasn't about to spend another $100 for the broken pipe. "We can't come out tonight," the DWP operator told me, clearly annoyed. "All our available personnel are helping the fire department re-route water lines to fight the fires. We might not be able to get out there tomorrow either. You'll have to turn the water main off to stop the leak."

"Where exactly is the main line, and how do I turn it off?"

"It's probably near the sidewalk in front of your house. Do you have a Crescent wrench?"

"No."

"Well, the best I can do is to try and get someone out there tomorrow morning. Cost you $25 bucks for emergency service. And I can't exactly guarantee that either. There's no telling if we'll have any available techs by then if the rioting continues."

"Fine." What the hell was I paying these people for anyway? "And if water comes through the floorboards and wrecks all my stuff, I'll bill you. Thanks for nothing." I hung up and called my landlord. His machine picked up, of course. I told his machine what was going on, hung up, and called my father. I knew he'd have the right tools and be able to find the main water line.

I met my dad in my driveway as he pulled up ten minutes later. Before getting out of his car he reached into the back seat for his tool box, and then into his glove box and pulled out a hand gun.

"What the hell is that for?" I had no idea my father owned a gun.

"There's a riot on, in case you haven't heard." He got out of his Chrysler LeBaron and put the gun in the waistband of his pants, for easy access, I guess.

"And what are you going to do with it?"

"Shoot anyone I have to." He said it so casually. "Now where is this leak?"

I just stood there. "This is absurd. What are you thinking? By the time you take that thing out of your pants, anyone aiming at you would have shot you already. Why are you carrying that thing around?"

"This is the United States of America, young lady. I have a legal right to carry a weapon to protect myself and my family, and that is exactly what I intend to do. We are under a curfew tonight. I'm not supposed to be out of the house as it is. And I'm not here to get into a political debate with you. I'm here to fix your leak. So where is it?"

I shook my head with a heavy sigh and led him to the side of the house, showed him the flood then we went out to the sidewalk to turn off the main line. Except we couldn't find it. We rooted around in the ivy looking up and down the street for a good ten minutes, until a lone car came cruising slowly down the vacant street toward us.

My father straightened as he watched the old beater Volvo slowly come to a stop in the middle of the street directly across from where we stood on the sidewalk. All the windows were down and faces of five or more Black guys stared at us. My father didn't say anything, but he slowly rested his hand on the gun in his waistband, his potbelly obscuring the small handgun from view.

"Dad, don't!" I whispered harshly. The bangers silently stared, not even talking among themselves. "Ignore them, dad. Let's just find the goddamn water main. Okay?"

My father didn't move. He stood there, staring back at them with his hand on his gun. I felt like I was in a movie, frozen in a standoff at the O.K. Corral. I had to do something or someone was going to get hurt. "Hey, you guys," I yelled to the bangers casually.

"Shut up, Rachel," my father commanded in an angry whisper.

My heart racing, I plunged ahead. "You guys know where the valve for the water main might be? Our pipe busted. Can you help us out here, before the DWP makes me homeless?"

The driver smiled a huge white grin. "Don't know nutin bout dat. But ya outta watch yoself out here, bitch. Yo ain't heard? Cops is trigga happy."

"En so are we," yelled the guy in the back seat. They all cracked up laughing and the driver floored it, laid half his tires on the road speeding away. Jerks.

"That was a stupid thing to do, Rachel. You could have gotten us killed." My father was literally shaking as he yelled at me. The entire scene was almost comic, had it not been so profoundly sad.

"Forget it dad. They're gone, okay? Can we just find this stupid valve and turn my damn water off, please."

My father was more interested in watching the street than finding the valve. He didn't move for at least five full minutes, rooted to his spot looking up and down the street, wide-eyed and hardly blinking. I went back to looking for the water main lid. It took us another three quarters of an hour, but we finally found the box with the water valves and turned the main line off. When I hugged my dad goodbye I felt him looking over my shoulder, eying the street. The bangers never came back, and my father made it home without shooting anybody.

In my entire life I'd never seen my father that afraid of anything. And I despised those bangers for making me witness that. I lay in bed salivating for a buzz and fighting myself over calling Lee. The last thing I remembered before falling asleep was hoping those guys in that car tonight would slam into a wall and die.

-

Chapter 29

I woke the next morning to no water, no shower, not even hot tea, and with more anger than I'd ever felt towards any group of people in my life. I turned on the TV immediately, filled with all that hate. The actor, Edward James Olmos, was telling everyone to come down to Central L.A. and help clean up.

My first thought was ASSHOLE! You people wrecked it, YOU CLEAN IT UP! But then the camera panned the street. Black people were sweeping up glass and putting back what was left of the produce in some Chinese guy's store. For the first time in three days the media was showing people of color helping instead of hurting. Although there was still minor looting, and a few buildings burning, the police had finally come out in force. The National Guard had been called in and armed soldiers were roaming the streets.

Then the man himself, Rodney King, got on the air, crying. He sounded like a high school dropout, but one thing that came across every TV and radio that morning was his plea we "all just get along." And I was suddenly humbled by this ignorant man.

I called the KTLA news department. "I want to know where to go in L.A. to help with the cleanup." I needed to do something to repent my sin of racism.

"We don't know," a woman at the station said. "Call the AME church downtown. They probably know."

"What are you talking about? You're showing Edward Olmos on your station right now. He's asking for volunteers. What number did he give you to call?"

"Not sure."

"Then ask your reporter to ask him." What was wrong with these people?

"Hang on," she said curtly and put me on hold. Ten minutes later she was back on the line. "The reporter with Olmos is already on his way to another site. The police are telling us we can't ask people to go down there yet because there's still rioting going on. We would be liable if anyone got hurt." Leave it to the media to cover their ass while exposing everyone else's. "We're really busy here. I've got to go. Good luck. Bye." She hung up before I could cuss her out.

I clicked the receiver down to call the AME church, but when I started dialing I heard Lee yelling through the phone, "Rachel...Hello...Ray...What are you doing?"

"Oh. Hi. Sorry. Didn't hear you on the line. I'm trying to call the AME church to see where I can volunteer to help clean up some of the looted stores."

"What!? Are you crazy?" He practically shouted. "This is no time to play martyr. Especially if you're White. I don't want you going down there." He said it like a command.

"I don't care what you want, Lee. This isn't about you, or us. It's for me. And I'm going." I pulled on an old pair of jeans and my hiking boots.

"This is not a good idea, Ray." He paused. "Are you watching TV?" It was a rhetorical question. "They're still killing each other out there. I don't want you to be next."

"Well, that's sweet and all, but I need to go down there and see for myself what's going on, help out if I can. I'll be fine, don't worry."

"Famous last words. I'm sure Mr. Denny felt the same way before they dragged him out of his truck and bashed his head in with a brick."

I sighed. He sounded like my mother.

"Is this a noble thing? I mean, what are you trying to prove by going down there? You're not going to change anything mixing it up those lazy, whining pricks?"

"I'm hoping to change me, Lee."

"Well, call me a racist then, because I don't give a shit if every one of them bites it down there. Save the taxpayers the bill of throwing em all in jail."

"Wow. Was your humanitarian persona just to project the proper image?"

"Don't get self-righteous, honey. I'm concerned for your safety. I just think this is a really stupid idea."

"Duly noted." I finished tying my laces and stood up. "Look, I've gotta go."

Long pause. "Yeah, okay." He knew he couldn't win. "Call me the moment you get back, okay? And be safe out there."

"Okay. Have a nice day," I mocked. "Bye." I sighed heavily, shook my head. The man was a consummate hedonist, as were most all addicts. I left the plumber I hired in the crawl space under the bathroom, got in my car, and onto the freeway, and spent the first twenty minutes of my drive trying to figure out why the hell I still wanted Lee to want me.

I wasn't scared going to South Central L.A. I knew the media made a mockery of reality. The first time I realized they were more than just exaggerating, they were out and out lying was the winter storm of '81 that destroyed part of the Santa Monica Pier. News showed a debris filled parking lot, complete with seagulls drifting around on what looked like a small lake. Excited to see this rare occurrence, I took my Nikon and drove to the beach. The pier parking lot had some minor puddling as I cruised over to the collection of news vans. Several reporters from various stations were standing around a twelve foot wide area of standing water. A camera was on the ground near the waterline and I realized they'd shot the puddle from the ground to make it look larger. Some young lackey packing up threw the rest of the sardines in the water he'd been tossing into the puddle to attract seagulls. Until that moment I believed what I saw on the news was real. I hadn't realize the myriad of ways they faked it.

I swung onto the 110 and passed the tall buildings downtown thinking about that storm. Again I craved a joint so badly I could almost feel the tingling lightness creep across my scalp. The buzz would surely relieve the weight of my guilt, and lift my profound sadness.

Took the Washington St. exit. It wasn't near as obliterated on the street as the news made it look. There were a few more burnt out buildings then usual, but the area had always been a wreck. Graffiti on the walls and empty lots filled with junk dominated the scene for as long as I could remember. There was one major difference. The National Guard was everywhere, with guns and in tanks. Like, what the hell were they going to do with tanks. This was L.A., not Czechoslovakia.

I came to a red light, rolled down my window and asked some old Black guys hanging out on the corner where they needed volunteers to help clean up.

"I think they started cleaning up the Stater Brothers on Central a few blocks down. They're probably looking for help over there," a guy said.

"Thanks." I rolled up my window and drove down a few blocks, then turned into the Stater Brothers parking lot. About fifty people were in the process of cleaning up the burnt out store. They had brooms and shovels and were filling three huge dumpsters in the parking lot. News vans were grouped together at the far end of the lot. Reporters were interviewing some of the volunteers. A tank with National Guardsman sitting on it, drinking sodas and coffee, was parked on the sidewalk to the side of the store.

Like Ralph's, the market had been fire bombed. It would have burnt to the ground had the fire department not soaked the roof, which had caved into the market. The sidewalls were standing, but the store had no ceiling, and the glass front was gone. Ralph's had burned only minimally and was cleaned up the same evening it was bombed, but this store was a wreck, completely destroyed. I grabbed a shovel and helped one of the sweepers clear the parking lot of glass and debris.

"Hey, thanks for coming down and helping in the clean up." He smiled, gleaming white teeth against chocolate brown skin, young, maybe early-twenties.

"Sure, no problem." I spoke as I lifted the filled shovel and dumped it in a bin. "I'm really sorry this happened to you guys."

"Yeah. Me too." He swept vigorously, his hard arm muscles bulging under his long sleeve shirt. "We're really devastated about this whole thing. I've lived here ten years and nothin like this has ever gone down. This market employed at least fifty people from the area. Now all these people are out of a job until they rebuild. If they rebuild." His big brown eyes seemed to dim as he filled the shovel with glass and water soaked pieces of ceiling. I struggled to lift it into the dumpster. "Hey, let's switch." And he handed me the broom.

"Thanks." I took the broom, and we switched places. More people came to help as the morning wore on. By the time most of the parking lot was cleared there were a good hundred people out there. Or I should say a hundred good people. Some women set up a stand with drinks and sandwiches for the volunteers. The crowd was all Black. I was the only White person there. Funny thing about that was I didn't feel White. Everyone treated me like just another volunteer. Except to the press. They kept bugging me for an interview. I finally went ballistic on the fifth reporter who asked me why I came to help in the middle of a riot. "Why are you here?" I glared at the preppie White reporter. "Fisting the first amendment doesn't absolve you from promoting hate, nor your audacity in filming the effects. So get the fucking mic outta my face, pick up a shovel and help clean up the mess you helped create." I went back to sweeping. The guy with the shovel flashed me a wide smile as he lifted the trash into the bin. The reporter went back to his cronies. No one asked me for an interview the rest of the day.

When the parking lot was cleared we went inside to help with the cleanup. Shelves were still standing, but most of the produce and products were gone, looted. Some remaining items were floating in filthy water that rose to my ankles. While volunteers cleared shelves and shoveled soaked boxes of food and pieces of ceiling into trash cans, a continual stream of Latino families came in and stole anything they could get their hands on.

I was among the volunteers appointed to stop looters from taking food items out of the water, which the firemen assured us was full of asbestos from the fallen ceiling. A Latino girl about 15 years old joined me as an interpreter.

"Don't take the food from the water, and don't feed it to your children. It could kill them. It's poison. Do you understand?" I did the hands around neck choking sign, the interpreter repeating my words in Spanish.

They didn't listen. Not one of them. They lifted bags of chips, bars of butter and cartons of milk out of the dirty water, then put the stuff they collected in Hefty bags. After the twentieth time we'd said it I looked at the young interpreter and saw tears in her deep brown eyes and streaking down her soft, oval face.

"They won't listen to us." She had only a slight accent, probably first generation born here. "They are illegals and trust no one. They are poor and desperate to feed their kids."

"I'm sorry," I said, lacking words of wisdom to bolster her. "I am so sorry."

She came to me and hugged me tightly then broke down

completely, literally sobbing. I held her, stroked her long brown hair and tried to be the strength she needed, but the truth was I could hardly breathe.

"It'll be OK," I whispered in her ear. "The bags are sealed. The kids will be fine," I lied, then held her face in my hands, dried her cheeks with my sleeve. She flashed a soft smile but I felt her lingering doubt. I took her hand and lead her to another family looting who didn't listen to us. In a flash of anger I grabbed the Hefty bag partially filled with water-soaked groceries from who I assumed was the mother, emptied it then filled the bag with what remained of cereal boxes on a shelf. The Latino interpreter spoke to the woman in Spanish the entire time in the same angry tone as my actions. I don't know what she said, but the woman left with her four kids after that, and the Hefty bag free of toxic food.

The remaining food and looters gone, we went back to cleaning up. With every shovel I threw away, a little of my hate went with it. The place was as spotless as it could be by the time the National Guard chased us all away, reminding us of the curfew. I was exhausted on the drive home. And though I was without hate, blackness consumed me. Images of the day flashed before me; all those people that had lost their job; immigrant parents dragging their children through the aisles while looting; the Latino girl's beautiful tear-streaked face.

I didn't even try to stop the tears blurring my vision on the drive home. Until today, it was more concept than reality there were hungry children in L.A. Where were the famous actors doing infomercials for our starving kids? My heart ached, a physical pressure in my chest for the inequity of our beginnings, and the status quo we all tolerate. I got off the freeway and onto the streets of my clean, upper-middle class neighborhood. "Here by the grace of god go I," I said aloud as I pulled into my driveway. And I don't even believe in god.

My phone was ringing when I came in the back door but I didn't run to answer it. I sat on the kitchen floor, let Face rest her head in my lap, stroked my dog and cried. I finally got up and took a blazing hot shower, then gathered the filthy clothes I'd worked in all day and threw them away. In my bedroom, I slipped on jeans and Lee's soft white shirt, flopped on my bed and clicked on the TV. Most stations were showing small gatherings of volunteers helping across L.A. And though it sparked a flash of faith in the human race, I settled on reruns of Rosanne.

The TV did not absorb me. My mind kept cycling over the absurdity of chance, the entropy of luck born solidly into the middle class, and White. Only could have top it born rich, and male. And every part of me carved a buzz right then, detach from the reality that it takes millennium to make a dent in human cognition. We're still breast beating monkeys, without the emotional maturity to manage the technology we're creating. It was likely we'd nuke ourselves into oblivion before making the transition to unification.

The phone ran for the third time in an hour and I finally picked it up. "Hi." I said flatly.

"Hi." Lee's tone was somewhere between anger and relief.

"Are you?"

"Why?" He paused. "You wanta be?"

"You bet." I sought to get as fucked up as possible, craving the lightness of simply being, and to breathe. "Can you come over?"

"Well, there is a curfew on. But I'm willing to risk it. Give me half an hour. If I'm not there by then I'm either busted or dead."

Lee was at my door twenty minutes later and we spent the evening getting high over games of Tavli. He left me at close to midnight with a heartfelt hug which I returned in kind, glad he'd come, marveling how easy it was to be with him as I shut the front door. I wasn't sorry I'd gotten high tonight, but it didn't detach me from the world outside completely like I'd sought— narrow my focus to my own existence, as most seemed to live. I lay in bed staring at the ceiling afraid to close my eyes. Every time I did I saw images of the day and the faces of the damned.

-

Chapter 30

The riots ended three days after they began. Over fifty people were killed, over two thousand injured, millions, perhaps billions in property damage. Though the media still sought and exploited any conflict for weeks after the riots, there weren't many left. L.A. settled into a tenuous peace in the early summer heat, the thick brown air and grid-lock traffic. Most everyone seemed edgy, afraid of each other. Of the police. Of the collapsing economy.

Lee and I continued playing ball three times a week, chatting with the familiarity of good friends over Diet Cokes in the lobby after our games, and often sharing a joint on walks immersed in intimate talks before departing from the club. All that really changed between us was we stopped doing regular dinners and spending weekends together. And no sex, of course. We met at the courts and left separately. He kept the appropriate distance, an L.A. kiss upon greeting, a hug when parting, and I followed his lead. I had it in my head if we kept playing, stayed connected, that it wouldn't take much to talk Lee back into pursing a relationship, regardless that I knew we should never get back together. I clung to hope that my latest personal ad would yield someone closer to my ideal. 'Hope springs eternal,' until reality sucks it dry.

Over the next several weeks I talked to over thirty different respondents to my ad, met eight for coffee dates, and went out with four twice. I felt little connection on the phone and none in person, and no one came close to what I already shared with Lee. By the second date I was so bored interviewing them and feigning interest in their replies I hardly engaged. I was tired of pretending to be impressed by their MBAs and careers in Marketing and Finance. And I didn't agree Rodney King deserved what he got, or that the cops should burn in hell, or that Michael Milken was the fall guy for the savings and loan scandal and didn't really do anything wrong.

Suzanne gave me notice in the beginning of June. She couldn't afford the rent on her limited income teaching music and was moving back in with her parents. Panic set in that I too would become one of the damned as weeks went by without any response to my ad for a roommate. Though I consistently had work, laying out $1,500 for July's rent, along with all my other bills would require going into my savings. And I needed every penny I could collect to move to the Bay, the other safety net in my head. The voice of reason assured me escaping L.A. and my family would be the best thing for me, even if it meant hurting my mom, which I'd resisted for years since her love was the only unerring love I'd ever known.

Towards the middle of June, Lee and I were in the racquet club lobby by the soda machine. He got a Diet Coke for me per usual, then one for himself, then leaned against the wall and opened the pop-top then looked at me.

"I've met someone," he said with a haughty smile.

It felt like he slapped me. "Good for you, Lee." And the ground opened up and swallowed me.

He stared at me. "Ah, Ray. You know I'll always love you. But being together is a constant reminder of the man I'll never be. I think we need to make a clean break and separate. It's time for both of us to move on."

And just like that, Lee and I were done. I was back to alone, abandoned, sucked into the black hole of want.

7/31/92

Runnin the rim of black space;

Wonderin if I want to keep up the pace;

If I let myself fall in the hole;

Ain't quite sure I can get out no mo'.

No Lee, or weed to lighten me, and the darkness descended through the sweltering dog days of summer. My 34th birthday came and went with only my mother's acknowledgment. When I wasn't writing copy and designing direct mail campaigns, I wrote in my journal, but that was about it. Writing fiction that I'd probably never get published anyway seemed pointless. Building, drawing, taking pics seemed equally pointless. I didn't need any more furniture, and what purpose did putting pictures on walls serve anyway? I played racquetball with Jon and Lavonne, but it was intermittent and quite frankly boring, having become a much better player than either of them since playing so consistently with Lee. I didn't really need the workouts for weight control anymore since I wasn't eating much anyway. Depression is a great diet aide.

Late summer Frankie was in town from the Bay to visit her family. She talked me into meeting her at Palermo's in Hollywood for dinner. The place was packed, per usual, ten or more people standing outside sipping glasses of wine, complimentary for the wait, but Frank stood out among them. Tall, slender, dressed in a tight red cashmere sweater, black jeans and ankle high black boots, the epitome of chic with her thick dark hair cropped short, almost butch, but framing her angular, yet feminine features.

Over our meals she rambled on about the joys of finally having money, her husband, Craig, supporting her every endeavor— her latest going back to school for a BA in psychology in the fall. It took her well over an hour to get that I wasn't barraging her with questions when she finally inquired what was going on with me.

"I hate what I do for a living. It's beyond unfulfilling, on par with demeaning that the extent of my creative achievement is selling people lies and crap they don't need, made even worse with computers stripping away any semblance of art. The notion of spending the rest of my days sitting in front of a monitor hacking out grid system designs is abhorrent. I'm way beyond lonely, on par with suicidal. And while time marches on, and I'm still childless, I'm stuck in hell I can't seem to get out of," I said flatly.

Her eyes narrowed on mine. It was hard to tell in the dim light in the restaurant, but she was angry, I think. "Rachel, for the past ten years you have been waiting for some guy to come along and save you. Assuming you don't meet Mr. Right, do you really want to spend the rest of your life doing shit you hate to get by and waiting around to die?" It was a rhetorical question. She didn't let me answer, but she couldn't ignore the look on my face. "Well, I won't let you. You are one of the most talented, creative people I know—"

"Yeah, well, that and a dime won't buy me a cup of coffee, Frank. There's no money in the arts, except for one in a million, and I ain't one of em. Clearly."

"Your work is amazing. Why do you think I have it displayed all over my house?" She glared at me dumbfounded. "Somewhere down the line if you keep working at it, you'll find someone interested in repping you. Guaranteed." She stared at me then shook her head." Look, you've told me you loved teaching college. So go back to school, get a teaching credential and teach full time. Do fine art on the side. You're gonna have to make up your mind and do something. Waiting around for a knight isn't working. Clearly."

She was right, of course. I did love teaching. It had value, unlike advertising. But it was easy for her to say go back to school with her honey and his money. How was I supposed to pay tuition when I could hardly afford rent? And while becoming all I could be was important to me, it paled in significance to giving life, the evolutionary purpose of enduring womanhood.

"It's not just about making it in the arts. I want kids, Frank, a family of my own." I sighed heavily.

"You don't need a man for kids, Ray. Adopting, even having kids on your own is all doable today. And teaching is virtually impossible to get fired from, a guaranteed income, and enough to raise a kid or two on."

"It's selfish at best to assume I'd be enough for a child. And I'm scared out of my mind of burdening my kids with my insanity. I want a husband to raise children with, inject some balance, stability, model the discipline I so sorely lack."

"Why do you always sell yourself short? You work your ass off. And you're complex, not crazy. You'll give your kids a broader perspective then most parents do. You don't need a man to save you, Rachel, no matter what your parents say. Save yourself. Make the life you want."

I gave her a vague smile but her words did not soothe. She had no clue what living in my realm felt like. Frankie was married to a millionaire, poised to have kids without worrying about making an income or raising them on her own. She had Craig till death do them part, her loving husband providing her financial freedom and a built in support system, a best friend to share her life with. And I did not.

Driving home it was hard to breathe, envy consuming me. I wanted everything Frankie had, but knew for me it was an impossible dream. I wasn't beautiful and confident verging on arrogant after being pursued by most every man out there since puberty, as she had been, though like most women, I'd wished to be. And right about then I wanted to be anyone but me.

Stopped at 7-11 on the way home to get a Diet Coke. I'd used all my cash at dinner and opened my glove box to retrieve the Altoid tin I kept change in and saw the bottle of Vicodin Lee's sister had given me in Oregon to administer to him when he was sick.

Half an hour later, I sat cross-legged on my bed and emptied the bottle into my hand. More than enough pills to disconnect, shut down fear, and want, forever. For a second I felt strong, in control of my fate, male. Then I saw myself in the deco mirror on my dresser, and felt stupid and small. My face looked ghost white against my mess of dark hair. My eyes were swollen from crying half the way home, and through my blurred vision I looked translucent, almost transparent, which modeled how I felt, and lived most all the time now. I stared at the pills in my hand. Take them all and put an end to the gnawing ache of solitude.

Stop, my distant intuition whispered. *Think.*

I poured the pills onto the comforter in front of me, went to the bathroom for a glass of water and resumed my position on the bed. I looked out the window. Face was bounding after a squirrel in the front yard's orange light with the encroaching sunset. Bolt lightning with fluid grace. I looked around the room. Nothing of value I'd leave behind, and no one but my mother to mourn me. Face wouldn't, of course. She'd be fine without me. My mom or sister would surely take care of her. And being as linear as dogs are, she'd probably never miss me.

My black ring binder notebook lay on the blanket within arm's reach, open to the journal entry I'd written earlier.

8/30/92

Nothing lives on when we die. There is no such thing as a soul.

What makes us unique, different from each other, is simply our combination of chemistry, which begins at conception and ends at death.

Awareness—pleasure, pain, love, lonely only exists while physical.

No heaven. No hell. No afterlife awaits us. And we're not reborn to live again.

Upon dying our bodies decompose, the atoms that remain scatter, and we are no more.

We feel no more.

And somehow, there is peace in that.

Flipped the journal closed with a nod of confirmation to this truth. But no one wants the truth. That's why there's religion. And no one was going to want to be with me. I was a devout empiricist, a realist, overwhelmed by harsh realities most normal adults ignored or compartmentalize to survive. People don't want to touch depression. That's why there's Prozac, and alcohol, and weed. Doesn't matter now. The life I wanted, the man I longed for, the family I desired, the world I hoped for was an illusion, unobtainable.

No partner through this malaise, and no family. I'd affected no one. Nothing would change with my exit. The glass wall that damned me to the outside was almost opaque now. And I didn't care anymore. I was so fucking tired of chasing illusions, ideals, of wanting, wishing, waiting...

I stared at the pills nestled in the blanket. I felt exhausted. I'm done waiting... Take the pills. Go to sleep. Be done.

The phone rang. I just stared at it. No point in talking to anyone. If it was my mom or Jon they'd probably ask me what was going on, and I couldn't make up anything quickly right then. My mind wasn't processing at its usual sonic rate. The phone's ring was loud and jarring. Go away! People can be such a bother. Who was it that said they loved humanity—it was people they couldn't stand? Snoopy, I think.

Answering machine finally picked it up. No message. They hung up. A minute later it rang again. Machine picked it up again. They hung up again. Another minute and the phone rang again.

I grabbed it. "What!?"

"Hi." Lee. We hadn't spoken in almost three months.

Thought I felt a spark of a rush hearing his voice, but if it happened at all the airless blackness inside me diffused it. "What do you want?"

"I want to talk to you." He paused. "I've missed you." He paused again, as if awaiting my response but I had none. "I've been thinking a lot about us. I miss you being in my life. I'd love to see ya, get together and just talk. You busy? Can I come over?"

"Why?" I sighed. "I could have dropped off the face of the earth and you wouldn't have known about it. I haven't heard from you since June, when you moved on. So what happened to the woman you were seeing? Oh, don't tell me. You broke up and that's why you're calling me."

"That's bullshit. We broke it off a month ago. She didn't want to wait for me to get you out of my system." He paused, either waiting for my response or carefully choosing his words. "Look, I've been thinking about this basically since we broke up. I really want to talk to you. Can I please come over?"

"No. Whatever you have to say you can tell me over the phone." It really didn't matter what he said. I stared at the little pile of pills on the bed.

"OK..." but he hesitated. "I love you, Rachel. Get it? I'm madly in love with you. Okay? I want you to bear my children. I want to support you so you can pursue your dreams. I want to spend the rest of my life with you."

If I had any brains I would have hung up. Instead I sat there holding the phone trying to decipher how I felt about what he'd just said. The problem was, I didn't feel much of anything. "Lee, you've told me all this before and walked away."

"I wasn't ready yet. I wasn't ready to make a lifetime commitment to you then. But I am now. I'm turning 40 in three months and I want to get on with life, to make a life, a home, a family. I know you want that too. And there isn't a woman I've known that holds a candle to how I feel about you. You excite me, Ray. You challenge me to my limits and beyond. And yeah, that scares me. I've never been with a woman like you. But I want to try and work it out between us. I know there are issues, but I'm willing to work on them, on us, if you are."

I noticed the pulse of my heartbeat thrumming in my chest and throat. And suddenly I recognized excitement, the first positive feeling I'd had in days. A fragment of light was penetrating the perpetual gloom. And while Lee may be the freight train comin at me, he was on the line, professing his love and wanting to be with me. I was no longer invisible, nothing, to no one. He'd been the best part of my life for almost a year, blackness descending only after his departure. And addict or not, he was easily the only man I'd considered a life with since Michael. "How can I trust you," I whispered.

"I promise you I won't leave this time. No matter what."

A twist of fate, if I believed in such a thing, but more likely the entropy of timing, and unintentional though it may have been, Lee was saving me from myself tonight. My life forward did not have to be alone and childless, or no life at all, if I agreed to try again with him. I listening for the counter inside my head to give me guidance but heard none. I hadn't trusted my intuition, and now I couldn't hear it. I wasn't sure what to trust anymore.

"Trust me," Lee said, as if reading my mind again.

I couldn't help smiling, followed by a pleasing warmth engulfing me just beyond the numbness.

"If I asked you to get back together and give it another try what would you say?"

"Are you asking?"

"Only if you say yes."

I'd put the pills back in the bottle after hanging up, and put the bottle in the wooden box on my nightstand. I'd been ready to play the hand that had always sated me in my darkest times— that I was in control of my destiny, could be the master of my demise when living was too hard for too long. The pills would be there if blackness descended again down the line. In the meantime, I had my best friend back, possibly my knight, and this notion lifted the smothering darkness. But every so often my scalp would tingle from a sudden flash of insight. Getting back together with Lee or swallowing the bottle of Vicodin was basically the same thing. I was still running away from myself, looking outside for something or someone to save me.

We went back to playing racquetball three times a week, hung out together after the games and every night in between. Weekends we went to movies, plays, concerts, explored museums and tide pools, new restaurants and old favorites. Lee bought a $3,000 Japanese block print of Mt Fuji because I said I liked it, and a $2,500 Stratocaster even though he couldn't play guitar. Saving money was clearly not on his agenda. We got high consistently as well, having agreed we could use together until we married and were ready to work on having kids.

I was trying to be compromising. That's what all my friends kept telling me, what my mom and sister had been selling me all these years. Relationships were about compromise. And smoking weed seemed a small thing, especially compared to real drug addicts or alcoholics. Oddly, even the buzz did not shut down the gnawing awareness I needed to quit using, and stop running from myself. But I felt scared to feel too deeply, afraid of the darkness descending again if I examined the larger picture with Lee, the one that extended beyond our shared moments.

We slept at his place or mine on Friday and Saturday nights, and went back to weekly sex as well. I still insisted he use a condom. I was depressed, not stupid, and creating a baby with Lee would be, especially while still using. Weeks flew by and life moved forward. I applied to UCLA's graduate Education program for the winter quarter to begin the process of getting my Teaching Credentials. It felt like I was on the road to changing my life, finally back on track, coming out of a long, very dark tunnel.

Lee had gone back to pudgy over the summer, but within four weeks of playing ball he'd drop much of the weight, though, like me, he'd probably always be smooshy vs hard. He invariably ordered the heaviest, fattiest foods on the menu, and insisted on following the meals with extravagant desserts. I generally took a bite or two of Lee's and then let him finish the rest, which he always did. I tried not to let his gluttony bug me since racquetball was keeping him in shape. I became accepting, a safe harbor. We didn't fight or argue virtually at all. In fact, we had only one minor conflict the entire six weeks we'd been back together.

Early October, over dinner at the Chart House in Malibu, Lee told me he'd planned a trip to Vegas with Mitchell and Mike before we got back together. He'd been putting them off but his friends kept pestering him about his promise and he felt a need to live up to his word. He assured me he never intended to gamble, was going merely to 'assist his good friends,' having committed to teach them some tricks at poker and introduce them to off-track betting.

I shuddered, afraid to open my mouth, lest recriminations pop out, but could not help myself from injecting reality into his Weekend with the Boys in Vegas fantasy. "Aren't you tempting fate with your... proclivity to gambling?"

"I want you to come with us." His Cheshire grin spread across his face like he was ten paces ahead of me. "I want to prove to you I'm a man of my word, that I can and will abstain from gambling. It's important to me. Please come."

"Lee, how come you didn't mention this trip to me before now?"

"I'm absolutely sure you know the answer to that, my dear." He glared at me with comic indignation. "So, you can be mad at me, or forgive me and join us, which would suit everyone since I'm not going without you."

"I'd feel like a jerk with you and Mitchell and Mike, like a fifth wheel. I don't want to intrude on your weekend of male bonding. Why don't you just go and I'll sit this one out."

"Then I'll tell em to forget it."

"No! Don't. They'd hate me. I'm sure they're looking forward to going and I don't want to be the bad guy wrecking it for everyone."

"Then come. It'll be fun. We won't hang out with them. They're just going to want to gamble all night anyway. We can go to a show, or walk around and look at the lights, have a nice dinner somewhere. Please come."

So I agreed. I considered rescinding my offer the entire three weeks before the trip. But I didn't. Be accepting, trust him, though I couldn't. My intuition knew who he was, how he was, and perhaps felt it was time for me to dismantle the fantasy I'd constructed with Lee.

-

Chapter 31

Mike and Mitchell were at Lee's door when we stepped off the elevator Saturday morning. Lee sparked a J and handed it to me then went upstairs to throw some clothes in an overnight bag. I felt like Yoko Ono with the boys in the band as we stood there. With little to say to them, and my presences clearly stifling their dialog, only the joint passed between us.

We stopped for bagels and lox spread on the way, which Lee paid for. I listened to them chat about business, their exchange more pissing contest then friendly banter. Lee touted his income from '91, and his percentage gains over the last few years. Mike talked of his start-up with his Stanford buddies— something about a 'browser' for the 'internet,' whatever that meant. Mitchell claimed to be in stealth mode while he whittled a contract with Turner Broadcasting for his new cable music channel. He'd brought a case of cassettes and insisted we listen to new rock that I didn't know, and didn't want to get to know, but I was working hard at not being contentious so I lied when he asked what I thought of the music. We stopped for gas outside Barstow. Lee went inside the station to pay. Mike, to pee. Mitchell and I waited in the car.

"So, how long have you and Lee been back together?" he asked casually.

"Little over a month now. I'm sorry if I wrecked your weekend. I told Lee I was more than happy to stay home but he insisted—"

"You didn't wreck our weekend. I really hope it works out for you guys this time."

"You don't sound very confident it will."

"I don't know, Rachel. You seem really up front to me, ya know, down to earth. You guys are very different. I know Lee probably better than anyone. We've been friends since high school. And he's not what he plays himself to be."

"What's that supposed to mean?" I glared at him. Judas! Then I saw

Lee and Mike come out of the mini mart carrying sodas and munchies.

"All I can tell you is Lee's probably the best salesman I've ever met. He's so good in fact, more often than not he even sells himself."

"Hey, you trying to pick up on my girl, Mitch," Lee said as he got behind the wheel. "Or you telling her all my secrets?" He gave me a quick kiss then handed me a Diet Coke.

"I was telling your girl here that you're a schmuck, man, and she ought to run for the hills, but she won't listen to me," Mitchell said with good cheer.

"That's 'cuz she loves me," Lee said. "Right, sweetie?"

I didn't say anything. Lee started the car and I thought we were leaving but he looked at me then put his hand on the back of my head, pulled me to him and kissed me. I felt both boys watching us and almost pulled back, but didn't. Instead I kissed him back, tongue and all as not to shame him.

We didn't go into Vegas but stayed at State Line, a blight in the middle of the desert that consisted of a few garish hotels on either side of the freeway at the Nevada border. It was late afternoon by the time we got to the Balizar Hotel and Casino off I-15. Lee got Mitch and Mike a room connected to the one he got for us and paid for it all, in cash.

I felt ill as we rode up in the elevator together, the boys chattering with excitement about what to do first. Our rooms were on the 12th floor, all identical with a shower/tub in the small bathroom, two double beds and a color TV with a VCR built in that sat atop the long, laminate six-drawer dresser.

"What's up, man?" Mitch came through the connecting door moments after Lee and I entered our room. Mike followed. "Let's cop a buzz before we go play." The boys looked at Lee expectantly.

Lee set his bag down near my backpack on the floor and looked at me. He took the Marlboro pack from the pocket of his leather jacket, pulled out a joint and sparked it then handed it to Mitch as he settled on the edge of a bed. Mike and Mitch sat on the other bed and passed the J between them. I stayed by the dresser, leaned against it for physical, and emotional support.

"So, what is it you guys want to do?" Lee asked.

"What we came here to do, dude." Mike took a deep hit off the joint then got up to pass it to me. "Let's gamble!" He arched his eyebrows and flashed me a grin.

I didn't smile back as I took the joint from him and took a hit. I avoided eye contact with all of them. Instead I focused on the joint and took another hit before I was finished exhaling the first one, hoping the renewed buzz would dissipate my growing anxiety.

"How about we go into Vegas and get some dinner first?" Lee asked diplomatically.

"Yeah. Okay." Mike's brow narrowed slightly on me.

"Fine by me," Mitch chimed in.

I took one more hit and handed the joint to Lee. He looked at me as he took it.

"Okay, Ray?" Lee practically whispered as he stood. We were eye to eye.

He'd betrayed me, but I felt pressured to oblige. "Sure. Let's do it." I stared at him, tried not to glare at him with the boys eying me. I'd expected we'd be staying in Vegas, on the Strip, not State Line, and having dinner on our own as he'd suggested when he'd initially asked me to join them. Of course, I couldn't exactly remind Lee of his words to me in front of his friends.

I managed to keep up the light pretense after sharing another joint on the drive into Vegas. I was beyond feeling too deeply when the boys agreed to save time by eating at a dive diner off the strip. The place was a wreck, as were the three waitresses, seemingly in their late 20's but looking rather haggard, with that blankness in their eyes of mind-numbing boredom.

"Ready to get onto the evening's festivities," Mike said as he pushed his plate aside and threw his paper napkin on the remains of his Mexicali Platter. "I say we park at Caesar's Palace and walk wherever we want from there."

"Good with me," Mitchell added, glassy-eyed over the rim of his Diet Coke glass before taking a sip. He stared at me, as if assessing me.

I looked at Lee. He stared down at the bun crumbs of the double beef, double cheese hamburger he'd just consumed, then finally looked at Mitch and Mike sitting across the booth from us. "Okay.

Here's the deal. I hang for a few hands of poker, show you both a few tricks, then Ray and I are off and away and you're on your own for the night."

His declaration gave me ground, reestablishing our connection and I grasped his hand beside me and held it tightly between us on the sticky plastic bench. Staying at State Line and missing a nice dinner together were minor indiscretions or even possibly miscommunications. The real test of his word was following through to spend the evening with me sightseeing, and not gambling, which he'd just made clear he had every intention of doing. The boys begrudgingly agreed to Lee's terms.

We all shared another joint in the car on the three block ride to Caesar's Palace, but left half of it in the ashtray since the boys, even Lee didn't want to wait to finish it once we parked. I did. We held hands as we walked, and I felt his grip tightened and his pulse quicken when we rounded the corner and saw the garish facade of the casino. As we passed the oblong fountain with giant horses guarding the corners, Lee nodded towards the sculpture on the center pedestal of two men virtually raping a woman, and flashed me a grin, with what looked like pride. His stride became wider, faster as we moved under the columned, layered concrete canopy, then up the few steps towards the entrance. He let go of my hand as we came through the sliding glass doors, and without glancing at the fountain with three topless women, swaggered across the enormous marble lobby and into the casino area. And even very high I knew my knight had vanished. More likely I'd never possessed him at all.

Flashing lights, ringing bells, ticking of spinning roulette wheels assaulted me as the boys and I followed Lee to a craps table. I practically gagged on the choking stench of hard liquor, cigarette and cigar smoke. We went from craps to roulette to baccarat for close to an hour, Lee explaining in fine grain detail the subtleties of the games. It was surreal being in there, the woman among the men, like I was stuck in some 1940s gangster saga, moving in slow motion through the glitz and glitter of it all. But when Lee sat on a stool with Mike and Mitchell at a poker table it felt like he'd hit me. I stood next to him unable to move or even speak, outrage amping my heart, pounding so hard my chest ached.

"Sit," Lee patted the seat next to him. "It's fun. I'll teach you what you need to know."

"No, thanks," I grumbled, practically growled.

"You're going to have to leave the table if you're not playing, Miss," the mid-30s, impeccably stylish dealer said.

"And Lee can't stay either if he doesn't play," Mike said, glancing at me.

"We'll do just a few hands, he'll show us some stuff—" Mitchell added.

"Then I'm yours for the remainder of the evening. Give me half an hour and we're out of here. Promise." Lee shrugged, like what else could he do, then took $80 out of his wallet and put it on the table. The dealer took the bills and gave him four chips.

I wanted to sweep the table clean as I'd done with the weed at his condo months back. But I didn't. I walked away, seething. I was shaking so hard it was difficult to keep moving.

Asshole! Addict. Lee or me? Both.

With no particular place to go I wandered around the noisy, crowded, smoky, flashing bright casino and waited for Lee. The stupid, desperate part of me still clung to the notion he was simply showing his friends some moves in poker as he'd promised, and he'd walk away from the tables in half an hour and meet me as he'd said.

Slot machines were the least offensive and cheapest option I could think of to kill time. I picked one and fed it quarters with a self-imposed $20 limit. About thirty minutes of mindlessly pressing buttons I was up $350 and bored out of my mind. I cashed out and went back to Lee. He was still at the same table I left him with Mike but Mitchell was gone.

"Hey, Ray," Lee said coolly. Suddenly he was Mr. Vegas. Grinning, smug, confident, aloof, untouchable. He put his arm around my waist and drew me close, gave me a little pat on my ass and introduced me to the dealer and three other men at the table as his "little good luck charm." I felt ill. "Havin fun doll?" he asked.

Doll? My skin crawled. "Yeah. Here." I put the cash I'd won on the poker table in front of him. The money felt dirty. I had to get rid of it.

"Well, you ready to learn how to play poker with it?"

"No. You wanta take a walk or something?" I asked as casually as possible.

"Not right now, babe." Babe? "I'm up $2,500 bucks. You're doing pretty well yourself. We can't quit now!" He patted my ass again and returned his attention to the dealer who politely informed me that if I wasn't going to place a bet I'd have to leave the area. I left and walked around the casino, then got a cup of tea at the buffet cafe. Half hour later I went back to Lee. Mike was gone.

"Lee, can we go take a walk now, see the strip, watch the volcano or something."

"Not just yet. Give me a couple more minutes, would ya? I'm down a few hundred. I want to try and make it up." He said it like it was the same as being up $2,500. He wasn't depressed or angry. He was totally and completely absorbed into playing poker. A bullet train could have run through the place and he wouldn't have noticed. "Hey, you went away and I started losing. Stick around and play a hand or two, be my lucky charm?"

"No, thanks." I wanted to scream, You sick sonofabitch! "I'm going for a walk."

"OK. Have a good time," he said as he placed a few chips on the table. "I'll be here."

"I'll bet on that," I walked away, through the maze of tables and machines out of the casino and into the warm October evening.

I walked up one side of the strip and down the other. When I got back to Caesar's Palace an hour later Lee was still at the same table. He was down $1,750. His mood was a little less amicable. He was doing his best to fake it though. "Hi there. Have a good walk?"

He acted like I'd been gone ten minutes. "Yeah. It's nice outside. You wanta come check it out, maybe get dessert somewhere?"

"Maybe a little later."

"Where are Mike and Mitchell?"

"Not sure. Mitch was tapped out, then lost the $50 I fronted him. I gave him my car keys so he could go get high. I haven't seen Mike in a while. They're probably hanging in the car getting buzzed. Why don't you go join em."

"You wanta come?"

"Nah. Not right now. You go ahead though."

"Wanta get a room upstairs and fuck?" The dealer heard me and cracked a smile.

Lee laughed. "Maybe later. Why don't you go catch up with Mitch and Mike for right now."

I couldn't think of anything else to say so I left. I went to the car. Mitch and Mike were inside the Mercedes listening to music and getting high. I felt like I was intruding but by that point I didn't care. We hung out in the car an hour or so talking about Mitchell's music channel and Mike's start-up until I got bored and went back to the casino to find Lee. The smoke tempered my outrage only slightly, but helped me narrow my focus to the moment at hand. It was after 1:00a.m. by then. He was still sitting at the same table playing poker.

"You ready to go. I'm really tired," I said flatly.

"I'm winning here. The last four hands I've made back almost $400 bucks."

"Lee, we've been here almost five hours. I want to go back to the hotel now."

He ignored me for a few minutes while he finished playing his hand. He won. $100 bucks. "See. You are my lucky charm, babe."

"Lee, I want to go."

He looked at me. "Okay. Go find Mike and Mitch, then we'll go."

"Mike and Mitchell are probably still in the car getting high."

"Well, just go make sure they're there because I don't want to spend a lot of time searching for them, Okay?" He wasn't asking.

"Fine." I couldn't exactly lift him from the table so I walked away seething again. When I got to the car the boys were gone. "Fuck!" I said aloud to no one. I went back into Caesar's and found them in the sports area watching thirty or more TVs showing games from that day. Lee joined them just as I did.

"Well, I just about broke even," Lee said as he pulled me into him and held me close with his hand on my waist. "How'd you guys do?" It was a stupid question, knowing the boys had lost to their limit hours ago. "Okay. Tell you what I'm gonna do. I'll put $500 on two games tomorrow. If I win, I'll split the winnings four ways. That way we all win."

Mike and Mitchell loved the idea.

"Split it three ways," I said. "I don't want any part of this. Are we going or what?" Before anyone could say anything I removed Lee's hand and walked away. Lee went to place the bets with Mike and Mitchell following close behind him.

We shared another joint in the car on the way back to our hotel. Mike, Mitchell and Lee chatted about the upcoming games, the point spreads…etc. I didn't say a word. I took hit after hit trying to ignore the burning in my lungs, in my heart, in my guts and in my eyes. I stared out the window so no one would see the tears streaking down my face. Stoned wasn't working. There wasn't a drug on the planet that could get me high enough to mute my intuition repeatedly insisting it was over with Lee.

I wiped my face and eyes on my sweater sleeve as we pulled into the parking lot of the hotel. We said good-night to Mike and Mitchell and went into our room. Lee locked the adjoining door. I went and took a shower. A few minutes later he came into the bathroom and asked if he could join me. The thought of getting intimate with Lee right then literally made me sick. A wave of nausea rose up in my throat I couldn't swallow back. "No. I just need to relax in here by myself for a few minutes, Okay?" I wasn't asking.

"Oh," he seemed surprised. "Yeah, I guess." He left, shutting the bathroom door behind him. A few minutes later he came back in. "You know, Ray, I just want a little affection from you," Lee said through the shower door. "Why are you being such a bitch?"

I got out of the shower, grabbed a towel, wrapped it around me and glared at him. "You completely ignore me all night long while you sat there playing poker after you promised me you weren't going to gamble at all this weekend. 'Just going to show Mike and Mitch some tricks,' you said. Now you want affection? Well, so did I. Where the hell were you all night?"

He stood there staring at me, his full lower lip slightly pouting, eyes and countenance contrite, like a basset hound, or a pudgy little boy being scolded. "I get you're mad at me, and I guess I don't blame you. I took it further out there than I'd planned tonight. I was just trying to show Mike and Mitch a good time.

Bullshit, but I didn't say it. He'd never hear me if I reminded him again of his promise not to gamble at all since he'd cloaked his addiction with the fiction he was being magnanimous.

"I'm sorry, Ray. Really." He kept his sad eyes on mine, as if trying to penetrate the wall between us. "I want to make it up to you. Tell me what you want and I'll make it happen."

Good question. What exactly did I want from Lee at this point? "For you to be different, or want to be." I sighed heavily and shook my head, went back into our room and put on some clean jeans and another sweater that didn't stink of smoke and booze.

"I really am sorry, Rachel." Tears were streaming down his cheeks now. "I'm sorry I'm not who you want me to be. I really thought I could be. I'm sorry."

He'd broken my heart tonight, and shattered my last remaining delusions of a future together, but it was clear I'd hurt him as well. I suddenly felt bad for being a bitch. He'd acknowledged screwing up, regardless that he wasn't taking responsibility for his inability to reign his behavior. There was no point in continuing to harp on him. Lee was still a boy, masquerading as a man. And I knew this about him from the beginning. I just didn't bother listening to my intuition.

I wanted to get out of there, and away from the twisted characters inhabiting the place. I could feel them through the wall of our room. "Let's get out of here. Go take a drive, look at the night sky." The only good thing about any desert is their endless sky.

We drove north on a small highway for several miles until we were clear of city lights. He lit a joint and offered it to me but I declined. No point. I'd be partaking out of pure habit. Reality grounded me now, and I knew I wouldn't cop a buzz. He parked on the side of the road and we got out and sat next to each other on the warm hood, leaned back against the windshield and stared up at the black velvet dome twinkling with a million tiny diamonds. The Milky Way glowed soft white and arched across the heavens above us. The air was still, cool and dry. We didn't say much, except to point out constellations, and exchange Wows and Look! at the flash of a falling star. We marveled at the vastness of it all, and though I felt his affection, the electric connection between us was gone.

"Is it over? Are we done, Ray?" He'd read my mind again, or maybe just a good guess with my silence.

"Truth is, we were over before we started, Lee," I said grimly.

"We were just having too much fun to care." His delivery was lilted with humor. "So, you're not still mad at me?"

"No. I'm sad we can't make it together, but I'm not mad." I had no energy left to be mad at him anymore.

"Makes me sad too, breaks my heart, actually. I know you hated me when I was playing poker tonight. I hated myself for disappointing you. The truth is, I will again and again. I'll never live up to the potential you see in me."

"I know," I whispered. And it stung I'd set him up to fail, knowing who he was from day one, whether he did or not. "I'm sorry, Lee. We should never have gone beyond friendship."

A brilliant light streaked across the sky from east to west, leaving behind a blazing white tail for a blink of an eye.

"Look!" Lee shouted, pointing at the light as it disappeared beyond the hills. "Did ya see it?" He was exuberant, his sense of wonder one of the many things I adored about him.

"Yeah. It was beautiful." I stared at the sky in awe hoping for another falling star.

"I really do love you, Ray. And I don't want to lose you. Can we still be friends? At least play racquetball, since you're the best partner I've ever had?" He looked at me but it was too dark to see his expression clearly.

"Right back at ya." I paused, listening inside for guidance. "But I do believe we're gonna have to cut the cord completely to quit each other, Lee."

-

Chapter 32

Face was ecstatic to see me when I came in the back door late Sunday afternoon. She had food and water as always, and access to the yard through the doggy door, but it was rare I left her alone overnight. She jumped all over me wagging her tail wildly, whining in greeting. I sat on the kitchen floor welcoming her wet licks of affection. I stroked my dog and we revealed in each other's company a moment. All affection should be this easily exchanged. Ah, to be a dog...

"We're on our own again, baby. No more Lee." I bit my lip to keep from crumbling. "We're done this time. Fait accompli," I said to Face, who rolled onto her back for a tummy rub.

Pathetic spinster, ugly old maid echoed in my head, as the words always did when I was back to alone. It was time to resume my search for a partner, though the notion of putting on a face for the next 20 dates from ads and fix-ups gave me an instant headache, especially after not wearing one so much of my time with Lee. I was 34 years old, and felt *so done* competing with all the young cover-girls here. I really had to get out of L.A., away from the menagerie my siesta town had become. I had to ignored my family's continual barrage of devaluing messages that a woman's worth was giving birth. I wanted more— to *be* more than a sparkly but not too bright wifey. It was time to cut the cord with my parents, from the perceived security they offered and stop allowing them to undermine me. And it was suddenly obvious how to close the chasm between awareness and action.

I got my duffel bag from the closet, packed it with the clothes I'd need. I'd wasted far too much time searching for a man to validate me. The truth was, and had always been, I was going to have to do that for myself. It was time to change the trajectory of my life, to live where I wanted, and become who I wanted to be instead of what I was told by everyone from my mother to the media women *should* be. With or without a man, kids were doable with the right income, and I'd find a way to make the money to raise a family of my own if need be. My longing for a partner to share life's journey would likely never leave me, but I didn't need a man to save me from Lonely. My imagination did that quite effectively, and it was time to celebrate it. I'd start with writing a novel on this last year with Lee, perhaps be the voice of reason for other women who believe their value comes from fitting into antiquated roles constructed for us, roles we no longer need to remain in.

I called Frankie, told her I was coming up to San Francisco to find a work and a place to live, then asked to crash in her guestroom for a couple of days. She graciously invited me to stay as long as I needed, then asked why I finally decided to make the move up to the Bay. I repeated her words to me a month earlier, "It's about time I stand on my own, create the life I want, right?" I grabbed my portfolio, called Face to come, and we headed out the back door.

I rolled down the window half way as I accelerated onto the 101. The dog stuck her nose out and her jowls flared with the wind. The setting sun reflected the black cover of the notebook I'd left on the dashboard and obscured my view out the windshield, so I moved it to the passenger seat. I noticed writing scrawled across the cardboard back cover from almost a year ago, and laughed at myself for the wisdom I chose to ignore, and swore right then—

never again. From here forward, I'd trust my intuition to guide me.

10/26/91

Intuition is a flash of insight. Neither telepathy, nor stroke of divinity, its enlightenment comes from empirical evidence, consciously or unconsciously attained. Intuition may not tell you what you want to hear, but if ignored, you're basically fucking yourself.

-

♦ ♦ ♦ ♦ ♦

-

Major depressive disorder (MDD) (also known as clinical depression, unipolar depression, or as recurrent depression in the case of repeated episodes) is a mental disorder characterized by pervasive dark or negative thoughts and persistent low mood that is accompanied by low self-esteem and by a loss of interest or pleasure in normally enjoyable activities. MDD is a leading cause of suicide.

Studies have shown major depression to be about twice as common in women as in men.

For information, as well as resources for treatment and support for those suffering from depression, please contact **The National Institute of Mental Health**:
http://www.nimh.nih.gov/health/topics/depression/index.shtml

or the **World Health Organization**:

http://www.who.int/mental_health/management/depression/en/

-

♦ ♦ ♦ ♦ ♦

-

About the Author

J. Cafesin is a novelist of taut, edgy, modern fiction, filled with complex, compelling characters so real they'll linger long after the read. Her debut novel, _Reverb_, hit #1 in Kindle Store Contemporary Romance, and #4 overall in Amazon's Best Sellers Rank during a recent promotion. Recent reviews: "Riveting; Compelling; An original and unique read." _Reverb_ was also #1 in Read Our Lips Book Reviews 2013 Year In Review.

Other works include her fantasy YA/NA/A crossover series, _Fractured Fairy Tales of the Twilight Zone_. In Volume #1, _Fractured Fairy Tales_ Meets _The Twilight Zone_ in this collection of four "uniquely captivating," edgy, fantastical character-driven tales, each sprinkled with a touch of magic, and a powerful message that lingers long after the reads... "5 Stars. Great read for young adults, and even some not-so-young adults!"

The Power Trip (the first in the upcoming techno-thriller series) follows the misanthropic adventures of four Stanford students, who implement an online game in which players manipulate each other using predictive modeling. Due to release summer 2017.

Her essays and articles are featured regularly in national

publications. Many of the essays from her ongoing blog have been translated into multiple languages and distributed globally: http://jcafesin.blogspot.com

She resides in the San Francisco Bay Area with her husband/best friend, two gorgeous, talented, spectacular kids, and a bratty, but cute Shepherd pound hound. Find her on her author site: http://jcafesin.com, or on Facebook and Twitter.